Something for the Weekend

PETER SIMMONS

FOREWORD

As you, gentle reader, may discern from the somewhat episodic format, this work began life as the script for a television series - I thought the re-enactment world was ripe ground for a gentle comedy taking an affectionate look from within (rather than a sneering look from without). Unfortunately, none of the companies or competitions to which I submitted my script seemed to agree (or maybe it requires a screenwriter of far greater skill), but rather than abandon the idea completely, I set about turning the screenplay into the novel you're about to (hopefully) read. Much of the subject matter is from personal experience, the rest is invention or exaggeration. Similarly, many of the names used are those of people I have encountered over my years of re-enactment - having initially used them simply as placeholders, it became hard to separate them from the characters as they grew, so I let them be. It may be, then, that you come across someone who you think you recognise (maybe as yourself) and it may indeed be that you share more than just a name. However, all the more extreme characteristics of certain individuals in the book are mere invention and should be treated as such, with no offence taken. As they say in the movies, any resemblance to any persons living or dead is purely coincidental...

CONTENTS

PROLOGUE

Smoke crept over the ragged fields like sea-mist, swirled by the thump of cannon and lit from within by the lightning flashes of muskets. Above the fog, thickets of pike-points jabbed the clear blue sky and gallant colours fluttered in a light spring breeze tainted with the rotten-egg stink of sulphur. The whisper of wind was enough to part the reeking smoke shrouding the opposing armies, allowing the sun to spark off those helmets and breastplates that had not been dulled by rust or lamp-black.

Drums hammering, Harding's Regiment of Foot advanced into the inferno of musketry and cannon fire, swifts flicking low across the grass before them like dolphins beneath the prow of a ship. Within the packed ranks of the pike division, the reek of gunpowder was kept at bay by the mingled stench of sweating bodies, damp wool and seasoned leather. Oxygen was a luxury, the broiled air a foetid blanket, and Daniel Bowers was already struggling to keep in line. The heavy pike threatened to slip from his shoulder with every uncertain step, rattling against the steel helmet that seemed intent on reshaping his skull. With his ears folded flat by the cheek flaps, the cacophony of battle was reduced to a distant underwater murmur through which his laboured breathing wheezed like a broken tin whistle. Beneath the constrictive metal plates of back-and-breast armour, the stifling coat of blue wool was already heavy with sweat, though he would have sworn that there was no more moisture to harvest from his desiccated body. This was Hell, a nightmare of sweat and confusion, and he shouldn't even be here. It wasn't his fight, he should never…

His head snapped back, jagged rivets biting into his skull like iron teeth. The discordant clang of his helmet ricocheting off the armour of the man in front throbbed in his ears, though it did not drown out the ripple of laughter that shivered the ranks. None of his comrades had missed the order to halt, and their easy surety forged a bond of shared experience that left him excluded - not through malice, but because he was yet to be measured. He would be tested soon enough.

'March on!'

The pike officer waved his division forward with a lazy flick of his hand. Tall and spare-framed, he barely blinked when a cannon blast punched the air, though Daniel - fingers clumsy in thick leather gauntlets - had to snatch his pike with his free hand as it toppled forward, the pressure of the discharge buffeting him like a giant fist.

'Ranks and files!' came the shout, though no one else had missed a step. 'Keep your ranks and files!'

Recovering his pike, Daniel clamped the shaft tight to his shoulder, the derision of the veterans far outweighed by more immediate concerns - not fifty yards ahead, a block of grey-coated musketeers levelled their weapons in his direction. He shortened his steps, but the man to his right grabbed his elbow and propelled him on.

'Here it comes, chaps,' drawled the officer.

'Give fire!' On the heels of the distant command came the spluttering roar of a volley. The immediate horizon vanished in a smear of dirty flame-shot smoke. Daniel tucked his head into his shoulders, though the snaps of flame seemed so far removed from their grim potential that it was hard to believe the enemy were shooting at him.

'Let's have them! Port your pikes!'

Daniel slid his left hand a third of the way up the shaft and lowered the pike to forty-five degrees as he had been shown, ringing the helmet of the man in front like a bell.

'Charge your pikes!'

By extending his right arm behind him and touching the knuckles of his left hand to his chin, Daniel levelled the pike in the "charge" position, though he forewent the sharp, savage shout barked by his comrades. The ill-balanced eighteen-foot spear dragged on his arms, the silvered tip drawn inexorably toward the floor. He fought to keep the shaft level, all the while trying not to trip over his own feet as he shuffled forward. Would he have the strength to actually thrust it into someone? No matter - seeing the formation bristling with charged pikes, the enemy musketeers fled.

'Stand!' yelled the officer.

This time, Daniel managed to avoid clattering into the man in front, though the great green flag that fluttered above the ranks carried on forward.

'Stand!' came the call again. 'Get your points up! Advance your pikes!' With quivering arms, Daniel hauled his pike back to the vertical, but still the flag plunged on, making its way out into the no-man's land between the two armies.

'Stand! Come back!' There was a note of desperation in the officer's voice, but it had no effect on the determined ancient who tottered forward with the banner, rheumy eyes set behind thick round glasses, grey hair streaming behind him. His sword hung low, almost trailing on the ground so bent was he by the weight of the great standard, but he ploughed doggedly forward as if the gentle breeze was an ocean gale, teeth gritted beneath a straggling beard. 'Trevor! We've stopped!'

'Oh my God,' rasped a voice from the flank. 'What's that senile old bugger playing at now?'

Face puce beneath the broad brim of his plumed hat, belligerent posture marred by the slight curve of his belly, Colonel Barry Reynolds was obviously not impressed by Trevor's antics - the bellicose expression did little to iron out the hang-dog sag of a man who demanded the highest standards and expected only disappointment. His knuckles whitened around the shaft of his polearm, as if imagining a scrawny neck beneath his fingers, while the pike officer corralled Trevor back into position like a recalcitrant tortoise.

'Order your pikes, guys.' The command came from within the ranks. Trying to mirror the practised moves of his fellow pikemen, Danny managed to get the butt of the pike onto the ground by his right boot without mashing his toes.

'They're sending in their pike.' The officer at Reynolds' shoulder had an expression that was paradoxically both dreamy and intense, like a psychotic sleepwalker.

'Thank you, Kenneth.' Cupping a hand around his mouth, Reynolds hailed the pike officer. 'Julian!'

Julian flapped a hand in acknowledgement. He cut a far more impressive figure than the colonel in Danny's eyes, breastplate and helmet polished to an eye-watering sheen, the lace trim and gold-tipped cords of his uniform elegant and unruffled. By contrast, Reynolds' scuffed leather jerkin hung open over a faded red coat and the metal plate around his neck was speckled with rust. The brief exchange between the officers obviously meant something was about to happen, the expectation heightened by a rhythmic thumping as the vast mound of sweating flesh beside Danny systematically bashed his helmeted head against his pike shaft.

'I don't think you're up for this, Nick,' smirked the tall pikeman behind the Falstaffian giant.

Nick screwed up his round, red farmer's face and gave a colossal rolling belch that drowned out the crackle of musket fire, a cavernous rumble that increased in both pitch and tempo until it reached a grotesque vibrato finale garnished with the stink of sweat and stale booze. 'Born ready, Stevie-boy. What we waiting for?'

'Who we got, Mike?' Steve called to a front-ranker.

Of a height with Steve, Mike could have been his twin - they both shared the same broad, wry features, though Danny had earlier been told, as if it was a tiresomely frequent misconception, that they weren't related. 'Northern.'

Nick growled, picking up the pace of his helmet-banging to an almost climactic frenzy. 'Fucking brilliant. Tossers.'

Danny peered between the broad shoulders of the front rank. Apart from a few lads about his age - dressed in kit as ill-fitting as his own borrowed uniform - the advancing enemy were a tough-looking bunch, bent-nosed and gap-toothed like a pack of gnarly rugby forwards, their experience hammered into their scuffed and dented armour. It was some comfort that his own comrades looked equally hard-bitten - and, in Nick's case, hard-biting.

Beyond the wavering pike tips, cavalry charged and wheeled through the smoke, though they were reassuringly distant - he didn't fancy a ton of wild-eyed, shit-smelling, tooth-baring equine tank hoofing toward him under the purported control of some braying Hooray Henry (or Henrietta) intent on sticking it to the plebs. A cheer went up from the rather small crowd behind the rope barriers as the cavalry thundered past, little kids waving paper flags to show the allegiance their parents had bought for them that afternoon. What side was he meant to be on? He should have paid more attention to Tab's explanations, but her words had been just background noise as he'd gazed on the perfect, cream-complexioned, high-cheeked face that was the sole reason for him being here. Speaking of which...

He found Harding's musketeers some twenty or thirty yards away, their powder-blue coats distinct despite the battlefield haze. It had come as a surprise that there were uniforms of sorts, each regiment being identified by their coat colour - where were the Roundheads in striped rugby jerseys and hinge-tailed helmets, or the resplendent Cavaliers in silks, ribbons and plumed hats? Hollywood and key-stage education apparently had a lot to answer for, as here there were no such clear-cut lines between the opposing forces, adding to the confusion about which side he was meant to be fighting for.

Where was Tab? He could pick out individuals in the pungent fog but was unable to find the face that dominated his dreams. Had she been hurt? He wrung his hands around the shaft of his pike. Anything could have happened to her - it was dangerous out here, with explosions and horses and... No, there she was, thank God, kneeling behind the musket lines with some stocky geezer thrusting a rod down the barrel of her gun. She had her back to Danny but there was no mistaking the blonde pigtail hanging down beneath the odd rolled cap that she, like most of her fellow musketeers, wore in defiance of Hollywood myths. The bloke inspected the end of his rod with a satisfied nod, breaking it down into sections that he stowed away in a sausage-shaped bag. Tabitha rose to her feet and Danny rasped his tongue along his shark-skin lips. The grey regimental britches were far from flattering on most people - widening the hips and shortening the legs - but Tabitha's moulded her shapely rear to perfection as she sashayed back to the front line. Slinging his bag over his shoulder, the sturdy-looking bloke picked up his own gun and followed her, pausing to pat out the fledgling flames on a wiry musketeer's shoulder. Almost unrecognisable in the finery of an officer, Keith Winters - Tabitha's dad - gave an approving nod.

A horrifically damp hawking shattered the burgeoning fantasy of what Tabitha Winters wore beneath her britches. 'What they waiting for?' Nick spat a gobbet of crusted phlegm onto the ground.

'Easy, tiger.' Clinging to his pike, Steve bobbed and writhed like a pole-dancing Sasquatch. 'We'll go in a minute.'

'Just waiting for the musket to bugger off - we're too tight in here.' Julian, sauntering along the ranks, had picked up Nick's impatient comment. Earnest, slightly protuberant eyes locked onto Danny, the prominent Adam's apple lending an air of august competence. 'Alright, Danny?'

'Er, yeah, cheers, great. Thanks.' Of everyone, even Tabitha and her parents, Julian had been the only one to go out of his way to make him feel welcome. Everyone else treated him with polite - or not so polite - disdain. Well, sod them. Bunch of sad gits. He didn't want to be here anyway. He was only here for Tab.

'Good lad, good lad. We'll be going in soon. Keep tight, keep your head tucked in, and push your bollocks off!'

Julian strolled on and Danny found himself standing a little straighter, knees locked against the faint tremor running through his legs. There were probably generations of Julians going back centuries who would say things like "Come on, chaps, let's charge that machine gun, what?" or "I know they've got boiling oil, but we can't let the side down, can we?", and the dewy-eyed plebs under his command would throw themselves willingly - gratefully even - into the jaws of death.

Danny's own jaws of death - the opposition pike block - ground ever closer. Nick was growling deep in his throat, his unblinking eyes distant, while Steve bounced to the steady thump of drums. The drummers themselves - both female, though one much more obviously so - stood at the rear of the block. The shorter of the two, a determined little ferret of a woman whose femininity was well-disguised, nudged her younger companion to remind her to beat her drum rather than make eyes at the lads in the approaching pike block. The girl's mane of red hair and nose stud probably weren't strictly in keeping with the period - the artfully applied make-up definitely wasn't - but the effect was certainly striking, and the ornate drummer's coat gave the rib-nudging impression of a principal boy in a pantomime that was never intended for an audience of kids. Noticing Danny's attention, she fluttered him a quick wink, brazen features bunching into a flirtatious smile. Cheeks igniting, he made a show of examining the regiments ranked behind them - a glorious array of reds, greens, blues and yellows - before tracking Keith Winters and his musketeers as they charged whooping and hollering into hand-to-hand combat. Tabitha, a mile-wide smile showing through the smudges of black powder, jabbed wildly with her musket butt while the dark-haired guy next to her flashed away with his sword like a 1930s matinee idol. He had the looks for it as well, and a stab of jealousy snuck under Danny's breastplate, although his concerns were somewhat mollified by the number of opposing musketeers of the female persuasion queueing up to be the swordsman's next victim. Many of them were to remain unskewered - at a shout from Keith, the blue-coated musketeers turned and fled, leaving a pile of bodies behind them along the crowd line. Some nutter dressed in priest's robes had been busy haranguing the audience, but now, with a tormented howl, he turned his attention to the heaped bodies (most of whom were shifting into more comfortable positions). Overcome with theatrical horror, he dropped to his knees, narrowly avoiding catching one of the flashy swordsman's willing victims in the head. Casting a shifty look around, the priest placed a hand on her tumbling brown locks and mouthed a devotion while the fingers of his other hand traced around the inside of her fallen headgear. Finishing his prayer, he rose to his feet and, on the pretence of smoothing his dark, drooping moustache, gave his fingertips a crafty and most unclerical sniff.

'Advance your pikes!'

Julian's clipped tones thankfully jerked Danny's attention away from the priest's antics. His fellow pikemen had their weapons up in three crisp movements, shaft tight to the shoulder, butt cupped in the hand, and he heaved his own up to join them - if he'd arrived last night with Tabitha and her family instead of getting picked up at the train station that morning, he would at least have had chance for a bit more practice.

'Straight in at the push, chaps. We're not going to point. Close order!'

The ranks closed in around Danny, as did the frenetic realisation of what was about to happen. The opposition block ploughed on like a steamroller.

'March on!'

Crammed in tight, Harding's pike inched forward. Their opponents - Northern? - were just feet away, pikes vertical, front rank low and bracing back against the pressure building from behind. There were two styles of pike fighting, Julian had explained earlier. Point, where they'd jab at their opponents (the pikes, of course, had wooden, silver-painted tips, not lethal steel points), and push, where the block would lock together, pikes at the vertical, and slam into the enemy. Not strictly authentic, Julian had said, pulling a face, but reminiscent of the brutality and physicality of close-quarter combat in the 17th century - and enormous fun, he'd added with a grin, like an armoured rugby scrum.

'Closest order!'

The front rank dropped to a crouch, affording Danny a view over their helmets into the faces of his enemy. Close up, they weren't any more appealing - particularly the grim-faced veterans, though even the younger lads (who looked as though they'd be more at home outside the off-licence on a Saturday night) twisted their features into feral, if self-conscious, snarls.

A sudden surge from behind shunted Danny into the man in front. Before he had chance to set himself to drive, the two blocks snapped together with the force of a low velocity car crash, the shock of the impact enough to snatch the breath from his lungs - the clamour of metal on metal was almost drowned out by the explosive exhalations of forty men and women. The press of bodies compacted like plasticine laced with steel, neither block yielding an inch, and Danny's feet actually lifted from the ground, his armour squeezing him like toothpaste in a tube. A scarred face was inches from his, snarling, spitting, and then cracking into a smile.

'Come here often?'

Danny had no breath for an answer. His armour had found what little spare flesh there was and was pinching his sides like a steel vice. Worse, his right hand - cupping the butt of his pike - was trapped between his breastplate and the armour of the man in front and was being ground with bone-cracking pressure despite the thick leather gauntlet. With the armour crushing his chest, it was impossible to drag any more air into his lungs and his head was starting to feel dangerously distant. It was like one of those nightmares where you couldn't move, where you were trapped in a tiny little space that was shrinking by the second and filling with water. Then, just as lights began to star his vision, the pressure was off. His feet dropped back to the ground and the block piled forward into the disintegrating opposition.

'Reform on your colour!' bellowed Julian.

Picking his way around the fallen who rolled like turtles as they tried to get back to their feet, Danny dragged himself back to where Trevor - belt held firmly by Julian - stood with his standard.

'Fucking straight through them!' hollered Nick, forming a new front rank with Mike and Steve. Danny hovered, but someone grabbed him and shoved him into line, ramming him into Nick's broad back.

'If you ain't hurt, get in!'

He *was* hurt! His side felt as though it had been hammered by a steak tenderiser and he daren't flex his stiffening fingers. At least he could breathe now, though each breath was coaxed with an effort from the super-heated miasma that hung around his helmeted head. Sweat streamed down his face and his legs were liquid, but was that a flicker of elation in his belly? No, it was probably the chips and foot-long hotdog he'd stuffed down two hours ago.

'Close order!'

Not again! Danny dropped lower this time, determined to keep his feet on the ground. They went in quicker than before - he barely heard the command for 'Closest order' - and when they hit, Nick didn't budge an inch. Danny, unfortunately, did. The weight from behind drove him on and he found himself chewing on the giant's backplate. Add possibly chipped teeth to his list of woes. Bollocks to this. He drove his boots hard into the turf, straining every muscle against the broad back in front of him. He went to the gym three or four times a week but running on treadmills and lifting weights was no preparation for this! Every tendon, every joint, creaked and protested. His arms were crushed into his sides, the edges of the armour gnawing at his skin through the rough woollen coat, and hob-nailed boots scraped down his shins with excruciating precision, shredding skin through the thick socks. He tried to back up, but the weight from behind had him pinned. Something had to give - his knees, more than likely. Then, just when the mill of metal, wood, wool and flesh tipped beyond bearable, they were through, the release of pressure as their opponents crumbled once more as welcome as it was sudden.

They reformed but did not go back in. Instead, Julian ordered them to open their order - Danny translated this as "spread out a bit" - then called for water.

'After two fucking pushes?' Nick was incredulous. 'Pussies!'

Leaning against his pike, Danny sucked in breath after shuddering breath. With the ranks open, he could at least get some air in, but he still felt like he'd just run a marathon. Through treacle. Two pushes had been enough - surely there wouldn't be any more?

'Here!' Steve thrust a leather-covered plastic bottle into his hands. 'Get it down you.'

Not caring how many lips had already been around the bottle, Danny gulped down three or four mouthfuls of tepid water, his throat like a twig.

'You okay, love?' In britches, blue coat and wide-brimmed hat, the matronly Mrs Winters - Tabitha's mum - took the bottle from him and slung it over her shoulder to join the others jostling at her waist. A quick appraising glance evidently assured her that he wasn't in imminent danger of collapsing - if only he shared her conviction. 'Make sure you take on plenty of water - that goes for you too, Nick!' She'd spotted the tarnished hip flask that Nick was surreptitiously slipping into a waist pouch.

'Yes, Jane.' Nick's face twisted in disgust, as if someone had suggested he drink his own piss.

'You're bleeding a bit, love.' Giving Nick up as a lost cause, Mrs Winters dabbed Danny's lips with a moist cloth. 'Nothing to worry about.'

Tasting metal, Danny ran a tongue along his teeth, probing to make sure none of them moved before spitting an alarming gobbet of blood onto the ground. *Come for the weekend. It will be a laugh. Right, yeah. Dress up like a prat and get my face smashed in!* Was it enough of an injury to warrant him sloping back to camp? Julian's shout closed off this avenue of escape before it could be explored further.

'Water out! We're going again!'

'Let's fucking have it!' roared Nick.

1 SHOTS FIRED

Cocooned in a fug of sweat-laced steam, Harding's regiment trudged laughing and joking through a labyrinth of caravans, campers, cars and tents. The battlefield exploits they relived would, by later that evening, be far enough exaggerated to take their rightful place in the dusty regimental mythos.

'How was that then, Danny?' Danny's backplate rang dully beneath Julian's companionable hand.

'Yeah, yeah. Good. Great. Awesome.' There were no reserves left to spark his voice with any enthusiasm - after the first two pushes and a token engagement at point, his battle had devolved into scrum after endless scrum, his world condensed to the few square feet of armoured flesh around him. It had been non-stop slog and his legs felt as though they were made from wire coat-hangers lashed together with elastic bands. Thankfully they'd been allowed to break step once off the battlefield and out of sight of the public - there was no way he'd have been able to march all the way back to camp. Everything hurt, from the blisters forming in the ill-fitting boots to the nagging ache of his teeth. Sweat trickled down his neck and his head itched horribly. He stank, too - but so did everyone else.

Julian eyed him speculatively. 'Good lad, good lad.'

He owed Julian more than a cursory response, despite his exhaustion. These guys did know their stuff, and once or twice out on the field he had felt a frisson of what could have passed for excitement - but when all was said and done, it was still dressing up and playing soldiers. Keith Winters, straps and buckles creaking and jingling, saved him from having to force an answer - it was hard to believe that the tall sweat-and-powder stained figure, dripping with lace trim, was his dad's best mate.

'How was your battle, mate?'

'Not too shabby.' Julian ducked his head and removed his gleaming helmet, shaking free a thatch of sandy hair. 'Went clean through Northern!'

Keith pulled off his own plumed hat, though he had little, if anything, to shake free. 'Bet they hated that, eh? You won't remind them about it in the beer tent later, will you?' Keith turned his gaze to Danny. 'And how was your new recruit?'

'Came through in one piece.'

'Said you'd survive, didn't I, Dan?'

'Yeah, cheers.' The eyes above the beaming smile and Roman nose were warm enough but Danny, as always, was a little wary of the father of the first naked female body he'd seen. Not that he'd ever let it dissuade him from trying to get a second showing, but the fallout from the first (even though both he and Tabitha had been about five years old) still sometimes woke him in the night with cold sweats.

'Good stuff!' Keith's avuncular affability gave no indication of any homicidally protective intent. 'Well, now you've got down and dirty with the pike boys, how do you fancy cracking off a couple of shots? There's powder left.'

'Go and have a pop, Dan!' urged Julian. 'You won't get a chance tomorrow.'

All he wanted was to strip off the sweat-sodden kit, let the spring air cool his body, and sink a beer or three. Those muskets looked bloody dangerous - more for the musketeer than for anyone foolish enough to wander in front of one. 'No, it's alright, I'll…'

'Tab!' shouted Keith. 'Tab! Take Dan and let him crack a few off.'

On the other hand, now he was here, he might as well experience all that was on offer. Ignoring the muffled sniggers from Mike and Steve, he gave a nod - interested but casual enough not to appear too eager. Or so he hoped. The object of his unrequited affection was talking to the burly bloke who'd helped her earlier, leaning on her gun with her hips tilted at an angle that was never in any military manual, 17th century or otherwise. One knee-length woollen sock had ridden down, showing an inch of creamy flesh.

'Come on, dad! I need to wash my hair!' The sour pout did nothing for her classically-cut features. To someone more poetically inclined, the porcelain skin, delicate cheek-bones, fine-arched brows and dollish ruby lips would have been redolent of the classic English rose, a disdainful beauty with hidden fires burning beneath the ice. To Danny, whose mind was of a less flowery, more functional bent, she was fit. Bloody fit.

'You'll have plenty of time for that! Go on, it's the least you could do after we press-ganged him.'

Tabitha shot a look of pure poison at her father before favouring Danny with an expression that suggested he was sleeping in a shop doorway covered in piss-soaked cardboard - a hint of pity but mostly contempt. 'Oh, come on then.'

'Leave your stick and armour here,' said Julian. 'I'll see they get back.'

'Cheers.' Danny fumbled with his chinstrap. Once he remembered to remove his gloves, he undid the helmet on the third attempt while Tabitha glared murder - mostly at her father but with just enough left over for him. Snatching the sopping woollen cap from his head, he ran a hand through his sweat-dampened hair - he'd never get it back into any sort of style.

'Come on,' muttered Tabitha, tapping her foot and looking skyward. Danny scrabbled for the straps on his armour, but it took Julian's help before he finally removed the cumbersome plates. The kiss of the fresh air as he undid his coat was almost as welcome as the chance to spend some time alone with Tab. He'd do anything to be with her, he'd do anything for her and, given half the chance, he'd do anything to her.

'Ollie!' yelled Keith. 'Do me a favour and pop along to keep an eye on them.'

'Sure,' replied Ollie - he of the flashing blade. 'I'll just ditch some kit and catch them up.'

'Tab's been firing less than a year,' Keith explained to Danny. 'Best Ollie goes with you. Just in case.'

Keith Winters gave a rueful shake of his head as his daughter strutted off with Danny trailing in her wake like a kicked dog. The poor little sap would throw himself off a cliff if she asked him to, but she was sensible enough not to go getting involved with anyone this close to her 'A' Levels.

Julian gulped water from a leather flask. 'Right, I'm going to go and knock myself up something to eat.'

'Not just yet you're not.' Keith had just seen the belligerent figure heading their way, accompanied by his ever-present shadow.

Barry Reynolds, CO of Harding's Foot, was not a happy man. Even the dachshund tucked under his arm seemed to wear a disapproving scowl. 'Julian! What the hell were you playing at out there? I needed your block supporting Keith, not buggering off by yourselves in some sort of cock-measuring contest with those Neanderthals from Northern!'

'Sorry, Barry, but we had orders from brigade to...'

'Bryn?' Barry's face grew as crimson as his doublet. 'That Welsh idiot? You take orders from me! Your colonel! Not him!'

'Bryn really should follow the chain of command.' Ken - at Barry's side as always - held his hat in his hands, greying breeze-ruffled hair the only sign of animation. The high, wide forehead gave the overall impression of a slightly bemused frog. 'He shouldn't be issuing orders to...'

'I'm going to Peter!' The lines of Barry's face deepened until he resembled a crumpled cushion. 'What the hell was he doing promoting that leek-muncher to...'

'We did somewhat break Northern though, Barry.' Julian interrupted the tirade. 'Went through them quicker than a cheeseburger from "Frying Tonight".'

'And we didn't need pike support,' Keith added. 'We had that flank secured.' By ensuring half his block was loaded at all times, no one had been able to come near them.

'But pike wouldn't have abandoned their musket division.' Ken's strangely childlike face at last sparked with some life. 'They'd have been sitting ducks.'

'Just as well we're not actually refighting the civil wars then, Kenneth!' Keith tried to keep the sarcasm as gentle as possible. Mustn't mock the afflicted, though Ken was everything the man in the street would expect a re-enactor to be and Keith found solace in the mild cynicism that cut him adrift from those whose fanaticism made them count the buttons on every coat and check the weave on every pair of hose.

Ken's mouth worked soundlessly before he found his voice. 'But if we're not authentic then...'

Julian flapped his hands. 'I know, I know, but we do have to strike something of a balance, otherwise we'd have one man and his dog watching.'

Like today. 'And the dog wouldn't be all that keen.' Bring back the days of the big battalions that, even then, never outnumbered the crowds. With time and money at such a premium these days - and with so many alternatives that required so much less effort - re-enactment was a dying hobby.

Barry tugged at the dachshund's ears. 'Just make sure you take your orders from me and not that sheep-botherer! Man's an idiot - he couldn't handle a company, let alone a brigade. Clear?'

Julian nodded, a faint smile playing at his lips. 'As crystal, Barry. That's authentic Louis the Fourteenth crystal before you ask, Ken.'

It seemed the debrief was over, but before Keith could retreat, Barry jumped back in like Columbo. 'One more thing.'

Julian sighed. 'Yes, Barry?'

'Trevor - he's a liability. He nearly had my eye out with his flourishing - and I've seen more aware objects standing around a garden pond with fishing rods. Floating turds move with more purpose.'

Keith couldn't really disagree. Poor old sod. 'But he's been with the regiment for years, Barry. It's his life. It's all he's got.'

Barry raised a sandy eyebrow 'So what? What am I? A bloody St Francis for the geriatric and terminally bewildered? Come to me all you who are infirm in mind, body or bladder and I will give you succour! You want me to spoon-feed that bimbling Methusalah his milky tea and rusks just because no one can be bothered to put him in a care home? We're not a charity!'

'Actually we are,' said Ken. 'Registered charity number…'

Julian cut across the 2IC. 'I know he has a tendency to drift off, but what else can we do with him?'

Barry fiddled with the lace collar beneath his rusting gorget. 'I can think of several things - the glue factory, for one. He leaks as well. I thought something had died this morning!'

Julian nodded solemnly. 'Well, just try and keep upwind of him and…'

'No, that death-trap of a camper van he rattles around in!' Barry scrutinised Julian's face as if he knew he was being deliberately mocked. 'One careless match and we'll all be joining the choir invisible! Or we'll find him in there one morning stretched out like bloody Imhotep.'

The whiff of gas *had* been somewhat pungent that morning around Trev's battered old camper - like its owner, it should have passed on with dignity several years ago. Still, no one really wanted to be ensign - Keith's own tenure had been a necessary, yet tedious, evil. He couldn't blame his lads and lasses for avoiding it - they wanted to fight, not ponce around with the colour, and it was the same with Julian's pike. 'Okay, Trev's not ideal, but he does a job and leaves…'

'Job?' Barry's tightening grip prompted a look of bug-eyed concern from the dachshund. 'Carrying the colour is an honour! If someone gets made up to ensign, they'll be bloody well made to appreciate it!'

Ice was forming in Julian's eyes, though he kept his voice calm and reasoned. 'Can't we just leave it for this season - give us chance to butter someone up for next year and find a way of softening the blow for Trev?'

Barry appeared to give this some serious consideration, his brow furrowing in the shadow of his hat. 'Okay,' he said eventually, 'but we can't afford for him to make any more cock-ups. Peter's on my back over this and that's something I can do without!'

'Peter?' snorted Keith. Peter was Lord General of the King's Army, a real-life, old school galloping major. 'He's too busy having tiffin or letting his current filly have a blow on his hunting horn!'

A brief, rare smile flickered across Barry's saturnine face. 'Probably. Francesca's in the saddle at the moment, isn't she? Or is it Wendy? Philandering old fruit. It'll rot off.' He placed the dachshund on the ground. 'Heel, Rommel! Kenneth.' Adjusting the hang of his sword, he raised an eyebrow to Julian. 'You broke Northern?'

'Obliterated them.'

'Excellent!' A full, genuine grin ironed most of the discontent from the rumpled features. 'Can't wait to see the Cock of the North's sweaty face in the beer tent tonight.'

The dutiful laugh died in Keith's throat - something awful was happening to his leg. Even through the leather of his bucket top boot he could feel something bashing his calf like a demented jackhammer - apparently the same something that had wrapped furry limbs around his knee in a lustful embrace.

'Well, carry on.' Barry gave a curt nod. 'Rommel! Leave!'

Keith reached for the water canteen at his hip, but Barry's voice was obviously enough to cool the canine ardour. Head hanging down, but with a look back at Keith that suggested this was only adieu, not goodbye, Rommel slunk away after his master. As did Ken.

'That thing's a sex maniac.' Keith brushed at his britches, careful not to let his fingers linger too long on the coarse wool. 'Thank God Barry's downsized.'

Julian was struggling to keep the grin from his face. 'Yes, remember General Wolfe? If he was humping your leg you'd let him finish - and light up his fag afterwards.'

God forbid. 'If only he'd stopped at legs! We never did see Roger again, did we? Or Wolfe, come to that.'

'No. Barry reckoned he was a cross-breed, didn't he?'

Well, they did attract all sorts. 'Roger? That could explain...'

'No, you prick, Wolfe.'

'Bollocks!' The beast had been a menace, genuinely terrifying, Cerberus with a deficit of heads - one had been more than enough. 'Half nothing. That thing was all wolf - the only dog it had in it was what it could pick from between its fangs. Probably had someone's sweet, grey-haired old grandmother in there as well.'

'More than likely. Talking of grey-haired, what to do about Trev?'

'God knows. It's not like he's the oldest on the field. You know old Bob Seymour from Ballam's? He's been drumming for thirty years!'

'Really?' Julian smirked. 'His arms must be tired by now!'

'Not non-stop, you arse!'

The men and women of Julian's pike block trooped past trailing their weapons. With blood and bruises around lips and noses - Steve had a blackening lump below his left eye - Keith was glad that his time in the block was done.

'Get some ice on that, Steve.' Jane was working her way through the walking wounded, checking their bumps and bruises.

'Yes, Jane, I will, Jane.'

'And Nick, would you please take on some water before you start chucking more booze down your neck?'

Nick grimaced. 'Yes, Jane. Come on, boys - beer tent's open.'

Jane, her duty done, slipped an arm around Keith's waist and gave him a peck on the cheek. 'Good battle, love?'

'Not too bad, though the way Barry goes on...' His musketeers were trooping off in the wake of the pike and, knowing he owed a pint later in the beer tent, he called to the burly figure bringing up the rear. 'Terry! Cheers for sorting out Tab's gun.'

'No problem.' Cocking a stubby thumb, Terry screwed his broad features into a smile. 'Just got her touch-hole blocked by some wadding.'

'And I see you had to put Ray out again!' Just a little fire caused by the proximity of sparks and wool. Happened all the time - but to some more than others.

'What, the human torch?' Terry gave a gap-toothed grimace. 'He's been lit up more times than a dogger's headlights!'

Jane gave a tut of disapproval. 'He's a liability!'

It was obviously Keith's day for defending the troops. 'Yes, but his heart's in the right place.'

'Pity his eyebrows aren't,' grunted Terry. 'Or his fingers.'

'And just remember who has to patch up the collateral damage next time he goes off,' added Jane. 'At least Danny came through okay.'

'Poor love - he looked terrified!' The diminutive Annie caught Jane's last words as she came past, rattling her sticks on the rim of her drum. 'He's a good-looking lad though, isn't he?'

'Oi! You're a married woman!' Terry sucked in his paunch and puffed out his chest. 'Why would you look at a scrawny little pup like that when you've got this?'

I know - sometimes I just can't believe my luck!' Annie blew him a kiss, the frizz of dark hair she shook free from her Montero cap instantly softening her features. Men's kit did her few favours in Keith's eyes, unlike his Jane, whose winsome curves ensured her femininity whatever her attire.

'Did Danny enjoy it, Julian?' asked Jane.

'Hard to tell. Doesn't say much, does he?'

'He's a lovely lad. We've known Sarah and Paul for years, haven't we, Keith?'

Longer than he cared to remember. 'Cracking couple.'

'Did they never fancy a bash?' Julian started strapping Danny's armour over his halberd.

'Not really their thing.' Keith tried to imagine dapper Paul Bowers in the garb of a pikeman and failed. 'Nor Danny's, I suspect. He's only here for one reason, mucky little sod. Still, if it brings in the recruits...'

Jane slapped him across the shoulder. 'That's your daughter you're using as a recruiting sergeant! God, it's like something out of Dickens!'

The cordoned-off meadow on the outskirts of the campsite echoed to dull cracks as trainee musketeers were put through their paces. Smoke hazed the reddening sun that shone fractured through the pine trees. Wrinkling his nose against the acrid, eggy stink that was slowly becoming familiar, Danny lifted the rope barrier for Tabitha to duck under.

'So Ken is second in command to Barry.' Tabitha straightened up, adjusting her cap that had caught on the rope. 'Look, you're not really interested in this, are you?'

'I am!' insisted Danny, his constant questions having been the only way of carrying their stilted conversation through the campsite. Taking the route over the top of the barrier, he snagged his hob-nailed boots and only a series of frantic hops saved him from a humiliating fall. 'Honest! What's your dad?'

'Captain of the musket division.'

'Got it.' Divisions, companies, regiments, brigades, matchlocks, doglocks, partisans, halberds, captains, sergeants, majors, sergeant-majors. The words were as endless as they were incomprehensible, but at least while she was talking on a subject she loved she was treating him nearly as an equal. 'And that Julian bloke - the posh one - runs the pike, yeah?'

'That's right. And he's not that posh. It's called being cultured - the only culture you've got is growing between your toes.'

'Easy! I've got feelings!' To keep the conversation from flatlining, he recalled the other characters who had caught his attention that afternoon. 'There was a bloke dressed up like a vicar...'

'Kev?' The perfect - if petulant - bow of Tabitha's mouth turned down. 'He's a bloody perve!'

Having observed Kev's antics, Danny couldn't disagree, but her answer threatened to curtail the conversation. 'Yeah, but what does he do?'

'Pervy things!' She folded her arms protectively across her chest.

Seeing he'd get no more out of her regarding Kev, he chose a different target. 'What about the old boy with the flag who keeps wandering off?'

'Trevor? He's the ensign - it's the least dangerous job they could give him after he lost his licences. And don't let Barry or anyone else - especially Ken - hear you call it a flag. It's a colour.'

'Colour. Right. Got it.' A flag was just a bloody flag, wasn't it? Something else she had just said struck him as rather ominous. 'Licences?'

'Shotgun and explosives licences.' Tabitha lifted her musket. 'For this. They're not toys, you know. Oh no.' Her face dropped.

'What?' What had he done wrong? He hadn't even got his hands on her musket yet. Not that he was overly keen. Nothing safe needed a licence, let alone two. However, following the line of her gaze, it became apparent that her dismay was reserved for the thick-set guy stomping toward them. With his tall wide-brimmed hat and sombre black coat, he looked like an archaic undertaker.

'Richard Macintyre,' Tabitha said. 'He's the Parliament Lord General - among other things.'

Showing that imitation was indeed the sincerest form of flattery, the oily-looking guy slinking along at Macintyre's shoulder was dressed almost identically, though the short, plump kid walking behind them with a standard slung over his shoulder - smaller than Trevor's great banner and embroidered with gold script - was dressed a little brighter in plum-coloured coat and emerald britches. A West Highland terrier scampered between the three pairs of trudging feet.

'Parliament?' Gripping his hair, Danny sifted through the torrent of information that he had half-absorbed already today. 'Is that us? Is he our boss?'

Tabitha threw up her arms. 'No. We're Royalists, for the hundredth time.'

'Afternoon, Tabitha.' Macintyre's Scottish accent matched his appearance - thick-set and dour - and he somehow seemed to speak as if he had an imaginary cigar clamped between his teeth.

'Hello, Richard.' Tabitha forced a smile onto her face. 'Ian. Hi, Sophie.'

'Hello.' Ian - the oily bloke - showed a yellowing smile of breath-taking insincerity, his tones dripping with obsequiousness. 'And who do we have here?'

'This is Danny - one of our new recruits.'

'First time, eh?' Ian seized Danny's hand, pumping it up and down with each syllable. 'Enjoying it? Of course you are! Good, good, excellent! Still, if you'd rather see what the view's like from the winning side, then...'

'Hands off, Ian! We saw him first!'

'Can't blame me for trying!' Ian released Danny's hand. Danny fought back the urge to wipe it on his jacket. 'So, you and he are...'

Tabitha wrinkled her nose. 'Oh, no, no! Nothing like that! He's a friend of the family, that's all. Dad's been trying to get him along for years. No, God, no.'

'So what made you want to come along this time then, Dan?' The plump kid had a surprisingly soft voice with the merest hint of a Scottish accent. Danny's rusted cogs grated into place. "Sophie" apparently wasn't any sort of nickname and the penny dropped fully when the standard bearer pulled off his - her - hat to reveal dull blonde hair yanked back into a bun.

'Don't know really.' Danny shrugged, Tabitha's protestations having stuck two fingers up at the pathetic reason for his being here. However, there was a passive appeal to Sophie's cheerfully plain features that invited candour and, though he could not reveal the depth of his obsession, he could at least give an answer that her amiable enquiry was more deserving of. Also, the longer he kept her talking, the longer he was kept away from the unpredictable muskets - perhaps they'd run out of time altogether? 'Thought it would be a break from revising.'

Cornflower eyes sparkled with genuine interest. 'You as well? Uni in September?'

'Hope so, yeah.' It still seemed so far in the future as to be another life, but in four short months, if all went well (and he had no reason to suspect that it wouldn't), he would be moving out of the house he had called home for all of his eighteen years. It was a daunting prospect, and one he tried to avoid dwelling on, but her words had cast a dark shadow over the bright spring afternoon. 'If I get my grades.'

'I'm sure you will.' A gregarious smile split her round face. 'Exciting, isn't it? I can't wait! What are you stud...'

Macintyre gave an impatient cough. 'Come on, Sophie.'

'Okay, dad. Catch you later, Tab. Nice to meet you, Dan.'

'Oh, yeah, same.' It was always the fat ones that were friendly - the sort described by their friends as having a "really great personality". Great personality or not, he all but forgot Sophie as Ollie sauntered up, dark hair riffling in the breeze, coat hanging rakishly open. His companion, the red-haired drummer, had stripped off her ornate jacket, and the sweat-dampened shirt clinging to her heroic contours was dangerously transparent in places. Danny managed to drag his gaze to her face - only to be pinned for a second time by the predatory flare of her smoky eyes. Once more his cheeks flamed like those of a little kid caught peeking into the girls' changing rooms, and he studied the lacings of his ankle-high boots.

'Sophie!' Ollie threw his arms around Macintyre's daughter in a fraternal hug. 'Hi!'

'Hi, Ollie!' Sophie pressed her cheek to his and waved to the girl. 'Mandy!'

Macintyre ground his teeth 'Come on, girl!'

Sophie disentangled herself. 'Coming! See you later, guys.' She fell in behind her father and Ian, stepping around the terrier which, showing no signs of wanting to leave, bared its teeth at Danny.

'Leave him, Fairfax!' snapped Macintyre over his shoulder. 'You'll no want to chew on a Harding. You'll catch worms.' Giving one last snarl for form, the dog trotted away.

Ollie vaulted the rope. 'Come on then, Dan, let's go and have a pop.'

'A quick pop,' added Tabitha. 'I want to get ready for the beer tent.'

Which would probably involve quaffing from horns while pounding the tables in time to rousing ditties in which "huzza" and "hey-nonny-nonny" would be all too prevalent. 'Shouldn't that be mead tent?'

'Don't be a twat, Danny. Now watch.'

He tried to look interested as Tabitha loaded her musket, though he was too conscious of Mandy's appraising gaze for the unnecessarily complicated process to make any sense, let alone sink in. With broad cheekbones and a wanton upward lift to the centre of her lush upper lip, Mandy's charms were a little more robust than Tabitha's trim, old-fashioned beauty, but no less alluring. The redhead exuded a heated magnetism, an easy sexuality that made every move, every look, a sultry invitation.

Tabitha had the loaded gun at her shoulder, left leg slightly extended and head tucked into the stock - the glowing cord (match, she'd called it) looked horribly close to her face. Her finger tightened on the trigger, sending the match dipping toward the pan. The priming flared with a vicious hiss and, a split-second later, Tabitha's trim frame gave a slight judder as the gun roared, kicking back in response to the flame jetting from the muzzle. Jesus! Anyone standing too close would have been cooked! The red-orange tongue had licked out a fair few yards and the dry thump had battered Danny's eardrums with more ferocity than the massed volleys of earlier. Smoke rolled away over the meadow.

'Right, I'll load it and then you can have a go.' Dropping the musket smartly to her side, Tabitha began the laborious loading process.

'Nothing to it,' Ollie assured Danny. 'Just keep your head down or you'll get a face-full of pan.'

'Right, yeah.' The rotten-egg stink of gunpowder tickled the back of his throat - at least he didn't have to load the bloody thing. The match still glowed between Tabitha's fingers as she poured powder down the barrel. Was that safe? It couldn't be safe!

'Keep it tucked in nice and tight to your shoulder. Lean into it. You won't get much recoil as it's not firing ball, but you'll still know it's gone off.'

'Right, yeah.' The thought of being so close to such a violent discharge left him queasy. It would be like holding a backfiring exhaust in his hands.

'Here you go.' Tabitha handed the musket to Danny. He took it with the tips of his slick fingers - it was heavier than he'd expected. 'It's not going to bite you!'

Did he really need all his fingers? Making sure he kept away from the trigger, he nestled the butt into the angle of his chest and bicep, left hand cupped under the barrel, right hand wrapped around the stock. Tilting his head away from the smouldering match, he slid his left hand further forward as the barrel dragged downward. Tab must be stronger than she looked.

'Pull it into your shoulder!' Tabitha's tones were strained with exasperation.

'Right, yeah.' He shifted the butt a little higher, the mesmerising red-orange ember glowing like a tramp's dog-end.

'No, higher. Into your shoulder. No! Look here, I'll show you.'

Like a primary school teacher snagging a recalcitrant pupil, she took a firm hold of his unprotesting arms and pressed in close behind him. The involuntary sigh that whispered past his lips shivered the match's thin trail of smoke. He dumbly allowed her to tuck the butt into his shoulder, the cool touch of her fingers enough to make his flesh simmer even through the thick wool. His legs, weary from the exertions of battle, threatened to crumple beneath him and he locked them rigid, his backside burrowing into her taut abdomen. He was grateful for the cool wood against his cheek.

'Careful!' Mandy's voice dripped with syrupy promise. 'I think it's about to go off!'

Ollie's laugh was easy and free from malice. 'Well, it is his first time.'

'Leave it out, you two!' Tabitha stepped back. 'Ready, Danny?'

Danny nodded, though whether he had the nerve to pull the trigger remained to be seen.

'Right, open the pan and squeeze the trigger.'

'Have a care!' hollered Ollie.

'What?' Danny had heard the same cry frequently throughout his cursory pre-battle drill and the engagement itself, but he had no idea what the arcane order meant. 'Why?'

Mandy dipped her eyelashes. 'He's just warning people you're about to squeeze one out!'

'Oh, right, yeah.'

'Off you go then, mate.' Ollie gave him a nod of encouragement.

Danny blew out a shuddering breath and sighted along the musket. The stretch of grass and trees blurred into a green morass, the steel barrel snapping into sharp focus. Sweat stung his eyes. He wanted the loo. Or to puke. Or both. He blinked, and his finger crept toward the trigger. Then crept back. What if it blew up in his face? Then again, what if Tabitha thought he was a wimp? Sod it! With a convulsive jerk, he snatched at the trigger and squeezed his eyes shut, waiting for the world to erupt.

There was no hiss, no flare of ignited gunpowder, and no deafening explosion. Slowly, he unhunched his shoulders and peeled his eyes apart.

'Typical!' The disappointed pout on Mandy's face was at odds with the bawdy mirth dancing in her doe-eyes. 'What a disappointment for a girl! Must be nerves!'

'You didn't open the pan, did you?' Tabitha's expression prayed for deliverance from idiots. 'Better blow on the match - if you haven't knocked the coals off.'

'What?' The warm flush on Danny's cheeks seeped through his skin to mire his senses in marshmallow.

'The match. You've probably stubbed it out. The tip needs to be glowing.'

'Uh?' It was like when you'd drifted away during a lesson and the teacher picked you out with unerring accuracy, whipping the class into a bewildering carousel of sniggers while you tried to search for the answer to a question you hadn't even heard.

Tabitha looked skyward. 'Just blow on it - and try not to burn your lips.'

'Blow? I've got this!' Mandy eased herself into Danny, the seething whirlpool inside him hitting critical mass. He tried to pull away from the intimate press of her breasts, but a hand dropped to his arse and took a firm hold, a gentle squeeze telling him to stay where he was. Drained of all strength, his body thrummed like an electricity pylon, her soft breath tickling his ear and skimming across his searing cheek to coax the match back into life.

'Nice and red now,' purred Mandy. 'There's nothing like a nice glowing tip.'

'Right, open the pan this time.' Tabitha's tone suggested that her patience had long since flown and he fumbled for the pan cover, taking four attempts to slide it open while Mandy's sensuous blowing ignited nerve endings in the furthest-flung reaches of his body. Curling his toes against the excruciating assault, he thanked God everyone was standing behind him - the baggy hang of his britches could only hide so much. After a last appreciative squeeze of his buttock, Mandy released him, though the evidence of her handiwork remained.

'Now,' said Tabitha. 'F…'

He yanked at the trigger, screwing up his eyes against the hissing fountain of spark-riven smoke, welding his muscles tight against the expected recoil that never came. His ears - somehow locked down against the anticipated explosion - opened like flowers. The thing hadn't even gone off!

'Misfire.' Tabitha somehow made it sound like his fault.

'Aah, shame,' cooed Mandy. 'Never mind. Perhaps we can try again in a minute.'

Cocking open an eye, Danny lowered the musket, making sure the unpredictable contraption was pointed well away from him.

'Wait!' yelled Ollie. 'It might be a…'

With a hellish roar, the gun erupted, bucking like a live thing and kicking back between Danny's legs. Only the proud results of Mandy's attentions saved his balls from savage punishment, though nothing cushioned the jet of terror-laced adrenalin that drilled through his core.

'…hang-fire.'

The beer tent could never have been prosecuted for false advertising. It was a tent - a vast white marquee jam-packed with sweating humanity - and it sold beer. Cask ales were racked behind the long bar, possessed of a variety of gut-wrenching names that promised a rollercoaster ride come morning, though the more prosaically named ciders were no less potent. Two token lager pumps hung forlornly from the chipped formica, and rickety trestles groaned under the massed ranks of wine and spirit bottles - it was no place for the abstentious, or for those who wished for a quiet conversation. A noisy gaggle of grass-stained kids weaved between the adults, though their shrieks and laughter were drowned out by the rock band belting out covers on the low stage where dry ice hung like musket smoke and blue strobes pulsed through the murk.

The lager Danny sipped from a plastic glass was going to have to last him - it had taken about ten minutes to get served (through a combination of mime and pitied comprehension from the pretty Goth behind the bar) and he was in no hurry to repeat the process. The barmaid's black-eyed contempt - and the practised ease with which everyone else ordered their drinks - only served to further distance him from the riotous jamboree. At least his fears had been largely unfounded - it was no ersatz banqueting hall and there was not a "nonny" to be heard. It was almost like a gig or festival, but in jeans and a tee-shirt, he was somewhat under-dressed - or over-dressed, depending where he looked. Most of the blokes retained at least a vestige of their uniforms - the muggy stench of sweat and damp wool mingled with the rustic scents of the crushed grass floor - or wore even more lavish costumes. There was everything from Spartans to space-age stormtroopers, but it was the girls that caught his eye - they had come dressed to impress. Those in 17th century costume were corseted to eye-watering degrees of immodesty, while others sported the sort of skimpy outfits usually seen in an Ibiza nightclub.

The band finished their quick-fingered version of "Whiskey in the Jar", launching into the next number before the shrill whistles and applause had died down. The thump of the bass jabbed an invasive digit up Danny's backside to stir the lager churning in his guts, while the buzz of the guitar cut through his deadened senses like a chainsaw. Contorted silhouettes writhed amid the strobe-shot fog, and the occasional familiar face appeared through the haze. Ollie was throwing some fancy shapes, mimicked by a gaggle of admiring girls, while Jane and Annie pogoed furiously alongside Tabitha and Mandy. Cinched tight into her dress with her honey-coloured hair loose over bare shoulders, Tabitha was like a fairy-tale princess, though she looked almost frumpish next to Mandy, whose every gyration threatened to spill her ample, corset-enhanced charms out of the wisp-thin blouse. She was working her way closer to a group of bare-chested lads piling on top of each other's shoulders with whoops and yells - the rookies from the pike block Harding's had shattered on the field, though none of them looked the worse for that. A familiar barb twisted in Danny's guts, but Tabitha was paying no heed to their antics. Maybe he should go and join her? Someone would have to hold his drink, though - if he put it down on one of the cluttered tables, he'd never find it again. The erratic pulses of the strobes highlighted half-recognisable faces amidst the smoky gloom. Obviously bewildered by the festivities, Trevor stood drinking from a pewter tankard, dressed as if posing for a Van Dyck painting. Mike, Steve and Nick were at the bar, exchanging good-natured abuse with their erstwhile opponents, while Keith and his musketeers laughed and joked in a tight-knit little group. Lurking in the shadows, Kev eyed the dancers over the rim of a clay jug, no longer wearing his priest's garb but dressed in a tattered Harding's blue-coat. Julian stood alone, drinking sparingly with a faint smile on his lips. The divide remained as unbridgeable as ever - there was little choice but to remain a frustrated onlooker.

'Listen to those bastards!' Richard Macintyre, huddled with his inner circle in a gloomy corner, jerked his head toward the bar. Not even the jet-engine decibels of the band could drown out Harding's celebrations. 'What the hell were Northern playing at, getting trounced by those idiots?'

Ian sipped at his pint like a cat lapping milk. 'Wouldn't have happened in your day, Richard.'

'Aye, mebbe not, but I couldn't stay CO for ever.' Before making the jump to Lord General, Macintyre had commanded the Northern Association - one of the brigades making up the Army of Parliament.

'At least we win tomorrow,' said Ian by way of consolation.

'We won today! Not that you'd know! Oh no, not now.' Barry and Ken, wearing shabby Harding's blue-coats rather than their officer's finery, had just sauntered into the beer tent. Macintyre had friends all across the society, even in Royalist regiments, but Harding's? Just because they were one of the biggest regiments - outnumbering a Parliament association by themselves on a good day - they conferred upon themselves the status of Immortals, a self-righteous Praetorian Guard. Insufferably assured in their own superiority, self-imposed guardians of authenticity and historical fact, fanatically devoted - some would say deludedly so - to the noble legend of the real-life Colonel Harding, they had been unbearable even before Gruppenfuhrer Reynolds had taken over a couple of years ago.

'And as for Northern' - Reynolds' voice was deliberately loud - 'I've dipped sturdier soldiers in my egg!'

Bastards! Macintyre clenched his fists. 'Cocky c...'

'Just ignore them,' said Ian.

'What's that, Ken?' Barry had overheard. 'Do I hear the Whingatron 5000 being cranked up? Or is it bagpipes? Oh, evening, Mac. Hope we didn't damage Northern too much?'

If you took out the newbies who'd bolstered Northern's ranks - and there was no substitute for experience - Harding's had had a bigger block. There had been no shame in losing to them, so why did it feel like a knife was being twisted in his guts? 'They'll be up for it tomorrow.' They better bloody be!

'So will we.' Barry brushed the sleeve of his battle-worn coat. 'Pity the

Newton tribe got banned, isn't it? Bet Northern miss them in the block! That's a lot of weight to lose!'

'Wanker,' muttered Macintyre under his breath. The Newtons had been the mainstay of Northern since he'd been a callow pikeman, and once their progeny had been old enough to take the field, the association had been nigh on unstoppable. Reynolds was right. They were missed. 'Just wait until they're back.'

'Back?' Reynolds' face was suffused with dark glee. 'They won't be back! Not so long as I'm in the society! And with days like today, my friend, that's going to be a long time! A very long time indeed!' His fake cough did little to disguise the grunt of "tosser".

'We'll see.' Was there anything that could puncture Reynolds' supercilious air? 'We've been recruiting. We'll replace them.' Friends of friends of friends who were treating it like some sort of music festival - an excuse for drinking, screwing and probably more. Still, maybe one or two would snap into shape eventually.

'Yes, I can see your new recruits.' Reynolds' eyes narrowed when he saw who Mandy was gyrating with on the dance floor.

'Their kit was a disgrace!' said Ken with a disapproving frown. 'I know we have to encourage newbies, but desert boots and welding gloves? And the state of them now - they'll be fit for nothing tomorrow morning.'

'One way or another,' smirked Ian.

'Just keep their paws off my daughter!' Reynolds ignored Ian's subtle dig but still gave Macintyre the opening he'd been waiting for.

'I think it's more a case of keeping…'

Reynolds closed the gap between them in an instant. 'What's that meant to mean?'

'What's what meant to mean?' How far would Reynolds go? His face said all the way, but there were better ways of cutting him down to size.

'What you just said!'

'I didn't say anything!'

'Yes you did! Go on, say it again!'

'It.' Childish, but more than worth the flare of anger in Reynolds' unrelenting eyes. 'Again.'

'Dickhead,' muttered Reynolds, not quite quietly enough to be ignored.

'What?'

'I didn't say anything.'

'You did!' Two could play Reynolds' game if he didn't have the balls to throw a proper insult. 'Say it again! Go on!'

'It. Again.'

This was getting tiresome. 'Oh, for f… Grow up, man!'

'When you do!' The muttered "dickhead" was again just too faint to give offence.

'What?'

'Nothing. Come, Kenneth, we'll leave them to their Puritan revels - must be nearly time for them to break out the turnip juice!'

Reynolds swaggered off. Making to follow, Ken stumbled over Ian's outstretched foot. It could have been an effort to maintain his balance or a feeble attempt at a back-hander, but Ken's flailing arm knocked Ian's pint from his hand and showered beer over Macintyre's retinue who, until now, had merely been interested observers.

'Whut the fuck?' rumbled Tam, a fellow Scot with grey hair you could lose a regiment in and forearms like Forth Bridge girders. Ken backed away.

'Look what you've done, Rain Man!' Macintyre wrung beer from his shirt. 'I'll…'

Reynolds was back at Ken's shoulder like a shot, that animal Nick Owen looming behind him. Maybe Nick could be pushed far enough into earning himself a ban like the Newtons, but Macintyre didn't fancy having to patch his face back together for the privilege.

'You'll what?' enquired Reynolds politely.

Let him go - revenge was a dish best served cold, as they said. 'Enjoy tonight! Tomorrow?'

Scowling beneath the beer dripping from his brows, Ian drew a finger across his throat. Nick growled like an angry bear, but the rest of Harding's pike had arrived by now and they ushered him away while hurling choice insults at the cream of the Parliamentarian high command.

Macintyre waited until Reynolds and Ken had departed with their triumphant cohorts. 'Right, that's it!' Bloody Harding's. They'd get theirs and bugger the consequences. 'Sean! Sean! Over here! Now!'

A squat figure detached himself from the nearby huddle of men and women who still wore their riding boots as badges of distinction. The feared Ironsides. 'Yes, Richard?' Sean's Yorkshire accent was thick as gravy and he wore the dour, rumpled expression of a fading comedian in a working men's club.

'There's going to be a slight change for your boys and girls tomorrow.'

'Aye?' Sean cocked a bushy eyebrow.

'Reynolds and his mob - they need bringing down a peg or two.'

'We won't be near them - the script is the same as today.'

'I'm changing the script.'

Even at a distance from the dancefloor, the numbing clamour of the band was having a strange effect on Danny's right ear. It felt horribly warm and moist, with a high-pitched buzz-saw grinding through the muted, vertiginous ache. Fuck! His eardrum had burst! Only a gentle tug on his sleeve stopped him from seeking urgent medical attention.

The girl with her mouth millimetres from his ear was vaguely familiar. When she dropped down off of her tiptoes, she was shorter than him by several inches, affording him an agreeable view down her inflated cleavage. Whatever else he took away from this weekend - cuts, bruises, possibly dysentery - the corsets would stick with him.

'What?' he bellowed back at her over the hard-rock din. She raised herself up on her toes again, but whatever she yelled into his ear, she may as well have yelled it in Swahili. He answered her anyway. 'Yeah, I know. It was!' It was a broad enough reply to cover most options.

'What?' she mouthed. Her full lips, easy to read, pricked his memory. He had her now! Sophie or whatever - the Scottish bird. God, she looked different! Not fat, just curvy - as showcased by her dress - though neither the round glasses nor the unflattering curtains of dull blonde hair did anything for her. Okay, so not fat, but still not a looker, though her plump features were cheerful and easy on the eye. At least she seemed keen to talk to him - however futile that may be.

'I don't know! What did you say?' This really wasn't going anywhere fast.

She put a familiar hand behind his neck to pull him down to her level. 'I said cheer up! It might never happen!'

'What might not?'

Her next words were lost in a crescendo of fizzing rock music. The band's guitarist - sixty if he was a day and thin as a stick - was wind-milling for all he was worth.

'What?'

'I said... never mind! Come on!' Sophie grabbed his unfinished pint, downed it in one easy pull, and led him by the hand out onto the dancefloor, elbowing her way through the packed crowd with good-natured ferocity. Finding a space, she began to dance - although the ear-splitting rendition of "Ace of Spades" meant it was little more than frenzied bouncing up and down. Still clutching her hand, Danny had little choice but to join in with her enthusiastic leaps - it would be fatal to remain still among the jostle of bodies, and the sweating press and ferociously pounding anthem were antidote enough for any vestiges of self-consciousness. The wizened guitarist swooped into a fizzling solo, eyes closed and head shaking as if in pain. Swept up by the searing guitar-work, Danny bumped chests with Sophie - not an entirely disagreeable experience - and slid his fingers from hers to throw himself into a wild spin. Sophie mirrored his moves with a whoop and he whipped around again, getting snagged mid-spin by a wildly gyrating girl sporting a pair of scandalous hotpants. She ground her semi-exposed backside against him, black-rimmed eyes startlingly bright as she laughed over her shoulder, then whirled away into the crowd to let him bring his frenetic rotation full circle.

Sophie had gone. Porcelain features animated only by the mesmeric strobing, Tabitha extended her hands. Was this happening? Careful to keep his eyes on the face that had filled his dreams since well before puberty, Danny took her cool, slender fingers in his. Her rigidity tempered his abandon, her moves precise, affected and totally lacking Sophie's sheer exuberance. She danced for an audience, not for him. It was like dancing with a mannequin, and it was no disappointment when the song ended and she walked away without a word. Nevertheless, his exertions had taken a toll - sweat dripped from his brow and his tee-shirt clung to his armpits - and he needed a drink. Forcing his way back through the heaving crowds, he managed to make it to where Steve, Mike and Nick were propping up the bar.

'Ah, young Danny! Drink?' It was Steve who asked. Without their broad faces constricted beneath helmets, and with no armour to disguise their figures, it was easier to tell Steve and Mike apart. Where Steve's broad frame suggested at least a modicum of regular gym work, Mike's equally robust figure was already well on the cheerful road to dilapidation. He was also more blessed in the hair department - the light gleamed pink from Steve's shaved skull - and had an expression tinged with semi-permanent cynicism. Had Mike offered him a drink, Danny would have been suspicious, but as it was Steve…

'Yeah, go on. Lager, please.'

'Saw you with Tab out on the dance floor.' There was a smirk on Mike's florid features. 'You fancy your chances, then?'

God, was it that obvious? 'Nah, we're just friends, that's all.'

'Yeah, right!' Mike raised a cynical eyebrow. 'We've seen the way you look at her.'

Nick shifted his bulk around, moon face red and sweat-bobbled beneath his bird's-nest hair. 'Can't blame the lad!'

Mike's smirk grew to Cheshire Cat proportions. 'No, one false breath and we'll be scooping them back in with warm spoons!'

Steve joined in. 'And you could rest your pint on Mandy's! Pity she's got a thing for Parliamentarians.'

Nick belched, dragging it from deep within his cavernous guts. 'She's a box of mixed creams alright!' The permanent sheen of sweat glistened beneath the pulsing lights. Danny had never seen anyone so moist.

'Here you go!' Steve handed Danny his lager. 'So, enjoy yourself today?'

Danny gripped the plastic cup a little too hard, slopping lager over his fingers. 'Yeah, yeah. Great.'

'Bollocks! You're only here because of Tab!' Draining his pint, Mike reached for the next one.

'No! No, I'm not!' He couldn't reveal the true depths of his feelings, not to this lot, though the strength of his denial ran counter to his intentions.

'Methinks he doth protest too much!' proclaimed Steve. 'The ice maiden! Good luck with that - even if you got anywhere, Keith would kill you!'

'Don't worry, Dan.' Mike patted him on the shoulder with a heavy hand. 'Plenty on offer around here. Good-looking young lad like you - fresh meat! You'll be beating them off with a shitty stick - if you put yourself out there!'

'Yeah, otherwise you'll only be beating yourself off!' Nick's crude gesture was accompanied by another leonine belch.

'So get stuck in!' Steve slid an avuncular arm around Danny's shoulders. 'Once Tab sees you with a girl or three on your arm, you'll be in! Nick! Let him have a dribble of your special! He's going to need it!'

Danny tentatively took the small stone bottle Nick handed him, sniffing at the narrow neck. It certainly had nose - notes of apple (and was that honey?), a trace of berries and a distressing taint of damp vegetation. Or that might just have been Nick. By the hawk-like interest with which they were watching him, it was obviously some sort of test, and he took a quick sip that would hopefully stamp him with approval - it would be a lonely night otherwise.

It tasted no worse than it smelt - a syrupy mix like gin-laced cider with a cocktail of fruit flavours - though it oozed down his throat like the makeshift napalm made of boiling water and sugar they were rumoured to use in prisons. It took an age, millimetre by searing millimetre, and his eyes streamed as he held back a choke that threatened to strip the flesh from his oesophagus. The worst was yet to come. It hit his stomach like molten lava, the aftershocks sending acid pulsing back up to froth at his nostrils. He handed the bottle back, the ear-blasting music receding into a hazy background hum, and gulped lager to cool his throat. The toxic mix of Nick's special and the carbonated fizz set his guts whirling like a troop of acrobats. Fire-breathing acrobats. With feet of ice.

'Good stuff, eh?' Nick took a generous sip himself. 'Brew it myself!'

'Just don't ask what's in it!' was Steve's advice. 'Nick doesn't have a washing machine - all his dirty kit goes down to his still!'

'Bullshit. Nothing but the finest ingredients. All natural.' Nick belched again. 'My round. Lager, Dan?'

Forlorn flecks of foam decorated Danny's empty glass. How had he finished it already? Still, the firestorm in his guts had died down, leaving a cosy glow of bonhomie. 'Yeah. Yeah, okay. Cheers.'

These were great blokes. Really great. They'd not let him put his hand in his pocket all night. Top geezers. The lads. The guys. The boys. Fucking great laugh - and they understood as well.

'I love her,' Danny said without shame. They understood. They knew. Top blokes. 'I do. I love her. I really love her.' He lifted his beer to his lips, the plastic crumpling against his chin to spill lager down his already soaked tee-shirt. He tried to heave himself up, but his palm slipped in a puddle of beer and he slumped back down, skinning his elbow on the bar. Bastard thing.

Nick passed the bottle back to him. 'You should tell her, mate. Tell her how you feel.'

'Yeah,' said Steve. 'You've told us enough times.'

Danny took a generous swig. It hardly burned now. Great stuff. He could drink it all night. 'He'll Keith me - her dad. You said kill will Keith me.' Jesus, those lights were bright! Why wouldn't they stop moving? And who had put the band underwater?

'Keith'd?' Mike waved away the bottle. 'Nasty!'

'Go on!' urged Steve. 'Go for it! What's the worst he can do? It's Keith or be Keith'd!

Yeah! Fuck him! What could he do? He couldn't stand in the way of true love. These guys knew. His mates. 'Yeah! She wants me! She must do! She asked me here! We've known each other for years. It's... what is it?'

'Fate,' said Nick.

'Destiny,' said Mike.

'Karma,' said Steve.

'Yeah, one of them!' His hand was spread on the bar like a deformed spider, looking somehow alien, detached almost. How did his fingers work? They didn't feel right. Like someone else's. 'It is, isn't it?'

'Of course it is!' Steve relieved him of the bottle, turned him round, and gave him a friendly shove. 'Now, you go out and get her!'

Tabitha Winters. Yeah, she was his! His feet seemed to have ideas of their own, but if he concentrated, he could make them go roughly in the direction he wanted. The crowd parted magically before him. There she was, twisting artfully on the dance floor. God, she was gorgeous. Hair flowing like honey and face, well, face was... was... pretty. And look at that figure! Look at the arse! Look at the pink wobbly bits above the corset. Every girl should wear one. They should be mandatory. Right. Enough looking. He sidled up behind her and wrapped his arms around her waist, nuzzling her neck.

She jerked free and whirled, face like thunder. God, she was beautiful! Utterly terrifying, but beautiful.

'Danny! What the hell are you doing?'

What was her problem? She wanted him - the boys had told him that. His mates. They wouldn't lie. He'd just surprised her, that was all. 'Let's dance! You and me!' Under his fingers, her blouse slithered over the warm flesh beneath.

'Get off!' She slapped his hands away.

Was she on the blob? Frigid? Probably too overcome with emotion.

Yeah, that was it. She just needed a little bit of persuading. 'Come on! You know you want to!'

'You're drunk!'

'No, no I'm not. I've got to tell you how I feel!'

'Oh, really? And how do you feel?'

'I feel...' When had it got so warm? The back of his neck was on fire. Sweat broke on his brow. He needed to sit down. That would stop the tent from spinning. And what was wrong with the light? The shadows looked... weird. All crazy angles and sinister shades which did nothing for the sudden weight in his stomach. 'I feel sick.'

As if a dozen tiny sluice gates had been opened, his mouth filled with saliva, the precursor to the inevitable. Something white and fuzzy flashed past his feet and his stomach erupted like Vesuvius to blurt an acidic stream of yellow-brown, semi-liquid gunge onto the floor. Another heave, and another splat, full of satisfying chunks and meaty goodness. And another. And another. Oh great. For a moment, he tried to hold back the next heave, surrendering when the foul-smelling paste burned his nose. He emptied the rest of his stomach onto the floor, a flurry of frantic yaps drowning out the wet slap of puke.

Jane had seen what had been going on, and while she had no objections to Danny, he'd never normally have the courage to approach her daughter so forwardly. As she raced to save his blushes, Fairfax - Richard Macintyre's terrier - got under her feet and Danny was spectacularly and violently sick before she could reach him. Over the floor, over Tabitha, and over the unfortunate Fairfax who shot away yapping with chunks of what looked like diced carrot tangled in his fur. Over by the bar, Barry convulsed with laughter.

'Oh, for God's sake!' Tabitha brushed a fleck of mustard vomit from her blouse. 'You idiot!'

Danny staggered, trying to hold himself upright though his legs apparently had different ideas. 'I'm sorry. I'm really sorry. Don't let your dad Keith me!'

'Keith you?' Tabitha shook her head, scrubbing her blouse with her knuckles though she had already removed the few specks of sick. 'What the hell are you on about?'

Ignoring the all-pervading smell of vomit that was so familiar from the wards, Jane got an arm around Danny to hold him upright - and to shield him from her daughter's wrath. 'Too much to drink, love? Don't worry, we've all been there. Come on, let's get you to your tent.' The sooner he got some fresh air, the better. He belched ominously and she braced herself.

'I'm sorry.'

'Of course you are, love.' The threatened deluge did not burst forth and she relaxed a little. Judging by the steaming mess on the floor, there couldn't be much left to come out. 'Give me a hand, Tabitha.' He was a strapping lad and she didn't rate her chances of getting him back to his tent. She wouldn't leave him, though. Aside from the fact that she'd known him since he was in nappies, her instincts would not let her abandon anyone in his condition. At eighteen, he was judged to be responsible for himself, but no one, no matter how old, could be classed as responsible in that state. 'Tab?'

'No way!' The china-doll features were pitiless. 'I'm not touching him! Dad brought him, get him to help you!'

Jane ran a hand through the tousled hair of the handsome youth slumped against her shoulder. 'He's only here because of you - you know that.' Poor lad. She'd never understood why Tabitha had never given him a chance - not that he had any kind of hope after tonight.

'Then he's a bigger idiot than I thought!' Tabitha flounced off, replaced by an equally irate Richard Macintyre. Fairfax, tucked under one arm, presented a sorry, bedraggled sight.

'What's up with him?' Macintyre eyed Danny with suspicion.

'Just got a bit carried away on his first muster.' She couldn't throw Danny to the wolves - not when he was due an extended period of frostiness from Tabitha.

'Some bastard puked on Fairfax!' Accent thickening, Macintyre lifted the dog as evidence. It adopted a suitably put-upon expression and whined like Greyfriars Bobby. 'Was it him? Did he soil my dog? Did Barry put him up to it?'

'Don't be silly, Richard. Danny's not been sick - not yet!' Shuffling forward to hide the evidence, she tried not to grimace at the acidic warmth seeping through the leather of her shoes. 'If you don't let me get him some fresh air though...'

Macintyre backed off. 'I'm watching you! All of you!'

Somehow, Jane managed to manoeuvre Danny - now in state of soupy semi-consciousness - outside. She should really get him back to her caravan - it would be bad for all concerned if a new recruit choked to death on his own vomit inside his tent - but she'd never make it alone. Her arm was already straining at its socket, but just when she was about to leave him and go for help, the drag of the dead weight eased.

'Someone's enjoyed themselves a bit too much. Need a hand?' Sophie Macintyre had an arm around Danny.

'Oh, bless you, Sophie, yes please. He's a bit of a lump.'

'Sick,' mumbled Danny. 'Feel sick.'

'Whoops.' Could they get him over to the bushes behind the portaloos in time? 'Here we go.' Between them, she and Sophie managed to get

Danny into the scrubby undergrowth where he dropped to his knees and was noisily sick.

Sophie winced, though there was a deal of sympathy on her face. 'I suppose Nick and his crew got their hands on him?'

'Yes. Oh well, boys will be boys. He's not the first.'

'No.' Sophie removed her glasses and polished them on her blouse. 'Someone puked on our dog - was it him?'

'I'm afraid so.'

Sophie's half smile was a world away from the dour, ever-present scowl of her father. 'I won't tell dad.'

'Thanks, love. He already thinks Barry put him up to it. They're as bad as each other, those two! Sorry, I know he's your dad, but...'

'He can get a bit carried away. I know.'

Danny made a horrendous noise, like a parrot gargling razor blades. Jane rubbed the rippling back. 'That's it, love. Get it all up.'

'Oh God!' moaned Danny.

'Ah, the battle-cry of the beer tent warrior!' Sophie, with a rueful shake of her head, stroked Danny's neck. 'We can't put him to bed in this state!'

'No. We'll get him back to my caravan - he can sit there for a bit.' Sophie was such a sweetheart. Not a patch on her Tabitha for looks, of course, but far more straightforward - and nothing at all like her father.

'Not much of a night for you.'

'I'm more than used to it.' At least Keith was past those days now - for the most part anyway - but he'd had his moments. They'd thrown away their first tent - years ago now - after he'd redecorated the interior after one particularly heavy night. 'You finished, Danny?'

Danny looked up, wide-eyed and pitiful. 'Sorry. I'm sorry.'

'Of course you are.' Jane - with Sophie's help - hauled him to his feet. 'Come on, let's get you cleaned up.'

The evening's festivities were drawing to a close. The band was silent at last and even the die-hard drinkers were leaving the darkened beer tent, wading through a littering of discarded plastic cups, cigarette butts, ketchup-stained polystyrene trays and the dribbling figures of those revellers who'd decided their tent was just too far to walk. The long queue before the brightly lit serving hatch of "Frying Tonight" - one of several food vans plying their trade at this late hour - was testament to the effect of alcohol over experience.

Mandy and her lucky paramour - one of the rowdy Northern recruits - exchanged saliva in a steamy clinch before she led him behind the portaloos. As the amorous couple disappeared, a salacious figure detached itself from the shadows and followed in their wake. Kev smoothed his moustaches and hunkered down, his smirk widening in direct correlation to the pitch and urgency of the muted cries of passion.

Burger in one hand, bottle in the other, Nick ploughed head-down through the gaggle of chattering girls around Ollie. Ollie's *sotto voce* quip was greeted with tinkling feminine laughter and a departing belch from the shambling man-mountain.

Keith, mildly buzzing, walked with Barry, Ken and Julian. What had happened to Jane? More importantly, would she be in the mood for anything frolicsome when he got back to the caravan?

'Right, time for a night-cap?' Barry veered around a guy rope as they entered the Harding's enclave. 'I want to go over some plans for the August Bank Holiday muster. The Battle of Little Felcham...'

'Technically it was a skirmish,' said Ken.

'The Battle of Little Felcham.' Arriving at the door of his caravan, Barry glared at Ken. 'The last stand of Harding's Regi...'

What Keith took to be the face of a Greek Fury appeared suddenly at the caravan window - pinched, shrewish and haloed with wild platinum hair. Ken jumped and let out a little whimper. Julian's eyes flickered. Barry's head drooped.

'It will keep until tomorrow. Coming, dear.' With a regretful look at his subordinates, Barry slipped into the caravan. As soon as the door shut, a shrill voice whirred into life to drown out Barry's mollifying tones.

Julian winced. 'Looks like Alice is still under the weather!'

Keith wasn't sure even Barry deserved Alice. 'Is that woman ever over the weather? Must be her "Crone's" disease playing up again!'

Ken frowned. 'Oh, I don't think it's a digestive disor...'

Tough crowd. 'No, I meant crone, not Crohn. You know, like a wit...' As if possessed of preternatural hearing, Alice sprang back into view like a hellish Medusa jack-in-the-box. 'Jesus!' Abandoning Ken and Julian, Keith fled into the night.

'Feeling better now, love?' After a couple of hours of sipping water and apologising in the Winters' awning, Danny at least had control of his legs now, though Jane still had a hand on his arm as she guided him toward the little blue and grey tent. "2 Persons" it said on the front, though it was hard to see how even just Danny would fit in there.

'Yeah. Thanks, Mrs Winters.' Danny dropped to all fours, fumbling for the tent's zip.

'Jane. Come on, how long have we known each other? It's not the first time I've put you to bed.' Her headtorch illuminated his blushes - at least it was an improvement from the deathly white of earlier. 'You sure you're going to be alright?'

Danny twisted himself into the tent like a butterfly that had given up on life and decided to regress to childhood. 'I'll be fine. Sorry for…'

'Don't worry about it - it will all be forgotten by tomorrow. Get some sleep - you know where we are if you need anything. Goodnight.' Zipping up the tent for him, Jane set off through the darkened avenues back to her caravan, following the bobbing circle of light from her torch.

Rolling through the campsite, guided only by animal instinct, Nick side-stepped to let Jane hurry past. His trailing foot caught a guy rope, tumbling him to the ground with the impact of a respectably sized earthquake. Neurons sparked erratically as he searched for landmarks. Where the fuck was his tent? It was here somewhere. Like a dying elephant trying to find its fabled graveyard, he hauled himself over the ground until he came to a familiar blue and grey tent. The rosy glow of contentment faded when he reached for the zip and his fingers grazed taut, smooth fabric. Bollocks! Where was it? Had to be here. It was his tent - how could he lose the zip? The tent rippled beneath his questing fingers. What the fuck? Some bastard had moved his door! Twats! Load of rubbish! Who made a tent without a bloody door? He fell on the flimsy shelter with both hands, raking the quivering walls in the vain hunt for the missing door. Probably nicked by Northern. Bastards.

Wrapped in his sleeping bag, Danny wriggled until he achieved the optimum position to ease the rolling weight in his guts. Swallowing the sour taste fouling his mouth, he managed to quell the riot of random thoughts that kept his brain from powering down, welcoming the grey fog that set him on the journey to sweet oblivion. It was almost as if someone was rocking him to sleep and… No! Shit! Everything was moving! What the hell? His eyes flared open as the fragile walls billowed with a nylon hiss. An animal growl booted up long-dormant instincts - those that had saved his most distant ancestors from becoming a messy lunch as soon as they stepped out of their caves - and he hunkered deeper down into his sleeping bag, pounding heart threatening to start a chain reaction that would be cataclysmic in the confines of the tent. The walls bulged under another frenzied assault, a giant paw falling on his backside and startling him into movement. Like an arthritic caterpillar, he jerked and wriggled his way across the groundsheet, risking one look back at the monstrous shadow thrashing distorted limbs against the tissue-thin fabric. Who the fuck brought a bear to a campsite? And, more importantly, what did it want if it got in?

*

Bloody door. Where was the bloody door? Nick took one last swipe at his tent and then sunk down onto the ground. It was comfortable here and not too cold. He could have a rest, just for a minute, and then find the elusive door. Closing his eyes, he burrowed his head into the welcoming earth.

***

A golden spring dawn broke, heralded by a seraphic fanfare of birdsong. In the woodlands around the campsite, a variety of improbably fluffy creatures no doubt gambolled and frolicked beneath the pink morning sun in total defiance of the visceral nature of... well, nature. In the Living History camp - the authentic village of white canvas tents where people ate, slept and worked as if they were living in the 17th century (if work back then consisted of continually stirring pots of indistinguishable brown sludge or turning endless wooden bowls on pole-lathes) - fires were being prodded into life by men and women dressed in grubby shirts and shifts that showed far too much hairy leg.

In the so-called plastic campsite (the modern site where most of the re-enactors spent their downtime away from the 17th century) the smell of gas was already hazing the air. Mandy Reynolds - hair dishevelled, corset in hand and loose blouse clutched over her impressive charms - hurried barefoot through the Harding's enclave, side-stepping a snoring mass resembling one of those mysterious giant globsters that occasionally washed up on Pacific beaches.

The aroma of cooking bacon tickled Nick's nose. He sniffed, snorted, and then, cocking open an eye, heaved himself to his feet like Leviathan rising from the deep. He gave one last glare at the tent that had denied him, snuck a peek at Mandy's low-slung backside, then clocked the blue and grey tent some ten yards from where he stood. Realisation dawned in the soupy fog of his consciousness. That was his - and the door was on the right side!

Jane had been up and about early. After emptying the chemical toilet, she'd wandered back through the Parliament camp where Richard Macintyre had been hosing down a miserable-looking Fairfax. Keith and Tabitha had still been sleeping when she'd got back to the caravan, so she'd got the first of the bacon on and brewed some coffee. Filling a plastic cup with the steaming black liquid, she poured in some sugar and gave it a quick stir. Danny liked his coffee dark and he wouldn't want milk curdling in his stomach this morning. Slapping a generous pile of bacon rashers between two slices of bread, she dumped the sandwich on a plastic plate and hurried over to Danny's tent.

There was little sign of life. 'I've brought you some breakfast, Danny. Danny? Are you okay? Danny?'

The unintelligible grunt at least assured her that he had survived the night - though whether that was a bonus only he would be able to tell.

'Feeling better?' Her question was answered with another simian grunt. She placed the coffee and the bacon sandwich down by the tent flap, wafting the tantalizing aroma with her fingers. In her experience, the scent of bacon usually worked Lazarus-like miracles. 'I'll just pop it down outside. Make sure you get something down you - you'll feel better for it.'

Once she was sure there was going to be no further response, she left him to it. Keith and Tabitha would be shouting for their own breakfasts by now and a duty of care only went so far in the face of her own family's demands.

Slowly, painfully, the front of the tent unzipped a few inches. A trembling white hand reached out, grasping the sandwich as a drowning man would grab a length of flotsam.

Sunglasses shading his eyes and Panama hat jammed over his balding pate, Keith sat huddled in his camping chair with a Conference League hangover doing just enough to further ruin his morning. Bloody Barry, calling a meeting first thing on a Bank Holiday Monday! Most of the regiment was assembled before the CO's caravan on folding chairs, deckchairs, stools or the ground. The man himself stood on the caravan steps, Ken at his side.

'Right, I won't keep you long. This is just a quick heads' up for our August Bank Holiday muster. The Battle of Little Felcham.'

'The skirmish of Little Felcham,' muttered Ken.

'The Battle of Little Felcham.' Barry sipped coffee from an oversized mug. 'You should all know the story. For those of you who don't - Kenneth?'

Ken cleared his throat and tried to climb up onto the steps. When it became clear that Barry was not going to relinquish his position, Ken clasped his hands behind his back, looked to the sky, looked at the ground, shuffled left, shuffled right, and then turned his reddening face to his audience.

'July 1645. The king is on the ropes after Naseby.' Ken spoke quickly, robotically almost, and Keith had to crane forward to hear - not that the story was news to him. 'Harding's Regiment, on garrison duty since the storming of Leicester, hear of the king's defeat and head south, gathering stragglers as they go. Camped outside Little Felcham, they're attacked by elements of the New Model Army. The rag-tag force is overwhelmed but Harding's regiment take shelter in the village. The Parliamentarians demand their surrender but Harding refuses and, to spare the villagers, leads the regiment out into the open where they are slaughtered to a man.' It was most likely sweat that Ken cuffed away from the corner of his eye.

'Very moving, Kenneth.' Barry stretched himself up onto his toes. 'Right. There you have it. Harding's last stand. Little Felcham. Kenneth and I are going down there in a week or so for a recce. The battlefield's sorted, we think we've got a campsite, but we will need a village.'

A meaty hand rose into the air. 'I can knock that up for you - I've still got a few bits and pieces laying around from last time and I can rig up a few more. If I can get down to the site, what, two days before everyone else starts arriving, I can get it all put together.' Good old Tel. Keith gave him a mental pat on the back. Mr Fixit. Salt of the earth.

Barry gave a curt nod. 'Thank you, Terry. I'm sure you'll do an excellent job as always.'

'Will it burn?' Ray's narrow features glowed with a fevered intensity beneath the salt-and-pepper stubble, making him look more than ever like some wizened Wild West prospector.

'What's that, Ray?' Barry craned his neck, looking out over the crowd.

'Will it burn?' Ray trembled with suppressed anticipation, the blue smoke of his cigarette curling into the clean air. If there was ever a man more ill-suited to black powder, Keith had yet to meet one, though Ray had all his licences and, despite the occasional conflagration, had never killed anyone. Yet. 'Can we burn it? I could rig up some pyros and...'

'But they didn't burn Little Felcham!' Barry stamped his foot, the iron-framed steps on which he stood wobbling dangerously. 'That's the whole point of Harding's actions!'

Ken's forehead creased. 'There is evidence to suggest that some outbuildings were fired, Barry.'

Ray's eyes lit up. 'And the audience always loves an explosion!'

Ken scowled. 'They set light to a barn or two, Ray! They didn't blow anything up!'

'Artistic licence! Come on, Barry, what do you say? Explosions! Fire! Smoke! It'll look great!'

'But it didn't happen! Not like that!' Ken's voice had taken on a strangled pitch.

'Bums on seats, Ken!' said Ray, lighting a fresh fag from the crushed dog-end in his fingers.

'Be still, Kenneth!' Barry looked into the middle distance, as if seeing the blazing village and a horde of awestruck public. 'I like it, Ray. The barns go up, the villagers flee into the vengeful arms of Parliament, and we march out against a backdrop of flames!' He gradually reeled his focus in. 'Yes, you're on, Ray - as long as there's no repeat of last time!'

Like a particularly ragged Guy smouldering on his bonfire, Ray was engulfed in billows of smoke as he choked on his cigarette. 'That wasn't my fault, Barry.'

'I don't care whose fault it was! We can't afford anything like that again!

Now… where are you two going?'

Mike and Steve folded their chairs away. 'We're doing a cameo with Peter and Kev at twelve, down on Living History.'

Barry's mouth formed an "o" of horror. 'Oh my God - don't do anything to discredit the regiment!'

'As if we would!' Steve looked offended, though Keith could well understand Barry's apprehension. Kev had been known to overstep the mark on occasion and that would be catnip to those two clowns.

'And make sure you're back here for form-up at 1.45.'

'Of course, Barry. Come on, Steve.'

With a low murmur of excited - or not so excited - voices, everyone else started packing their seats up.

'That's not a signal for you all to bugger off!'

'Aren't we done, Barry?' Julian looked indecently fresh.

'I suppose so. For now. Just remember - form-up at 1.45.' Draining his coffee, Barry retreated into his caravan, leaving Ken at the foot of the steps like an abandoned child.

'More hurry up and wait.' Jane folded her camping chair.

Keith rose stiffly, filling his lungs with the invigorating smell of the camp - a mix of wood-smoke, gas, bacon and gunpowder that was a little like Bonfire Night when he'd been a nipper, though richer, more evocative, speaking to the part of him that was as old as the universe. Though the society was no longer what it had been, the smell was still in his blood, could still excite him like a raw recruit and take him back to late nights steeped in booze and companionship and battles with a cast of thousands. Still, last night had been a throwback to the good old days and he stifled a yawn. A mid-morning doze was in order. 'Well, why walk straight to the battlefield when you can hang around for an hour first? Have you seen Danny this morning?'

'I heard noises when I took him some breakfast earlier - he's definitely alive! Probably just a bit embarrassed, poor love.'

Thank God those days were behind him. A mild headache and a slightly queasy tummy were more than enough for him to deal with these days. 'Well, it's not like it hasn't been done before - except for puking on Mac's dog! That was special.'

'I don't think Mac saw it that way - and he was in a foul enough mood to start with!'

Keith rubbed his hands, the prospect of battle driving away the last traces of his headache. 'Well, let's see if we can improve it this afternoon!'

'I shall have you arrested for sedition, you yammering clapperdudgeon! Get yourself from my sight before I have my men beat you!' Magnificently whiskered and wearing a fine suit of blue and scarlet silks, Peter Beesley cut an imposing figure, wearing his mantle of authority with the air of one to the manner born.

The cringing Puritan preacher - Kev in another of his endless guises - raised a leather-bound bible in the face of the blue-blooded belligerence. 'Beat me, you say? For defending the truths contained in this book against the avarice and papery of your king?'

Peter dashed his plumed hat from his head, his snow-white hair seeming to curl in indignation. 'My king is no papist, sir! He is the rightful king, and you would do well to remember it!'

'There is one king only! King Jaysus!' The pious tones were thick with godly bile and archaic inflection.

'Treason, sir!' bellowed Peter, rapping Kev on the head with his silver-topped cane and provoking a nervous titter from the small crowd standing among the smoke-shrouded canvas.

'It is no treason to follow the Lord. We shall see later who holds sway over men's hearts - King Jaysus or Charles Stuart!'

'You have been warned, sir, but you have tested my patience! Beat this rapscallion!'

'Oi!' Mike nudged Steve in the ribs, tearing his attention away from a couple of young mothers in gauzy summer dresses. Bugger! Missed his cue. Flexing his leather-gauntleted hand, he curled it into a fist which he hammered into Kev's stomach, pulling the punch at the last second so that his knuckles barely grazed the stained shirt.

Kev doubled over. 'Urrgh! So this is your King's Justice?' His voice dropped to a hoarse whisper. 'Again! Do it again!'

Mike joined in, twisting Kev's arm to expose his heaving midriff for the next blow. Flesh spread like dough beneath Steve's knuckles, but Kev was still not satisfied. 'Harder!' he urged softly. 'Do it harder!'

Each to his own. Kev was getting far more out of this than he was, but the horrified gasps from the audience as a third punch hit home with a sound like a cabbage being dropped were worth dipping a toe in the murkiest of waters.

'Lovely,' moaned Kev. 'More! More! Come on, put your back into it!' The savage knee that Mike drove into Kev's groin connected with his inner thigh rather than what was swinging in his grubby britches, but he threw his head back and shrieked piteously.

Peter's rich tones rolled over the cries like treacle. 'My lords, ladies and gentlemen, boys and girls, behold the price of treason! Make sure to be here at 3 o'clock, when my army will chastise the rebellious curs of Parliament.'

Following Mike's lead, Steve grabbed Kev's arm and forced him to his knees. For added effect, he kicked him in the ribs with his size twelves. Too much? Apparently not.

'Oh, that's good. Lovely job. Come on.'

Taking hold of Kev's greasy collar, Steve shoved him forward to sprawl on the ground. He really should charge for this highly specialised abuse - he could probably get extra if he put on his uniform and brought his handcuffs along.

'I will not beg for my life!' howled Kev. With a wink at his tormentors, he dropped his voice to a low, lascivious rasp. 'Finish me off.'

'Hah!' Mike's sword (thrust into the ground beneath Kev's armpit) was the catalyst for the grand finale, setting off frenzied death throes of theatrical proportions. Kev screamed. He howled. He jerked like a landed fish. He cursed his tormentors. He cursed the king. He cursed the crowd (rolling across the ground to get a more advantageous view up the floating skirts of the two young ladies who had already caught Steve's eye) and he called on God. Never had any Hollywood cowboy drawn out such a lingering death, lurching between his grieving companions as his life seeped between his fingers. Finally, as the faces of several children grew tearful with concern, Steve drew his own sword and thrust it into Kev's guts. Kev rolled over once more and then was still - except for the spasmodically twitching fingers of his left hand which coaxed nervous applause and a child's wail from the crowd.

The bacon sandwich and coffee had gone someway to making Danny feel human again, though he still dared not leave the stifling sanctuary of his tent to face the low voices and laughter outside. Flashbacks from the previous night flickered like a ghastly highlight reel - just when he thought he was over the worst, another hazy memory would stab him with a fresh spike of shame. Had he really tried it on with Tabitha? And what about her mum? He had vague recollections of an earnest discussion in the Winters' awning and an overwhelming gratitude toward the matronly Jane but, please God, let the phrase "I've always liked older women" be part of the nightmares that slopped over the mercurial rim of recall - he'd already dismissed the bear assault as such. There was no disputing that he'd been sick - his teeth were still coated with the residue and the smell was woven into the fabric of his discarded clothes. Oh God - had Jane stripped him? No telling, as there was no telling what else he had got up to last night, though an irate Scottish voice echoed through his hammering skull. Had there been a dog? There had. A little white one - the same bastard thing that had snapped at him yesterday. He'd puked on it. Oh great. Its owner was some big shot in the society, wasn't he? Well, it didn't matter. He was never coming back.

The temperature was building, the sun gently cooking the inside of the tent. He was busting for a piss, but he'd filled every available receptacle during the night through some latent talent of self-preservation. He had to go - especially as the uproar disrupting his lower regions was on the march downward. His bowels rumbled like a coffee percolator.

He was dripping with sweat (45% proof, probably) by the time he'd finished thrashing his way into his clothes. Unzipping the front of his tent a millimetre at a time, he satisfied himself that there was no one around, scrambled out, and dashed for the closest portaloos. The unfairly bright sun sheared through him like a laser and a horde of shrieking kids erupted from between the clustered tents, battling away with wooden swords. He veered away from them like a fleeing ghoul with the village mob hard on his heels, wasting precious seconds. The delay was almost fatal, but he made it just in time, slamming the cubicle door behind him and blocking out the intrusive sun. Thank God the portaloo had been cleaned - he'd heard stories of veritable Everests of shit piled up over the rim of the seat - and there was toilet roll.

After a distressingly explosive five minutes, he was feeling a little better about life. True, his head was still being clubbed from the inside by a tribe of Neanderthals, but the bulging sensation behind his eyes had gone and, though his stomach still pitched and rolled, things were a lot less urgent lower down. He pumped the handle, flushing the slopping evidence away in a swirl of blue chemicals, and scurried back to his tent unchallenged. Before he could dive into his fusty sanctuary, a hand fell on his shoulder. Shit. It was Keith come to kill him, or that Scottish bloke.

'Caught you at last!' Danny started breathing again - the gently amused tones were Julian's. 'We thought you were hibernating! Come on - form-up in half an hour! You are coming on today?'

Where were the recriminations, the accusations? The total lack of reference to the previous night was almost disappointing. 'I thought I'd give it a miss. I'm not feeling so great.'

Julian's wide eyes sparkled with lazy humour. 'You'll soon get over that once you get stuck in! Just get plenty of water on board - you're not the first to go on with a hangover.'

'It's not that - well it is that - but...'

'Last night? Don't worry about it - you're a legend already!'

Danny took a last-ditch attempt to excuse himself from action. 'No, it's the whole thing - dressing up and that. It's not me. I'm not that sort of person.'

Julian laughed. 'So what sort of people do you think we all are? You don't have to be a sort! Just enjoy it while you're here! After today you'll never have to see any of us again. Your choice, but you'll only be sitting by yourself feeling like shit while we're all off enjoying ourselves. Sophie!' He waved to the plump figure in voluminous white shirt and bottle-green britches picking a path between the tents. 'Hey, Sophie!'

Oh no, not her. They'd danced last night, hadn't they? She'd been enthusiastic, as he recalled. That was all, wasn't it? A vague recollection of gentle hands and a soft, sympathetic voice plucked at his memory, but that was all part of the delirium, surely? Bollocks! She was coming over! What if they had…

'Morning, Julian!' she said brightly. 'I've just been down to traders' - what do you think?' She held up a leather flask.

'Very nice.' Julian made a show of admiring the leatherwork. 'Cost you much?'

'Me? Nothing. Cost my dad twenty-five quid, though.' She peered at Danny through her round glasses. 'Hi. Still alive?'

Shit - wasn't her dad that Scottish bloke? The one whose dog he'd puked on? 'Just about,' he mumbled.

'Danny's not so keen to come on today. Just been trying to convince him. Why don't you have a go, Soph?' Julian clapped Danny on the shoulder. 'Form-up at 1.45. See you there.' He sauntered off, leaving Danny alone with Sophie and the Atlantic breakers in his innards.

'Still feeling rough, then?'

'Yeah.' Please God, they had just danced, hadn't they? Laced into her corset in the dim light of the beer tent, she wouldn't have looked too bad after a few pints - and he'd sunk more than a few last night. The early part of the evening was there, if a little hazy, but later? He racked his brains but all he got was a gleefully obstinate blank. There were no clues on her face, just a gentle concern, but he had to know. 'Look, last night…'

'Don't worry about it.' She rubbed his shoulder. 'I won't tell my dad.'

He jerked back as if scalded, stomach plummeting in flames. 'What…'

'About Fairfax.'

'Who?'

'Our dog. The one you gave a makeover.'

'Oh, yeah.' Of course. Thank God. Well, that was two worries off his mind in one hit. Perhaps the day was looking up. 'Sorry about that.'

'It wasn't your fault.' Sliding her glasses down her little snub nose, she peered coyly over the rims. 'I won't tell him about what happened later, either.' Oh, shit. He knew it. 'It was amazing - and you were incredi…' Her snort of laughter terminated the artful gushing and halted the rising bile in his throat.

'You're winding me up?'

'Sorry, I couldn't resist it!'

He sunk back into his shoulders. 'What a fucking mess! I can't remember anything.'

'Relax.' His flesh tightened as she patted his stomach. 'I didn't take advantage of you and neither did Jane. And you weren't in any state to try and take advantage of us!'

Huh! As if. Still, she was a breath of fresh air after Tabitha and her icy ways. Apart from Julian, she was the only person here to have treated him like he didn't have some sort of social disease - at least without having any ulterior motives. Or so he hoped. 'Sorry.' She was quite sweet in her own way and whether the apology was for last night's behaviour or for his initial boorish appraisal, he wasn't sure. Maybe for both. 'And thanks.'

'No problem.'

Squinting up at the cloudless sky, she polished her glasses on her shirt. She didn't show any signs of wanting to leave and he had nothing better to do except skulk in his tent, though the conversation was in dire need of a jump-start. 'What's that?' The leather flask would do as a catalyst.

'This?' She held it up for him to inspect the neat hand-stitched seams. 'Just a water bottle.'

'Where does all that stuff come from?' He'd briefly been shown "Traders' Row" after yesterday's battle, a double row of white canvas tents where you could buy anything from buttons to weapons - the sheer scope of industry involved in setting up a row of makeshift shops in the middle of nowhere had been impressive, if nothing else.

'Most of the traders make their own or sell stuff that other people have made for them. Some of it comes from abroad - mostly the guns.'

Oh, right.' The conversation faltered again, but it couldn't end yet - speaking to her helped block out the shame of last night. He searched the distance for inspiration, the plateau on which they were camped affording him superb views over the vale sprawled beneath an achingly blue sky. There was no sound save for the sleepy buzz of insects, and he could see for miles over the patchwork sea of green fields slumbering beneath the midday sun, only the distant silver flashes on the hazed horizon hinting at civilization. For a fleeting moment he actually got it and a blanket of calm settled over him, filling him with a wistful sense of isolation that was far removed from loneliness.

'March on, boys!' Calling to the phantom army that presumably followed him, Trevor stumbled past. The grass riffled in his wake - the wind, of course - and, the spell broken, Danny exchanged a bemused smile with Sophie. 'So, what do you do? Musket, like Tab, or...'

'Nothing so exciting.' She grimaced. 'I carry my dad's standard, run messages on the field, that sort of thing.'

'Oh, yeah.' Of course, he'd seen her with the flag yesterday.

'I really want to go pike, but he won't let me.'

'You're not missing much.' He rolled his shoulders, the aches and bruises coming out to play now his hangover had taken second fiddle.

'You pussy! So that's why you're not going on today?'

'No! Told you, I'm feeling a bit rough.'

'Ah, diddums!' Her full lips bowed into a pout. 'So, what are you going to do? Mope around here all afternoon feeling sorry for yourself?' There was no malice to her gentle teasing and her smile was infectious.

'Better than running around on a field with a bunch of nerds!'

'Oh, so that's it! Nothing to do with a hangover - you just think we're all a bunch of freaks!'

'No!' Bugger. He'd offended her - all he'd meant to do was match her friendly banter. 'I mean, not all of you are!'

'Just some of us then?' Her voice had cooled, as if he'd touched some source of inner hurt.

'You're not. You seem okay.'

She clasped her hands to her chest and fluttered her eyelashes, the warmth returning. 'Be still my beating heart! So, haven't you enjoyed yourself even a teensy wee bit?'

The barely-there Scots lilt burred across his fraught belly like the caress of a velvet glove. 'A little bit, I suppose.'

'That's all that matters then! Sod what anyone else thinks! Or are you that shallow?'

'Maybe.'

She put a hand on her hip. 'Well, it's your choice. No one's going to put a gun to your head and force you, but I think you should. Then you'll never have to see any of us again - unless you want to come back!'

'Let's just get this afternoon out of the way first, shall we?' Come back? No way. This was a one-off - and had been a total disaster. Tab was as futile a goal as ever - more so, if anything.

'So you are going on, then?'

'Haven't decided yet.'

'Well, you haven't got much time to make your mind up. Speaking of which, I need to get back.' She darted in, the peck on his cheek as natural as it was innocent. 'If I don't see you again, nice to have met you, but I hope you come back.'

Absurdly, his cheeks warmed. 'Really? Why's that?' Hopefully his breath didn't smell as rank as is tasted.

'Don't get carried away!' Once again, her mask of pure impudence twisted his own features into a reluctant smile. 'It's just nice to have a new piece of man-flesh who's not over fifty and doesn't need a crowbar to pry him out of his seat - and who's not lacking in the social skills department, although you might have a bit of work to do on that after last night!'

'Cheers. I think.'

'See you later, then. On the field - after we've beaten you!' Poking her tongue out, she hurried away between the tents.

*

The incessant rattle of drums called Harding's Regiment of Foot to arms. Streaming from the jumbled lines of tents, men and women fastened coats, tightened helmets, adjusted armour and checked their equipment as they scrambled to the form-up point.

Keith cast an eye over his two sleeves of musket as they assembled either side of the pike. No absentees. More than could be said for the pike block. 'Doesn't look like Danny's coming on then.' He'd have to make sure there were plastic bags readily available in the back of the Mondeo.

'He'll be here,' said Julian with an easy smile.

'You think so?'

'Oh yes. Here he comes now.'

Looking as though he'd dressed by guesswork, Danny endured the welcoming chorus of retches and barks with sheepish good humour. Tabitha didn't join in, her face a mask of icy disdain.

'Glad you could make it! Your kit's all over the place though. Come here.' Julian took hold of Danny, tightening straps and tucking in stray cloth. 'Now pick up a stick and get in line!'

'Quiet in the ranks!' bellowed Ken over the racket of the noisy hero's welcome Danny received from the pike block. 'Have a care! Advance your arms by division! March on the colours!'

Weapons were raised to greet Trevor's meander along the assembled ranks. Barry rolled his eyes while Ken ushered the ensign into position.

'The regiment will march to the right!' hollered Ken. 'By division. March!'

The two armies faced each other before a much larger crowd than Sunday - Mondays were always busier, Steve explained to Danny. Finding his comrades much more forthcoming after surviving his messy initiation, Danny dared not respond. If he opened his mouth, he'd spew. To try and take his mind off the pounding cannons that rattled his skull, he ran his eyes along the serried ranks of the two armies, drawn up in battle order with ensigns flourishing their colours to the fore. The square banners swooped and whirled like great kites, the acrobatics limited only by the dexterity of the respective bearers. Trevor twirled the Harding's colour about his head with arthritic panache, each stuttering revolution barely concluding with enough energy to fuel the next. Round it went like a scythe, knocking the standard out of the hands of the ensign to his right before sweeping back to clatter the man to his left across the helmet with a dolorous ring. As a finale, Trevor ended up with his own banner wrapped around his face, gaping through the silk like a pinscreen sculpture. Jane hurried forward to free him.

Hooves pounded as Peter galloped past at the head of the Royalist cavalry, two attractive horsewomen of middling years jostling to get close to him. One, with a mane of raven hair flowing from beneath her hat like a plume, had a banner set against her stirrup, much to the apparent chagrin of her blonde companion. Peter reined in and waved a regal hand, face like that of a lecherous walrus behind the bars of his helmet. 'Fight well, my boys, and you shall have the pick of the plunder! We'll have their baggage and their women! Colonel Reynolds?'

'Sir?'

'Take your rogues forward and sting these dogs into action!'

The battle had been building for some twenty minutes, and after the initial sparring of cannon and musket the armies were closing. Through the smoke, Macintyre caught sight of his opposite number on the far side of the field. 'Look at that arse prancing about!' No other Lord General had ever thought it necessary to puff himself by jumping in the saddle. 'Never seen a horse with two cun…'

Ian pointed off to the left. 'Harding's shot are engaging Northern now.'

'Bugger them!' There were no bragging rights to be had there. 'What about the pike?'

'Just moving up now. They're going in! They're going in!'

Even at a distance, the clash of metal as Harding's pike block rammed into Northern like a bulldozer was clearly audible. Macintyre's heart sank. 'I don't believe it! Straight through again!' Time to show Reynolds, a mere colonel, who had a whole army under his command. 'Right. Sean! Sean! Now's your time!'

Raising a gauntleted hand, Sean led his dour Ironsides - all buff leather and blackened armour - out onto the field.

Danny's hangover, while not gone, had taken a back seat. Harding's pike raced back to reform once again, Northern picking themselves up off the ground in their wake.

'You're doing great!' Julian slapped each of his charges on the back as they hurried into position. 'Each one of you…'

'Is worth ten of them!' Mike finished for him.

'Exactly!'

Barry was hovering near the pike block, practically skipping with savage excitement. 'Get 'em packed in and go again! One more shove will break them! Go! Go!'

'Hold on, Barry. They're watering.' Julian pointed to Northern who, now reformed, were in no hurry to re-engage. 'Open your order! Water in!'

Danny sucked greedily at the water bottle Jane handed him. Exhausted already, he was nevertheless glad he had come on the field. He was sweating pure alcohol, cleansing his body - if not his mind - of last night's excesses, and the mantle of acceptance sat easily on his shoulders.

'Northern are taking ages!' Barry complained. 'What are they playing at?'

'Buying time?' suggested Ken. 'Taking a breather?'

Barry thumped the butt of his partisan into the ground. 'Come on, Northern! Water out! Water out! We're ready! Julian? Close them up!'

'We can't go anywhere until they're ready for us - we may as well take the breather.'

A voice suddenly crackled from the flanks. 'Horse! Horse!'

Barry shot Trevor - for it was he whose frail tones rose in warning like an ancient soothsayer - a withering look. 'What's that old fart on about now? We don't get charged by horse. It's not in the script.'

'Probably ours,' Ken said, though Danny gripped his pike shaft more tightly at the faint tremor beneath his feet.

'Don't worry, mate.' Steve gave Danny a nudge. 'They're not after us today - same as yesterday.'

'You reckon?' Mike was already crouching, his pike angled outwards. As Ken's eyes widened, Danny turned to look at what had so alarmed Barry's subordinate.

The Ironsides pounded in from the rear, rocking the earth. Spread out in a line, swords raised, the armoured figures were giants, steam curling from the nostrils of their plunging, wild-eyed steeds.

'We're watering! We're watering!' Ken waved his arms above his head as the riders bore down on him.

'Charge for horse! Charge for horse!' chanted Trevor, whirling like a spindle-limbed Dervish.

'Ignore that and ignore them!' countered Barry. 'Trevor, you ever give an order on the field again and I'll…'

'They're not stopping!' Ken clutched Barry's arm. 'This isn't in the script!' He raised his voice. 'You can't charge us while we're watering!'

'I don't think they care, Ken!' Julian was already hauling Jane into the centre of the block. 'Charge for horse!'

Despite the flurry of movement all around, Danny's brain could only churn out slurried commands that his stodgy limbs had no hope of translating. Standing immobile and isolated, it took Steve to haul him into the protective clump.

'Tighten up, Dan!' Steve braced the butt of his pike against his right foot and dropped to a crouch. 'Don't let them through!'

Heart racing in time with the thundering hooves, Danny copied Steve and angled his pike out at forty-five degrees, the butt hard against his foot. The horses rushed past scant feet away, great stinking monsters with hooves like sledgehammers and evil yellow teeth, and the pike was nearly dashed from his hand as an Ironside clattered it with a meaty blow from his sword. 'Fuck!'

'Just keep a tight grip, Dan,' said Steve, a grin plastered across his face, 'and make sure you don't twat the horses!'

The initial charge surged past and the Ironsides turned to look for easier pickings, unable to penetrate the bristling hedgehog of pike. Julian held a corner, halberd raised, and Jane and the drummers sheltered in the middle of the block, but not everyone had made it to safety. Ken jabbed at a circling horseman with his polearm, but Barry simply stood with his hands behind his back, jaw clenched. If he didn't admit their existence, his expression said, then the Ironsides couldn't be there.

Keith led his scattered musket divisions toward the sanctuary of the pikes, dodging through the whirl of horse-flesh. Clutching her hat to her head, Tabitha sprinted in wide-eyed fear, an Ironside on her heels. A yard or two from safety, she stumbled to her knees, and her pursuer wheeled his horse to avoid riding her down. She froze like a rabbit in headlights, pinned to the ground in terror as hooves flashed all around her.

With little time for thought - if his head had been a split-second sooner than his heart he would never have moved - Danny dropped his pike and, shrugging off Steve's hand, darted out into the whirling chaos. Tabitha looked up at him with dull eyes, tears cutting through the powder smears on her cheeks. 'They just came out of nowhere!'

'Come on!' Grabbing her coat, he hauled her to her feet and threw her toward safety. A horse thundered past, buffeting him with the wind of its passage, but he picked up his pike and shouldered himself back into the block where the musketeers were now sheltering between the angled shafts.

'Thanks.' For once, the cold contempt was gone from Tabitha's crystal eyes. 'And sorry - I was a bit of a silly cow, but it's the first time I've been caught out in the open.'

'Don't mention it.' Could one selfless act wipe out an evening of shame? He hoped so, and Tabitha's faint smile told him it could. 'Look, last night, I'm so…'

'Oi, hero!' Danny's head rang as Nick clattered his helmet with his pike. 'We ain't done yet!'

Barry and Ken had finally sought refuge amongst the pikes. Northern were advancing from the front and the Ironsides still circled, all except one who stalked the solitary, bumbling figure outside the block.

Trevor was still smarting from Barry's dressing down, though the tears pricking his eyes were surely from the smoke. He'd saved the regiment! Now all he had to do was find it. He stumbled across the uneven ground, the colour dragging his shoulder down. Which of the clumps of pike was Harding's? A tug at the colour slewed him to a halt, and he whirled around to find an Ironside reaching from his saddle with the hallowed silk twisted in his gauntleted hand.

'Here! What are you doing?'

'It's alright,' rasped a Yorkshire accent. 'It's been arranged. Give it here!'

Had it? Had anyone told him? Possibly. Probably. It was so hard to keep track these days. Still, if this fellow said it had been arranged, then most likely it had. He couldn't risk mucking up the script - that would bring an even more savage reprimand from Barry.

'Arranged? Oh, that's alright then.' And, though it filled him with shame, Trevor released the colour.

'What's he doing? What's he doing?' Barry was incredulous.

'Oi!' bellowed Mike as Sean punched the air with the captured colour. 'You bastard!'

'What's up?' Danny asked.

'The colour!' Steve's amiable face was twisted with rage. 'He's taken the colour! You can't do that unless it's been arranged.'

'And there's no way Barry would ever agree to that!' Mike raised a finger in salute to Sean. 'Bastards!'

A terrible scream sounded from the ranks, a cement mixer filled with bricks combined with the bellow of a wounded elephant, the sort of shriek of rustic rage that was usually followed with the words "geroff moi land!" or "get your hands off my sister, she's mine!". Nick threw down his pike, face crimson and eyes far gone, and burst from the ranks to charge at Sean.

'Come on!' Steve dropped his pike.

'Where are we going?' Danny threw down his own weapon.

'To get our colour back!' Mike charged off in Nick's wake.

With an angry roar, Harding's surged forward. Northern were almost upon them, but the enraged bluecoats ignored the levelled pikes and steamrollered through, using fists, elbows and knees to force a path. The two rookies Danny found himself up against were no bigger than him and their faces were pale with hangover and shock. He also had the advantage of having his hands free and he threw himself forward in a kind of double rugby tackle, grabbing each of them round the waist and bearing them to the ground.

'Easy, mate.' The complaint came with a metallic clang and a waft of vomit.

'Bastards!' Danny screamed in their faces, caught up in the moment, and then gagged as someone jerked him to his feet by his collar.

'Want to play do we, boy?' Craggy face testament to years of brutal service, the pikeman was virtually square, as if someone had challenged themselves to cram as much human into as small a space as possible. Pinned by the iron grip, Danny could only watch as a gauntleted fist was cocked. Then the salty veteran was gone, hammered to the ground by Mike's flying shoulder charge.

'Come on!' Mike gave Danny a shove and they scrambled clear of the melee.

Growling like a Rottweiler, Nick had Sean's bridle in one hand and the Harding's colour in the other. Sean's dour face was alive with panic and he looked to Barry, picking his way over the wreckage of Northern.

'Call him off, Barry! If he hits me, it goes straight to the top.'

'Then it can go alongside the complaints I'm putting in against you!'

'We didn't know you were watering - and I think there was a misunderstanding with the colour. We heard that...'

'Bullshit! Take your donkeys and get out of here! And tell that Scottish bastard I'm out to get him!'

'Barry!' Ken tugged his colonel's arm. 'We're retreating!'

'But we just creamed the buggers!'

'The script, Barry.'

'The script? Fu...' Ken's beseeching, puppy-dog eyes halted the tirade in its tracks. Like the unquiet dead, the defeated Northern pikemen were hauling themselves to their feet. In the distance, the Royalist cavalry were in flight. The Parliament regiments were advancing, colours flying. Barry's head dropped in meek subjugation. 'Of course. The script.'

The overladen Mondeo estate, caravan rocking behind it, pulled up outside a neat suburban house in a neat suburban street. The neat suburban couple waiting on the garden path had a smaller version of Danny between them.

'Cheers, Keith.' Danny threw his rucksack onto the pavement and clambered out after it. 'Thanks, Jane. See you, Tab.'

'See you, Danny.' Much of the ice in Tabitha's features had thawed.

'Bye, love.' Jane flickered her fingers.

'Cheers, Dan.' Keith gave a nod to Danny's parents. 'Paul. Sarah.' He winked at the young boy. 'Reece.'

'Keith.' Danny's father nodded back. His mother smiled. Reece - Danny's twelve-year old brother - said nothing, merely curled his lip in contempt at the state of his sibling.

'Said I'd get him back in one piece,' said Keith.

Danny's mother wrinkled her nose. 'One not very fragrant piece! Shower!'

'Enjoy it, son?' asked his father.

Danny was beyond tired and his body was a mass of bruises, but there was a soupy contentment grazing at the back of his thoughts. 'Yeah! Yeah, it was great.' He ignored Reece's hiss of "sad". He'd get him back later, though the jibe did make him wonder how he was going to square this with his mates. Laughing it off as a chance to get into Tabitha's pants seemed cheap now.

'Really? Did he do alright, Keith?'

'Like a veteran!'

His father looked at Danny and the three Winters as if they were all playing a massive joke on him. 'Going to go again?'

It had been one hell of a weekend. The noise, the smells, the thunder of hooves, the crash of muskets, the clash of pike, the ridiculous (but uplifting) pride of reclaiming the colour, the camaraderie, the corsets - don't forget the corsets. The Winters were all giving him encouraging nods, even Tabitha. He couldn't deny it had been a laugh, but could he handle the inevitable piss-taking from his mates? Catching the sparkle in Tabitha's eye, he took a deep breath.

'Oh yeah. Yeah. I'm going again.'

2 DECLARATION OF WAR

The luxuriant leafy surroundings, marbled frontage and grandiose Doric columns failed to combat the dreary office block's stark functionality, though the shorter of the two men walking down the sweeping steps had more successfully disguised his austere exterior with flash and dash. The blue suit was tightly tailored with creases that could cut diamonds, the polished brown shoes ended in a modish point. Dark hair was slicked and piled around a face puffed by intemperance, though the taut sheen showed where surgery had ironed out the worst ravages of excess. A wide smile further tightened the ostentatious features. Councillor Simon Chatsworth was a happy man.

'Well, that went better than could be expected. You were a great help in there, William.'

Despite the florid features of an avid whisky consumer, William Sneath retained a military bearing, back ramrod straight beneath a steel grey suit cunningly tailored to disguise an un-martial paunch. The regimental tie, close-cropped iron hair, neat moustache and hard, pale eyes completed the image.

'My pleasure, Simon - I do hope it won't go unrewarded?'

'Of course not. Early days yet, though, and there's still a considerable hurdle to jump.' Everyone had their cross to bear - Chatsworth's was the whinging, hand-wringing beard-and-sweater brigade. Still, they were about to meet their match. 'Bloody heritage council, living in the past. No offence.'

Sneath gave a wolfish smile. 'None taken. Believe me, I'll take a deal of pleasure from this. The petition's up and running. Your hurdle won't be a problem for long. Leave it with me.'

'Oh, I will. We can't let nostalgia stand in the way of progress, can we?'

Sneath winked. 'Or of profit.'

Chatsworth laughed off the insinuation. 'Indeed!'

Juggling the sombre leather folders under their arms, they shook hands before going their separate ways beneath a shower of fresh spring rain.

3 THE RECONAISSANCE

Ken's Honda Civic rattled along the twisting country lane at a steady forty miles an hour, the frequent bumps a maddening half-beat from synchronising with the thump and trill of Baroque music.

'Haven't you got anything else?' Two hours of harpsichords, mandolins and hooting shawms were enough to test anyone, no matter how dedicated to the 17th century, and Barry's only wish was that he could meet one of the long-dead composers responsible for the assault on his eardrums so he could shove an authentic instrument somewhere authentically painful. Rommel, at least, was untroubled by the eldritch shrieks and wails, as evidenced by the gentle snores from the back seat.

Ken flicked down the volume, though the muted shawms still prickled Barry's nerves like super-charged party squeakers. 'Military Marches of the World? Folk Tunes of the Peninsular War? Around the British Isles in One Hundred Hymns?'

Barry gripped the sides of his seat until he could feel the springs corkscrewing into his palms. Ken was excellent in his role as 2IC - dedicated, determined, unquestioning - and his 17th century knowledge was second to none. Unfortunately, that all came at a price. 'Anything more contemporary? Like post nineteen hundred?'

'Vera Lynn and the…'

'Post nineteen forties. I meant post nineteen forties.' That Ken worked in I.T was a constant wonder - then again, considering the cold logic and lack of human interaction such a career doubtless involved, maybe it wasn't such a leap.

'Well, I have got some Coldplay.'

Barry ramped the volume back up with a savage stab of his finger and slammed his head back into his seat. There couldn't be that far to go now, though the leafy fringes gently rolling by weren't familiar. 'You sure this is the right way? I don't recognise anything.'

'It's a different route, that's all. It takes us by the Lace Museum and...'

God, no! 'No time for that, I'm afraid. Especially if you've got us lost.'

Ken's bottom lip quivered. 'I know exactly where we are - and exactly where we need to be.'

'Presumably you know how to get between the two?' They'd be late - and Barry hated to be late, especially on an important weekend like this. There was a battlefield to look over, a campsite to find, and some PR schmoozing to be done - although Ken could be something of a hindrance in the schmoozing stakes. 'There's someone up ahead. Let's stop and ask.'

'No, no! No need!' Ken's knuckles whitened on the steering wheel.

'Look, I'll do the talking...'

'No, I know where we are!'

'So do I - the middle of bloody nowhere!' The solitary walker was already a receding dot in the rear-view mirror. 'Take the next right - I'm sure that will swing us back toward the dual carriageway. Eventually.'

'No, no, we can't do that! I've planned...'

'For God's sake, Kenneth, the fairies won't come and steal you away if you go off piste! The best laid plans and all that. A good officer needs to be able to adapt.' Barry opened the glovebox and began to sort through the neatly stacked papers inside, ignoring the whimper of protest. 'There must be a map in here - I can't even get a signal on my phone, it's so bloody desolate around here.' His fingers closed around a CD case. 'Hello, what have we got here?'

'Look!' yipped Ken. 'A signpost! Little Felcham 8 miles. I knew it! Sure there's no time for the Lace Museum?'

'This is a working trip, Ken, not a chance to indulge your hobbies!' He ran a finger down the CD's track listing. That would do! 'Now this is more like it!'

Ejecting the incumbent disc, Barry tossed it onto the back seat where hopefully Rommel would ensure that it was never inflicted on him again. The new disc slid home, Rommel cranking open a sleepy eye as the opening notes of "Ride of the Valkyries" swirled around the car.

Little Felcham was a pleasant little market town, barely more than a village. Turning off the main road, Ken pulled up outside a sprawling public house full of "olde world charm" - at least that's what the chalk board outside declared. To be fair, the original structure appeared to be 18th century, though subsequent renovations and improvements masked much of the original stonework. The swinging sign, with Charles I looking loftily down on them, proclaimed it as "The King's Head". The quaint cottage next door - all ivy and rose bushes - had a B & B sign in the window.

'I said we'd make it, didn't I?' Ken was first out of the car. 'We'd have had plenty of time for the Lace Museum.'

Fascinating as Barry found many facets of 17th century life, his interest did not extend to what sort of lace the denizens of that period draped around their necks. He let Rommel out of the car, fastening a lead to his collar. 'I wanted to get checked in. We should have time for a bite and pint before we meet this lass from the local rag.'

Ken tugged his hair fretfully. 'I do hope it won't be another one of those articles portraying us all as crackpots and anoraks.'

'God forbid.' Could Ken be packed off to the Lace Museum for the duration? 'She's just doing a bit on the history, that's all - with a mention of our muster, of course. Any publicity is good publicity.'

Barry pushed open the B & B's heavy oak door, ducking into a low-beamed reception hung about with a faint, musty smell that was welcoming more than unpleasant. The dusty silence only reinforced the impression of a country church or a cottage museum, as did the antique prints and portraits hung around the faded cream walls that had Ken scurrying around like a kid in a sweetshop. Might even stop him banging on about the Lace Museum. Ringing the bell on the polished oak desk next to the staircase, Barry arranged his face into its most cordial setting, the lines of which soon faltered when no one emerged from either of the doors leading out of the foyer.

'Look!' Ken exclaimed, hovering by a particular portrait. 'Prince Rupert!'

'If he's not manning reception, then I don't care. Does anyone actually work here?' A second ring failed to elicit a response, and when a further two proved equally ineffectual in summoning assistance, Barry took to flicking the bell so rapidly that the chimes melded into one insistent ring, as if a pocket-sized hunchback capered across the desk.

The tintinnabulation faded back to merge with the onrushing silence. Barry sucked his fingernail, though his wound was well-earned when the door behind the desk creaked open. The woman who shuffled into the foyer, a vague smile decorating her seamed features, was from another world, a world of sepia tones and carbolic soap - the archaic pinafore and black chambermaid-style dress would have been in vogue around the time Kaiser Wilhelm had a slight fallout with his cousins. A Miss Faversham, lurking like a wizened spider in her white-shrouded chambers, forever waiting for the guests that never arrived. Taking a moment to orientate herself - maybe the hairpins fastening the tight grey bun acted as a compass - she began her advance on the desk. Each step took a considerable amount of thought before the foot was placed down, accompanied by a deliberate shake of the head that dislodged wisps of hair from the corralling bun. There was a hypnotic - almost horrific - stop-motion stiltedness to her movements, and Ken retreated toward the front door, a vacuous Perseus confronted by the Stygian hotelier. Barry stood his ground, willing her on. Glaciers ploughed their way seaward quicker - Trevor would look spritely by comparison - but after what seemed an age, she reached the desk in a choking cloud of lavender.

'Oh! You should have rung!' Her voice was as desiccated as her appearance, and she blinked as if it was the most unexpected thing in the world for someone to be standing in her lobby. 'Can I help you, gentlemen?'

'You're Mrs Muir?'

'Sorry, dear? You've got rather a low voice.'

'Oh, for God's sake,' said Barry under his breath. *Why me?* He cleared his throat and filled his lungs. 'Are. You. Mrs. Muir?'

'No, dear, I'm Mrs Muir. Now, were you after a room?'

'I have a room booked, Mrs Muir. I'm Mr Reynolds.' He leaned over to Ken. 'Don't hold your breath - if she's even got the booking down I'll be...'

'Ah, yes, here we are!' Mrs Muir tapped a leather-bound tome, sending up a cloud of dust. 'You're the Roundheads, aren't you?'

Ken tensed, and Barry waved a frantic hand at him. As it was, this could take the rest of his life. 'Close enough, Mrs Muir.'

'Sorry, dear?'

'Never mind!' Was she related to Trevor? His mother, perhaps? 'We do have the room? I take it I booked it during one of your lucid spells?'

'Lucy?' The wrinkled brow creased further. 'No, Janet usually takes the bookings. Lucy hasn't worked here...'

'God help us.' Barry abandoned any attempt at keeping his asides low. 'Can we just sign in? We do have someone to meet before Doomsday.'

Mrs Muir gave him a beatific grin. 'You'll be wanting to sign in and get unpacked, won't you?' A bony finger traced a trembling path down the ledger and she gave a dry chuckle. 'Oh dear. There appears to have been some sort of a mistake.'

Of course there had. They'd end up sleeping in the bloody Civic. 'Mistake, Mrs Muir? What sort of mistake?'

'Only a slight one, nothing to worry about. You booked a twin room, according to this.'

Barry had an awful feeling he knew what was coming. 'A twin room, yes. A twin room, for two people, with two beds. Not an unusual request for a B & B, I wouldn't have thought? So, what is it? Wrong date?'

'Oh no, all present and correct, it's just that we've put you into a double.'

'A double!' With Ken? God, no. 'Well, change it, woman!'

'Would you believe that we let out our last twin room just ten minutes ago?' She gave a dry-lipped smile of apology.

'Are you sure they weren't just in here to read the meter?' Barry's weekend was going downhill rapidly. 'God knows how many bodies she's got stacked in the attic,' he said to Ken out of the side of his mouth. 'All those poor bastards who came in here for afternoon tea or to service the boiler and wound up spending the rest of their lives trying to tell this dotty old bat that they didn't want a room!' Placing his knuckles on the desk, he stared into the rheumy eyes of the elderly hotelier. 'Well, tell them there's been a mistake! Give them the double and let us have the room we booked!'

'Oh, I couldn't do that! Such a charming pair of gentlemen.'

'Right. We're off! Come on, Ken.' No way. No way was he sharing a bed with Ken. It was bad enough that they were sharing a room.

'We're the only place around here that allows pets in the rooms.' Mrs Muir eyed Rommel as if judging his weight in gold, the avaricious glint belying the dusty facade.

'And that should have been a giveaway.' Rapacious old bag!

'There's nowhere else - only the Premier Lodge down the road, and they won't have Rommel.' There was a mute plea behind Ken's eyes - the prints on the walls obviously trumped the notion that he'd been lured into a witch's gingerbread cottage. 'It doesn't bother me - we can go top and tail! It will be fun!'

'Fun?' Sour bile bubbled in Barry's throat. 'Unlike you, Kenneth, sharing my bed is not a novel experience.'

'Perhaps you could have a chat with the gentlemen?' suggested Mrs Muir. 'They seemed very pleasant. Ah yes, here we are - a Mr Macin...'

'Dear God, no.' Barry squeezed his eyes shut. No need to ask whose heavy footsteps shook the staircase. *Who have I offended?*

'That's a lovely wee room, Mrs Muir.' The Scottish burr drilled into Barry's skull, homing in with uncanny accuracy on the part of his brain that hung by a thread above the chasm of psychosis. He forced an eye open. Macintyre and Ian Riley stood at the foot of the stairs, grinning like top-hatted villains who'd just secured their first ever damsel to the railway tracks.

'Ah, Mr Macintyre! These two gentlemen were wondering if there was any chance you would consider swapping your room for their double? Our mistake, I'm afraid, but they did request a twin when they booked.'

'Well, that's a shame, isn't it?' Mock concern weighed down Macintyre's broad face. 'We're all settled in now, I'm afraid. Nay mind - I don't think they're as bothered about sharing a double as they're making out. I'm just surprised you allow their sort in here!'

The sly wink that accompanied the sordid insinuation snapped the creaking chains of Barry's self-control. Fortunately, Ken had the presence of mind to throw his arms around him before he could hurl himself at Macintyre.

'I'm not sure I follow you, Mr Macintyre?' Mrs Muir peered over the top of her spectacles.

'No?' Macintyre's grin was threatening to unhinge the top of his head. 'Look at them now - all over each other! You could at least wait until you got into your room!'

Barry fought free of Ken, any vestiges of dignity long since flown. 'That's it! We're off! We'll sleep in the car if we have to! I'm not staying under the same roof as bloody Rob Roy!'

'What are you doing here anyway, Ian?' Ken placed himself between Barry and the stairs.

'Just a little bit of publicity,' Ian said airily. 'Got a recruiting gig in the town.'

'But this is our muster! You can't!' A crimson glow illuminated Ken's neck, creeping up to cover his cheeks like an animated map of the expansion of the Roman Empire. At least he could give voice to his anger - the swelling bubble of vitriol in Barry's chest rendered him speechless. Sneaky Scots git!

'Says who? There's this as well!' The cover of the hardback Ian flourished was decorated with the portrait of a man Barry knew only too well, despite the gulf of three hundred and seventy years that separated them. The title itself was little short of blasphemy. "Harding's Babe-Eaters: The Real Story of Little Felcham".

Ken hissed like a scalded cat, baring his teeth. 'It's slander, nothing more! I've read about it - populist theories and questionable evidence. It's a disgrace that it was ever published!' He snatched the book from Ian, veins bulging in his forehead as he set his teeth and tried to rip the sturdy volume in two. The cover bent beneath his hands but remained stubbornly intact, and after straining like a constipated toddler for a futile minute he contented himself with tearing out a few pages and throwing the book into a bin.

Macintyre had watched the pathetic tussle with ill-disguised humour. 'You can have that - we got a few freebies. You should have said - I could have got you a signed copy!'

Barry found his voice at last, doubling his fists and squeezing until the knuckles were like polished ivory. 'He's here? William Sneath is here?'

'Oh yes. He'll be at our recruiting drive later today! And tomorrow he's doing a battlefield walk. Anyway, what is it you say - any publicity is good publicity?'

'Right!' Somehow, Barry managed to maintain a semblance of control. 'Kenneth - the bags! We're staying!'

The bar of the King's Head was, as promised, full of "olde world charm", though for Barry - skulking at a dim corner table with Ken - that charm was currently being diluted by Macintyre and his noisy compatriots intriguing the locals up at the bar.

'It's outrageous!' Barry took a sip of lager, quashing the urge to down it.

'The room is nice, though,' said Ken, brushing a froth of foam from his top lip.

'Not that!' Going to bed with Ken was the least of his worries now. 'Him! The Gay Gordon over there. I'm taking this to the top! This is our territory.'

'Oh yes, of course! And that bastard Sneath - how he can sleep at night after denigrating the memory of heroes…'

'Sneaking Scotch git, getting a highbrow academic on board.' If a meteor suddenly hit Little Felcham, wiping the village from the face of the earth, Barry would have gladly sacrificed himself if it meant ridding the world of Macintyre and Sneath.

'I wouldn't call William Sneath highbrow.' With studious concentration, Ken arranged four beermats into a perfect square. 'He's just regurgitating spurious evidence that was discredited years ago - not that the idiots who buy his books seem to care.'

'Well, he's not my main concern right now - what I'm worried about is Mac and his boys getting first crack at any recruits!' That was the unwritten rule of the society - if it was your gig, your regiment got first dibs on any recruits it attracted.

'We've got our own recruiting day in a couple of weeks.' The mismatching logo on one of Ken's beermats ruined the symmetry of his square, and he hunted around for a replacement.

'It will be too late by then! They'll have already picked up all the potentials. Bastards!' A familiar figure slipped past Macintyre's enthralled groupies. 'Ah, here's Julian. Julian! Julian! Over here!'

Julian sauntered over and pulled up a chair. 'This is a bit unexpected, isn't it? I drove up past the battlefield - they've got quite a sizeable camp up near Harding's Stone. Even saw a couple of horse boxes, and they've got an awning up in the town square. William Sneath is here, apparently.'

What the fuck did Mac think he was playing at? Barry shredded one of Ken's beermats between his fingers. 'Yes, the conniving bastards have got him on board as well.'

Julian eased back in his chair. 'I hear his book is a bit speculative?'

'Don't!' Barry started on a second beermat. 'I've only just got Ken settled. So, where are you staying?'

'Lovely little place about ten miles down the road - quite close to the Lace Museum actually.'

'Penny with you?' Barry asked, before the faraway look in Ken's eyes could manifest itself more vocally. She was a good girl, Julian's wife, cracking company. A shame she didn't come to musters any more.

For once, Julian's shell of languid self-assurance seemed to crack. 'Er, no, no she's not.'

'Ah, lone wolf for the weekend, eh?' Pity if she'd taken a set against the society, but a lot of them did, like golf or football widows. Still, at least Penny had the decency not to shadow her husband with the sole, sour intent of ruining his weekends. Unlike some.

'Er, yes, yes, something like that.' Julian seemed keen to change the subject. 'So, what are we up to today?'

'We need to recce the field at some point - we can probably leave that until tomorrow, especially now Mac is here.' The battlefield was pretty much a given, but Barry wanted another look and the camping facilities still needed sorting. 'We've got a chat with this lass from the paper - if she shows up - and then we'd better have a sniff round and see what Mac's up to.'

'And give William Sneath a piece of my mind.' Ken took a swig of his bitter then started to gather in beermats from those tables within reaching distance. 'Do you know he claims that Harding and his men were actually chased from the village after making free with drink and the populace? He says it was Harding who threatened to burn the village - he's even started a petition to have Harding's Stone removed!'

'I've heard about that petition - it's got the historical society in a bit of a state.' The girl who had appeared next to their table smiled at the shrill wolf-whistles from the bar and brushed a lock of dark hair back from her face, hazel eyes flicking over the three Hardings. 'Most of them think this William Sneath is a bit of an idiot, but there are a few on his side. Which one of you is Barry Reynolds?'

'That'll be me.'

'Melanie Halliwell, Felcham Echo.'

'Oh, at last!' Trust the paper to send some moppet fresh out of university instead of a proper reporter - though all was not lost if her journalistic skills were on par with her somewhat Mediterranean good looks. 'Take a seat.'

There were no chairs available, but Julian rose and offered her his. 'There you go, Miss Halliwell. Forgive me, it is "miss"?'

'Yes - and likely to be for a while! Please - it's Melanie. Or Mel.' She sat down, crossing her legs with a hiss of denim.

'Well, I suppose that leaves some lucky chap out there somewhere. Can I get you a drink, Melanie?'

'Thank you. Just a water, please - I like to keep a clear head while I'm working.' She pulled a notepad from her handbag. 'Sorry, I didn't catch your name?'

'No, Barry didn't get around to the introductions, did he? I'm Julian.' He extended a hand.

'Pleased to meet you, Julian.' Melanie took his hand with a coy smile, her dark eyes flashing over him with brief appraisal. 'You're not a Jules, then?'

'Oh, I think I'm a bit staid to be a Jules.' His eyes flickered with lazy mischief.

'I don't believe that for a minute!'

Julian bestowed one of his benevolent-lord-of-the-manor smiles upon her. 'Well, some of my more intimate acquaintances have been known to refer to me as Jules from time to time, so do feel free.'

'I'm Ken.' The stack of beermats Ken had been constructing fell to the floor. 'Short for Kenneth.'

'Jules it is, then.' She spared Ken barely a glance.

Barry cleared his throat. 'If you're going to the bar, Julian, I'll have a lager. Kenneth will have another pint of "Frisky Fox" - and that'll be your last, Ken. I'm not having you raising the duvet all night.'

'There was a mistake with the rooms,' Ken explained to Mel while Julian raised a Roger Moore eyebrow. 'They've put us in a double! We're not, you know, funny.'

'Do stop wittering on, Kenneth. We're behind schedule as it is! If you hadn't realised, Mel is here to interview me! I thought you were off to the bar, Julian?'

'Right you are, Baz!' Sketching a salute, Julian headed to the bar.

'He's got a bit of old-fashioned charm, hasn't he?' Mel said wistfully.

'Has he?' Barry kept his voice off-hand - he'd seen before how young women were powerless before Julian's charms. It was the faint whiff of class, had to be. 'Can't say I'd ever noticed. Now, where shall we...'

'Very urbane.' She traced a pattern on the table with a slender finger. 'Sophisticated - not like the apes you get around here who think the local chippy equates to haute cuisine and who expect a quick bunk-up behind the swings in the local park after buying you half a... Sorry, my turn to witter on. He is a charmer though, isn't he?'

'If you say so - old, as well.' God, if he could only bottle Julian's secret. 'And married!'

'Old? He can't be more than forty-five - and he looks good on it!'

Ken weighed in. 'And he's going through a rough patch with his...'

'That's enough, Kenneth! We're not here to discuss my subordinates! We're here to talk about me - I mean the regiment.' Well, the colonel was the regiment, wasn't he? Time to get started before Ken got onto lace. 'Got your notebook, Mel? Good!' He'd rehearsed this interview a thousand times. 'Right, how about "Barry Reynolds sits across the table from me, a modern man but cast in the mould of the heroes he so faithfully emulates. It's not hard to imagine him as..."'

Mel stopped him with a raised hand. 'I'll just start with a few questions if that's okay, Barry?'

'Baz, please.' She really was very attractive, with her olive skin and smoky eyes.

'But you hate…'

Barry worked an elbow into Ken's ribs. 'I think Julian needs a hand with the drinks, Ken. Off you go.'

Ken slunk away like a kicked puppy, allowing Barry to give Mel his undivided attention and what he hoped was an avuncular smile. 'Now, Mel, let's get started.'

Mel's pen blurred across the pages of her notepad. The interview had gone well, all things considered. Barry Reynolds, once he'd settled, had been an informative, if not enthusiastic, interviewee and, despite the constant interruptions from Ken, Julian had shattered any preconceptions about the re-enactment scene. Now that noisy crowd around the Scottish bloke had buggered off, it was pretty much just the four of them left in the bar.

Fingers drumming on the table, Julian was finishing his latest anecdote - one of many that had invigorated her notes. 'So I just said, "When in Rome, dear boy", and walked away!'

As well as lifting the lid on Julian's reserved exterior to give an intriguing snapshot of the mischievous schoolboy beneath, each story had provided a sparkling insight into a hitherto unknown world, transcending the cloistered parochialism that saw the re-enactment scene paint itself in such unflattering shades. 'I bet he was fuming!'

'He did turn a somewhat intriguing shade of puce, I must say!' Julian's hand slid across the table, his little finger brushing hers with warm confidentiality.

Ken leaned forward, spraying saliva in his eagerness to share a story of his own. 'What about the girl down on Living History that time who was wearing sixteenth century lace? Do you remember? It was hilarious - she thought it was authentic! So I said to her… said… when in… no… it was… Well, I said something to her.'

Ken slumped back with an uncertain smile, and with the conversation not only killed, but butchered, bagged and buried, even Julian seemed unable to find a witty little gem to resurrect it. 'Thank you for that, Kenneth,' Barry said after an uncomfortable few seconds of silence that seemed more like minutes. 'Most entertaining. I think Mel has got enough material now.'

'Yes, I have, thank you. More than enough, if anything.' Julian's finger crept on top of hers, pressing gently. Come off it, what was he playing at? Not that the gentle pressure was objectionable - and there was no wedding ring. He couldn't be that married.

'You might even find something useful once you've thrown out all of Julian's "amusing" anecdotes.'

'Oh, I might keep some of them in - they add a bit of colour and they get away from the idea that you're all a bunch of anoraks.' Julian lifted his finger a millimetre or so from her hand - a question, an invitation maybe? Missing the warm touch of his skin, she raised her own finger to reinitiate contact, intrigued. Had she misread the signals? There was no harm in finding out, especially after the fraught couple of months she'd had.

'Oh, our Ken's very fond of his anorak!' chuckled Julian. 'I'm more Barbour jacket and tweed, while Barry likes a black leather trench coat.' His face crinkled into a smile. 'Well, now you've clocked off, so to speak, I can get you a proper drink - unless you've got something...'

Those lazily intense eyes were fixed on hers, stripping away the barriers of restraint. She shifted in her seat, the rasp of her jeans irritating her skin with a pleasant, if slightly lewd, friction. 'Oh, no, no. I'm done now - I'm yours for the rest of the afternoon if you want me!' She cringed at the unconscious innuendo in her words.

'Well, let's start with a drink, shall we?' His eyes told her everything she needed to know, and a warm yet welcome flush stung her cheeks.

'Julian, we've got work to do!' Barry glowered across the table. 'I've got calls to make - and we need to see what Mac's up to.'

'And go and have a word with William Sneath!' added Ken, his expression that of a rabid ferret.

'Ugh.' Mel could still smell the whisky-soaked breath, still feel the coarse tickle of the military moustache as he'd whispered in her ear. 'I interviewed Sneath yesterday. He's got a very high opinion of himself. He was slobbering all over me the whole time - he even asked me out for dinner, though I could tell he was after more. I don't think he could quite believe I turned him down.'

'Sounds a dreadful chap,' said Julian. 'I can't say I'm too fussed about meeting him. I'll continue with the press liaison role, I think. Come on, Melanie, let's get you that drink.'

Smoke hung over the garden like the fog of war, full of the promise of exotic marinades, worryingly pink meat, and a healthy dose of the trots in the morning. Keith, beer in hand and sporting a frilled apron that had to have been a Christmas present, shoved blackened lumps around the barbecue.

Danny had escaped from his family but had not yet succeeded in cornering Tabitha for anything longer than thirty seconds. There were over twenty people gathered among Jane Winters' rosebushes and Tabitha seemed intent on talking to every one of them before him. He was just looking for somewhere to deposit his empty lager can when Jane rushed though the patio doors, phone in hand.

'Keith! Phone!'

'Who is it?' Keith flinched as the barbecue flared with a greasy hiss.

'Barry.'

'Oh God, what does he want? You could have said I was out.' He took the phone, fixing a glazed smile onto his face. 'Barry! Hi! How are you doing, mate?' Even from ten yards away, Danny could hear the voice crackling down the line. 'Oh yes, yes, I remember. How is it? Really? Macintyre?' Keith winced, holding the phone away from his ear. It was almost a full minute before he spoke again. 'Well, that's not on, is it?' He looked to the sky as if searching for an excuse among the wisps of cloud. 'Tomorrow? That could be awkward, got a bit of a do. We'd have to leave early and the amount I intend to drink tonight, I'd still be well over the limit!' His face dropped. 'Oh, right. Kevin? Great, good. Spare gun for Ken? Sure. Yes, yes, see you tomorrow, mate. Bye.'

Jane folded her arms across her ample bosom. 'Well?'

Keith cleared his throat. 'Taking a trip out to Little Felcham tomorrow. Apparently Macintyre's pulling a fast one and Barry's trying to…'

Seizing a bottle of wine, Jane filled her glass to the brim. 'Really, they're worse than children! Well, I can't make it - and you won't be in any fit state to drive!'

Keith gave her an encouraging smile, though it carried a faint air of desperation. 'Don't worry, it's all organised. Kevin's picking a load of us up in his van.'

Jane snorted into her wine. 'Well, good luck with that!'

'I'll make sure I get the front seat! Tab! Danny! Fancy a trip out in the country tomorrow?'

More dressing up? His mates had been merciless since his first trip to what they called "nerd camp", but the chance for another day with Tab was worth any amount of piss-taking. Sold.

The atmosphere in Mrs Muir's lobby crackled like a Battle of Britain operations room. Barry hung up the Bakelite telephone with a satisfied smile. 'Sorted! Action this day - well, tomorrow.' *Shove it up your arse, Mac!*

'How many have we got?' asked Ken.

'Enough - Keith's bringing a spare gun for you, Terry's got powder, and Steve is bringing a few pikes. Ten or twelve of us, but that should be plenty. Kev's doing a few pick-ups, Terry's bringing Ray - oh, and Trevor's coming.' Now for the opening skirmish. 'Right, let's go and see Mr Sneath!'

*

The market square of little Felcham was everything you'd expect the market square of an English market town to be, with the ubiquitous war memorial, hanging baskets, and a little huddle of stalls set out on the quaint cobbles. Today though, the alcoholics clustered beneath the bandstand (large enough to accommodate a one-man band and no more) were being treated to sights far stranger than they were accustomed to - even those whose cider-fuddled brains could still recall the infamous day of the living statue. Today, the Army of Parliament held the square.

Sentries with pike and musket stood at every corner, handing out leaflets and posing for photos with an enthralled public. The two horses standing alongside the war memorial tossed their heads as they were petted and stroked by a constant stream of admirers, though the Ironsides in their saddles remained suitably dour. Richard Macintyre was well pleased. It was a large enough turn-out without making it too obvious that they were treading on - no, crushing - Harding's toes. Still, all was fair in love and war, and Harding's would never have given William Sneath their patronage. A little white awning had been erected - with no little effort - on the cobbles, flanked by a giant poster showing the man himself (looking suitably academic yet soldierly, his disapproving expression vowing to bring the devilish Harding to long-overdue account) and a blown-up version of the cover of "Harding's Babe-Eaters". Everyone in the long queue snaking over the cobbles clutched a copy of the book while they waited patiently for a signature from the author, sweating in his grey three-piece beneath the canvas. In return, it was hoped that they would sign the petition that lay at Sneath's right hand. Little Felcham was rightly proud of its heritage. The battlefield - a little way outside the modern-day village - had a small information board and a modest plaque commemorating the battle. All well and good - Macintyre was fully in favour of keeping the past alive, he wouldn't be here if he wasn't - but the field also had Harding's Stone. Nestled among a tangle of bushes at the foot of a gentle slope, the lump of dressed granite with its silver plaque extolled the alleged heroic actions of Colonel Harding on that fateful day back in 1645. It stuck in his throat that a man like Harding could garner plaudits from future generations when he was little more than a butcher. The stone was a travesty and its presence on the battlefield a nose-thumb at history. The petition, when he'd last looked, had only a handful of signatures, but the more who read the book, the more would sign. By placing the awning close to the war memorial, they'd hoped to prick consciences by reminding people of real heroes, not the swashbuckling fantasies conjured years after the events by Victorian romanticists. By the end of the summer, there would surely be enough signatures to get the local council to sit up and listen and remove the monument to barbarity. A cosy fog of contentment settled in his stomach, marred as two figures lurking on the edge of the square suddenly stood out in high definition. What the hell were they up to?

'Look at them! Look at them! They can't wait to sign up! Bollocks, bollocks, bollocks! I thought we'd have a clear run at this place in a couple of weeks! Bastards, bastards, bastards.' Every person who took a flyer or held a weapon or tried on a helmet was a knee to Barry's groin. Fucking Macintyre!

'And look at the queue for Sneath!' moaned Ken. 'They're actually buying that rubbish!'

'Hello there, gentlemen!' Macintyre swaggered over, hand on the hilt of his sword and Fairfax scurrying at his heels. 'Would two such fine upstanding specimens as yourself be wanting to join the Army of Parliament?'

'Get stuffed, Mac.' Society rules dictated that officers should treat their superiors with respect, even if they fought for the other side. Society rules could do one.

Macintyre's grin was unassailable. 'Of course, you'd have to put aside your less salubrious habits - quite against our Puritan sensibilities. Historically speaking of course! Does nae bother me what the pair of you get up to behind closed doors. How is the room, anyway?'

Barry ground his teeth. 'It was an administrative error and you know it! If it wasn't for Rommel, I'd have found somewhere else!' Hopefully he was even now pissing up Mrs Muir's rosebushes or doing something violent to her ageing and sullen ginger tom - Ken had needed to be escorted past the chair where the spiteful creature lolled in swollen splendour like a Roman emperor.

Macintyre soaked up every word, forging it into barbed ammunition to fire back. 'Ah, your wee sausage dog - we know how much you like a bit of sausage!'

'Bastard!'

'Children present, Barry!' Macintyre wagged a finger. 'Remember we're representing the society!'

'You are! I'm just a member of the public - for now.'

'What do you mean, for now?' The Scotsman's eyes narrowed, as if he'd spotted a discarded penny on the far side of the square.

That's got the bastard! 'You'll see.' A ball of white fluff flurried around Barry's ankles. Time to stir the porridge. 'I see you've brought Fairy with you.'

'Fairfax. His name is Fairfax!'

'Odd name for a girl.'

'He's a boy!'

Loaded, aimed, now fire. 'Well, Rommel didn't seem to think so the other year, did he?' Rommel's first muster - and he'd been a little over-excited. Barry would have let the unmentionable act continue out of sheer devilment, but Alice and a bucket of water had come to Fairfax's rescue.

'It's no my fault your dog's confused!' The Scotch brogue deepened to a growl.

'You can hardly blame him with your little bitch leading him on! At least he was giving, not taking!' Sensing he was being talked about, Fairfax looked up, a world of hurt in his eyes. Barry rubbed his hands - reference to the canine French Mistake aside, he'd given Macintyre enough to worry about. 'Come on, Ken, we're off!' He turned to go, but Ken was not at his side. 'Ken? Kenneth? Oh my God, no.' Copy of "Harding's Babe-Eaters" in hand, Ken was waiting in line to see Sneath. He wasn't too far from the front and Barry dashed over. 'Come away, Kenneth!'

'Not until I've got my book signed!' There was a look of vacant determination on his face.

'You've bought it?' After all he'd said, Ken had forked out money on that tripe? 'You've actually bought it?'

'We're running low on toilet paper.' Ken shuffled to the front of the line. 'Ah, Mr Sneath! Ken Howard. Long-time fan, first-time reader.'

Sneath was visibly wilting in the heat, yet the corners of his moustache twitched in a smile. 'Well done, well done! I'm sure you'll enjoy it! Dispels some of the more fanciful notions and paints that rogue Harding in his true light. Do you know much about the story?'

'Oh, a fair bit.'

'Well, why not come along tomorrow? I'm leading a battlefield walk, starting and ending at Harding's stone - you know I've got a petition to get the stone removed? The man was an animal!' Sneath tapped the petition with a meaningful finger.

Barry jumped in. 'We're both busy tomorrow, I'm afraid.'

Sneath's pale eyes flickered to him. 'And this is?'

'This is Barry,' said Ken, 'my, er...'

Catching Macintyre's disgustingly graphic gesture, a disapproving frown split Sneath's brow. 'Ah, say no more. Each to his own, what?' He gave a wary chuckle, obviously not wanting to discourage two more potential signatories, whatever their persuasion. 'Leaves the path clear for us real men to have a crack at the ladies! Like that little filly from the paper! Damn fine-looking bit of totty - think I'm in there. I'll have another crack at her later - she's interviewing a couple of saps from Harding's Regiment today. Probably another couple of left-footers, eh? No offence! Still, I'm sure she'll be in the mood for a real man after that, what? Now, who am I signing this to?' Taking the book from Ken - careful to avoid making skin contact - he placed it on the table and flipped to the inside cover. 'Just to Ken? Or to the pair of you?'

Ken smiled - the sort of smile only ever seen racing from the green depths just before a luckless swimmer became lunch. 'If you could just write "To Ken. I'm sorry, I am a piece of human refuse who would not know objective research if it came up and tweaked my starchy nipples. My book should be sold on a roll, in packs of four, as it is only fit for wiping the arses of those who rightly honour the memory of those who I so shoddily and inaccurately denigrate!" Oh, you could add "Love William" if you like.'

'What?' Sneath's jaw dropped.

'Or if that's too much, you could just write "My name is William and I am a c..."'

'Ken!' yelped Barry. They couldn't insult a respected historian - even one as odious as Sneath - in full public view. The repercussions could be fatal to the muster.

Sneath's eyes paled further. 'Right, I think you... aagh! Shit!' Ken had slammed the book shut on his fingers and was pressing down with all his might.

'Whoops! You've smudged it!' Tossing the book to the floor, Ken drew himself up for a parting shot. 'Still, it won't make it any less legible than the rest of the drivel in there!' With that, he was gone, striding away across the square with self-righteous dignity.

Ken's departure left Barry facing the incandescent Sneath, the incredulous Macintyre, and the approaching Roundheads. Time to leave - but Ken's pugnacity had awoken a mischievous imp that refused to let him go quietly. 'Sorry,' he trilled, blowing Sneath a kiss. 'It's her time of the month!' Then he took to his heels.

Mel was drunk. Not too much, just a pleasant light-headedness that was probably due more to drinking while the sun was still bright than to the actual amount she'd consumed. She still had control, though one or two more drinks would further loosen the shackles of restraint. Still, maybe they could do with loosening, but she had to be careful - she didn't want Julian thinking she was no more than a silly kid, especially as he'd drunk nothing but mineral water all afternoon. It would be easier if he let himself go rather than holding himself with such amused dignity. Had she made a fool of herself yet? Her mouth was certainly flowing far more freely than usual, but she'd said nothing untoward as far as she could remember. 'Why don't you have a drink? A proper one!'

Ice clinked in his glass. 'I'm driving, remember? I will need to get back to my digs at some point.'

'Do you have to?' It would be a shame for the afternoon to end now - she hadn't laughed so much in weeks. Months, if she was honest. And there was that intriguing undercurrent…

'I think I've done enough sleeping under the stars this month - and I don't think I'd fancy snuggling down between Barry and Ken.' His eyes - those dreamy blue eyes that made you feel like the only person in the room - twinkled.

'You could always stay at mine,' the gin blurted for her. 'I mean, just so you can have a drink - I've got a spare room.' She did mean that, didn't she? He was good company, sure, but that was all wasn't it? Anything else was purely the drink. 'I didn't mean…'

'Well, we'll see.' The way he raised his eyebrows over the rim of his glass sent a vulgar pulse coursing through her - the humid vehemence of her body's natural responsiveness far more acceptable after a few G & Ts.

'What are you playing at, you fuck?' The gravelled voice shattered the prurient tension. As if from nowhere, a brawny, tattooed arm shot past Mel's face and a beefy hand grabbed Julian's collar.

Julian said nothing, just looked down at the hand that was twisted in his shirt front then up into the face of the young man who held him.

Mel's knotting stomach soured the sensuous buzz that had been building. Not him! Not now! 'Mark! For God's sake, get off him! We're through, I told you!'

'No we're not!' Mark's open, almost boyish, features were made harsh by the drink she could smell on his breath. God, he was an idiot!

'Yes, we are! It's over - how many chances did you think you were going to get?'

'You're dumping me? For grandad here?'

'I dumped you a long time ago. What I do and who I see now is my business, not yours!' Muscles rippled beneath Mark's taut tee-shirt, and she could almost feel the crushing embrace of the slabbed arms once more. God, he'd make mincemeat of Julian! Could she stall him until the barman, Aiden, returned from the cellar? The bloodshot eyes told her she couldn't.

'Bloody slag!' Was it just drink? Or something more?

Julian's polite cough was ludicrously gentile in the face of such belligerence. 'I'd appreciate it if you didn't use such language toward a lady. I'd appreciate it even more if you'd take your hands off me!'

Mark's brow wrinkled, as if the words couldn't quite penetrate the fug of alcohol. 'What are you? A poof?'

Julian's eyes, so warm and relaxed a moment before, were suddenly cold. 'I think you should leave.' The curt, almost robotic tones fell like lead slabs and sent another chill rush through Mel's body.

'Yes, Mark, you should go.' *Please go.* The air was fraught with tension, thick with the promise of imminent brutality, though the outcome of the impending violence was not so clear-cut as she'd assumed seconds before. Julian's frosty calm was unutterably more menacing than Mark's drunken bluster.

'I ain't going nowhere!'

It was a wild punch but, powered by Mark's gym-bred strength, it would have felled a calf - had it landed. With almost balletic grace, Julian swayed aside, his movements sure and unhurried as he grabbed the extended arm and twisted it casually behind Mark's back. 'Now I really think it's time to go, don't you?'

Red-faced, Mark struggled in vain to free himself. 'Get off, you bastard!' His eyes went to Mel - pleading, hateful, she couldn't be sure - and she had to look away.

Aiden reappeared from the cellar, all six and a half reassuring feet of him. 'You again, Mark?' He put down the case of mixers he was carrying. 'Come on, out, or I'll let the gentleman break your arm! You're barred. Again!'

'Allow me!' Julian manoeuvred Mark to the door and helped him into the street. Aiden went with them and Mel's fingers tightened on her glass at the raised voices, though Mark's eventually faded into the distance. It sounded like he was crying.

'My hero!' she said when Julian returned. The levity was a little forced and the hammering of her heart stirred her stomach.

'Eight years in the Signals and ten in the Met before I found a cosy little desk job!' Julian wiped his hands on a bar towel, not even out of breath. 'Who was that tacky little hood? An ex?'

'Yes. A recent ex.' She was compelled to defend Mark - after all, they'd dated for nearly a year and in defending him she also validated herself. 'He's a nice enough guy, believe or not, until he's had a drink. Then he's an idiot.'

Julian regarded her gravely. 'Drink does tend to make idiots of the best of people.'

'Tell me about it.' Time hung suspended for a moment, his face with its gentle, shrewd lines filling her vison and those blue eyes boring into hers. Then their lips met.

She'd never kissed an older man before, not with passion, and the depth of the experience shook her. There was no rushing, no crude groping, just an unhurried sense of being explored, tasted, with the press of lips firm yet tender. Okay, so he was married. Tough luck, sister. If you're not going to appreciate him then he's going to have to find himself someone who does. He broke the kiss after what seemed like an age, but it was not enough and only the gentle hands he placed on her shoulders prevented her from going in for more. Was he teasing? Playing with her? She darted her head forward, lips parted, but he jerked away. 'What's up? I thought you...'

'I do... I think. I'm not sure.' He ran a hand through his hair. 'It's... complicated.'

'It always is!' She shouldn't have rushed in like that, but he'd wanted it as much as she did. Still did. She could see it in his eyes. 'Look, I like you, you like me, what's the problem?'

He looked suddenly ten years older. 'I wish I could tell you.'

'It's your wife, isn't it?'

'No, no it's...'

Look at him, fumbling for excuses! 'Bloody men!' The drink-fuelled anger was directed as much at herself as at him. What had possessed her? For all his beguiling, old-fashioned charm, he was no better than the rest of them, though why the sudden cold feet? A conscience? Or was this how he got his kicks? 'You're all the same! Stringing me along all afternoon while you've got a wife sitting at home! I feel sorry for the poor cow! Bastard!'

She drained her drink, resisting the urge to sling the glass at his head, and barged out past Barry and Ken who were just coming through the door.

'She's in a hurry, isn't she?' Barry was in a buoyant mood as he strode into the bar. 'Must have heard that Sneath has his sights on her! Had a good afternoon, Julian?'

Despite the worm of self-loathing twisting through his guts, Julian forced a smile. 'Yes. Lovely. Thanks.' He should go after her. Explain. But what then? Another kiss? More? Was that what he wanted? Really?

'As have we!' If Barry noticed anything was up, he hid it well. 'Shoved it up that bastard Sneath and then had a look around the field. We'll be fighting on the actual site! And there's plenty of room for camping.'

'I'm sure it will be great, Barry.' For all his efforts, Julian's voice came out flat and dead. Barry frowned

'Don't sound too enthusiastic, will you?'

***

Keith paced his drive, the jingle of chains and buckles persisting in questioning the wisdom of the last couple of double whiskies in front of the chimenea last night - or earlier this morning. Tabitha, also in full kit, had her arms crossed and wore one of her more acerbic faces.

'About time!' She'd spotted Danny - in jeans and tee-shirt - running down the road toward them.

'Come on, love - Kev's not even here yet.' Keith ran his eyes over the bags and gun cases heaped in the drive. Everything was present and correct - there was even a spare colour bundled with the polearms.

'Why do we have to go with that creep?' If possible, Tabitha's expression chilled by several degrees.

'Oh, Kev's alright - in small doses.' He was in no mood for her airs and graces this morning. 'And there's no way I was going to drive after last night! Morning, Dan! Bright-eyed and breezy?'

Danny took a second to gather himself, panting hard. 'Er, yeah, yeah. Alright, Tab?'

'Hi, Danny.'

'Enjoy yourself yesterday?' Keith swallowed the yawn forcing its way up his throat.

'Yeah, cheers.'

'And your folks?'

'Yeah, yeah, I think so. Dad was still snoring when I left.'

Tabitha's smirk would have frozen lava. 'At least you managed to get through the evening without decorating the patio with puke!'

'Now, Tab, no need to bring that up again, eh, Dan?'

'Sorry, Danny.' She sounded almost genuine.

Danny shrugged. 'Forget it. What are we actually doing today, anyway?'

How much had he told them last night? It was all a bit hazy. 'Off to Little Felcham - that's where we're putting on the August Bank Holiday muster and...'

'He knows all that, dad. He's not stupid - well, not totally.'

'Alright, alright.' Tabitha answered his scowl by poking her tongue out at him. 'Well, Barry and Ken - you remember them, Danny? - are there sizing the place up, looking over the campsite and battlefield. Julian's there as well. It turns out that Parliament have got the jump on us and snuck up there in force to put on a "call-to-arms" - a recruiting drive. Barry's hopping mad - can't say I blame him - and we're going as damage limitation to see if we can steal back a bit of land after Macintyre's Blitzkrieg.'

Danny looked none the wiser. 'Yeah, yeah, but what are we actually going to be doing?'

For all his vehemence, Barry had been sketchy on details. 'You know, I have no idea! Barry's hatched some plan to stitch Macintyre up - he'll brief us when we get there.' Where was Kev? 'If we ever get there.'

'Oh, right.' Danny's honest blond features were troubled. 'Is it, you know, okay? In the rules or whatever?'

'Probably not, but Macintyre's well out of order so it'll even out!' Any comeback would be on Barry. They were just following orders - as they'd said at Nuremburg. Besides, it had been a pretty shabby stunt Macintyre had pulled the other week, sending his minions to convince Trev to give up the colour - the poor old fella had nearly been in tears after the dressing-down he'd received from Barry. Retribution was long overdue. 'It should be a bit of a giggle as well!'

Tabitha couldn't resist another dig. 'Just try not to puke on Macintyre's dog again!'

Danny's brow furrowed further. 'Does he know it was me?'

'I don't think so. I wouldn't worry - I think Barry's already got you down for a medal! A mention in dispatches at the very least!' Keith flicked his eyes to his watch. 8.40. 'Where's Kev?' As if in answer, a distant car horn wheezed through "Dixie". 'Ah, that'll be him now!' The two kids exchanged scathing glances and he couldn't blame them - even when that particular horn had been in vogue, he hadn't found it amusing.

Heralded by a backfire that would have eclipsed a volley from the entire Royalist army, a rusty white Transit rounded the corner. Belching black exhaust fumes, it hurtled along the sedate avenue and rattled to an unsteady halt inches from Keith, horn labouring through its tune like a 60-a-day man wearing an aqualung to end on a horribly triumphant inflection. Kev jumped out of the driver's door, his soiled "Harding's Regiment of Foote" tee-shirt a graphic menu for whatever roadside café he had visited en route.

'Oh my God,' moaned Tabitha, her face a smorgasbord of negative emotions.

'Morning, Keith. Tab. Young'un.' Kev's trailing moustache seemed to crackle with excitement. 'Throw your kit in the back with the others. I saved the front seats for you and Tab, Keith.'

'Excellent.' Keith kept his eyes from his daughter's - he could feel the heat from her gaze anyway. 'Let's get loaded then.'

'What about me?' Danny was giving the rusting bodywork a speculative inspection.

'In the back. Plenty of room!' Kev bounded to the rear of the van like an enthusiastic monkey, the doors grinding open on the fourth attempt. Blinking in the sudden light, the three ashen-faced passengers sprawled among bags and boxes were keeping their distance from a soiled mattress.

'Light! Thank God! Morning all.' Ollie, nudging what appeared to be a rubber hood with his foot, looked particularly queasy, though Nick, blithely chugging lager from a can, didn't seem too bothered.

'Back for more, young Dan?' Mike gulped the fresh air. 'Hope your stomach's a bit stronger today! If you don't puke on us, Nick'll be pissing all over us before long!'

Nick crushed his can and tossed it into the darkness. 'Nah, I'm good for another couple of hours. Got the failsafe anyway.' He held up an empty 5-litre water bottle.

Thank God he wasn't travelling steerage. Keith passed the gun cases into Ollie and then threw in the kitbags. Kev slid the polearms in. 'In you get then, Dan - need a bunk up?'

Danny hauled himself up into the van, scrambling away from the helping hand Kev slapped on his backside to fall amongst the sacks with a rattle of chains. The rubber hood unfolded to gape a silent scream at Keith, the blank eye-pieces witnesses to untold horrors.

Mike curled his legs in. 'We saved you the mattress, Dan.'

'Oh, cheers.' Danny rolled onto the grubby bedding. 'It's a bit sticky...' The burst of raucous laughter was shut off as the door slammed. Tabitha looked sick.

'Right! In we get!' Climbing back up into the driver's seat, Kev swept a stack of magazines onto the floor. With a dexterous foot, Keith flipped over a cover showing a stern-looking woman in corset and stockings as Tabitha urged him into the middle seat. There was barely time to buckle up before the engine caught (on the second attempt) and they were launched on their way with another pitiful fanfare and a thunderous backfire.

Travelling in the front of Kev's van was infinitely preferable to riding in the foetid darkness of the rear but it was still everything the distressed exterior of the vehicle had promised. Surely even Kev could derive no pleasure from the stained seats that jolted with every bump on the narrow country road to give Keith's prostate the sort of attention usually only administered by a medical professional's lubricated digit. The smell, while not overpowering, was quite something - exhaust fumes, the ghosts of a thousand takeaways, and something distressingly fungal. Keith dared not look at his daughter, though the few times he'd caught her reflection in the wing mirror there was murder in her eyes. The song choices of choirmaster Nick - unseen but definitely not unheard - were apparently doing nothing to lift her spirits.

'Oi 'ad 'er, oi 'ad 'er, oi 'ad 'er, oye ay.' Nick's disembodied voice was thick with West Country vowels as it rolled out a familiar old folk tune - though the words were not quite so rustic. Mike, Ollie and Danny joined in, well-rehearsed by now.

'Oi 'ad 'er, oi 'ad 'er, the West Country way. She was so pretty and only sixteen!' Kev smirked, Tabitha banged her head against the side window, and Nick gave the last line everything. 'So I showed her the works of my threshing macheeeeeenaaaa!'

The answering howls of the three-man chorus transported Keith back to his rugby days. 'It's a grand old hymn, isn't it?'

'It's disgusting!' spat Tabitha.

Nick threw himself into his next ditty. 'The mayor of Bayswater has got a pretty daughter' - if Tabitha thought the last one was bad, she was going to hate this one - 'and the hairs on her dicky-di... uh-oh. Hang on!'

'What's up, Nick?' That was Mike.

'I need to go! I need to go! Where's the bottle?'

'Here it i... Jesus, no! That's not it!' Ollie's voice cranked up an octave. 'What the f...'

'Don't ask.' The strain was discernible beneath Mike's too-nonchalant tones. 'Just put it back.'

'Hurry up! Hurry up!' Nick was growing frantic. 'I can't hold it!'

'Here it is.' It was Danny who came to the rescue.

'I love you, Dan. You don't know what this means.' The release, when it came, was explosive, like a high-pressure hose being directed into a plastic bucket. 'Ooooh, yes.'

Keith made a show of looking up into the sky. 'Looks like being a rare old day, eh?' The torrent petered out but the shaky smile he exchanged with his daughter turned to a wince when it became apparent that Nick had not yet finished. Now, though, there was less echo and more splash. 'Work okay, Kev?'

'Can't complain - well, I could but it wouldn't do me any good!'

The stream faltered. Tabitha gave Keith a tentative glance, but the respite was temporary.

'My goodness!' Unbelievable. Like a leaking gutter during a summer storm. 'So, wonder what Barry…' He cocked an ear. Dripping silence. Thank God - surely Nick had finished this time? 'I wonder what Barry…' The pause was a mere coda. Nick began squirting short, frequent bursts. Eight, nine, ten. That was it. Keith waited a few seconds for good measure. 'As I was saying, I wonder what…'

The tap was turned back on at full stream, though what little echo there was sounded dangerously tight. Nick's worried tones confirmed the sum of all fears. 'Bugger! Shit! It ain't stopping! It's nearly full!'

'That's not possible!' Ollie's cry was accompanied by a frenetic scrambling.

Possible or not, Nick was fretting. 'Find something else! Quick!'

Danny's voice was nearly lost amid the frantic thumps that suddenly rattled the rear of the van. 'What's under there?'

'Kev's cloak of human flesh, probably.' Mike was on the verge of hysteria. 'Or scalps.'

'Oh God, mother!' screamed Ollie. 'Blood! Mother!'

Nick was not amused. 'Stop dicking about and find me something! This isn't funny! What you got, Dan?'

'Bucket.'

'Nothing in it?' Mike wanted to know. 'No bones or anything?'

'No, it's clea… well, it's empty.'

'Here you go, Nick!' There was a hollow plastic *thunk*. 'Start bailing!'

'In two hundred yards, turn right.'

Keith jumped at the authoritarian female voice. Had Kev got a stowaway?

'In one hundred yards, turn right.' The cheap-looking sat-nav wobbling on the dashboard had suddenly sparked into life. 'Turn right.'

With a misty-eyed smile, Kev pressed down on the accelerator. The Little Felcham turning flashed by.

'Kev! You've missed it!'

'Turn right!' ordered the sat-nav, accompanied by what sounded like a whip-crack. 'Correct your route immediately!'

'Kev...'

'Correct your route immediately!'

'What am I?' simpered Kev. 'I'm a very naughty boy!'

'Correct your route this instant!'

Barry would be waiting, tapping his foot and growing more crimson by the minute, but Kev seemed content to drive on indefinitely under the tongue-lashing. They could be at the coast before he submitted - and God knew what that would entail. 'We are in a bit of a rush, old boy.'

'Correct your route now!'

Kev's gaze flicked from Keith to the sat-nav and then to the rapidly approaching roundabout. Blowing out an unsteady breath, the distant sparkle faded from his eyes. 'Yes, mistress,' he said humbly - if not a little sulkily.

They were still travelling at a fair old lick when they entered the roundabout. Keith braced as a shrieking Tabitha was hurled against him, the nearside wheels seeming to lift from the tarmac as Kev hauled the van through a tight 180 degrees. It must have been terrifying in the darkened rear, though when the crashes and curses had settled, a sinister buzzing remained.

'I hope to God that's his razor!' said Ollie weakly.

'I don't think so,' replied Mike. 'Ah-ha!' The buzzing intensified, like a steroid-fuelled hornet of nightmare proportions and dubious tendencies.

'Get it away from me! Get it away from me!' Ollie shrieked. 'Not in the ear! Not in the ear!'

'No? How about here?'

Ollie's muffled yelp was drowned out by Nick's bellow of laughter.

Barry paced the country lane, flitting in and out of the dappled shadows cast by the overhanging trees. Most of his elite squad was here - Ken, Julian, Steve, Ray, Terry, Annie and four or five others stood by the cars drawn up on the verge - but they couldn't do anything until... A distant backfire shattered the rural peace and, second's later, Kev's van careered around the corner and slewed to a halt. Nick's baritone filled the lane, rolling out the tune of "The Old Hundred", though the words weren't in any hymn book. 'As I was walking through the hall.'

A chorus of voices - Barry identified Keith and presumably Tabitha among them - bellowed out in response. 'As I was walking through the hall.'

'A man came up and grabbed my ba...'

Barry banged on the side of the van. This was Dieppe, the raid on

Entebbe, the Iranian Embassy, Cockleshell Heroes. 'Keep it down! Mac's lot might hear you!'

'I called for help, but no one came.' Nick continued in a hoarse whisper.

'I called for help, but no one came.' The hushed refrain was broken by muffled laughter.

'And so he grabbed my balls again!'

'Come on, out you get!' The leafy surrounds could hide countless curious ears and eyes. Mac and his boys should be a mile or so away, but you never knew.

Keith and Tabitha scrambled from the van. Kev hopped from the driver's seat and headed round to release the passengers from the rear. Nick jumped down, rolling his neck. Danny looked on the sunlight as if he'd never seen it before. A pale-faced Ollie spat onto the ground and scrubbed at his teeth with a finger. Mike dropped to all fours and crawled toward Steve. 'Water! Water!'

Keith threw a rucksack to Danny. 'Here you go, Dan. Get kitted up.'

'What, here?'

'You ain't got nothing we ain't seen before,' Nick told him. 'Go behind a tree if you're shy - or in the back of the van.'

With a shrug, Danny stripped off his tee-shirt, exposing a lithe, muscled torso. *Gosh.* Barry couldn't blame Tabitha for sneaking a quick, red-faced glimpse. 'Okay, that's all of us I think - apart from Trevor. He'll have to catch us up - as usual. Keith? Did you bring a spare gun for Ken?'

'Yep.'

'Good - I want as many firers as possible. Go and see Terry for your powder - only four shots each.'

'I brought a spare colour as well. Just in case.'

'I can go ensign until Trevor gets here,' volunteered Julian. 'Steve can go sergeant and look after the pike - we're not going to be doing anything fancy, are we?'

'No, good idea. Right, listen in. Sneath's starting his walk at Harding's Stone. The whole tour should take two hours, tops. Kev, you know what you're doing?'

Kev, already half-dressed in his best (or worst) beggar's outfit, was busily applying prosthetic deformities to his face. 'All sorted, Baz.'

'Good lad. Now, I need a couple of volunteers for a secret mission - stealthy, light-footed. Get your hand down, Nick!'

Tabitha stuck her hand in the air. 'I'll do it.'

'Me too!' Hopping around in an attempt to get his second leg into his britches, Danny raised his hand and promptly tumbled to the ground.

'Oh my God.' Did the boy not understand stealth? 'Maybe Tabitha should go by herself?'

'He'll be okay, Barry.' Keith helped Danny to his feet. 'I don't know what you've got planned, but I don't want her going alone - and no one else here fits the ninja bill, do they?'

True enough - burly pikemen or musketeers the wrong side of fifty. 'I suppose not - just don't cock this up, Danny, okay?'

If Tabitha was keen to take Danny along, she wasn't showing it. 'What's this mission then, Barry?'

Barry pulled his secret weapon from his satchel - a box of Rommel's biscuits. 'Listen in.'

"IN MEMORY OF COLONEL HARDING AND HIS REGIMENT, BY WHOSE SELFLESS ACTIONS THE PEOPLE OF LITTLE FELCHAM WERE SPARED THE VENGEANCE OF THE PARLIAMENTARIAN ARMY. AUGUST 15TH 1645"

Reading the inscription aloud, Willian Sneath quelled his seething stomach by telling himself that the abomination would soon be removed. For good measure, he spat on the jagged lump of granite to which the plaque was attached before turning to face the battlefield walkers assembled at the foot of the shallow rise that shadowed the monument.

There were some twenty or so people in hiking gear - mostly middle-aged men, though thankfully that little filly from the newspaper was there. He let his eyes linger on her tanned legs, delightfully school-girlish above the hiking boots and rolled-down socks. Her shorts showed a gratifying amount of firm thigh. Damn, she was a little tease! She wanted him, must do, but there was a job to do first.

'All here? Good, good. Everybody got a copy of my book? It will help if you've read it, and I'll have some more copies for sale once we retire to the King's Head. Ah, Miss Halliwell! Couldn't stay away, eh?'

She shot him a spirited look that made him glad he'd swapped his usual suit for a pair of shapeless canvas trousers. Looked like some breaking in might be in order. 'It's part of my assignment, unfortunately. And, whatever your views, whatever the truth, you shouldn't be spitting on the memories of brave men.'

'My dear, the man was the lowest sort of scoundrel! Have you not read the book?'

She smiled. 'Oh, I tried - gave me the best night's sleep I've had in a long time!'

Those lips! Pert little madam. Still, once she got the sniff of money in her nostrils she'd be like a bitch in heat. He knew her type. Macintyre, standing with an escort of pikemen, came forward apologetically. 'I'm afraid she spent rather a lot of time with those idiots from Harding's yesterday - filled her head with all sorts of nonsense.'

'Ah, then I look forward to filling you in later, my dear.' He detected a slight tremor beneath the silky skin as he seized hold of her arm. Encouraging. 'Right, off we go! Come, my dear. You can walk beside me - I can give you my personal attention!'

With Mel's hip bumping pleasingly against his, Sneath led his tour party off. Macintyre and his men fell in behind, a small white rear-guard trotting behind them.

'Come on, Fairfax.'

The hedgerow was not what it had been back in 1645, though it was still tall and thick enough to present a formidable enough barrier to hide what Sneath knew lay on the other side. He snuck a sideways look at Mel, her bosom jiggling as she scribbled in her notebook, then cleared his throat to address his audience, quelling the urge to rush through the words. It would be done soon enough, and then...

'So, a Forlorn Hope of musketeers and dragoons, under a Colonel Tyrell, made their way through the underwea... undergrowth to this hedgerow, where they could finger - I mean fire upon - the right flank of the Royalist army.'

He was expecting it, but the punch of shots still made him jump. Smoke billowed from the hedge and, after the initial shrieks and laughter, the walking party gave a smatter of applause.

'And we're all very grateful to General Macintyre and the Army of Parliament for lending such an air of authenticity to the day! Now, on we go!'

Sneath led his adoring public on. None of them saw the two blue-coated figures creeping through the bushes on the far side of the field.

No matter how many times he told it, Sneath never got bored of the damning history of Harding. The *apres-ski*, so to speak, would be the icing on the cake. He gestured expansively at the fields around them.

'By now, the villagers had driven Harding's men from Little Felcham and... what the f...'

The beggarly figure shambling from the trees like a George Romero extra was truly repulsive - face riddled with sores and pustules - and only Macintyre's hiss of 'Kev! What the bloody hell are you doing?' convinced Sneath it wasn't an apparition summoned by his justified denigration of Harding.

'This is part of your show, Mac?' Bloody dress-up artists! What did they know about soldiering or war? He only tolerated that Scottish baboon Macintyre because he was a keen supporter of his campaign. Man had a daughter, too. 'Jolly good! Local colour, what?'

Macintyre shuffled his feet. 'Oh, aye, yes.'

'Alms for the poor, eh? Come here then, wretched fellow.'

Swivel-eyed and muttering, the beggar made his way toward Sneath, bowl in hand. Faces wrinkled as he passed. There really were some sad cases in this re-enactment lark. Nevertheless, Sneath had a public facade to maintain and rummaged in his pockets.

'Let's see what I can dig out for you. What do you have there, my good man?' The beggar tilted the bowl and the sweet smell of corruption overwhelmed even the authentically fusty odour woven into his rags. 'Good God!' Sneath pinched his nose, recoiling from the maggot-infested pig's trotter festering in the wooden dish.

The beggar screwed up his face, holding a finger beneath his nose. 'A... a... achoo!' he bellowed theatrically, launching the maggots in a foetid shower.

Sneath was in no position to avoid the stinking vermin that fell on him like rancid hail. 'You incompetent arse!' His hair seethed, and he rasped frantically to dislodge the little beast that writhed on his moustache. 'You cretin!' He raised his hand to strike the beggar, but the eyes of the tour party were on him and he dropped his arm. 'Ha ha. Good show.'

'Sergeant!' roared Macintyre. 'Take two men and get that wretch out of here!' As two pikemen bore down on the beggar, Macintyre dropped his voice to a whisper. 'I don't know what you think you're playing at, Kev, but...'

'Just a bit of comic relief.'

'If I want comic relief, I'll go get myself wanked off by a clown!'

'Ooh, now you're talking! I think I've got a Pierrot costume in the back of the van.'

'Fuck off!'

The pikemen seized hold of Kev - none too gently. 'No, have mercy!' he howled. 'Mercy! Aah! Ugh! See how the ruthless scum of Parliament treat a simple beggar, for all their pious ramblings! Harding's men fed me! Clothed me! True gentlemen and heroes all!'

'Get him out of here!' bellowed Macintyre.

'I don't find this sort of thing amusing, Macintyre.' As Kev was dragged screaming into the trees, Sneath ran a hand through his hair, dislodging maggots. Macintyre and Ian hastened to brush him down.

'I can only apologise - he wasn't meant to do that, I can assure you. He does tend to get a bit carried away at times.'

Sneath shook off the fawning hands and, rank stench still in his nose, stomped off toward Harding's Stone.

Mel let Sneath get ahead. Luckily, she'd been nowhere near him when he'd been showered with maggots - just a shame there hadn't been chance to take a photo. Yesterday's indulgence still sat heavily on her stomach - she'd downed most of a bottle of gin and half a tub of ice-cream once she'd got back to her flat - and she breathed in the clean air while she was free of Sneath's cloying presence. Macintyre's dog snuffled around her feet, chasing after the maggots that wriggled through the grass. She crouched down, but before she could run her fingers through the white coat, Fairfax's ears pricked up and he bounded off. Great, even dogs were rejecting her now. No, it had stopped by a clump of bushes, stumpy tail waggling furiously. As she watched, a biscuit looped out of the undergrowth and the dog snapped it from the air. A second biscuit followed, this time landing a foot or so closer to the bushes. It, too, was gobbled up, as was a third, but before Fairfax could snatch up the fourth, a pair of hands reached out from the bushes and dragged him into the undergrowth.

The grand finale. Harding's Stone. Full circle. Hands clasped behind his back, Sneath launched into his closing address.

'And it was here, if you believe the false history propagated to create a hero, that Harding's Regiment made their last stand, having nobly quit the village to spare it from being sacked! Poppycock! They were chased out by the villagers and cut down as they fled - brutal, maybe, but in keeping with the time!'

'Rubbish!' snorted Melanie.

Sneath favoured her with a pitying look. She just needed educating - and there was a lot he could teach her. 'Do you have a degree in history, young lady? Have you spent years of your life studying the civil wars? Have you investigated the pattern of shot derived from the musket balls that have been dug up over the years? No, I don't think so! I know we all love a hero, but I'm afraid that this stone is a travesty! It should not be here and, if I have my way, it won't be here for much longer!' He raised his fist skyward, but the expected applause did not materialise - his audience's attention was fixed on that lunatic from earlier, gliding from the treeline in priest's regalia. 'Oh no, what's this idiot doing now?'

Kev stepped reverently toward the stone, eyes on the heavens. 'Oh Lord, look with pity upon these jolt-heads who scorn the truth with their greed! Raise up the spirits of those heroes who gave their lives at this place that their fellows may live and bring down their vengeance on those who would denigrate their memory!'

A drum thumped out a solemn tattoo and pike-tips bobbed on the crest of the low hill above the stone. Snatching Sneath's moment, Harding's colour appeared over the rise and the battlefield walkers applauded the small but disciplined body of blue-coated soldiery that followed the banner down toward the memorial.

'Ladies and gentlemen,' declared Kev, 'the true heroes of Little Felcham! Harding's Regiment, come to honour their fallen comrades!'

The lump that Kev's words provoked in Barry's throat threatened to choke off his commands, and it was Ken who halted the company, allowing him time to compose himself. The applause of the crowd - and the identical looks of apoplexy on Sneath's and Macintyre's faces - lubricated his vocal cords and kept the tremor from his voice.

'Present!'

Barry raised his partisan. It had been several years since he'd had command of a block, but the sweep of the polearm had lost none of its panache.

'Give fire!'

The small volley spattered out over the forlorn fields, startling a flock of crows into the air. Barry rested on his polearm, waiting for Macintyre.

'What sort of shabby trick is this, Reynolds?'

'Here he comes,' Barry murmured to Ken. 'The Cock of the North.' Raising his voice, he was unable to keep the triumph from his tones. 'This? This is a memorial party, that's all. Just a coincidence that you happened to be here - we've had this booked for months!'

'Bollocks!'

'Language! You're representing the society, remember?'

Macintyre gave them a long, hard look and then simply turned on his heel and strode away. Mel laughed out loud, choking off when she saw Julian standing with the colour. Sneath himself took a step toward Barry, saw Ken's bared teeth, and turned and followed Macintyre.

'Hey, Mac!' Barry called. 'You've dropped your sporran!'

Purple bow between his ears, Fairfax trotted out of the trees. Macintyre's face went as pink as the tutu around the dog's hindquarters before turning a dangerous shade of red.

'Bastard! You English bastard! Why don't you go and...' A second volley from the memorial party drowned out Macintyre's words, but the implication was clear enough. He was still going when the echo of the shots died away. '...and then when you get there, pull it out and...'

A solitary shot - Ray clearing a misfire - rang out.

'...unt!' finished Macintyre.

Mel sat at the bar of the King's Head, the scribbled pages of her notebook stubbornly refusing to be translated into something worthy of her journalistic skills. The satisfaction of seeing Sneath put in his place was tempered by the unwelcome shock of seeing Julian again - yesterday was still far too raw for that. At least he wasn't here with the rest of Harding's (working their way through a carvery dinner), but every raucous burst of laughter prodded her with fresh fingers of humiliation and she closed her notebook and headed out to the beer garden.

The scent of fresh flowers and the gentle breeze were a godsend after the turbid air inside. Maybe she'd be able to get these bloody notes finished now and start drinking again. Further alcoholic oblivion seemed an incredibly attractive option, so much so that she could almost smell spirits on the whispering wind. No, she *could* smell whisky. The sour waft seeped into her senses, summoning a pale-eyed phantasm that lurched from her thoughts and into reality when a hand clamped around her wrist.

'Off so soon? We have some unfinished business, I think?' Sneath was drunk, she could tell that from the broken-veined eyes and the fumes on his breath, but something else had hold of him, something far worse. His free hand drifted across her bare thigh and she felt him tremble.

'I really don't think we do.' She tried to pull away, but he was strong despite his years.

'Really? Your face obviously doesn't agree with you - you want it, I can tell.' His slid his arm around her waist and pulled her close, the hairs of his moustache scratching her neck and his prying hand sliding higher. 'Come on, my room!'

'Get your hands off me!' The walls of the garden rose high around her, the chill shadows chasing away the heat of the day. The gangling rose bushes twisted and leered, crowding in with pink-faced salacity.

'You don't mean that!' He hauled on her arm and the sharp flare of pain in her shoulder suddenly made it all real. His breath was already coming in short, heated wheezes and the devil raised inside him would not stop until sated. She couldn't fight him - his trembling limbs were locked like steel while hers had turned to water. Surely this couldn't be happening, not here, not to her, but the fingers that plucked at the hem of her shorts and dug like knives into her side told her differently. The garden spun around her like a carousel in a nightmare fairground.

'I think the lady asked you to get off.' Julian yanked Sneath away by his collar, the sound of ripping cloth bringing her swirling senses back to earth. 'Now, bugger off! You really are a tedious little arse! I've got half a dozen guys in there who'll willingly tear you limb from limb, but if you lay another hand on Mel I'll do it myself. Clear? Good! Now go and write a book or something - a decent one this time!'

With as much dignity as he could muster, Sneath adjusted his shirt and strode away, a little unsteady on his feet. Even when he'd gone, the steel still circled Mel's wrists, the rigid fingers still clawed and probed, the hot sweat-stink of stale booze still wrapped its dank blanket around her. It was not so much the fear, it was the memory of her own helplessness and the absence of the silver-clear clarity she always told herself she'd possess in such situations - and it was being rescued by him.

'Thanks,' she said grudgingly. 'Again. I could have handled him, but thank you.'

'My pleasure.' Face held in a stiff mask, Julian turned to go.

She could have left it there, but that would have been petty, childish. 'Wait! Look, yesterday. I'm sorry.'

He stopped and turned back to her. 'No, I'm sorry. Really.'

'Friends?'

'Of course!' At last his features cracked into a smile. He opened his arms and she stepped into them, the safe, comforting smell of honest sweat and leather driving away Sneath's reek.

Sunday roasts demolished and a couple of pints apiece (or somewhat more in Nick's case) downed, Harding's assembled outside The King's Head. Danny, Ollie and Mike clambered into the back of Kev's van while Nick emptied the water from four new five-litre bottles.

Barry, a pleasant buzz on, still couldn't keep the smile from his face. 'Well done everyone. See you in a couple of weeks - should be a good one! Storming the castle, night attacks, fire pikes. Safe journey home.'

Emergency receptacles drained and ready, Nick was finally loaded aboard. Kev jumped in alongside Keith and Tabitha, gunned the accelerator and pulled away with a belch of smoke. Nick's voice came floating back over the farting exhaust.

'As I was walking through St Ippolits. A man came up and grabbed my nipplets!'

Bathed in golden sunlight, Harding's Stone kept watch over the fields that had once seen so much bloodshed, still and tranquil beneath the warm twilight. Only the drone of a labouring engine broke the silence, a battered camper van rumbling and bumping over the field before clattering to a halt before the stone.

Trevor, in his full finery, climbed arthritically from the driver's seat. Adjusting his glasses, he blinked in mild surprise at the empty field, gave a shrug, and hauled out the Harding's colour. He marched stiffly to the stone, colour dipped in solemn respect. The sunset pinked the horizon and still he stood, eyes distant. A dog barked in the far distance and, as if someone had flipped a switch, Trevor turned smartly and marched back to his van, sliding the colour reverently into the back before he took his perch in the driver's seat. With a grinding of gears, the camper turned a clumsy circle and bumped back over the field.

The sun sank into the west, laying mellow golden fingers across the waving crops as the uncouth voices of crows welcomed the evening.

4 THE BLACK HAWK

'Kern… Kerny… Kerny Jabrowlski?'

Peter's snowy moustaches drooped as he tried to get his mouth around the tricky pronunciation. Francesca - dark-haired and sublimely aloof - rubbed his shoulder in encouragement.

'Čierni Jastraby, Peter.' Barry basked in the glow of his own perfect enunciation. 'Based in Eastern Europe, though they've got members all over the continent.' The fledgling bloom of superiority soon wilted before the louche opulence of Peter's caravan - it never failed to ruffle Barry's proletarian sensibilities. Horse prints were very much in vogue, and the decommissioned Baker rifle on the wall had once been used in anger - as had the crossed basket-hilted broadswords. The primly delectable Francesca was just another ornamentation.

'Well, close enough,' huffed Peter.

'It means "The Black Hawk",' Ken informed him.

'Very dramatic.' Francesca tried to fill his teacup and Peter waved her away. 'Not now, m'dear. So, Barry, these chaps do medieval, eh?'

'Mainly - Christ knows what they'll be like now they're being let loose on black powder.'

'Enthusiastic, I should imagine.'

'Very.'

Peter hooded his eyes. 'And it's your job to make sure they don't get too "enthusiastic".'

'Why us?' Great. There went his weekend.

'Because I said so!'

'But I've seen their sort before,' Ken protested. 'They'll be a liability.'

Resting his chin on steepled fingers, Peter swivelled his eyes to Ken. 'Again, it's your job to make sure they're not a liability.'

Not fair! 'If some mono-browed Slavic cretin wants to blow himself to kingdom come, I'm not going to get in his way!'

'I agree, Barry - but it's up to you to prevent him from getting to that stage!' Peter's eyes hardened. 'They carry a deal of clout on the European scene, so I believe, and it will look bad on us if we - and by that, of course, I mean you - host them with anything less than red carpet treatment. *Entente cordiale*, Barry. Do I make myself clear?'

'As crystal, Peter.' Their fuck-up was his fuck-up. Great.

'Good, good. Excellent. When are they arriving, Frankie?'

Francesca peered deliberately over the top of her glasses like someone playing "sultry secretary" in the readers' wives section of one of Kev's more niche magazines. 'Sometime this afternoon, Peter, so they'll be in the battles both tomorrow and Sunday - and the night attack.'

'God help us.' Black powder novices and all the confusion of a night attack - what could go wrong? At least his affairs were all in order.

'Good show, good show.' Peter clapped his hands briskly. 'Right, off you go. Show them out, Frankie.'

Francesca ushered Barry and Ken to the door, rather like a palace flunky with ideas above her station and a pathological dislike of the lower classes. The jodhpur-clad blonde waiting on the steps was of an age with Francesca and her equal in looks, though after a more robust fashion. They glared at each other like alley cats.

'Ah, Wendy, m'dear!' boomed Peter. 'Do come in.'

The door slammed shut, startling that little Welsh dumpling Bryn who'd no doubt been sniffing around the caravan windows. Technically, as Brigade Commander (acting up until Peter found someone more competent and less eager), Barry should have dealt with him. The fact that Peter preferred to bypass Bryn and deal with Barry directly spoke volumes. Catching the look in Barry's eye, Bryn scuttled away.

'Bloody Peter!' said Barry savagely when he was sure Bryn was out of earshot. 'Why, Ken? Why has he saddled us with baby-sitting this bunch of cowboys?'

'Oh, I don't think they do Wild West. They're…'

'I know what they are! And I know why they're getting dumped on us!'

'Because Peter knows we're up to it?' Ken asked hopefully.

'No - we've got enough on our plate without having to worry about this. No, some little bird has been in his ear about our little stunt the other week - a fat, sweaty Scottish bird.' Bloody Macintyre! Just like him to go running to the board.

'You think so?'

'You think that Scots bastard would let me get one over on him? No, this has got his porridgey fingerprints all over it!'

'But we didn't do anything wrong!'

Barry sighed and started ticking off on his fingers. 'We showed up with no prior planning, no forms signed off, no powder clearance, and started blatting away on a farmer's field! Not to mention showering a prominent historian in maggots and kidnapping and feminising a dog!'

'But Macintyre…'

'Is a conniving, sneaky swine, but he's a devious, conniving, sneaky swine. He was out of order, but he did everything by the book. Bugger!' Barry kicked at an empty gin bottle protruding from a black sack beside the caravan. He missed.

'You think he's had a word with Peter?' Ken's hands wrestled like fretful spiders.

'And with the board. Whinging, back-stabbing git!'

'But Peter…'

'Is all well and good as long as he's left alone to play with his fillies and no one rocks the boat. He wants an easy life.'

'But we've not heard anything from on high - and Peter was civil enough just now.' Ken looked as though someone had just derailed his favourite model locomotive.

'Oh, read between the lines, Kenneth!' The weekend stretched ahead like a black tunnel - and the only light at the end was an oncoming train. 'They can't discipline us directly, not without Mac getting dragged in and the whole thing blowing up into something horribly messy. No, dumping "The Black Hawk" on us is a stroke of genius. We have to lick and grovel to them for the next couple of days, give them anything they want. If we upset them, it could close doors on the continent - and that will see us both back to the ranks. That's if we're lucky. On the other hand, any of their cock-ups will come back on us. Same results. Bastards!'

'So what do we do?'

'Like Peter said, we roll out the red carpet. Ply them with food and drink, let them make free with our women!'

'Surely not…'

'No, Ken, I was joking. About the women, at l…' The caravan door crashed open, a tearful Francesca stumbling down the steps and barging past them. 'Alright, Francesca?' The indignant little circles of her backside as she wiggled away were worthy of admiration.

'Bugger off!'

'Charming.' The velvet chuckle that drowned out Wendy's artful giggles stranded Barry halfway between admiration and disgust. 'Well, he's not going to let it ruin his weekend like it has mine, is he? I don't think there's one girl left in the Royalist horse who's not enjoyed a stint as his ADC. Come on, let's go and see if any more of ours have shown up yet.'

The campsite was situated in the sprawling grounds of a part-ruined medieval castle. A tarmac road - a rare luxury - ran through the centre of the camp to the tumbledown towers that shimmered lazily in the black waters of a swan-speckled lake. Seated next to a frosty Tabitha in the back of Keith's car, Danny craned his neck to keep the crumbling stone edifice in sight as they swung off the road and bumped their way through the maze of caravans, campers and tents until they reached a tall flexible pole topped with the Harding's colour. Any reservations had been left behind - after the (hopefully successful) conclusion of his exams, the summer stretched ahead like a four-lane motorway with no hint of traffic.

'Here we are! Home sweet home for the next couple of days.' Keith clambered out of the Mondeo, stretching his long legs. 'What could be better? Exams are finished, sun's shining, and tomorrow we get a night battle! You'll love it! Fire pikes, muzzle flashes in the dark - just a bit tricky loading, but nothing to worry about, Tab. And we're storming the castle!'

Burdened down with bags of travel sweets, Jane hauled herself from the passenger seat. 'Go on, go and get your tents up and leave me and your dad to get the caravan sorted.'

Danny pulled out his tent and backpack. Tabitha hauled out her own oversized rucksack, though that was only the vanguard of her luggage. The rest would be unloaded later.

'Where do you want to go, then?' Danny juggled his bags, the vast ocean of nylon, polyester and canvas rippling around him.

'Not too close to my folks - and not too close to Nick! Have you heard him snore?'

An ululating shriek announced that Mandy had spotted them. She raced over, delightfully fluent in tight tee-shirt and leggings, hugged Tabitha and then threw her arms around Danny. He froze, uncertain how to respond until the warm, eager press of her body melted his inhibitions. Dropping his gear, he hugged her back, though his attempted air-kiss somehow managed to find her cheek.

'You came back!' squealed Mandy.

'Yeah! Why wouldn't I?' What a welcome! Not that he was complaining, though Tab looked as if she'd bitten into a lemon.

'I thought we might have scared you off last time! I'm pitched just over there - come in next to me if you want. There's loads of room at the moment - get in quick before everyone else turns up.' She gave him a last affectionate squeeze.

Danny picked up his bags and Mandy led him by the hand to where her tent was pitched. It was only a one-man affair but blown up into something altogether grander, surrounded by fairy lights, flowerpots and a white plastic fence.

'There you go, Dan - get yours up next to my lady garden. There's space for you along there, Tab.'

Danny threw his rucksack down and unzipped his tent-bag to deposit a tangled mess of nylon on the ground. Unfurling the outer and inner, he found the poles and snapped them into rigidity. He ran his hand along the outer, located the slots, and tried to feed the first ungainly pole through. It was awkward with the pole flapping behind him, and Mandy took a hand.

'Where's this go? Oh, in here, of course! Okay, that's it, it's in.' Together, they had the poles inserted in seconds and hauled the tent upright. She passed him a tent peg and a mallet. 'Now, I'll hold it and you bang it in nice and hard!'

She was like a force of nature, impossible to resist. 'Brace yourself, then!'

It took two solid whacks to drive the peg in. Mandy fluttered her eyelashes. 'Ooh, you're strong! I bet you work out?'

'A bit.' Four or five times a week since the exams had finished, but he didn't want to boast.

She squeezed his bicep appreciatively, as if sizing up fruit. 'I'll say! No wonder Tabitha's been keeping you to herself all these years!'

The pressure of her fingers on his bare skin sent a swirl of heat through him. Dropping to a crouch, he hammered the next peg in, as wayward and ineffective as a toddler with a rubber mallet. Nevertheless, after a minute or two of feeble pounding, all the pegs were in. 'Job done!' He rose from his haunches to admire the finished product.

'Very impressive once it's up.'

Mandy's wink was full of promise and his core temperature rocketed to boiling point. *Calm down, she's just a bit flirty, that's all.* 'Yeah - now what do I do with the rest of the day?'

'We'll think of something to keep you occupied. Beer tent later? It's always chilled on a Friday night.'

Images of Mandy's impressive charms squeezed into - or out of - a corset did little for his composure. 'Definitely,' he croaked. 'Bit early now though, isn't it?'

She cocked her head to one side, rich red locks tumbling over her shoulder. 'We could always go for a walk in the castle grounds. Nice and secluded.'

'Yeah, okay. I'll see if Tab...'

'She's still sorting herself out. Come on.' She grabbed his hand, her fingers burning like ice.

He should really stay and help Tabitha, who was struggling to erect her own tent. 'I've still got a few bits and pieces to unpack first - and we should see if she fancies coming along.'

Mandy pouted. 'You can do that later - and she can catch us up. I want you to myself for a while.'

'You do? Why?' *Come off it, no way.*

'Why do you think?' She stepped closer, placing a thigh between both of his and forcing his legs wider.

'I… I'm not sure.' The sudden sense of vulnerability had his stomach (and lower) buzzing like warm lemonade.

'I don't really have to spell it out for you, do I?' she purred, smoky eyes twinkling.

Maybe she did, as his brain seemed incapable of accepting so obvious an invitation. Not so his body, which was giving urgent pointers while waiting for his mind to catch up. What about Tab, though? No, even if she had unthawed a little, there was no chance. She was up and down - okay one minute, cold as ice the next. Whereas Mandy was warm all the time. Sizzling in fact. 'What? I… oh… yeah, right… I…'

'All set up then, Mandy?' At her father's voice, Mandy slid her fingers from Danny's slack grip. Danny's heart leapt into his mouth, but if Barry - Ken at his side as ever - had noticed, he didn't show it, recoiling instead from the décor around his daughter's tent. 'Oh my God, what the hell is that?'

'Just thought I'd make it look nice!'

'Nice? It looks like an explosion in a poof's parlour!'

'I like it!'

'Well, as long as you're happy…'

Mandy poked her tongue out.

'You'll stay like that if the wind changes,' Ken warned her.

'Is that what happened to you, Ken?' she asked sweetly.

Barry bristled. 'You watch yourself, or you'll be up on a charge of insulting an officer!'

'Yes, dad. Sorry, dad.'

'Right, now make yourself scarce. I need a word with young Danny here. In private.'

Mandy's bottom lip hung out. 'But I was just about to show him the sights!' Another mushroom cloud detonated in Danny's abdomen.

'That can wait. Now go on - this is important.'

'Oh, for f… Okay. Catch you in a minute, Dan. Tab? You want a hand with your tent?'

Barry waited until Mandy was busy with Tabitha's tent. 'Making friends, eh? Good for you, Dan!'

Bugger off! There was an urgent press in his loins, and his libido was nudging him with a lewd elbow, but he forced a weak smile. 'Yeah. Right. What was it you wanted, Mr Reynolds?'

'That'll be Colonel,' Ken chided.

'Never mind that, Ken. Don't look so worried, Dan, just came to thank you for the other week. Mac's face was a picture after you'd finished dolling up his little bitch!'

'That's okay, it was a good laugh.' Thank God - he'd been steeled for the "hands off my daughter" speech.

'It was, but not completely above board, so I'd be grateful if you could forget it. If anyone asks you - anyone at all - you weren't there, okay?'

'Right, okay.'

'Good lad, good lad.'

'What's all that about?' Tabitha finally succeeded in sliding home the flailing tent pole.

'No idea,' said Mandy. 'He's come out of his shell, hasn't he?'

'Who, Dan? I suppose so.' Tabitha had recently come to the conclusion that maybe he wasn't the complete idiot she'd thought, but they were only back to what they had been years ago - virtually cousins. Why, then, did she often find herself sneaking sideways glances at him? Why did she feel suddenly protective, jealous almost?

'Quite fit, as well - and his eyes... oh. You're not... I didn't think you...'

'What, me and Dan? No way!' It could never work; their families were too close and away from all this he'd just be Danny again. A prat.

'It's just that you gave me a bit of a look.' Mandy curled a lock of ruby hair around her fingers. 'I didn't think you were in to him, not after the last muster, but if you've changed your...'

'I haven't, okay? Alright, he's not too bad looking and when he's not being an idiot he can be quite a good laugh - like the other week.'

'This was that thing that dad was on about? In Little Felcham?'

'That's right. We had a good laugh but that's it. He's more like a brother than anything.'

Mandy ran a finger over her lips. 'So you don't mind if me and him...'

'No, why should I? It's not like I fancy him, is it?' Then why was she so reluctant to allow Mandy to get her claws into him? She tried to sound casual. 'He's a bit young for you though, isn't he?'

'Oi! I'm only a year older.'

But so much more experienced. She almost felt sorry for Danny - almost as sorry as she felt for herself. 'Okay. Don't hurt him, though.'

Mandy gave an evil grin. 'Only if he asks me to!'

They both laughed, though Tabitha's was a little forced and she was grateful when Barry called to her. 'Tabitha? A word, please!'

Taking her chance, Mandy sidled over to Danny and led him away by the hand with a look of expectant panic plastered on his face.

Barry and Ken waited at the tree-shrouded entrance to the castle grounds. The check-in point for the campsite was manned by two members of

Godley's regiment - Brian and Phil, if Barry had their names right - but he wanted to make sure he was here to greet their guests in person.

'They won't have membership cards, but they should have an accreditation form.'

'I'm sure we'll recognise them, Barry.' Brian tapped a pen against his clipboard.

'They could be sneaking anyone in!' Ken, as ever, was fretting.

'For God's sake, Ken, I knew I shouldn't have lent you "Went the Day Well?"! They're not going to be coming in disguised as nuns and policemen! They just want a taste of the UK scene and to scratch up on their black powder handling. We should be proud that they've come to us - the best in the business! They've not come to steal our jobs, our homes or our women, despite what you read in the more lurid rags.'

'That's not what I meant! I just meant how do we know they're all members of Čierni Jastraby? How do we know they're all trained? They could be bringing wives, families, anyone!'

'If they've got any sense they'll have dumped the wives and kiddies at home,' said Phil with a grimace.

Brian gave a gobble of laughter. 'At least we'll be sorted if the plumbing goes up the spout!'

It was going to be a long, tense weekend. 'It's those sorts of stereotypes we need to avoid! Friendly faces! Welcoming! Try harder, Ken! And make sure they stick to the main drive, Phil - the verges are still a bit boggy. We don't want their coach getting stuck.'

'Right-o, Barry.' Although the weekend promised to be glorious, it had rained heavily for the past week. 'Could be them now.'

Heralded by a growling engine and grinding gears, a coach appeared at the end of the long avenue of trees leading up to the entrance. Barry rolled his shoulders, adjusting the hang of his Harding's polo-shirt. Should have changed into uniform. First impressions were important. 'This is it. Remember, Ken - warm and welcoming!'

'I'll try - but their kit better be up to scratch!'

The coach was approaching like the Bismarck steaming into action. From the state of the bodywork and the amount of black smoke, it obviously visited the same garage as Kev's Transit.

'They better slow down a bit.' Brian raised an eyebrow.

Phil stepped into the road, hand raised. If anything, the coach accelerated. 'Hey! Stop! Stop!'

'They're not stopping! Move!'

Brian got a hand on Phil's hi-vis vest and hauled him out of the way. Just in time. The coach careered through the entrance as if the Devil himself was at the wheel, roaring up the road toward the castle. About halfway along, left indicator blinking erratically, it slowed down with a crunch of gears.

'The idiots!' All Barry needed was a bogged-down coach 'Ken, go and stop them parking up on the verge - hurry, man!'

Ken set off at a run, making a handful of yards before slipping in the mud to land face-first in a puddle. He rose like the Tar Baby, eyes white and despairing amidst the filth. Though it was hopeless, Barry sprinted past his dripping subordinate, waving his arms and shouting for all he was worth.

'Nein! Niet! Nietski! No! Not the verge! Nicht der grass! Stop! You bloody idiots! Stop! Oh my God!'

The coach veered to the side of the road, its nearside wheels encroaching onto the grass. The inevitable happened. Furiously spinning wheels kicking up a magnificent shower of mud, the coach ground to a halt - an impressive gouge in the earth behind it - and sunk up to its wheel-arches. Barry let Ken catch him up and they approached the beached vehicle. Nothing moved behind the tinted windows, not even when the doors opened with a laboured hiss that made Ken jump.

'Hallo?' called Barry, like the first man aboard the *Mary Celeste*. 'Guten Tag? Bonjour? Willkommen?'

As with the benighted traveller before the moonlit door, only silence greeted him. Ken sniffed through his face pack, yipping when a silhouette flickered behind the dark glass, and Barry had to put out a hand to stop him from running as the first passenger appeared in the doorway, black robes merging with the coach's gloomy interior. Surely it couldn't be... it could! Picking up the hem of her habit, a nun descended the steps.

'What the...' A second nun followed, a third, a fourth, and then a whole stream of them, filing out to line the side of the coach like a regiment of penguins, faces obscured by their wimples. 'Oh my God!'

The first nun - a squat, dumpy barrel of a woman - waddled over. Only her nose and eyes - the fiercest Barry had ever seen on a woman (including Alice) - were visible and her voice was muffled by the rough cloth.

'Sorry, er, sister? I think you're in the wrong place - and you're definitely stuck. We'll have to ring round the local farms or call out the AA. We were expecting a re-enactment group - "The Black Hawks".'

'"The Black Hawk", Barry. Singular.' Ken looked as if he really believed a detachment of German paratroopers had just arrived incognito to cut their lines of communication - and their throats. 'He was a prince or something, I think. Some sort of folk hero.'

When the nun spoke again, the words "Čierni Jastraby" were clearly distinguishable. She was certainly getting animated and, with a sudden jerk, she threw aside her habit. Barry took a backward step. He had his own ideas about what sort of women took holy orders, but the luxuriant ginger moustache was a step too far. Did nuns, however masculine, usually wear doublet and britches beneath their robes? And the weapons! Sword, bandoliers, pistols, daggers - an arsenal of Blackbeard-esque proportions. The sword was out of its scabbard in a heartbeat, pressed to his throat while a face like a determined rabbit was thrust into his.

'We are Čierni Jastraby!' bellowed the erstwhile sister of mercy in heavily-accented English. 'Is jokes, no?' The other "nuns" - having cast aside their habits - roared with laughter. 'We are here to fight! To fire the muskets! And to make friends!'

'Not a great start then,' muttered Ken.

'You are wet and muddy, my friend! My English - not so good. What is it that you say?'

Barry gave Ken's shin a subtle kick.

'Welcome to England,' Ken said dutifully.

'Is good!'

With a delicate finger, Barry moved the ebullient little livewire's sword away from his throat. 'Who's in charge of this rabb... this fine body of men?'

'Is me! I'm the boss! Me! Lech! Lechslaw Maksymilian Klymzyn!'

What else? 'Lech it is. I'm Barry. Barry Reynolds, commanding officer of Harding's Regiment.'

Ken eyed "The Black Hawk" with despair. 'Not for much longer,' he said beneath his breath.

'Good! Is you I am looking for!' Lech seized Barry's hand in a bone-crushing grip. 'Come! You review my troops!'

Barry had little choice as Lech dragged him along the ranks of "The Black Hawk". They were huge - even the few actual women among them - and looked horribly hard-bitten despite being dressed like the most fanciful pirates Hollywood could imagine. There was a blur of names that Barry didn't catch, each accompanied by a steel handshake that left his hand like blancmange. Reaching the end of the line, Lech stood on tiptoes to clap the penultimate man on a broad shoulder. 'My son, Marius.'

The motley uniform aside, Marius looked like he should have been playing a Panzer commander in a World War 2 film - square-shouldered, blond-haired and blue-eyed. Poster boy of the Third Reich.

'Afternoon, Mary... Marius. First time in England?'

The clipped English, with the merest trace of an accent, only enhanced the air of blond superiority. 'No, sir, I was over here for two years studying. Is good to be back.'

Punching Marius on the bicep, Lech moved to the last of his charges. 'And my daughter, Suzanne!'

Sweet Jesus! She was a female version of her brother, a bloody Amazon. Big, breathtaking, beautiful. Wagner could have dedicated a whole opera to her. Her braided jacket, with the top few buttons undone, struggled to contain her, and Barry's neck creaked as he forced himself to look her in the eye. 'Ah, hello, young lady! A pleasure to welcome you to our green and pleasant land!'

The generous smile was even-toothed and dazzling - like her brother, she had to get her looks (and build) from her mother. 'Sank you.'

Lech waved a hand. 'Her English? Not so good! She is rider - winged Hussar!'

'I bet she is.' Barry risked a look at her snug riding britches and thigh-length boots. Best keep her to him… away from Peter.

'Sank you.'

'Well, we'll have to see if we can get her in the clu… in the saddle, won't we? I'm sure our horse will be glad to accomodate you!'

'No, is good. I have a name. Sean? Sean will provide horse for my girl!'

'But he's Parliament!' blurted Ken.

Lech frowned. 'Then who are we?'

'Royalists!'

'You mean we do not fight for the great Mr Cromwell?'

'No,' said Ken in a slightly strangled voice, 'we fight for the King!'

Lech shrugged. 'Is good, so long as we fight! And you, girl, do not think we go easy on you!' He shook his fist at Suzanne who poked out a perfect little pink tongue.

Barry clapped his hands. Time to get things moving along. 'Right, we've got a nice little spot for you to camp in - if you get your lads and lasses to unload, I'll show you where.'

'Coach is sunk.' Lech kicked a wheel. 'Is problem?'

That could wait for another day. 'Not at all, not at all. We'll get it sorted, don't you worry.'

The beer tent on the Friday night of a muster was always much more sedate than a Saturday or Sunday, and the marquee was only three-quarters full. Some people danced to the muted music from the P.A; most stood chatting.

Barry and Ken were introducing their guests to warm English bitter, though most of the Black Hawk opted for the premium lagers on tap. The conversation was limited at best and it was almost a relief when Macintyre sauntered past with Ian.

'How's your baby-sitting going? Lost any of 'em yet?'

Even the dour Scots growl was welcome after the thick Eastern European accents. Barry ushered Lech forward. 'Lech, let me introduce Richard Macintyre - Lord General of Parliament. Mac - Lech, CO of the Black Hawk.'

The two commanders shook hands. 'Alright? I met your lass earlier - bonnie wee thing. She's had a trot around with Sean.'

Lech frowned, obviously unable to decipher the gravelly tones. 'Repeat, please?'

'He's been staring at your daughter's arse while she bounces around on a horse,' Barry muttered, then turned on the stilted, overly loud tones he reserved for Lech. 'You'll have to forgive Richard. He's from north of the border and victim of an unfinished education.'

This apparently explained little to Lech. 'Please?'

'I'm a Scot!' Macintyre glared dirks at Barry.

Lech's leporine face lit up. 'Ah! Scots! Where is skirt?'

'Skirt?' Storm clouds gathered over Mac's brow.

'Skirt! All Scottish mens wear skirt!'

'You want to ask his dog about that!' sniggered Barry. This was great. A small victory, and probably his last, but all the more reason to enjoy it while he could.

Lech floundered. 'He puts skirt on dog? For why?'

'I do not! Just Barry's little joke - enjoy it while you can, Reynolds.'

This was proof - if any more was needed. 'I knew it! I knew it! Can't take a joke, you miserable Scots git! You've been in Peter's ear, haven't you?'

'I don't know what you mean.' The innocent tone was belied by the savage satisfaction smeared across Mac's face. 'Nice to have met you, Lech. Enjoy yourself on the battlefield tomorrow - don't hold back, will you?'

'You will be there?'

'Of course - with my army!'

'You wear skirt then?'

'It's called a kilt, man! And no, I will no be wearing one!' Mac's accent became so thick as to be unintelligible - even to a fellow Briton.

'Please?'

'Ach, have a good night.'

Lech twirled his moustache thoughtfully as Macintyre strode away. 'Tomorrow we will break his army! Then he will wear skirt for us!'

'We're scripted to lose tomorrow,' said Ken.

'Lose?' Lech's teeth became even more prominent. 'We do not lose! We never lose! We are Čierni Jastraby!'

Oh, well done, Ken. 'I'm afraid we have to,' Barry explained as gently as he could. 'Don't worry - we take the castle in the night attack.'

'So we win in end?'

'Yes, yes we do.'

'Is good!' The thick moustaches settled into more agreeable lines.

Ken couldn't keep it shut. 'But on Sunday we...'

Barry stamped on his foot. Ken whimpered.

'Is problem?' asked Lech.

'No, no, just treating his disease.'

'Disease?'

'Yes, he was born with it. Foot in mouth disease.'

'This is jokes? I do not understand.'

'Never mind. More drinks?' The universal language.

'Of course! But first, we toast!' Lech pulled out a hip flask, took a generous swig, and passed it to Barry. 'Čierni Jastraby!'

'Čierni Jastraby!' Barry took a pull on the flask, trying to ignore the aroma of old socks. Whatever it was hit his throat like an asteroid searing through the atmosphere, detonating in his stomach to send fiery shockwaves all through his body. He felt (and, horribly, heard) his eyes bulge. His toes curled. Upwards.

'Is good?' Lech raised an eyebrow.

Robbed of the power of speech, Barry nodded and passed the flask to Ken, careful not to let any drips touch his bare flesh.

Lech slapped Ken heartily on the shoulder. 'Will cure your disease, no?'

'Čierni Jastraby!' Ken took a swig. 'Good grief!' He held the flask up, smacking his lips appreciatively, then took another full-blown swallow.

It was a shame that Mandy hadn't donned her corsetry for the beer tent - or maybe not. As it was, her peasant-style top hung loosely from her shoulders, threatening to engulf Danny in a tumbling avalanche of unfettered pink flesh, and her denim miniskirt rode up to expose a tantalising length of smooth thigh as she swung her leg over to straddle him. Whatever she'd had in mind in the castle grounds earlier had been scuppered by the hordes of sightseers, but she was more than making up for it now. Firecrackers erupted across his body as she ground against him in a series of sinuous movements. Jesus, she was hot! Too hot! He was liquid between the eager grip of her thighs, powerless, every fibre alive and shrieking as if his skin had been replaced by satin and charged with static. His solitary fumbling encounter at a party last year seemed about as erotic as plugging in a USB stick in comparison, a stark, mechanical necessity to remove the shameful tag of virgin. It seemed a tag still deserved now, immured as he was beneath the voluptuous press of her body and tortured beyond endurance by the light expertise of her handiwork. The subtle, powdery scent of her perfume filled his senses and, beneath it, a secret, musky aroma slithered its intoxicating fronds around his most sensitive regions, coaxing the urgent heat that swelled him almost to bursting. God, no! He looked past the lustrous web of red hair, praying for a sight to delay the inevitable.

Jesus, that helped! Like a dash of cold water. Barry was chatting with those foreign blokes, seemingly oblivious to the fact that his daughter was merrily dry-humping not thirty yards away. Beyond them, on the dance floor, was Tabitha - he'd caught her eye a couple of times earlier, her expression unreadable. That blond geezer who'd turned up with the Czechs, or Poles, or whatever they were was there, too. Marius. He was garnering a lot of attention with his slick moves and Tabitha was dancing clos…

Mandy nipped his neck. 'Hey - you're with me, remember?'

'What?' Thankfully the building crescendo in his loins had faded to a dull, if pleasurable, throb.

'Tab - you haven't taken your eyes off her all night!'

He'd only looked at her once or twice. Maybe three times. Possibly four. 'I'm just keeping an eye on your old man, that's all.'

'Oh, don't worry about him! He's half-way to being pissed anyway!'

'Yeah, okay.' He took one last look at the dance floor, but Mandy put a forceful hand to his cheek, locked her lips over his and squeezed her squirming tongue into his mouth. Defcon 3 was reinstated, their tongues dancing together in a moist frenzy, the play of his fingers across her spine eliciting a muffled squeak of pleasure.

'That's better!' They parted, breathless, Mandy's eyes sparkling and a pleasing red tint to her cheeks. She slipped a hand under his tee-shirt, her fingers cool on his raging flesh. 'Look, forget Tab - I know you had a thing for her, but you'll never get close. You don't stand a chance!'

'I don't fancy her. We're just friends.'

'Yeah, right. Whatever.' She licked his earlobe, sending icy arrows screaming along his nerve paths. 'Anyway, you've got zero hope with that Marius around - he's well fit.'

'What's that make me then?' The cautionary voice in the back of his mind told him that this was never going to be anything permanent, but other regions of his anatomy had the reins tonight. He slid a trembling hand along the tanned silk of her thigh, hardly able to believe that she allowed his questing fingers to brush beneath the hem of her skirt.

'Lucky. Very lucky if you play your cards right!' Her own hand slid lower.

Everything she did, every move she made, verged on the decadent, making him feel like a schoolboy finding his first stash of porn. How much longer could he hold out? He snatched up his drink and downed it. 'Must be getting about time to turn in?'

'It's not even ten yet!'

He didn't care. He just wanted her. Here and now if necessary - and before she took even more notice of that Marius bloke. Still, he had to play it cool. 'Another drink, then?'

Her hand circled maddeningly. 'Are you trying to get me drunk? Go on then, make it a double this time! Don't get too carried away, though - I want you to be able to perform later!'

*

Danny floated to the bar, skin still prickling from the touch of Mandy's attentive hands. His jeans seemed to have shrunk several sizes, too. How would he last more than half a minute when she really got stuck into him? He waved a tenner at the nearest barmaid. 'Lager, please, and a vodka and coke. Double.'

'Danny, my son!' Nick was at the bar with the usual suspects. 'Get in there!'

Mike's hand descended on Danny's shoulder. 'Good work - usually takes about three musters to get a go on Mandy!'

'Must be my good looks.' Whatever her reputation, Danny was not going to miss out - not when it was such a sure thing. Anyway, Ollie apparently ended up with a different girl every muster and he was feted as a hero.

'Or sympathy!' said Steve.

In reply, Danny raised his middle finger.

Nick took a sniff of the erect digit. 'Not quite cracked it yet then!'

'Alright, guys, leave him alone! None of us would do any different in his shoes, would we?' Ollie was feeding a handful of change into his pocket. 'I know I didn't!'

'Or me,' said Mike and Steve together.

'Or me.' The cavernous belch on which Nick ended his statement billowed the walls of the marquee.

'Get stuffed! You're all old enough to be her dad!' She had some standards, surely?

'Oi!' Ollie managed to scatter change over the floor. 'Not all of us are!'

'None of us are,' added Steve. 'Not quite!'

'Nah, she's just got a thing for older men!' Mike ran a hand through his hair.

Steve trod gently on Ollie's fingers as he scrabbled for his change. 'Yeah, ask Trevor!'

'Sod off!' The enjoyable, if crude, banter was a rough form of acceptance - the trip in Kev's van the other week had broken down barriers - but they were beginning to erode his excitement.

'No, really.' Mike joined in with Steve, trying to trap Ollie's fingers beneath his trainer. 'Trev's only about thirty - that's the effect she has! Eh, Steve?'

'Burn out!'

Finally gathering in his recalcitrant change, Ollie got to his feet. 'No, seriously mate, she's a good girl. Good laugh. Just keep things in perspective, yeah?'

'What do you mean?' Why were they trying to ruin things for him? He knew the score. It was just a hook-up, no strings. Fine. If things developed, all well and good. He couldn't go on waiting for Tab - he'd be a born-again virgin.

'Things are different on camp. You're away for a few days in a different environment. You get people from all over the country turning up who never see each other from one month to the next, so what goes here is sort of separate, yeah? It's boxed away with the rest of their kit when they get home - just keep that in mind on Monday morning. It's just a little something for the weekend. Get it?'

'Yeah, yeah. I think so.' One weekend, one day, one minute, he didn't care. He was with Mandy tonight and, at the moment, that was all that mattered.

'Good. Just don't get...' Ollie froze, pint halfway to his mouth. 'Mother of God!'

Steve choked on his lager. 'View halloooo!'

'Jesus!' Mike missed his mouth, slopping half a pint over his shoulder.

Even Nick's permanently half-closed eyes opened wide. 'Bugger me!'

Like a hand-grenade thrown into a box of fireworks, Suzanne had just made her grand entrance. The riding boots accentuated her height, the skin-tight britches oiled the rolling gears of her hips, and the barely decent crop-top showed off her taut belly while promoting her more bountiful charms.

Ollie smoothed his hair back. 'If you'll excuse me, gentlemen, it's time for the Flashing Blade to get to work!'

'If you need a hand...' Mike called after him.

Why waste time drooling over the unattainable? Drinks served, Danny pocketed his change and took a gulp of lager before fighting his way back through the swelling press around the bar. Pulling clear, the sight that greeted him stopped him dead in his tracks, simultaneously punching him in the stomach and kicking him in the balls. Marius had moved fast - he now occupied Danny's chair and Mandy occupied him. They both, to put it politely, had their hands full.

'Whoops,' said Steve.

'Coming over here, nicking our women,' rumbled Nick.

'Never mind, mate. You'll get another chance.'

The sensuous pulses that had warmed his body turned to bitter shards. Danny shook off Mike's consoling hand and whirled away, though he had little idea where he was going. Anywhere away from her, so he didn't have to watch Marius smoothly slipping in to what he'd spent all day earning. Bloody slag! And bloody smarmy git! Bollocks, bugger, shit.

The vodka and coke was lifted from his unresisting hand. 'You shouldn't have!' It was Sophie, dumpy in jeans and sweatshirt.

'That's for... oh, sod it, you might as well have it!' There was no way Mandy was getting anything more out of him.

'He's a bit of a dish, isn't he?' Sophie took a sip of her purloined drink.

'That Marius or whatever he's called.'

'Oh yeah, he's Mr Bloody Wonderful.' Blond-haired, blue-eyed bastard! *Big*, blond-haired, blue-eyed bastard! Big enough to quell any impulsive thoughts of vengeance. 'Git!'

'Well, he thinks a lot of himself, that's for sure!'

'Tried it on with you, did he?'

'Me and every other girl! Looks like he's struck gold now, though.'

Twist the knife, why don't you? 'Yeah, great.'

Her hand went to her mouth. 'Oh - I thought it was Tab you had your sights on?'

'Yeah? Well, he'll be getting stuck into her before much longer probably.'

'He's only here for a day or two then he'll be gone - and standing scowling isn't doing you any favours!' She put a hand on his arm. 'Not everyone's under his spell, you know.'

'No? Well, Mandy is now - and Tab's been making eyes at him all night.'

Her touch was gentle, caring - inviting almost. Pity about the shapeless sweater - the memory of her soft contours reignited the fires dampened by Marius' brash opportunism. Without the glasses, hair freed from the drab little ponytail, maybe she'd... No, get a grip. Having been so rudely snatched from the pot of simmering expectation, he'd have jumped on Trevor if he put on a tight dress and made an effort with his hair.

Chewing a nail, Sophie seemed to be weighing her next words. 'Look,' she said eventually, 'you can tell me to mind my own business if you like, but you and Tab? I really don't think...'

'Mind your own business!' What the fuck was it to do with her?

Dropping her hand to her side, she gave him a little resigned smile. 'I suppose I asked for that. I was just trying to...'

'Yeah, I know what you were just trying to say. Look, where do you get off sticking your nose in?' The frustrating tide of heady anticipation and anti-climax had exposed black rocks, bitter, jagged and keen to bite. 'I fancy Tab, I was on for a shag with Mandy, and I'm not interested in you, so just fuck off, okay?'

She didn't deserve that, he knew that even before the downturn of her mouth told him what a bastard he was, but the hardened carapace of rejection was not so easily cracked. For the second time in as many minutes, he stormed off with little idea where he was storming to. From, that was the important bit.

'Lesbian. Has to be.' Ollie was not impressed when he arrived back.

'Didn't fall for your charms, then?' Mike pushed a fresh pint along the bar.

'Or anyone's by the look of it,' said Steve. 'Look at them - like flies around shit!'

Suzanne was fighting her way through a gaggle of admirers, fending them off with a friendly smile. Making her way through to the bar, she squeezed in next to a solitary figure.

Julian shuffled along the bar, giving room to whoever had just squashed in next to him. Multiple piercings glinting beneath the lights, the tattooed barmaid gave a bewildered frown as she tried to take the newcomer's order. Picking up a definite - and familiar - accent, Julian lent a hand.

'She asked for a vodka and coke.'

'Well, why didn't she say?' pouted the black-lipped barmaid.

'Sank you.' The new arrival gave Julian the full benefit of her perfect smile.

She was a beauty, no mistake, with striking Slavic cheekbones and big, blue eyes whose innocence seemed at odds with her Amazonian bearing. 'Don't mention it.' He raised a hand to the barmaid. 'I'll have a lager as well, please.' Turning back to the girl, his eyes lingered on the spun gold cascading past her shoulders before flicking to the toned, tanned belly. 'I'm surprised you made it to the bar in one piece - you seem to have picked up quite a crowd of admirers!'

Combined with the still-present - if bemused - smile, the frown did little to mar her features, instead imbuing them with an adorable quizzicality. 'Please?'

He was rusty, but not so rusty that her smile didn't widen in delight when she heard her native tongue. Even his accent was pretty spot on. She answered in the same language.

'I think that it is the drink makes them like this, no?'

'Of course!' Julian fished out his wallet as the barmaid returned. 'I'll get that, don't worry.'

'Thank you.'

'My pleasure. So, whereabouts in...'

Balkan disco - presumably in geographically incorrect honour of the Black Hawk - blared from the P.A. Barry and Ken joined Lech in enthusiastic, high-kneed dancing. Mandy and Marius slipped out, hand in hand.

'You come back to our camp! We have fire, we have drink, we have more drink!'

Barry skipped over a guy rope. He wasn't really a bad sort, old Lech. And Peter couldn't complain - they'd rolled out the red carpet as ordered. A few more drinks could really put the cap on the old *entente cordiale*, though the cold front no doubt awaiting him back at his caravan shone through the contented alcoholic fuzz like polished steel. 'I really should get back to Alice.'

'You come! Drink! See wife later!'

'Come on, Barry!' Ken bumped into him and spun gently away. 'Live a little!'

It wasn't that late, was it? Barry fumbled for his watch. Too dark. Couldn't see the damn thing anyway. 'Okay, okay. Maybe just one more.'

The Black Hawk had made themselves at home and a large fire crackled in the centre of their little enclave. They couldn't do that, *entente cordiale* or no! Rules were rules - especially with Peter breathing down his neck. 'Hey! No open fires!' The flames did look pretty though, with fire-sprites whirling up into the darkness.

'You're so stiff sometimes, Barry!' Ken slumped down into a convenient camp chair, taking the proffered bottle of spirits from a hulking Black Hawker. '*Entente cordiale*, remember?'

Different rules, different regulations. Make them feel welcome. With his head drifting several feet above his body, Barry fell into the chair next to Ken and took the bottle from him. *Entente cordiale.*

Having spent a miserable hour roaming the darkened castle grounds, Danny returned alone to his tent. He should have searched out Sophie and apologised, but he'd had enough humiliation for one night - or not, apparently. Mandy's tent was lit up with fairy lights, an enticing boudoir which should have been his bed for the night, and each low mutter or muted giggle twisted the knife a little deeper into his back. With a sensual hiss of nylon, a pair of superbly rounded buttocks bulged against the walls of the tent, replaced after a moment of two of frantic thrashing by an equally impressive, if not more muscular, backside. Resisting the urge to slam his foot into the gyrating protrusion, Danny clambered into his own tent and slipped into his sleeping bag, soothed to fitful sleep by the unabashed enthusiasm of his neighbours' frenetic rutting.

***

Barry managed to open one eye, the lid grating like a badly oiled gate. The other eye seemed unwilling to move, so he contented himself with one. The sun was less bright that way, only lancing a single shard of silver pain into his skull - a skull through which the whole Royalist army seemed to be marching with hammering drums. A troop of malicious imps trampolined their way across his guts. 'Oh God. Oh God. Oh God. Sweet mother of

Jesus, never again.' He ran a sandpaper tongue around his shrivelled lips while Ken woke beside him with a whimper. With a Herculean effort that made the top of his head fall off, Barry peeled open his other eye and sat up, rolling a dangerous tsunami through the choppy waters of his innards. He was still in the same chair as last night. The fire had died down, leaving only grey ash and a wisp of smoke, and there was no sign of Lech or his stormtroopers. God, the sun was bright - too bright to be dawn. A bolt of terror spiked him, overruling the noisy debate in his stomach. 'Ken! Ken! What time is it?'

'Time to die,' croaked Ken, slipping from his chair and curling up in the ashes of the fire.

'It's morning! It's morning! We've been here all night! Oh my God, she's going to bloody kill me!' Barry climbed to his feet, fighting against the grey that hazed his vision, forcing back the acid that bubbled up his throat, and clenching his cheeks against the concert of moans and gurgles that eddied in loose tides through his abdomen. He was a dead man.

Keith had gone to Barry's caravan first thing, hoping to get some more details on the day's activities. No go. Barry had not been outside drinking coffee - as was his norm at this hour - and the chalkboard on which the day's instructions were usually scribbled was still blank. There was no way he was going to risk facing Alice if Barry wasn't there to keep her on a tight leash, so he hovered. They were meant to be drilling with the Black Hawk at some point, but that wasn't down to him to organise. Munching on bacon rolls, Mike and Steve drifted past just as Barry appeared at the far end of the avenue of tents, staggering like a shipwreck survivor dragging himself from the embrace of the ocean.

'Well, well, well.' Keith recoiled from the speakeasy fumes wafting from the CO. 'Look what the cat dragged in! Where have you been?'

'*Entente* bloody *cordiale*!' Barry looked green.

'Not the only one,' whispered Mike so that only Keith and anyone within a ten-yard radius could hear. 'Anyone seen Mandy this morning?'

'Sssh!' Steve elbowed him to silence, though Barry showed no sign of having heard.

'Ah, mixing with our gallant European allies.' Julian strolled around the corner of the caravan. 'I had a chat with one of them last night. Suzanne. Charming girl!'

'Well, she doesn't get that from her father!' Every breath Barry took looked as though it could be his last. 'Man's a savage!' He nodded toward his caravan, fear replacing the pain in his eyes. 'Is she... up?'

'Most of the night, I think,' said Steve.

'Oh Jesus.' Barry straightened himself out as best he could, rubbing at his teeth with a finger.

Barely containing the bubbles of mirth that overwhelmed any sense of empathy, Keith pressed the waxy flesh of Barry's palm. 'Good luck, old chap.'

With the green giving way to a ghastly shade of off-white, Barry stumbled up the steps to the caravan like a man making his way to the guillotine, though a French aristocrat would surely have made his final walk with far more panache. Exchanging glances with the others as Barry disappeared inside, Keith could see the same mix of apprehension, sympathy and gleeful delight on their faces. Barry's muted attempts at mollification stood no chance against the shrill voice that whirred into life like a chainsaw on helium.

Julian winced. 'Well, she's taking that quite well.' He flinched at a ripple of smashing china. The suspension gave a tortured groan as the caravan started to rock. 'Maybe not,' he conceded, having to raise his voice over the burgeoning cascade of shattering crockery.

'Sounds like a Greek wedding,' snickered Mike, the caravan pitching and tossing now like a ship in rough seas. It was a full minute before an ominous calm descended and the caravan settled back onto its wheels. 'Do you think she's killed him?'

'From the look of him it wouldn't have taken much,' said Steve.

Should he escape now or stick around in case First Aid was required? Only Lech's arrival prevented Keith from pursuing the former course of action.

'Barry is here?' In full kit, the Black Hawk's CO was a picture of rude health - especially compared to the wan vision that had been Barry.

'Indisposed at the moment, old chap.'

The moustaches bristled. 'This is not good! We need talk - powder, drill, battle. I need to know these things! I go in!'

'I wouldn't,' Julian advised. 'Not just yet.'

'Last night he say to me "my home is yours"! Not to be stranger! Come whenever you want, door is always open! I go in. Is important.'

'I don't think he's going to take no for an answer,' Steve said helpfully.

He wasn't, either. With Ken presumably another victim of Lech's hospitality, Keith was the senior officer present. The buck stopped with him. 'Okay, old chap, but one of us will go and check first, make sure he's up to visitors.'

'Sure, I wait.'

Julian made a show of peering around the small group. 'Right, one volunteer. Well done, Steve.'

'No way!'

'Someone doesn't want to make sergeant, do they? Do it!'

'You bastard! Okay - but you owe me! Big time.'

Steve approached the caravan in a sideways shuffle, like an arachnophobe approaching a bed under which an eight-legged monster had just scuttled. Mike could barely keep the grin from his face. 'Be careful in there - we don't want to lose you!'

'If I don't make it back…'

'I know, I know.'

'Well, here we go.' Steve squared his shoulders. 'It is a far, far better…'

'Hold up! I've got an idea! Wait there!'

Mike dashed off while the reprieved Steve sagged against the caravan. Keith cocked an ear to the eerie silence. Hopefully Barry would resurface before Mike got back - then again, hopefully not, not while Marius was saying a passionate goodbye to Mandy outside her tent. Good Lord - surely they needed air at some point? As the amorous couple parted, Lech put his hand in the crook of his elbow and punched the air. With a wink at his father, Marius strolled away, Mandy only tearing her eyes from his taut backside when Danny emerged from his tent.

'Morning, Danny. Hope… oh.'

Ignoring her, Danny stormed off in the direction of the portaloos, almost colliding with Mike who was hurrying back with a small round mirror, the sort you'd use for putting in contact lenses in the field. He handed it to Steve who held it as if it was dog-shit.

'This is your idea?'

'Yeah. Perseus and Medusa. One look can turn a man to stone!' Mike raised his forearm as if protecting his face with an imaginary shield.

Steve brightened. 'Got it!'

With the others crowding behind him - at a suitably safe distance - Steve crept up to the caravan. Nudging the door open with a tentative foot, he took a breath and thrust the mirror inside. 'Barry? Alice?'

The reflected scene of destruction visible over Steve's shoulder was quite something to behold. Glass and broken china littered the floor. Food was smeared up the walls. Cushions and overturned stools were strewn hither and thither and a shivering heap of blankets showed where Rommel had taken refuge. The intrepid hero panned around for further signs of life - or death. 'Jesus!'

It may well have been a gorgon that suddenly filled the mirror - hair wild, eyes staring venom, and face capable of not only curdling milk but of turning it into frozen yoghurt - but it was probably Alice. Her mouth opened in a feral hiss, then the nightmarish image was gone as Steve dropped the mirror and tumbled out of the caravan.

'I go in now?' Lech wanted to know.

'Help yourself, Vlad,' Steve said from the security of Mike's arms.

Lech marched up the steps and into Medusa's lair. Keith considerately shut the door, sealing Lech in. How much *entente cordiale* would be extended?

As expected, the deranged outboard motor kicked back into life, the sort of tongue-lashing that could strip the flesh from a man's bones quicker than an acid bath. At an imploring look from Julian, Keith took hold of the door handle, releasing it again as the high-octane barrage petered out in fits and starts, punctuated by Lech's low, Bela Lugosi tones. That in itself was a feat pretty much akin to King Canute actually turning back the sea rather than getting the hem of his robe damp and salty, but Alice's ensuing girlish giggle was rarer than unicorn dung.

With the morning warming up nicely and the smell of honeysuckle in the air, the Black Hawk were being put through their paces alongside Harding's. It was not going well. Marching at the head of the musket division, with the pike on their heels and the Black Hawk shambling along in the rear, Keith risked a look over his shoulder. His boys and girls were in perfect step, as were Julian's pike. Sandwiched between them were the drummers, Mandy casting frequent looks back around the pike block to exchange smiles with Marius, swaggering like Davy Crockett in the front rank (if the dishevelled dog-leg could be called such) of the Black Hawk with a musket slanted across his shoulder.

'Form battalia to the left!' hollered Ken from the centre of the meadow. By his side, Barry winced and huddled deeper into his shoulders, hat low across his brow.

Using his partisan to direct, Keith wheeled his division to the left. In effect, the whole regiment should have snapped from column of march into line of battle, each division rotating 90 degrees on its own axis like Venetian blinds. The pike slotted into place to the left of the musket, the drummers between the two blocks, and even Trevor managed to find his spot without too much prompting. The Black Hawk, however, seemed content to carry on walking across the rear of the formed regiment until Ken rushed over to Lech and, with much arm-waving, eventually managed to get his men to shamble into position alongside the pike. Stepping short, and with Barry grimacing at every thud of the drums, the hybrid regiment crept forward.

'Stand!' shouted Ken.

The drums stopped without a rattle - though Mandy dropped her sticks - and Harding's slammed to a halt.

'Zastavit!' bellowed Lech.

The Black Hawk dribbled to a shambolic stop, each man screeching the order at his neighbour.

'Like a flock of bloody seagulls!' Barry's mutter carried far enough for Keith to hear it. 'Hurry up, Ken, let's get this over with!'

'Form horn battal!'

Lech's face twisted in confusion and he held a muttered conference with his cohorts. Barry had his head in his hands.

Sod this! 'March on!' Keith waved his block forward. Let the Black Hawk catch up - he wasn't going to wait around like an idiot.

'Co?' Lech finally cottoned on. 'Ah! Roh bitka! Roh bitka!'

Under Lech's orders, the Black Hawk shuffled forward, mirroring Harding's. Now both divisions of shot were in advance of the pike, like a pair of horns.

'Stand!' bellowed Ken.

'Zastavit! Zastavit!'

With the screeched echo of Lech's order, the Black Hawk came to a stop in a more or less ordered fashion.

'Captain Winters!' called Ken. 'Take over!'

'For God's sake keep it down, Kenneth!' hissed Barry.

This was going to be fun. Keith turned to face the regiment - the ordered blue ranks a sharp contrast to the piratical ensemble alongside them - and filled his lungs. 'Make ready!'

'For the love of God!' moaned Barry.

'Prichystat sa! Prichystat sa!'

The musketeers went through the motions of loading, Harding's smartly - as expected - and the Black Hawk with a deal of fumbling and entanglement in bandoliers. Waiting for the guests to catch up, Keith cocked an ear to Barry and Ken's muttered exchange.

'Have these guys even got licences?' Ken wondered.

'First thing I checked. Unfortunately, they have.'

'Have they passed any sort of test?'

'Apparently so - they're all passed off under their own group, so we have to lump it.'

'But if it's a safety issue…'

'Then it's our heads on the block. What can we do? Our hands are tied.'

'But…'

'Hush now, Ken.'

Harding's had their muskets at the "rest" position, showing they were loaded, and the Black Hawk looked close enough to ready. 'Present!'

'Pritomny!'

Amid the screeching of repeated instructions, forty-odd muskets were levelled. Pray to God that none of the Black Hawk had actually loaded. Keith raised his partisan and took a deep breath. 'Give fire!' He swept the polearm down.

'Dat ohen!' roared Lech.

Harding's shouted an ironic, if enthusiastic, "Bang!" that had the Black Hawk exchanging mystified glances until Marius bellowed "Tresk!". Then they all joined in, hollering at the top of their voices and falling about howling with laughter. It was that moment that Peter chose to stroll past with Wendy.

'Morning, morning! All going well? Excellent! Look forward to having you chaps on the field!'

Pushing past Keith, Barry hurried across the meadow, trying to catch up with Peter's long strides which were lengthening by the second. 'Peter, if I could just have a…'

'Well done, well done! Carry on!' Peter called over his shoulder. Wendy's backside jiggled fetchingly in her jodhpurs and the men of the Black Hawk - and one or two of the women - whistled and cheered.

'Silence in the ranks!' Ken bounced on his heels. 'Silence!'

The battle was well under way, a modest crowd watching from behind the blue rope barriers, and smoke hung heavy in the sultry, breezeless air as the two armies exchanged fire. Harding's held the centre of the field, presumably to keep the Black Hawk safely away from the crowd. As Parliament withdrew to a new position, Keith took the opportunity to report to Barry.

'They're not doing too bad, really.' They weren't either, if he was honest. 'They seem to know what they're doing - a bit slow, but I suppose they're more used to axes and broadswords.'

A Black Hawker sauntered past, trailing his musket. Frowning at the lock, he spat, blew on his match, and rammed home another charge before bringing his piece to his shoulder.

He'd spoken too soon. What was the idiot doing? Did health and safety mean nothing on the continent? 'No, no! Misfires to the rear! Don't try and clear it here! Stop!'

The musketeer grinned at Keith and squeezed the trigger. The discharge was deafening - they always seemed louder when fired individually and this one was double-shotted. Barry moaned and gripped his head.

'Bang!' The musketeer was still grinning.

Keith waved away the thick, acrid smoke. 'Bloody idiot!' He could have taken his hand off - or worse - and he had fired over the heads of the pike block. 'How much was down that?'

With a shrug of incomprehension, the musketeer hurried back to the ranks. 'You were saying, Keith?' enquired Ken.

'I said they knew what they were doing - I didn't say they followed our…' An urgent flurry of drums interrupted him.

'Oh God, no,' Barry whined. 'Leave us alone!'

'Charge for horse!' shrieked Ken. 'Charge for horse!'

'We can all see that! Keep it down!'

*

The opening pike pushes had been the perfect antidote to a morning spent brooding. Each trapped hand, each pinch of armour, worked out Danny's frustrations on his own body, the bruises tattooed into his flesh gradually eclipsing the deeper bruises hammered into his soul. Now, with the Ironsides sweeping forward, he braced the pike against his foot, the trembling earth massaging nerve-endings that still ached for release. Hopefully, Marius would get trampled to death, but the combined musketeers had formed a protective circle of their own. The drummers, however, sought shelter amongst the pikes and Danny returned Annie's smile as she squeezed past, though he jerked away from the imploring hand that Mandy laid on his bicep. Turning his back on her beseeching eyes, the vision thundering past all but erased her from his thoughts.

Riding with the Ironsides, Suzanne's golden hair streamed from beneath her helmet. She wore a wide smile but no breastplate, her braided jacket unbuttoned to the waist. Weaving her way between the formations, she curbed her horse every now and again, arching her back to sit high in the saddle and flaunt her magnificent physique.

'Lucky bloody horse!' moaned Mike.

Steve steadied his pike after a particularly enthusiastic blow from a circling Ironside. 'Yeah, too right! Wonder why she's not got a breastplate?'

'Because they haven't built one to take on the job! Look at 'em go! Over here, darling!'

Suzanne wheeled and galloped over, running her sword along the raised pikes. Cheers and wolf whistles followed her as she circled the block, and then she was off, blowing a kiss over her shoulder. Danny's admiration of her horsemanship was rudely interrupted by the clatter of Mike's pike against his helmet.

'Oi, Danny! I've got wood!'

'Here she comes again!' whooped Steve.

'She's not the only one!' gibbered Mike. 'I'm spent! Take it away - I can't takes no more!'

The Black Hawk started their own catcalls as Suzanne rode around them, yelling, hooting, whistling and making gestures that left no doubt as to their intentions should the luckless traitor fall into their hands. Lech loudly berated them, beating the worst offenders around the head.

'Gentlemen, please!' Julian called across. 'Show some restraint! And I don't think that last suggestion is physically possible - or legal, come to that!'

'You speak the lingo then, Julian?' asked Mike.

'I do. Picked up a bit in the forces.'

'Signals you were in, was it?' Steve peered with suspicion at his pike lieutenant.

'Most of the time.'

'What are they saying, then?'

'I couldn't possibly tell you!'

'It's upset her old man, whatever it is!' Mike pointed to the incandescent Lech. 'Go on, Julian, give us a clue!'

'Okay - but you cover your ears, Danny! You're too young! Essentially, they're just working out how many she could, er, accommodate.'

'Five!' was Steve's guess.

'Nah, seven!' put in Mike.

Dirty old bastards! Still, Danny gamely gave an opinion of his own - grossly inflated, as he couldn't get past three. 'Nine?'

Julian raised an eyebrow. 'They had it up to twelve, if you'll believe that.'

'Fuck off!' Twelve? Maybe five at a stretch, but...

Steve blew out an incredulous breath. 'Bloody hell - I'm watching the wrong sort of films! I should ask for a transfer to the vice squad! Twelve?'

'Yes, well, they're very continental, old boy!'

The cavalry came sweeping back with a thunder of hooves, though Keith was denied the pleasure of examining Suzanne's heaving frontage by Lech's shout of 'Pritomny!'

'No! Not at the horses! You never fire at the horses!' Hadn't the bloody idiots taken anything in? 'Hold fire! In Slavic!'

'Dat ohen!'

The Black Hawk unleashed a ragged splatter of musketry at the Ironsides, no more than 15 yards distant. Above the snorting and whinnying of rearing horses, Sean's shriek of 'You fookin' idiots!' was all too clear. When the smoke cleared, the Ironsides had fled, though one horse remained, standing with an empty saddle. The rider sprawled on the ground had blonde hair and a braided jacket. Throwing down his polearm, Keith raced to the rescue, but Julian beat him to it.

'Are you okay?' To cheers and whistles from the pike block, Julian was already helping Suzanne to sit up when Keith arrived.

'Yes,' she said, a little groggily, though her big blue eyes were filled with gratitude. 'Sank you.'

Julian was more than capable of holding her hand, so Keith made his way over to Lech, wary of the Black Hawk muskets - he didn't want his face blown off. 'What the bloody hell are you doing? You don't fire at the horses! Your daughter could have been hurt!'

'Well, she is bad girl for teasing my men! Anyway, was mistake. Sorry. Cavalry has gone, though.'

Give me strength. 'But we were meant to fall back from them! We lose, remember?'

'Oh yes. And win tonight! When we attack castle!'

*

The braziers on the castle walls warmed the darkness with an orange glow that sparked fire from the helmets of the men and women assembled below. The half-ruined walls weren't that high - once someone had scrambled up the grassy bank it was only a climb of seven or eight feet - but the gate was a much more preferable option, though not without its hazards. Ray was making his way along the ranks with a length of lit match, and as each pikeman lowered his weapon, he touched the match to the bundled rags wrapped around the tip, holding it there until flames blossomed. Dipping his own pike towards Ray, the soaking cloth making it top-heavy, Danny locked his arms as the orange fire took hold.

'Bugger!'

Fire sprouted from Ray's gloved hand and, spinning in a frantic circle, he flapped and blew until Jane came to his rescue with a bottle of water. Danny raised his pike, careful to keep it angled forward. The blazing ranks made an impressive sight - there was something primitive and pagan about the rolling flames and the ember-edged blackened strips falling from the points. Bloody dangerous though - with any luck that bastard Marius was somewhere he could get his fingers burned.

'Are you sure you're up for this?' Julian tapped Suzanne's helmet - with no horse involved, she'd joined the pike for the assault, much to Mike and Steve's breathless glee. 'That was quite a tumble you took earlier.'

The flames highlighted her perfect white teeth. 'I'm fine. You will look after me.'

'How does he do it?' muttered Mike. 'They're like putty in his hands!'

'Old school charm - perhaps we should try it?' suggested Steve. He and Mike locked glances. 'Nah,' they chorused.

At the head of the army, legs set apart, Peter waved his hand. 'In we go!'

'This is it!' called Julian. 'Just be careful where you stick those things, guys!'

'And you, sailor!' Mike called back.

Muskets crackled from the top of the wall, the sparking pans and flashing muzzles vivid, almost magical, in the gloom. An answering volley thundered in response and the massed pike of the Royalist army shuffled toward the open gate where Parliament waited with their own fire-pikes. Danny, in the second rank, dragged his heels, his night-vision ruined by the orange glows that traced intricate patterns on the black canvas. With an angry flare and a hissing shower of sparks, the first pikes clattered tentatively together beneath the stone archway like industrial-sized sparklers.

*

The assault on the gate was a pretty sight, with the blaze of orange painting an infernal sheen on the pikemen's armour, but Barry couldn't waste time admiring it. Keith and the musket block - and the Black Hawk - brought up ladders, setting them against the walls with solid thumps. Slinging their muskets, the Black Hawk threw themselves at the rungs and started to climb.

'Go on, my boys!' roared Peter. 'Huzza!'

Barry nudged Ken. 'We'd better get up there after them - God knows what they'll do if we leave them alone in there!' Taking hold of the rungs, Barry swung himself up, Ken, Keith and the musket block on his heels. 'Oh Jesus!' he breathed, his exertions reminding him that, while his hangover was gone, it was not forgotten. 'Oh bloody Hell! Bugger, bugger, bugger!'

It was only a matter of feet, but he kept his eyes fixed firmly on the wall as he climbed - not that he didn't trust Terry's handiwork, but the rickety ladder creaked and shuddered with every step and the gentle breeze that shivered the flames of the fire-pikes buffeted him like a hurricane. The vast darkness behind him seized hold of his coat, tugging him backwards, and his feet hesitated, boots dragging on legs that suddenly had no more substance than the air around him. He'd climbed far higher ladders, but they'd been properly made affairs - not nailed together from whatever wood Terry could find - and there had always been someone he trusted with a foot on the bottom rung. All he had was a horde of eager escaladers whose every step pulled the ladder away from the wall by several inches before it bounced back into place. A hand pushed on his arse and he scrambled on. He had to set an example - and the quicker he went, the less time there was for a mishap, though his feet slipped on every rung and his hands were greasy inside the gauntlets. Reaching the top, his shoulders and calves screeching in protest, he slung his leg over the parapet at the fourth attempt and dropped onto the ramparts. The scene in the courtyard had him turning to climb back down, but his way was blocked by Keith and his musketeers and so he was forced to watch as the Black Hawk unleashed their full skillset, honed on the medieval re-enactment fields of Europe.

Not a swash was left unbuckled, not a buckle left unswashed. Swords flashed in the firelight while Black Hawkers threw themselves from the tops of the walls, performing tumbles that would put Chinese acrobats, trained since footbound childhood, to shame. Somewhere, in Hollywood's Elysian fields, the shades of Rathbone, Fairbanks and Flynn smiled and raised their glasses.

'Oh God.' Barry peeked between his fingers as an elderly Parliamentarian - who looked as though a sneeze would finish him - was driven back by a flurry of glittering blows before a lunge to his stomach left him wheezing on the floor. A giant Black Hawker threw down his sword, ripped the helmet from a luckless Roundhead, and clapped balled fists against the man's ears as if clashing cymbals. A pair of Lech's marauders picked up a defender between them and hurled him screaming over the ramparts like a sack of potatoes. Ian's voice weaselled out over the din.

'Quarter! Quarter! We yield! The castle is yours!'

Lech seized Ian's sword and shoved him brutally to the floor.

'Hey!' complained Ian, not unreasonably.

'Quiet!' sneered Lech. 'You are prisoner! Lucky I do not kill you!'

Barry had no choice but to watch the battle dribble to a confused end. Maybe he'd enjoy it back in the ranks - or maybe he could join the Napoleonics.

Peter's voice floated up from below. 'That's it! Well done, everybody, well done! Let's form up outside and take a bow!'

From the glares, mutters and rough-housing of prisoners, Lech and his men were not ready for the battle to end. Barry clenched his fists until the leather gauntlets squeaked. 'That's it! All over!'

'No! This is not good!' Lech stamped his feet. 'We still have plenty of powder left!'

'Not a problem.' A sickening sixth sense suggested that things were about to go downhill. 'Just return it.'

The Black Hawk, however, had no intention of handing back their leftover powder. It was Marius who started it, throwing a handful of powder onto the closest brazier to make it flare like a stage magician's flash-pot, then they were all at it. Some scattered powder as if sowing seeds, reaping a hissing, spitting harvest, while those with paper cartridges threw them onto the flames whole, eliciting squibbish pops and showers of sparks. Lech stood amidst the rain of fire, a beatific smile wreathing his flame-tinted features, a grinning devil orchestrating the ghastly firework display that sealed Barry's damnation. Each spluttering crack, each billow of flame, was another torch tossed onto his funeral pyre.

Ken's hands went to his mouth, his eyes white and wide in the flame-shot darkness, and then he threw himself at Lech. 'Stop! Stop it! It has to be returned! You can't...'

'Bah!'

Lech thrust him aside, shunting him into Tabitha as she made her way along the battlements toward her father. She stumbled back - straight into the blast radius of a brazier onto which an enterprising Black Hawker had just thrown a handful of cartridges. Her scream as the flash of flame engulfed her was a fitting paean to sing off Barry's command, the horrific slow-motion spectacle of her dropping to her knees with hands clapped to her face a maroon-tinged scene from a no-punches-pulled war film. Smoke bloomed from her clothing, glowing embers eating away at the thick wool, and Barry found some small crumb of pride in the cool efficiency with which Terry whipped her bandoliers over her head and then pulled her hands away so that he could ease off her smouldering coat. Ollie, collecting bottles from the assembled musketeers, poured water over her head, plastering the blackened shirt to her skin. Good lads, looking after their own. His lads. For now, at least.

'Blasted idiots!' Keith elbowed his way through the milling soldiers. 'Are you okay, love?'

Jane hurried over, water spilling from the bottles clutched in her arms. 'Can you open your eyes?'

Tabitha shook her head, eyes screwed shut and tears carving rivulets down her blackened face. She buried her head in her hands once more - a pose that Barry felt very much like copying.

'She's fine, mate.' Terry had a hand on Keith's shoulder. 'Just shaken. We got everything off before it could go up - coat's a bit singed, though.'

'Thank you, Terry.' It was Jane who answered - Keith seemed robbed of the ability to speak, standing with gritted teeth and murder in his eyes. 'Come on, dear, let me have a look.'

Sobbing, Tabitha pulled her hands away from her face. Wide white eyes showed through the blacking.

Jane quickly assessed the damage, such as it was. 'Just a bit singed. Let's get you back to the caravan and cleaned up. Keith...'

But Keith had moved fast - faster than Barry had anticipated - and now had hold of Lech. 'You're a bloody menace! If you'd hurt her...'

Even if he got away with this episode, any damage to Lech would see Barry finished. He pawed at Keith's arm, though the musket captain's corded muscles thrummed like steel cables. 'Calm down, Keith. No harm done, eh?'

'Calm down? You're joking! Enough is enough - you'd better have a word with Peter. Or I will!'

'In the morning - when we've all calmed down.' *And when I've packed.*

'Bollocks to it.' Shoving Lech aside, Keith stormed off. Barry tracked his progress across the courtyard, finding Macintyre lurking in the shadows. Bastard. With a grin, Macintyre drew a finger across his throat.

With a couple of G & T's inside her, Tabitha's hands had finally stopped shaking, though she could still see the white-red flash that had erupted without warning to pepper her face with needles of fire. For one awful moment she'd thought she'd been blinded, but her instincts (and Terry's quick reactions) had saved her from nothing more serious than a few singed patches and a lack of eyebrows. Nevertheless, her parents had been reluctant to let her out to the beer tent, but she'd insisted. Her dad had come with her, but he'd left when Lech had walked in, glaring at Barry and leaving a half-finished pint. She'd never seen him that angry, not even when, as a child, she'd trodden on an upturned paint pot lid and trampled eggshell-white emulsion all through the living room.

'You are okay now?'

A pair of gentle blue eyes filled her vision. Marius. God, she must look a state, what with the after-sun her mum had slapped on her and her eyebrows gone. 'Oh, yes, yes, thank you. A bit shaken and singed, but I'm fine.'

His fingers circled on her forearm in a way that made her legs weak. 'I must apologise for the thoughtless actions of my group.'

'It's not your fault - you weren't throwing powder on the fire, were you?' His voice dripped like syrup in her ears, and those eyes...

'Er, no, no, but I feel responsible. I should have stopped them - and now you have been hurt.'

'I'm fine, really. I'd feel better for a drink though!'

He gave a smile that pretty much finished the job of melting her. 'Come, then. I will buy!'

'What happened with Tab?' Danny couldn't throw off a slight twinge of guilt. He'd all but forgotten Tab in the hormonal tsunami of the past day and now the rumours were buzzing about events in the castle.

Ollie's face was sour. 'Those bloody idiots - they were throwing powder on the fires! Went up like bloody fireworks. Tab got caught in it.'

'Jesus!' That sounded bad - A & E bad. What if her face had been scarred? 'Is she okay?'

'Yeah, yeah. Just got a bit singed. She's fine - it's not put her off anyway!'

'Off what? Oh.' With the second kick to the crotch of the weekend - delivered by the same smooth bastard - Danny followed Ollie's gaze to where Marius and Tabitha stood laughing together.

Ollie shook his head. 'Carry quite a torch for her, don't you? Drink?'

Getting absolutely bladdered suddenly seemed the most attractive idea in the world. 'Lager, cheers. Yeah, I suppose I do.' Without the others around, it was easy to talk to Ollie. 'I've always fancied her, ever since we were kids.'

'Didn't stop you getting stuck into Mandy last night!'

'She was all over me! Can you blame me?'

'Not at all.' Ollie passed Danny his pint.

'Cheers. Then that Marius git got his hands on her and that was it.' If only he hadn't gone to get another drink when he did!

'You'll get another chance with her - especially now he's moved on!'

Mandy stood in the background, scowling at Marius and Tab, but Danny still had enough pride to not try and finish what had started last night. The moment had passed. Still, if Marius could move on that quickly, surely Tab was clued up enough to see him for what he was? 'Yeah, but...'

'Tab? Mate, if you've been into her for this long and nothing's happened, then chances are it never will! Just enjoy yourself! You're young. You can't waste your life chasing rainbows!' Ollie glanced over to where Julian was chatting and laughing with Suzanne. 'How does he do it? Every red-blooded bloke on camp has tried it on with her and she's just brushed them all aside! Not him, though!'

'Maybe you should ask him for some tips!'

'Maybe I should.' Ollie stared into the depths of his pint. 'I can't go on like this!'

'Like what?' Danny caught the faint note of despair. Ollie was drunk, but not too drunk that he was just being maudlin. There was real feeling behind his words.

'Rocking up by myself at every muster, chasing around after a different girl at every one - I'm going around for the second or third time now, I reckon! It used to be a laugh, it was me, you know? Ollie, the dashing blade. All the girls like Ollie. Only for a night or two, though. It's about time I grew up and found a keeper. Is it me? Or is it that I always find the wrong girl?'

'Bit young to be thinking of settling down, aren't you?'

'You think so? I'm thirty in a couple of months! You know, I even found a grey hair this morning! I can't be the dashing blade forever!'

Danny drained his pint. 'Another drink?'

'Yeah.' Ollie tossed his empty plastic cup onto the floor as Suzanne and Julian left the tent arm in arm. 'Yeah. Reckon I need one.'

'You sure you are alright?' Marius, one arm around her waist, ran a finger down Tabitha's cheek.

'I keep telling you, I'm fine!' She kept her voice steady with an effort, her skin puckering in the wake of his touch. He was so caring, so thoughtful - and so handsome.

'If your pretty face had been scarred...' He kissed the tip of her nose.

'So you're only interested in my looks?' she joked, although in truth she didn't give a toss what he was interested in, as long as he was interested.

'No, no!' His fingers fluttered across her waist and she locked her abdomen tight to stop herself squirming like a novice. 'You are beautiful girl, yes, but also clever, funny. I've not met anyone like you before.'

'Not even Mandy?' Better get that out of the way first.

Marius had the good grace to blush, lending a boyish appeal to his looks. 'Aah. Mistake. I am new to your country, have never been abroad before. I am lonely and afraid, and she spoke kindly to me. You cannot understand what it is like in my country - things I have seen. Things I will not insult your ears by repeating. Then I come here - people are kind, there is no war, no hunger, no disease. You know, I was one of six children - now only two!'

'Oh my God!' What horrors had those blameless blue eyes witnessed? She slipped her arm around his waist. 'What happened?'

'War. Disease. Is no nice thing to see dead babies in street. I am lucky to be alive and every day I am thankful!'

He looked so young, so lost, though there was nothing maternal about the protective surge that swelled inside her. 'That's awful!'

'But now I am here, with you.' His head dipped toward her, the marquee lights haloing his blond hair, his full lips sliding smoothly over even white teeth. 'Like an angel.'

Her beleaguered defences were breached far too easily. She offered no resistance as he pressed his lips to hers. His arms tightened, drawing her into his crushing embrace, and she went limp as a wrung-out rag, overwhelmed by the heady scent of clean male sweat and leather and the taste of lager on the steel-boned velvet cushions of his lips. The muscles of her thighs twitched and loosened, a primal response to the fervid waves lapping at her body, but when his tongue probed slickly for hers, she still had enough self-control - barely - to pull back.

'Come.' His eyes were wide, hungry - and a little distant. 'Bed now.'

'What?' Had she heard him right? 'You what?' A welcome breeze ghosted through the beer tent, cooling her flaming cheeks and clearing away the pink candyfloss that tangled her thoughts.

'We go bed now?' His hand dropped to her buttocks, one thumb hooking into the waistband of her jeans. 'I keep from you bad dreams.'

'We've only just met!' Despite the prurient heat pulsing between her legs, she wasn't going to jump straight into bed with anyone, not even a blond Adonis like Marius. If his fingers didn't start behaving themselves though, she might soon change her mind.

'But I feel I have known you all my life! I feel for you. It is strange, but can it be love already?'

'If it is, then you'd wait.' It would be so easy to surrender, to allow him to take her and initiate her into that secret club whose plush, pink doors had stood enticingly ajar since puberty, that exclusive society of which so many (almost all, it seemed) of her peers were members. A path should be laid first, though, a foundation of mutuality, otherwise she'd be no better than Mandy.

Marius shrugged, his grip loosening. 'Sure, I wait. Of course I wait! It is just your eyes - they make me crazy!' He picked up his glass. 'Drink is almost gone.'

'My round.' Slipping out of his grasp, she bolted for the bar. Her head and body were such a riot of emotions that she needed time to think, to get things straight. Despite the sly, secret heat in her loins, there was no way she was sleeping with him, not tonight - she'd often fantasised about losing her virginity and, though Marius was more than a match for any of the fictional lovers she'd conjured, a quick bunk up in a grubby tent was far too tawdry. He'd wait, though - he'd said he would wait - and they had all of tonight and all day tomorrow to start constructing the footings that would eventually lead to a much more fulfilling conclusion. Waiting for her drinks, she couldn't resist craning round to look back at him, though the sight that greeted her burst over her head like a sack filled with flour. She wasn't sure who the blonde was, but there was no mistaking who was attached to her face. The little shit! Her drinks arrived and she downed Marius' pint - he had enough to occupy his mouth and hands now - before bolting her G & T. Bastard! It wasn't fair! The dammed waters he had stirred threatened to burst, the dull, frustrated ache in her thighs filling her with a yearning to be held, to be kissed, to be loved - and to stick one on him. Well, that was easily taken care of. Danny was making his way across the tent toward Sophie Macintyre and, with the lager bubbling inside her and the gin leaping into the driving seat, she moved to intercept him.

'How's it going?'

Danny blinked. 'Yeah, yeah. Good.'

The faint smattering of freckles across his cheeks lent his blond good looks an innocent, almost boyish, appeal. He was no Marius, but the doglike devotion in his clear eyes - as blue as Marius' but without the arrogance - told her he'd be putty in her hands. 'Come on, I feel like dancing.'

She led him out onto the dance floor, circling his waist with her arms. As if she was made of bone china, and with a glazed look on his face, he eased his own arms around her. She pressed herself into him, his body reacting as she ground against him, and when she was sure Marius was looking, she locked her lips onto Danny's. This time, she did not stop her tongue moving to find his, and though at first it was horribly like kissing a close member of her family, the growing warmth soon made it more natural, less forced.

Julian woke with the sun streaming through the walls of his tent and the ghost of alcohol sour on his tongue. He'd drunk far more than he should have last night - virtually unheard of. Still, sometimes a chap had few options left to block out the inner turmoil, if only for a few hours. He breathed in, a musty but not unpleasant smell hitting his nostrils, all the more familiar for its scarcity these past months. Crimson images of the previous night flooded his head, and he rolled over with an icy hand squeezing his stomach, knowing who would be next to him before he saw the tousled blonde hair.

Suzanne. She had a contented smile on her face, one perfect bare breast exposed by the sleeping bag. Had they? Of course they had - the lingering aroma of recent coitus told him that. For fuck's sake! His stomach rolled over and he scrambled out of the sleeping bag. *Don't let her wake up, not yet. Please.*

It was still early, the cool air a welcome relief after the thick, sticky atmosphere of the tent. He made it over to his car just in time, doubling over to vomit behind it, the gut-wrenching heaves purging his innards if not his soul. Spitting the last of the acrid mess from his mouth, he crawled to the wing mirror, hating the face that was reflected there and barely resisting the urge to put his fist through the glass.

Barry crept out of his caravan, scanning the surrounds. All clear. Now, if he could just get through today with…

'Off for a word with Peter, Barry?' Keith appeared as if from nowhere.

'Ah, Keith, I…'

'You promised, Barry.'

'It's not that simple…'

Keith slammed a fist against the side of the caravan. 'They're dangerous, they're incompetent, and they shouldn't be anywhere near black powder. Tab was bloody lucky! How is it not simple?'

At the end of the day, he had to look after his boys and girls, whatever the consequences for himself. Still, it was all very well making noble declarations - acting on them was a different matter. 'Fine, fine! I'll go and stick my head in the noose! Good old Barry, he'll sort it out! Well, remember that when I'm gone.'

'What the hell are you on about?' Keith scowled at the self-pity.

'Nothing, nothing.' Who would take over? Not Ken, he'd follow his CO into obscurity. Keith? Or would Peter appoint someone himself, someone more malleable?

'Oh, and Julian's gone home - wasn't feeling great. We'll need a pike commander for this afternoon.'

Usually, such news would descend like a black cloud. Not today. 'Well, that won't be anything to do with me by then. Thanks. Thanks a lot.'

Leaving Keith in his wake, Barry hurried through the campsite to where the Royalist command were camped. Rather now than later - get it out of the way while he was still in the mood. Peter was on the steps of his caravan, hand on the door.

'Ah, Peter.'

'Barry.' Peter gave a curt nod and stepped over the threshold. Crossing his Rubicon, Barry grabbed the Lord General's sleeve. Peter regarded the clutching hand as if it was leprous. 'Something you wanted?'

'No, no.' Peter raised an eyebrow and Barry sucked in a breath - it was now or never. Maybe it was better this way, falling on his sword. 'Okay. It's them. The Black Hawk.'

'What about them? Fine fellows. I thought!'

No one was going to upset Peter's applecart. Blithe old fart. Rattling along in the tumbril of his martyrdom, Barry pressed on, for his boys and girls - while they were still his boys and girls. 'Peter, they're maniacs! Did you see them last night?'

'Just high spirits!'

'High spirits?' Peter must have seen the reports, just as he had. 'Parliament have got two in hospital because of their high spirits, and Tabitha Winters nearly had her face blown off! Keith's spitting blood!'

Peter gently but firmly removed Barry's hand from his arm. 'So what are you saying?'

They couldn't be his words coming out of his mouth. They couldn't. 'If they're allowed on the field this afternoon with powder, it won't be under my command!'

'Ken is with you on this?'

He hadn't spoken with Ken this morning, but he would be alongside him. 'Yes.'

Peter nodded. Was that a glimmer of satisfaction in the narrowed eyes? 'Very well - you realise the implications, of course?'

Barry swallowed - not without difficulty - as the verdict hovered in the still air. 'I do.'

'Well, I've enjoyed working with you, and it will be a pain getting a new CO at such short notice, but...'

It couldn't be real, could it? 'You're dismissing me?'

'No, Barry, you've resigned your commission. I...' As he tailed off, Peter's already florid face went pink, then crimson, then a dangerous shade of purple. His mouth worked soundlessly. His eyes blazed with fire.

Pulling up his jeans, a bare-chested Marius wriggled out of a nearby tent. Wearing only a filmy white shirt that did little for her modesty, Wendy crawled out after him. If the vehemence of their farewell kiss was anything to go by, it had been one hell of a night.

Huffing and spluttering like a spoiled child denied his fourth helping of cake, Peter spotted Lech lurking in the background. 'You!' A trembling finger jabbed at the Black Hawk's CO. 'Yes, you! Over here! Now!'

Lech doubled over. 'Me? Is problem?'

'Yes, there is problem!' Peter loomed high above Lech - even without the advantage of the caravan step he'd still have been a foot taller. 'You! You, your men and your deviant offspring, Vlad the fucking Impaler!'

On hearing Peter's voice, Wendy tried frantically to disengage from Marius. Lech smirked. 'Aah! The women! He likes the women! Young, old…'

'Well, he's picked the wrong one this time!' Peter's rage was a joy to behold. 'And you will not be on the field this afternoon - if you are, it will be with pikes! You are dangerous, sir! A menace! You and all your chattering monkeys! The Pirates of bloody Prague!'

Lech balled his fists and rocked on his heels. For a second - the briefest second - Barry almost felt sorry for him. 'You do not do this! I do not understand!'

'Do you not? Then step inside, sir, and I will explain further. Carry on, Colonel Reynolds!'

The Sunday battle was over and Harding's - their pike block supplemented by those of The Black Hawk who had still wanted to fight - trooped back to the camp. Tabitha dawdled along by herself - no one would have blamed her for not taking the field today, but she'd needed to prove that last night had left no scars (other than the slight scorching that was now starting to tighten and irritate her face). Right up until the first volley she'd been unsure if she'd have the courage to pull the trigger, but the heat of battle soon drove away any lingering worries - at least about firing. She had weightier issues on her mind. Danny. She'd kept clear of him for most of the day while she tried to get her head straight. Last night had been… okay. The conversation that had lasted until the small hours had sometimes faltered, but when they had fallen back onto a more physical form of communication (all fully clothed and above board, of course) there had been no complaints - although, for her part at least, it had felt a little flat, slightly staged.

'Is it all over with you and Marius, then?' Mandy fell into step beside her, swinging her drum onto her back.

'I don't think it really ever started. You?'

Mandy grinned. 'One night was enough! He's okay, but God does he have a high opinion of himself. I ruined things for me and Danny, though. Pity. Still, I can try again once he's stopped sulking!

'Ah…'

Mandy's face dropped. 'Oh no! You're not?'

Tabitha shrugged. 'I don't know! We kissed last night, but was I just trying to make Marius jealous? I don't know - even now!'

Mandy peered closely at her. 'I think you do.'

'Maybe. We'll see.' She steered the conversation away from the tricky subject of Danny. 'He's had a hard life, hasn't he?'

'Who, Danny?'

'No, Marius!' Even now, she tried to find excuses for his behaviour. 'What with losing all those brothers and sisters. The things he's seen...'

'Oh, he fed you all that as well, did he?' Mandy snorted. 'It's all rubbish!' She mimicked Marius' accent. 'You are angel!'

The sardonic impersonation hit home with more fire than the flaring brazier. Wanker! The fact she had been so easily duped hurt more than any betrayal. She'd always thought herself too canny to be caught out like that - she blamed the shock. 'The sleazy git!'

'And it's not his first time in England - he was at uni here for a couple of years.'

'Lying bastard!'

'Yes.' Mandy tapped her teeth with a drumstick. 'You think we should get even before he goes?'

Revenge sounded good - but it would have to be harsh. Because of Marius, she was going home with one almighty mess dropped on top of her. 'How?'

Mandy's vicious grin suggested that the punishment would befit the crime. 'I've got an idea, but I need to go and see Kev. Meet me by the portaloos in ten minutes!'

Sauntering back toward his tent, borrowed helmet hanging from his hand, Marius reflected on what had been a successful weekend. Two in two days- not a bad return. Who had been better, though? The little spitfire or the older one from last night? Pity that frigid blonde hadn't been more forthcoming, but that was her loss.

'Marius!'

The voice snapped him out of his reverie. As if his wishes had been read, the blonde girl was standing there. They always crumbled in the end. 'Ah! Is Tasha!'

'Tabitha, but never mind that now.' She lowered her head, eyes coy as she twirled a lock of hair around her fingers. 'I've been thinking about last night, about all the things you said.'

'What do I say?' He said so many things to smooth the passage to the bedroom that he lost track.

Tabitha took his hand. She was shaking, of course. 'About how hard your life has been. You have to seize every moment, don't you? Well, I'm seizing mine now! Come on!'

Hips swaying, she led him over to a block of nearby portaloos, those hellish contraptions with the blue flush that did little to mask the stink of accumulated ordure. Well, no stink was going to put him off this, especially as the redhead was waiting behind the portaloos. Even with her hair hanging in sweat-laced rat-tails, she was hot, especially with her drummer's coat unbuttoned and the damp white shirt moulding her full breasts with slick perfection.

Mandy smiled sweetly. 'Think you can handle the pair of us?'

Two? At once? Holy Jesus! He'd been close before, but never this close. 'Me? No problems!' Handle them? Of course he could handle them - preferably while they handled each other. Beneath their encouraging - and admiring - gaze, he stripped off his shirt, though his hands paused on the fastenings of his britches when the redhead produced a pair of handcuffs. What was this shit?

'What's up?' Mandy's provocative pout was full of wicked promise. She ran her tongue around her lips. 'Surely a big, strong boy like you isn't scared of a couple of girls?' Her voice became a throaty whisper. 'We won't hurt you. Promise. And with you all tied up, we might have to...'

She let the unspoken implication hang in the sultry air, but the way she cupped Tabitha's backside told him more than enough and her sly wink feathered away the last of his inhibitions. He scrabbled at his waistband, britches sliding down legs that were suddenly like water. The two girls gasped with artful delight when they saw what was fighting to free itself from his underpants. 'I'm scared of nothing!'

'Good boy!' Mandy ran a playful hand over his chest. His nipple, when she tweaked it, seemed hardwired directly to his groin and he locked his legs to stop them buckling beneath him. 'Turn around, then.'

Stomach taut with anticipation, he shuffled around and meekly put his hands behind his back. Chill steel snapped over his wrists.

'You've been a very naughty boy,' purred Tabitha.

The heated revving of engines filled the air. The tractor - commandeered from a local farm - strained against the ropes while the coach rocked under the willing hands of the Black Hawk. Slowly, painfully slowly, the wheels pulled clear of the mud and the coach came free, cheered on by those waiting to embark.

Barry Reynolds, colonel of Harding's Regiment of Foot, was well contented as he watched the Black Hawk load their bags. Peter observed from a distance - presumably to ensure that no one got left behind. Francesca was at his side, a red-eyed Wendy looking on.

'We go now - as soon as idiot boy comes!' Lech bounded over to Barry. 'I must apologise for the behaviour of my men.'

Barry waved the apology away. He wasn't really a bad sort, old Lech. 'Oh, no need, no need. High spirits, eh?'

'Yes. You take this.'

Lech handed him a small paper package. Like the winner in a budget game of Pass the Parcel, Barry unwrapped it to find a cheap-looking metal ring surmounted by a crudely moulded hawk - or sparrow. Probably a hawk, though.

'Thank you. I, er, I'm afraid I've got nothing for you.'

'You look after us for weekend. Is good.' Lech opened his arms and wrapped Barry in a crushing bear hug. 'You come and see us one day?'

'Oh, yes. Definitely.' Not for a while though, a long while.

With a last wave, Lech clambered aboard the coach. Laughter erupted from behind the windows, but it was not directed at him - it was directed at the naked figure hurrying across the churned grass. With his hands cuffed behind his back, he was bent double in a vain attempt to mask his crotch, though this only served to promote the small paper flag - one of those sold for the audience to cheer on their favoured side - fluttering in the crack of his backside.

5 UNCHARTED WATERS

'How about it then, Barry?' Keith poured tea into Barry's cup, having already refilled Ken's, and sat back into his armchair. Mellow evening sunlight played across the cream walls of his lounge.

'Hmmm, not sure.' Barry blew on his tea, rippling the umber surface.

'A weekend on the coast with more powder than you could shake a stick at? What's not to like?' Ever since he'd received the call, Keith had been like a schoolboy looking forward to the end of term trip. *Come on, Baz, say yes!*

'These pirate types - they're never very authentic, are they?' Ken's face showed exactly what he though of "pirate types".

It was a fair enough point, but Keith was damned if he was going to let Ken spoil what promised to be a hell of a weekend. 'Some are, some aren't. What does it matter?'

'We don't want to get tarred with the same brush, do we?' said Barry over the rim of his teacup.

'We won't be doing it as Harding's,' Keith assured him.

'And it is very short notice.'

'I told you, their other group just pulled out, so they're short of redcoats. I worked with Jim a couple of years ago on that "Last of the Mohicans" gig, and he gave me a bell to see if there was anything we could do.' That had been a hoot, fighting off hordes of tough Liverpool dockers masquerading as Hurons. 'He's a decent guy and we'd be doing him a favour. Go on - it will be a laugh!'

'We've got nothing to wear!' Whereas Barry seemed open to convincing, Ken was dropping obstacles at every turn. Luckily, Keith had anticipated most of his objections prior to calling them over.

'We've still got a stash of red coats from when we did Sedgemoor a few years back - and me and Julian have got our "Mohicans" kit. Our blue coats will do for sailor's jackets at a pinch and I'm sure we can get our hands on a few tricornes - knock a few up, even.' He could see it now, a solid block of red with a skirmish line of blue-coated sailors flung out in front, Union Flag fluttering amidst the skeins of musket smoke. Shades of *Barry Lyndon.* Marvellous stuff.

Ken's protruding lip threatened to dip into his tea. 'But what period is it meant to be?'

While Keith was all for authenticity, there was always room for a bit of a sea-change, a chance for a blow-out, and who didn't like playing pirates? 'It's generic pirate stuff, Ken. Don't get too hung up on the accuracy, just go with the flow! There'll be a whole Living History site set up with public wandering through all day. We'll be playing the forces of law and order, hunting down the pirates. Think of the exposure - we can push the Little Felcham gig.'

'Guns?' Ken threw down another obstacle to be hurdled.

'Firelocks for preference. We should have enough - we can probably scrape up three or four Brown Bess's between us as well.' Personally, he was a magpie for guns - the safe in the loft had three matchlocks, a doglock, a Brown Bess and even a three-band Enfield.

'What about the non-firers?' Barry was starting to look interested.

'Most people have got swords - hangars will do as cutlasses at a pinch. And we can knock up some boarding pikes.'

'Well...'

Keith had promised himself he wouldn't beg, but he had his heart set on this gig. 'Go on, Barry - what have we got to lose? We've been working our nuts off toward this Little Felcham bash - this could be just what we need to let off a little steam. I've spoken to Julian - he's up for it and I think he needs it.'

Barry's cup thumped down on the coffee table. 'What's up with him, anyway?'

You tell me. Keith shrugged. 'He's having a hard time of it with Penny, I think. You know what he's like - plays his cards close to his chest - but reading between the lines, I'd say they've either split or are splitting.' Julian and Penny were friends with he and Jane - not once-a-week, drinks-at-the-pub friends, but they used to meet once or twice a year outside of the season and Penny had been a regular at musters until a few years back. 'He's been a bit down recently, whatever the cause, and he's really looking forward to this. And you can have a blast back in the ranks if you want - Julian and I can run the show.' They'd already got their characters planned - had spent a few hours giggling like schoolkids over it. Steve was on board as well.

Barry gave this a moment more of solemn consideration. 'Okay,' he said finally, like Dwight Eisenhower deciding a little bit of rain wasn't going to spoil his jaunt across the Channel, 'let's do it.'

Ken's face was as sour as any stiff-necked sea captain facing down a mutineer, but the sails were set and the open sea awaited. The Crimson Pirate, Captain Blood, Pirates of the Caribbean - Keith couldn't wait to get stuck into his back catalogue for a dollop of salty inspiration. 'Avast, ye'll not regret it, matey.'

6 PIRATES!

The "Crown and Anchor" was everything an ancient seafront pub should be - it had low beams polished black with age, a dry, musty smell of old stone seasoned with a salty tang from the nearby harbour, and a menu full of seafood. Jim, in turn, was everything a pirate re-enactor should be - sailcloth trousers, grubby white shirt, black neckerchief, a mop of pale hair, a thin moustache (with goatee) and a gold ring glinting in his ear.

'All your lot arrived then, Keith?' The broad Brummie accent detracted a little from the piratical air.

'Most of them, Jim. Got a few more arriving first thing - we'll have a pretty formidable force!'

'Excellent - well, we've got more than enough powder for you. Basically, most of my guys don't have licences, so they're on blank-firers.'

'You as well?' asked Julian. Thankfully, he was more or less back to his old self, though he was giving little away.

Jim puffed out his chest, unleashing a waft of authentic B.O. 'Oh no, not me. I've got all my licences - basically I'll be rigging up the pyros. It'll look great! How's the camping? Alright for you?'

'No complaints so far - it's a bit exposed though, isn't it?' The site of the "Pirate Festival" was a mile or so down the coast on the derelict site of a Victorian coastal fort. Keith had his caravan in the fort's car park - far preferable to the tents clinging precariously to the rough slopes above the sea. 'We're near enough on the beach and there's no fencing or security.'

'You'll be alright as long as none of you sleepwalk!' chuckled Jim. 'Basically, all plastic tents need to be away by ten in the morning, before the public start coming it. You've got your HQ sorted?'

'Yes,' said Julian. 'A couple of tents and an awning - all canvas, of course.'

'Good stuff.' Jim snapped his fingers. 'Oh yeah, this pair who are joining us, Mandy and Kev, basically we'll brief them in the morning and check their kit. Neither of them are firers, are they?'

'No. Mandy's our CO's lass - she fancied a break from drumming - and Kev is…'

'Getting executed? Yeah, we've been through it, basically. Has he done it before?'

Keith's mind vomited up images from the times when Kev's passion for the grislier side of history had run away with him - then there were his other pursuits. *God save us all.* 'That and worse!'

'Well, as long as he's safe! Ah, here's my first mate. Clogger? Clogger!'

A young giant in black shirt, black britches and heavy boots was forcing his way through the crowded pub, though all male eyes were on the mixed-race woman slinking panther-like at his shoulder. Tall, striking, and with a cloud of raven hair, her wickedly dark eyes were full of smouldering promise, though the jeans and tee-shirt, while snug, were a disappointment.

Clogger elbowed his way over. 'Alright, skipper? Everyone's set up and settled in.' The wispy beard straggling over his chin highlighted rather than hid his youth.

'Good stuff - meet Keith and Julian. Basically, they're running the government forces for the weekend. Gents? Clogger and Liz - aka Black Bess.'

'Original,' muttered Julian.

'Basically, Bess runs another pirate group - your lass, Mandy, will be in her crew.'

'Pleased to meet you both.' Keith offered a hand to the hulking Clogger, the round face red and babyish beneath the stubble and scowl. Another one who took his role far too seriously, oblivious to how ridiculous he looked. 'Why do they call you Clogger?'

'You'll find out tomorrow!' Leaving the offered hand hanging, Clogger dropped into a chair.

'Sounds terrifying!' said Julian.

Bess's eyes flashed and a smile touched her full lips. 'Yes, you won't want to fall into our hands - we know how to deal with government scum!'

Keith squeezed his thighs together - there could be worse fates than falling into her hands and being dealt with. Up close, she looked a little older than he had originally thought, perhaps just a year or two shy of him, but she had kept her looks. And her figure. 'And we, madam, know what to do with pirates!'

'I bet you do!' She gave another vulpine smile that had him reaching for his pint. 'Any volunteers yet?'

'For what?' asked Julian.

Jim fiddled with his earring. 'We usually like to take a couple of prisoners - basically get 'em back to camp and…'

'Show them the error of their ways!' Bess finished for him. 'Nothing heavy, just a bit of a show for the public.'

'I'm sure they'll be queuing up to be captured!' Take Clogger and Jim out of the equation and it didn't seem an unattractive proposition. Kev would be with them as well, though. Maybe not, then. 'We'll get you someone.' He knew who, too - as did Julian, who sniggered into his pint.

'Good old Danny!'

By night, the stretch of waste ground on which the Pirate Festival was to be held looked fairly unprepossessing - it was doubtful it would look any better by day. The crumbling walls of the Victorian fort - portions of which had been incorporated into a grubby café - dominated one corner. Opposite, across the rough grass and random protrusions of concrete, was a shabby children's playground, threatened by the woodland straggling down from the high ground to the rear. It gave the whole area a stark, depressing air despite the scattering of bright modern tents and the campfires that lit the darkness.

Sitting on a grassy hump with his arm around Tabitha, Danny found the view seaward much more appealing - although a little close. There was nothing separating the campsite from the ocean lapping gently at the rocky shore. A low sea wall ran along a cracked promenade off to their left and beyond that was a small, sandy beach, but the camping ground was bare and inhospitable. Still, the lights twinkling across the polished glass of the bay were pretty, the soft wash of the waves on the pebbles was soothing, and the girl he had chased for his whole life was with him. All in all, things could be a lot worse.

'Nice here, isn't it?'

Tabitha shivered. 'It's okay. Getting cold, though.'

'Here.' Danny eased his arms out of the sleeves of his jacket and draped it over her shoulders. Everything since the night they had got together had been like a silver-sheened dream, wrapped in gossamer that would tear if probed too hard - the fear that it would end as quickly and unexpectedly as it had started was a constant black cloud on the horizon.

'Thanks.' She snuggled into him, but a rowdy mob came bustling past, spoiling the moment. Mike, Nick and Steve carried on, skipping stones over the water, but Ollie stopped to talk. 'Alright, Danny? How's the sword work coming on?'

Give a kid a stick and he'd make a sword. Give a grown man an actual sword and he was happier than a pig in shit. 'Yeah, yeah. Okay. I had a practice with Tab earlier.'

'Who's going to be carrying the bruises for a week. Thanks.' She winced, rubbing at her forearm.

'Sorry.' His first attempts at sword play had been enthusiastic, though he'd been more intent on clashing blade against blade rather than trying to strike his opponent. When he had landed a blow, it had been accidental, though even his profuse apologies had not raised the temperature of her reproachful glares.

'You'll be alright, Danny. Just remember - you're trying to land one on your oppo, not his weapon, yeah? Hit with the flat, not the edge, okay? Then, even if you do get carried away, you're not going to do too much damage. I know they're blunt, but you'll know about it if you get cracked somewhere bony!' Ollie tapped an elbow by way of an example. 'Right, I'm turning in. See you in the morning.'

'Night, mate,' Danny called after him.

'Night, Ollie.' Tabitha stretched, prim and precise as a cat. 'Think I'll turn in as well.'

'I'll walk you back to your caravan.' A goodnight kiss would be all he could hope for, but that would be better than nothing.

'I can find my way… oh, go on then.'

Arm in arm, they picked their way over the waste ground and into the car park beyond the crumbling walls. The lights were out in the Winters' caravan.

'Here we are then.' Tabitha slid her arm free from Danny's and fumbled for her key.

He reached for her, but she frustrated his intentions by darting in to peck him on the cheek. It was like being kissed by a dry sponge and he dipped his head in for something more substantial.

She stepped back. 'Goodnight, Dan. See you in the morning.' Clattering into the caravan, she pulled the door shut behind her. *For fuck's sake.* Surely he had a right to expect more than the odd chaste kiss after a month? Still, anything was better than nothing. Wasn't it?

Jim and his crew had worked hard through the early morning to clear away the modern tents and transform the wasteland into a setting fit for the Pirate Festival. A village of white canvas had sprung up, populated by an assortment of characters straight out of the pages of Moonfleet and Treasure Island. The car park was already full and members of the public wandered among the tents, marvelling at the sights, sounds and smells of days gone by. Here and there, amongst the fisherfolk, parsons, woodturners, potters, wenches, lords and ladies, villainous faces watched the approaches from the beach.

To the beat of a single drum, the forces of law and order advanced from the sea. A skirmish line of blue-coated sailors armed with boarding pikes led the way, followed by a column of redcoats beneath a large Union Flag. Two officers minced along at the head of the redcoats, confections of lace and gold, bewigged, powdered and simpering. Their lordships had arrived.

Stepping carefully over the trailing wires that showed where the earth had been sown with pyrotechnics, Keith followed the blue-coated sailors - Nick, Mike, Jane and Danny - into the roped-off arena where all the set pieces would be played out. Jim had done a good job - and look at all the public! The redcoats formed a solid block in the centre of the arena, the sailors taking station around the edges. Time to get it on.

'You there! Ruffian!' Raising a quizzing glass, Keith pointed to Jim, mending a fishing net on the edge of the arena.

'Me, your worship?'

Keith kept his voice as an effete drawl. 'Unfortunately, yes. You, sir. Come here, sir, and be quick about it!'

'What a frightful creature, my dear,' lisped Julian, face blanched and a beauty spot decorating one cheek.

Jim shambled over and knuckled his forehead, eyes cast down in obsequious reverence. With a flourish, Keith pulled a lace handkerchief from his sleeve and held it to his nose. 'Do there be any pirates hereabouts?'

'Pirates, sir?' Jim's Robert Newton tones could not mask the Black Country timbre. 'No, sir. Basically, we be just humble fishermen, your honour.'

'That will explain the smell!' Keith waved a limp hand. 'Farage!'

Steve's moth-eaten green coat and mildewed tricorne, coupled with a dusty grey wig, gave the desired impression of a decrepit retainer, but the blank look was genuine. Keith mentally face-palmed. Julian had chosen the name - someone contentious and in the public eye - and from the titters around the crowd, it had worked. Perhaps they should have told Steve. It took some frantic mugging before the light of realisation dawned in his eyes and he shuffled forward, gait inspired by the absent Trevor. The decanter on his silver tray was filled with a ruby liquid, and though the delicate wine glasses looked to be of the most exquisite crystal, Keith had picked them up from a motorway services yesterday afternoon.

'My lord?' wheezed Steve, adding a damp cough for good measure.

'Drink, Farage, drink! Quick, man.' Keith took a sip out of the glass Steve handed him, suppressing a wince as the velvet liquid scoured the back of his throat. Port? At this hour? It was meant to be blackcurrant squash!

Little finger daintily extended, Julian drained his own drink with scarcely a flicker. 'Now, rapscallion, we have a charter from the...' He frowned. 'When is this supposed to be again?' he asked Keith out of the corner of his mouth.

'Try Queen Anne?' Keith took another mouthful of port. Couldn't waste it, after all.

'From the queen to rid the seas hereabouts of the scourge of piracy! I have no doubt that, at the very least, you have knowledge of these scoundrels. You may pass on the message that we will not rest until they are all taken and gibbeted!'

'What do you say to that, rascal?' Keith looked down his nose at Jim, his pulse picking up at what was coming.

'What do I say to that? Basically, I say… get 'em, lads!'

At Jim's cry, a motley horde of villains erupted from the trees to join those who burst from the crowd, whooping and howling. Pistols and muskets cracked, the sharp reports identifying them as blank-firers. Nevertheless, they elicited excited shrieks from the crowd. Keith dropped his hand to the hilt of his rapier. If they liked those little pop-guns, they were going to love what was coming next.

'Twenty guineas you owe me! I said the fellow was a rogue!'

'You did, my darling.' Julian beckoned the sailors back to the centre of the arena. 'Pay him, Farage! Front rank! Present!'

'Fire!' bellowed Keith.

The thundering volley punched him in the stomach like a lead-filled boxing glove, drowning out the feeble cracks of the blank-firers. The pirates pulled up in dismay, engulfed in thick smoke, and the crowd applauded wildly.

'Rear rank advance!' hollered Julian. 'Present.'

'Rear rank make ready.' Keith drew his rapier. 'Front rank. Fire!'

A second filthy volley roared out, pinning the raging pirates at the edge of the arena.

Down on the beach, children abandoned their sandcastles or ran splashing from the water's edge, flocking toward the thundering volleys. A pall of smoke hung above the waste ground.

Adjusting her bikini top, Alice Reynolds put her book down and, raising her oversized sunglasses, sat up in her sun lounger. She cocked an ear to the sounds of battle, listened for a moment or two, then shook her head, slid her glasses down, and picked up her book.

Six volleys were enough to break the pirates. With the twenty-yard safe distance, and the rolling fire by rank, they were unable to close on the redcoats and fled into the trees. Brushing his coat down, Keith put his hand behind his back and addressed the awed crowd.

'This village and all lands hereabout are now under our jurisdiction.

Pirates - ye be warned!'

The camp was now under control of the government forces. This meant little to the hordes of public passing through, except that there were now redcoats and sailors patrolling the avenues between the tents and a few less salty sea-dogs on show.

Mincing through the crowds along with Julian, silver-topped cane in hand, Keith was having the time of his life. 'Out of the way, poor people! Shoo, shoo!'

Julian raised his hat to a young lady in a floral dress, making an elegant leg. 'Morning, madam.' She giggled and hid her face.

Spying a small boy goggling at the sights, Keith addressed the lad's father. 'Sir, your monkey appears to have escaped! Secure it, sir, secure it!' He poked the boy with his cane. 'Dance, monkey, dance!' When the boy capered a few grinning - if bemused - steps, Keith pattered his hands together.

Julian peered at the boy with his quizzing glass. 'I do believe it to be a boy, m'dear.'

'A boy? Then you, sir, if you be his father - beat him well and beat him often!' Keith dismissed the pair with an effete wave of his hand - there were more tempting targets on offer.

'She looks game,' Julian whispered in his ear, beckoning to a rather well-endowed lady who was watching a woodturner at work. 'Madam! Madam!' She looked understandably startled at being addressed by the foppish apparition, shifting her eyes sideways to deflect Julian's attention, but he wasn't about to let her off the hook. 'Yes, you madam! You! D'ye care for a game?'

Trapped, she narrowed her eyes. 'What sort of a game?'

'Coinage in the cleavage, madam! Coinage in the cleavage! Farage! Fetch her over!'

Suspicion was evident in her handsome features as Keith and Julian looked her over with their quizzing glasses, her low-cut top perhaps a little too revealing for someone the wrong side of forty. Still, everything seemed ship-shape and, so to speak, Bristol fashion. Keith lowered his glass. 'Lud, m'dear, the playing surface is not flat!' It was tremendous fun - you could get away with pretty much anything as long as you camped it up enough, and he and Julian couldn't be more camp.

Julian craned his head to peer down her top. 'Indeed not.'

The pantomime tomfoolery brought about a twitch of her lips. 'What do I do?'

'Just stand still,' Keith said. 'Myself and Percy will do all the work!'

Julian adjusted her pose, putting a hand on her back to tip her forward.

'Lean forward a little, woman. Like so! You first, Fitzy!'

Keith tugged his purse from his belt and scooped out a faux gold coin. 'Stand clear! Brace, madam, brace!' With an extravagant flourish, he flipped the coin at her. It landed directly in her cleavage with a pleasingly fleshy slap. 'A hit! Into the valley!'

The woman's mouth formed an "o" of mock outrage that soon collapsed into a barely suppressed grin as Keith swept his hat from his head - clapping a frantic hand onto the curled locks as his wig threatened to blow away - and waved an elegant hand at the gathering crowd. They were already attracting quite an audience.

Julian slid an arm around their victim's unresisting shoulders. 'But it is not all the way in, is it, madam?' he asked huskily, trailing the ends of his wig lightly across her bare shoulders.

'No!' With Julian's powdered face millimetres from hers, she was fighting a losing battle to hold back her giggles.

'Then you may not keep it!'

Julian reached for the coin peeking out from the enticing crevasse. Saucy git! Keith rapped him across the fingers with his cane.

'Hold, Percy! I claim "Stickage"!'

'"Stickage", my dear?' Julian frowned, as if Keith had just made it up - which he had.

'Indeed!' This was going to be quite a spectacle! 'Bounce, woman, bounce! Dislodge, dislodge!' Finally submitting to her laughter, she began to jump up and down in a flurry of wobbling flesh. The overall effect was quite pleasing, as evidenced by the growing crowd. 'More, woman, more! More vigour! Farage! Help her!'

Steve wrapped his arms around her waist and made a show of trying to lift her into her jumps. After several seconds of frantic shaking, the coin disappeared.

'"Slippage"!' crowed Keith. 'I win, I win!'

'You'll not see that again!' said Julian.

'Indeed not! Do you give change, madam? Your turn, Percy.'

Julian flounced back a few yards, spinning on his heel and flipping his own coin at the enticing target. Bouncing off her chest, it set off a chain reaction of ripples and hit the floor.

'Hazard!' bellowed Julian.

Keith echoed his cry. 'Hazard! Hazard!'

'Let me play!' A younger woman had appeared alongside the first. While her top was, if anything, cut lower, she did not have as much to display. Julian peered at both women.

'A "Two's Up", my dears?'

'Damn risky!' How far could they actually push things before anyone took offence? Quite a way, apparently.

'Well, I'm game if the ladies are! Fitzy? Are you?'

'Always!'

Julian clapped his hands. 'First toss to you! Two to choose from and nothing for the crack in the middle!' Slipping his arms around their waists, he squeezed the two women into one magnificent target.

'Stand fast and point your puppies this way!' Keith had to keep his voice well in character - any slip could see him on some sort of register. Booted out of his post at the university, at least. The coin he flipped at the two willing players ricocheted between the pair of them, lodging on the chest of their original victim. 'Hazard!'

'You can nudge, my dear!' Julian told him.

'Of course!' Extending his cane, Keith tried to nudge the coin into a more advantageous position, but it fell to the floor.

'"Slidage"!' hollered Julian.

'Damn! Your turn, my dear.'

Julian examined the second woman critically, like a golfer eyeing up a tricky putt. 'Cross your arms, my dear! That's it, squeeze your elbows in! Make more of it, madam!'

Keith had been right. This was just what was needed to recharge the old batteries. A nice, relaxed gig with someone else picking up the tab. No authenticity Nazis, no big battalions to organise, and no overbearing Lord Generals or sneaky Scotch bastards to worry about. He didn't even have to issue orders - he was back in the ranks, plain old Private Reynolds. There was only one dark cloud (apart from Alice, skulking on the beach and no doubt compiling a list of complaints that would only be sated by a lavish meal in town) and that was patrolling beside him. Ken's sensitivities had been pricked by the mish-mash of cross-period kit - anything from 16th to 19th century. He was missing the point. This was all about fun. Barry touched his hat to Ollie and Tabitha, patrolling with slung muskets. Over by the arena, Nick and Mike were showing a group of kids their swords while Terry went enthusiastically through the loading procedure for his Brown Bess. The rest of the "government forces" were scattered among the tents, engaging with the public or looking suitably stern as they went about their duties. The occasional bellow of "Hazard!" punctuated the air.

'Those two seem to be enjoying themselves!' Was that the merest twinge of jealousy at knowing that Keith and Julian would get all the plaudits for this gig? Or was he envious about the attention they were garnering from the public?

'Glad someone is.' Ken's eyes were constantly on the move, each fresh anachronism adding another crease to his forehead.

'What's up? They've done a good job getting us this gig.'

'It's not very authentic, is it?'

'Balance, Kenneth, balance. Granted, it's not up to our usual standards, but look at the people coming through the gates!' To be able to attract this number of people was beyond his wildest of dreams - he couldn't remember when they'd last topped two hundred spectators and there were at least double that here already. 'When was the last time we had this many people through?'

Footfall apparently meant nothing to Ken in the face of so many crimes against history. 'But look! Over there! That girl - kit by Ann Summers! Tavern Wench Number One from *Carry On Cliché*!'

'Yes, I had noticed her.' As had every other male. Magnificent - a period wet dream come to voluptuous life. 'Just surprised their lordships haven't homed in on her yet - ah, there they go!'

'And when is this supposed to be set?'

'The Golden Age of Piracy, Ken.'

'Then half the kit is at least fifty years too late - as is this!' Ken unslung his musket. 'India Pattern! They weren't...'

'Steady, Ken, steady! Okay, a few liberties have been taken, mostly by that pair of clowns' - Keith and Julian were now hovering around the nylon-bloused wench who had attracted Ken's ire - 'but everyone's hearts are in the right place and there's some good stuff here.'

Ken was not to be convinced. 'And where's "here" even meant to be?'

'Oh, I don't know - the island of Generica!'

Ken stabbed an outraged digit toward another corseted beauty. 'Look! Look! Case in point! 17th century bodice, 19th century mob cap! And that lace! All wrong for any period - unless it was slung over the back of mother's armchair!'

A small boy, wide-eyed with excitement, ran up to Barry, saving him from having to try and placate Ken. 'Is that a real gun?'

'It is indeed!' Barry passed his musket to the boy, making sure to keep a hand wrapped around the barrel. 'Heavy, isn't it?'

'Yeah! Dad! Dad! Look!'

Ken moved in like a Bank Holiday squall. 'It's a Short Land Pattern Tower Musket - commonly called a Brown Bess. It's actually far too modern for what we are trying to portray, but...'

'Bang!' shouted the boy, ignoring Ken. 'Are you going to shoot anyone?'

Barry's trigger finger twitched. 'Not just yet.'

'Morning, my good man!' Julian inclined his head to a man taking in the sights with his son - father more interested in the wenches than the vintage trades being plied. Keith couldn't really blame him. That last one they'd accosted - good Lord!

'Morning.' The father tapped his son on his shoulder. The boy gave a wave.

'Is this your monkey?' Julian had taken a leaf out of Keith's book, but the boy just looked blank. 'You, boy! Are you a monkey?' The boy looked to his father and then back at Julian. 'What's up, boy? D'ye have no English? Are you a monkey?'

The boy's father mimed a monkey - hands beneath his armpits and a simian pout on his face - and then pointed to his son who smiled but still said nothing. A suspicion that the boy's reticence was down to more than simply shyness snuck up and wrapped an arm around Keith's throat like a mutineer dealing with the sentry on the captain's cabin.

Oh no. Oh shit. Julian, please stop! 'Julian…'

Julian, however, was in full cry. 'Cat got your tongue, boy? Eh? Eh?' He prodded with his cane.

Further frantic mimes from the boy's father still failed to elicit a vocal response. Julian threw his hands up.

'Are you deaf, boy? Deaf? Oh sh…' Julian's powdered face dropped as the father reached down to pull a hearing aid's earpiece from beneath his son's jumper and fix it in its proper location.

'Oh God! I'm so sorry!' Julian flounced off in a hasty retreat, leaving Keith to exchange what he hoped were understanding smiles with the boy's father.

Assembled with the rest of the sailors on the path up to the scrubby woodlands, Danny fingered the hilt of his sword - it gave you a swagger, having something like that swinging at your hip. He might even get a chance to use it soon - the air was ripe with expectation and Terry was doubling over from the awning that served as their HQ.

'Right, their lordships want a patrol up into the woods, see if we can locate the secret pirate camp.'

Mike snorted. 'It's just through there, Tel - you can see it!'

'Play the game, Mike! Right, you four are going up there - Ray and I will cover the path. Time for your big moment, Dan!'

Big moment? No one had said anything about a big moment. What the fuck was going on? 'What? You what?'

'Has no one told you? Mike? Nick?'

Nick was grinning fit to bust. 'Sort of slipped my mind!'

'I thought Jane would have filled in him!' Mike's shit-eating smirk was the mirror of Nick's. Even Jane had a smile on her face.

'Keith was going to tell him, I thought.'

Nothing good could be linked to grins like that. 'Tell me what? What's going on?'

The hand Terry clapped on Danny's shoulder was far from comforting. 'You're volunteering.'

'I'm what?' What the fuck were they railroading him into? 'Volunteering? Volunteering for what?'

'The pirates want a prisoner,' Mike told him.

'Yeah? And?' Did he really need to ask? Only in the vain hope of his suspicions being proved wrong.

'We've promised them you, sweet-cheeks!' said Nick with a wink.

Prisoner? 'No way! Get stuffed!' This was above and beyond what he'd signed up for.

'It has to be you, Danny love.' Jane's grin belied her sympathetic tones.

'Does it? Why?' The sun glittered treacherously off the ocean. It looked cool and fresh over there, away from the sultry pressure by the trees. 'Why does it have to be me?'

'It has to be one of us four. The musketeers aren't allowed to hand their guns over and it can't be me - it'll be too obvious I'm a woman!'

And what, exactly, was going to happen to this luckless prisoner? 'What about Mike? Nick?' He'd only been doing this for a couple of months - he didn't know what to do!

'Really?' Mike's lip curled. 'Look at us - how would they ever take one of us alive?'

'You, though?' Nick circled Danny's bicep with one sweaty paw. 'Easy prey!'

'No way! No way!' He was only here for a laugh - this sounded like proper re-enacting stuff, deep into character like Kev. Oh God - Kev was with the pirates! His arse cheeks clenched of their own volition.

'You've got to!' Terry shifted to block off any possible escape. 'They're expecting you!'

'But what are they going to do to me?' A bubble of sour acid burst in Danny's stomach.

'Come on, man up!' Nick's jowls crinkled as he fought back laughter.

'Jane...'

'You'll be fine, love. It's only make-believe! They're not really going to... you know.'

'No! No, I don't! What? What?' His mind sprinted away from grisly images of chains and red-hot irons. What sort of freaks were these pirate blokes anyway?

Nick could no longer hold back his mirth. 'Someone get a camera - I want to remember him just as he is!'

'Oh, this is bollocks! I'm not doing it!' They couldn't force him.

Mike could. 'Yes, you are! Go on! Just camp it up a bit! Scream and beg, you know the sort of thing!'

'And watch out for that big fella, Clogger!' advised Ray.

'Yeah,' added Nick, 'at least make sure he buys you a drink first!'

'Fuck off!' There was no escape. He was trapped, doomed to God knew what. If he tried to make a break for it now, they'd haul him into the woods. At least if he went voluntarily, he'd retain a semblance of dignity (for now) and have a better chance of legging it when it came to the crunch.

'Right,' said Terry, 'come on. We've wasted enough time - off you go!'

Nick, Mike and Jane moved off first, heading warily into the waiting woodlands. Terry and Ray took up positions either side of the path with their muskets, Terry raising a meaningful eyebrow. Mouth dry and stomach heavy, Danny hefted his six-foot boarding pike and, like a grunt on his first (and probably last) foray into the jungles of Vietnam, followed his shipmates.

It was a little cooler in the woods, the musty gloom scored with an oppressive soundtrack of insectoid hums and chirrups. Though the "hidden camp" was only fifty yards or so into the woods, the path moved along a series of increasingly steep switchbacks and sweat was soon pooling in Danny's armpits and dripping from beneath his borrowed tricorne hat to splatter on the leaf-mould carpet. The green hell closed in around him, each snapping twig or rustle of leaves whispering slyly of what awaited him at the end of the path. It would be fine, wouldn't it? It wasn't like they were really going to torture him. Nevertheless, it was like waiting for the dentist and it was almost a relief when the crack of a pistol shattered the pregnant silence.

With a roar, a dozen or so pirates sprang from the undergrowth to fall on the little patrol, all wild eyes and savage faces. Danny turned to run, but two villainous cut-throats blocked his way. Sod this! He put his head down and charged, driving the two pirates from his path with a wild yell and a savage scythe of his boarding pike, but the hand that snagged his collar snuffed out any hope of escape. His feet scrabbled impotently for a moment and then he succumbed to the inevitable.

'This is it then, Dan.' Mike threw him back into the faltering melee. 'Good luck, shipmate. Lie back and think of England!'

'No! Don't leave me!' It was like being abandoned at the gates on the first day of school, but he wouldn't be making new friends over the sandpit.

Jane and Mike backed away down the path. Danny made another attempt to flee, but Nick loomed up like a haystack and plucked the pike from his unresisting fingers.

'Don't forget your safe word!' Nick snatched Danny's hat from his head and unfastened his sword belt.

'My what?' Was there something he was supposed to know? Something he should have been told? 'I haven't got one! What's that for?'

His laughing comrades fled down the path, leaving him to confront both the pitiless faces of his captors and the dread significance of "safe word".

Terry and Ray levelled their muskets as the survivors of the patrol sprinted through the trees, a mob of pirates on their heels.

'Here they come!' Terry cocked his musket. 'Cover them! And for Christ's sake fire high - and wide. They're getting bloody close!' This was going to be tight.

Ray fired first - not aiming quite as high as Terry would have liked. Still, the booming report - amplified by the trees - gave the pursuers something to think about. Terry squeezed off a shot, then Ollie and Tabitha were there to add to the covering fire. By the time Terry had reloaded, the pirates were in full retreat. The breathless fugitives jogged the last few yards to safety.

'What happened? Chapter and verse, smartly now.' Terry played up to the crowd that had come flocking at the shots. Nick solemnly handed over Danny's hat.

'Ambush,' panted Mike. 'There was too many of them!'

Terry turned the hat over in his hands. 'Where's Danny?'

Nick's sob would have garnered few Thespianic plaudits, but he gave it everything. 'They took him. We tried to save him but -' he sobbed again '- there was nothing we could do!'

'Poor lad.' Terry handed the hat back to Nick. 'Oh well, nothing to be done now - let's report to their lordships!'

Tabitha grabbed hold of Mike. 'What's happened? Where's Danny?'

'Dead - if he's lucky!'

With his hands tightly bound behind his back, Danny was ushered along the path by his captors. Some he recognised - Jim, of course, and the hulking Clogger, who looked and sounded like something out of a Steinbeck novel. Various other scurvy wretches surrounded him, leering as they suggested the various unpleasant fates that awaited him, but the one who worried him most - Kev aside - was the woman they called Black Bess.

She was dressed as a pirate captain, with a long blue coat and a plumed, broad-brimmed hat, but her costume had far too many sensuous twists. The britches were indecently tight, the thigh-length boots added several inches to her already impressive stature, and the frilled white shirt did little to contain her most obvious assets. It was she who had tied his hands, her deft movements and the subtle (but, he was sure, deliberate) brushes against him almost summoning that notorious lubber, Seaman Staines. The rolling sway of her hips had already convinced him that being captured may not be the worst thing and, combined with the constrictive pressure of the rope, raked a hitherto dormant section of his brain into gibbering of submission and subjugation while conjuring all sorts of seedy images that left him badly in need of a cold shower.

'You know your stuff, Bess.' Kev tugged at Danny's bonds, somewhat ruining the moment. 'He's not going anywhere!'

'I've had plenty of practice!' The throaty purr slid silk-soft hands across Danny's lower regions, nearly causing him to embarrass himself in front of the sea-dogs.

'Really? These are a pro job.'

'I am a pro!'

Pro? Pro what? God, what had he been let in for? A dungeon door slammed shut on the agreeable images of mildly enforced titillation, raising a much more sinister rubber-hooded spectre of barely legal perversion. 'Kev?' Danny hissed. Kev was the closest thing he had to a friend here. 'Kev! What's a safe word? I haven't got one.'

'Oh dear - you're in for a long old day then!'

'Don't tease the poor boy,' scolded Bess.

'Sorry, mistress.'

The pirate's camp was nothing more than a crude assortment of low tents and canvas sheets draped over branches, dominated by a hoary old oak tree with coils of rope heaped by its twisted trunk. The fire in the centre of the clearing crackled and popped with heathenish intent while the unlovely collection of piratical rogues gathered around it rose to their feet to welcome the hapless captive with hoots and jeers.

'Don't you worry,' Bess whispered in Danny's ear, his hair prickling beneath the combing of her fingers. 'It'll be fine.'

'Right, Clogger,' said Jim. 'Get him comfortable.'

The fire flared with eager fury as Clogger seized Danny's arm. Danny dug his heels in but could only slow his progress toward the oak whose gnarly branches spread wide to accept him. Although he was pretty sure he wasn't really going to be skinned or burned alive, his involuntary reactions to Bess's sensuous touches had given birth to a bugbear that cavorted and howled in the black reaches of his mind, even though Clogger didn't seem like the tickling type. 'Hey! Get off!'

'Don't make it worse for yourself!' growled Clogger.

'Worse? How can it...' Clogger seized his ear, twisting it like a bottle top. 'Jesus! Alright, alright.' In order to keep his ear attached, Danny allowed Clogger to drag him to the tree with no further resistance. Rough hands spun him around as though he was no more than a kid, shoving him back against the broad oak. The ridged bark scored flesh from his knuckles, his bound hands crushed between his backside and the trunk, and the hoots of the pirates filled his ears as Clogger stooped for a coil of rope. Two girls in loose trousers and knotted shirts, their faces smeared with ash and dirt, hurried forward to help, looping rope around Danny's thighs with muffled giggles while Clogger set to work securing his torso. There were several girls among the hollering mob - Bess's crew, no doubt - mostly dressed like the two securing him, though there was one who looked as though she'd raided an adult fancy dress shop. Skirt slashed to her thigh to show the tops of her heeled boots, breasts almost spilling over the tightly laced bodice, she gave him a cheeky little wink from beneath the shadow of her plumed tricorne. Oh God! Mandy. The ropes snapped tight around his thighs, pinning his legs to the tree. Clogger yanked at his knots, crushing his arms to his side and driving the knobbles and bobbles of the trunk into his back.

'So, why do they call you Clogger?' Danny wheezed, chest compressed by the ropes. Might as well try to make conversation - it would save dwelling on the complex stew of emotions that Mandy's presence had thrown together.

Clogger stepped back to admire his handiwork, seemingly oblivious to the Mexican wave of sniggers that riffled through the scurvy assembly. He appeared to give the question some considerable thought before pulling back his fist and slamming a punch into Danny's belly. Though the blow was pulled, it was still like being butted in the stomach by a boisterous puppy. 'Because I clog people!'

'Taken, you say? Damn careless!'

Seated out of the sun beneath the awning of the redcoats' HQ, Keith reclined with a glass of port while the remnants of Terry's ill-fated patrol sweated in the midday glare, hats in hand.

'Damn careless! Not so hard, Farage!' Julian rapped Steve - who was massaging his feet - across the knuckles with his cane.

'There wasn't anything we could do to...' Mike began.

'Damn me!' barked Keith. 'The impertinence! You abandon your fellow and then you dare answer back to your betters! Have this dog flogged!'

'Still, m'dear,' drawled Julian, ''tis one less of the ruffians we'll have to pay now! Lud, we should have enough spare for another frame or two of "Coinage in the Cleavage!"'

'Capital idea!'

Jane scowled. 'You two are bloody loving this, aren't you?'

She did look very fetching in her sailor's garb. 'Another pert-tongued rogue! Perhaps you, too, need a lash of the cat!' Was there was anywhere they could slip off to?

'Just you try it!'

Julian had his quizzing glass out. 'The fellow appears to be one of our more, ah, curvy matelots!'

'Indeed! What do you have down there, my man?' Wriggling his fingers,

Keith made a grab for Jane's chest, but she slapped his hand away with a giggle.

'Oh God.' Tabitha's grimace showed exactly what she thought of her parents' antics. 'I'm going to be sick! What are you going to do about Danny, dad?'

A bead of sweat rolled down his wife's throat toward the inviting valley of her cleavage, and he mopped his brow with a lace kerchief. 'Nothing! It's all part of the script. They'll let him go - what's left of him - when they get bored!'

'But Mandy's up there with them!' Tabitha looked close to tears.

Mirth flickered in Julian's eyes, but he kept his tone suitably solemn. 'Then it truly could be a fate worse than death.'

'Some of the more lurid stories can be dismissed - there's no evidence of anyone ever being made to walk the plank - but any captives could expect a pretty rough time if the pirates thought they were withholding the location of their booty.'

Lolling against the tree while Jim's commentary droned on, Danny tried to wriggle some feeling back into his limbs. How long could one bloke talk for? The crowd of watching public showed no signs of boredom though, and their eyes once more swivelled with bloodthirsty eagerness to the bound captive.

'I'd have him talking in seconds!' Bess's syrupy tones slithered over him like a feather boa.

'I'm sure you would!' fawned Ken.

'I'm sure you would...?'

'Mistress!'

'Better.'

Jim continued his monologue, pacing in front of the crowd with a deal of animation. 'Any ordinary seamen would be invited to join the pirate crew - if they refused they would enjoy the fate of the officers and any wealthy passengers taken. Although the plank is basically fiction, there are plenty of recorded instances of unpleasant ends! Maria Cobham, wife of pirate Eric Cobham, was notorious for her treatment of captives. She once had the officers of a captured merchantman tied to a mast so she could practice her pistol-shooting and had the crew of another ship bound in sacks and basically thrown overboard. There were also a variety of methods for loosening tongues. A favourite was tying a rope around the unfortunate prisoner's forehead until basically his eyes bulged out of his head. Clogger?'

What the...? The rope that was looped suddenly around Danny's brow was yanked tight, gripping like an instant migraine while the coarse fibres prickled like a grandmother-knitted jumper. 'Oi! Watch it! Shit! Shit!' As the vice-like pressure ratcheted up, the skin of his face tightened as if his hair had been scraped back into a savagely taut ponytail. His eyes bugged - Clogger actually seemed intent on popping them out of his head. 'Shit!'

'Oh, good work Dan!' said Kev in admiration. 'Very convincing!'

'That's because he's bloody killing me!' His vision blurred, sending doubles rising from the watching audience to float amongst the darkening trees. 'Get off, you twat!'

'Clogger!' hissed Jim. Expression blissfully vacant, Clogger carried on twisting the rope in his hammy fist. 'Clogger!'

The rope creaked, and Danny tried to squeeze his eyes shut before they plopped from their sockets. No deal - so great was the pressure that it was impossible to force his eyelids closed. He must look like a bloody frog. 'For fu...'

'Clogger!' Jim had hold of the giant's bicep. 'Clogger! Enough! Or I'll take away Mr Snug...'

The rope was off in an instant, Danny's eyelids slamming shut like garage doors to plunge him into crimson-tainted darkness. A pulse thumped in his skull like a hammer, and only when the pressure behind his eyes deflated, like a punctured dinghy, did he dare open them again. Clogger stood motionless, eyes moist, a Frankenstein's monster once more waiting for a lightning bolt to activate him.

'That's it then, ladies and gentlemen,' Jim's voice was a little strained, like that of a man who had just seen a lawsuit flash before him, though the smattering of applause suggested that the audience had thought it all part of the act. 'Basically a little taste of what could be expected if you fell into the hands of pirates. Now, back in the main camp you'll be able to see the actual type of irons that any pirate taken prisoner would find himself clapped in, along with a few more instruments of torture and punishment. Well, I don't think we're going to get anything more out of this wretch - Bess?'

Striking a pose that set the male members of the audience drooling, Bess sighted along her pistol and fired - the blank-firer's report no worse than a Christmas cracker. That was it - all over, thank God. Danny slumped down, eyes closed and head lolling. He waited for the applause to finish before cocking open an eye. The spectators were filing away through the trees - he'd be following them in a moment.

'Can I go now?' Apart from Clogger getting a bit carried away, it hadn't been too bad really, though his arms and legs were aching for release. Perhaps he might get some sympathy from Tab when he got back.

'Not yet,' Clogger told him, back from whatever dark place Jim's unfinished threat had sent him to. 'We might want you for another show!'

'What? Oh, come on!'

Bess jerked her head toward a canvas awning slung between two trees on the outskirts of the camp. 'Bung him in there for now - and make sure he's secured.'

'Hazard!' bellowed Julian, his coin bouncing from the chest of their latest willing victim.

'Hazard!' Keith stooped to retrieve the coin, straightening up to come face to face with a rounded pair of breasts straining at the flimsy fabric of a tiny bikini top like a pair of tanned zeppelins. 'Good Lord!'

The girl - superbly bronzed and with tribal tattoos swirling down her thighs and arms and across her flat stomach - had obviously come up from the beach to see what the fuss was. A jewelled stud gleamed in her belly-button and a silver shark-tooth pendant swung above her enticing golden globes. 'Let me play!' She leaned forward, arms beneath her bosom to promote her cleavage - not that it needed much help. 'Like this?'

'Just like that, madam!' Julian pattered his hands together.

'Come on then!' she said with a pout. 'Get on with it!'

They'd caught a live one. Julian threw first, his coin swallowed by the tanned cleavage. Following up, Keith's eager throw went hopelessly wide, the coin slipping on sweat-slickened fingers. Not that it mattered - with the poise and suppleness of an Olympic gymnast, the girl thrust out a superbly rounded bottom and then arched herself backward in an eye-boggling manoeuvre that saw the wayward coin drop neatly between her breasts. Sweet Jesus! Keith fumbled another coin from his purse, rummaging blindly as he watched Julian's second and third projectiles go the way of his first. By the time he'd hauled out a handful of coins, Julian was already on his sixth throw. Greedy bastard! Like a clay pigeon launcher on rapid fire, Keith flicked out two coins of his own. Their audience was shrinking as women in the crowd dragged husbands and boyfriends away, but their delightful muse showed no sign of getting bored. He and Julian were going through their change quicker than a gambling addict on a Vegas slot machine, and wherever each coin was heading (and Keith was experimenting with some pretty challenging trajectories), she would throw her body into a mouth-watering pose and the ersatz doubloon would vanish. Having exhausted his supply of authentic coinage, Keith scrabbled in his pocket and dug out a pound coin. It was not as aerodynamic as the larger, flatter discs, leaving his fingers in an erratic flight path and defying the girl's supple contortions to end up lodged against her pendant.

'Hazard!' he said hoarsely.

She wiggled in a way that nearly finished him off - but what a way to go! 'Come and get it then!'

Swallowing hard, he crept forward, keeping his eyes fixed on the silver crescent nestled against the glistening flesh. 'I think this is in the way, madam!'

'Move it, then!'

Could he? Should he? Jesus, she was thrusting toward him like a lead in a Russ Meyer movie. Stay in character. For God's sake, stay in character. With trembling fingers, he flicked the pendant - brushing the smooth flesh beneath - and the coin dropped out of sight.

'Keith!' hissed Julian.

'There, m'dear!' If Julian wanted a go, he should have got in quicker. But no, it had been a warning - a shaven-headed guy with tattoos and muscles on muscles had pushed to the front of the waning crowd, the silver pendant nestling in the v-shaped crease between the inflated pecs identical to the one worn by the girl. 'Oh shit.' Jesus, he was massive! And not too happy! Unless... Oh God. The glistening Hercules pulled a mobile from the back of his Speedos, the encouraging nod indicating that the game should continue.

Sat against a tree stump in the closed awning, bound hand and foot, Danny tried to wriggle into a position that would relieve the relentless press on his numbed backside. Easing one cheek off the floor only increased the pressure on the other and he slumped back down, drawing his knees in. Shades of primary school, sitting on a dusty hall floor while assembly dragged on and on, though there would be no bell to mark the end of the torture. What if they left him here all day? They couldn't - it had to be against the Geneva convention or something. It could certainly be counted as cruel and unusual punishment - it would probably give even Kev pause for thought, but just as it became unbearable, the entrance flap was twitched aside. About bloody time. 'Have you come to let me go?'

'Don't be silly!' Mandy ducked under the awning, closing the opening behind her.

Was it suddenly much hotter in the already sultry awning? 'What do you want, then?'

'To make you talk!'

Wasn't the game over now? She'd obviously decided to freelance, and God knew where that left him. Her wicked little smile set his sweat-slick wrists rotating in tight, frantic circles, though his bonds remained stubbornly tight. He should call for Jim - she was sure to be far more inventive than Clogger, and there was no audience to rein her in. 'Come on, this is going a bit far! I don't know anything!'

She pouted. 'No, silly. I want you to talk to me!'

So that was all. Best keep her sweet - she could be his ticket out of here. 'I am.'

She blinked, lashes heavy with mascara. 'I suppose you are. About time.

I thought you were going to ignore me forever!'

'Can you blame me?' What did she expect after what she'd done to him? Flowers?

'Not really. Sorry.' She cocked her head to one side. 'Be fair, though. You did have your eyes on Tab all night, didn't you?'

He was in little position to argue. 'Yeah. Yeah, I suppose I did. Sorry.'

She shrugged, as if to say it didn't really matter. 'Friends?'

'Yeah, friends - I need all the friends I can get at the moment!'

'I'm not going to let you go!' Her eyes sparkled with a predatory fervour and she tapped a finger against her lips.

'So, what are you going to do? The Marius treatment?' His hands resumed their hapless circles.

'No, don't worry.' Working deftly at Kev's knots, she freed his ankles. 'He was an arrogant shit! You're fairly harmless.'

'Cheers.' He wiggled his toes, coaxing some feeling back into them, though his buttocks still felt like stone. 'I think.'

'Seems a shame to waste the opportunity though.' With exquisite deliberation, she slipped off his shoes.

'Hey! What are you doing?' Taking the top of his left sock, she rolled it primly down his calf, his skin prickling beneath the contrast of the coarse wool and her featherlight fingers. It was like the night in the beer tent all over again - but he was with Tab now. 'Mandy, I…'

'Shush.' She started on the second sock, her touch wonderfully cool on his wool-patterned flesh. Tossing the sock aside, she caressed the twitching muscles of his calf, and he bit his lip to stifle a moan. Her fingers moved down his leg in graceful, maddening swirls, leaving trails of fire and ice, but when her nails danced across the soles of his feet like tiny lightning strikes the stark realisation of her intentions hit him like a steam train. She couldn't! She wouldn't! Shit! The involuntary twitch of his feet kindled a devilish light in her eyes and, with precise movements, she drew the long ostrich feather from her hat and ran it across her smirking lips before holding it up for him to examine. The stark white canvas framed the fearsome object that bobbed with dire potential. Oh Jesus. He drew his feet in, but she eased herself into a sitting position and heaved on his water-weak legs - encouraging him with sharp jabs of her painted nails - until one foot was trapped beneath the warm silk of her bottom and the other was pinned on her lap, toes wriggling and sole open to her whims. The rope sawed deep into his flesh as he bucked and strained, but her mischievous grin - and the soft shake of her head - told him she was not to be swayed. The feather dipped toward his foot and he curled his toes in futile defence.

'Oh no! Please! Mandy! No! No!'

*

Patrolling the path to the woods with Ken and the remaining sailors, Barry's teeth were set on edge by the sudden scream that shivered the trees. Christ! What the fuck were they doing up there in the pirate camp? With Kev there, anything and probably everything - watching *Deliverance* the other night had been a mistake.

'What on earth are they doing to the poor boy?' Jane peered up through the trees to where the white shrouds of the camp screened untold horrors.

'Sounds like Kev's got hold of him!' said Mike with a smirk.

'Savages! They're savages!'

'It's only a laugh, Jane.'

Another scream sounded, rising to a tortured crescendo before trailing off. Barry gripped his musket a little tighter. What if Mandy was being forced to witness something unseemly? It was probably no more than over-enthusiastic play-acting, but there did seem to be a note of genuine despair in those pitiful howls - and he had heard rumours about these pirate types...

Jane winced at yet another despairing shriek. 'Does that sound like a laugh to you? The poor lad - I'm going up there to put a stop to this!'

It did sound as if someone was maybe taking things a little too far. It may not have been his gig, but Barry was still regimental CO and that was one of his boys in trouble up there. 'Not by yourself, you're not. Come on - we don't leave our men behind!'

The tattooed muscle-man - who had introduced himself as Chase once he'd finished taking pictures - had his mammoth arms slung around Julian and Keith, his head nestled between theirs as he massaged their shoulders. His girlfriend - the equally impressive Jade - was fondling the lace on Julian's collar.

'So, what you lads up to later?' asked Chase.

The bulging Speedos were pressed against Keith's hip with far too much familiarity. Oh God. The photos had been bad enough, but videos would no doubt be next, and Chase would more than likely be a very hands-on director. Luckily, help was on its way - Barry and Ken with the sailors in tow, though the thunderous expression on Jane's face told Keith that Chase wouldn't be the only hard time he'd face today. Still, explanations could wait. He was saved!

'Oh, thank God.' He ducked out of Chase's iron grip. 'What is it, chaps?'

Barry slammed to attention. 'Permission to lead a rescue party, sir.'

'For who?' Julian, too, extricated himself from Chase's clutches.

'Seaman Bowers, sir.'

'Seaman?' said Julian querulously, ignoring Mike and Nick's sniggers.

'You wish me to risk men for your misplaced seaman?'

Barry kept his face straight. Just. 'Yes, sir.'

'He could be a fearful mess by now, Reynolds,' said Keith, a fecund field of double entendre ripening before him. 'Splattered all over the place.'

Jade smirked, her grin widening as she looked Ken up and down. Ken stared at his feet before flicking a glance to Chase. After a brief inspection, Chase gave him a nod and a wink. Ken stepped behind Barry.

'That's a risk I'm willing to take, sir. It will be touch and go, but I think we're up to it.'

'Stop talking and do something!' snapped Jane above the bubbling mirth. 'We need to get him back - he's not used to this sort of thing!'

Barry nodded in solemn agreement, though his face threatened to burst at any second. 'You can hear him screaming, sir! Bad for morale, sir.'

'Very well.' Keith sidled further away from Jade, who still flashed meaningful glances at him. 'You have a plan?'

'Yes, sir. I thought we'd sneak around the back, hit 'em in the rear, and extract our seaman.'

Mike and Nick had to walk away.

'It's off script, though!' Ken popped out from behind Barry, saw Chase was still eyeing him like a foot fetishist regarding a pedicure, and popped back.

'They said we can freestyle!' Julian reminded him. 'Go for it, chaps. Bring our boy safe home!'

'Sir! We'll leave the pikes here, just in case they try anything while we're gone - I'll take the muskets! Redcoats!' Barry unslung his musket and snapped the flint back to half-cock. 'Fall in!'

As Barry led the rescue party toward the woods, Keith and Julian took their chance and made their escape from the bodies beautiful. Keith made only a couple of yards before he was collared by Jane.

'Oh no you don't! You've got some explaining to do!'

Up at the camp, the pirates were at their ease - drinking, snoozing, playing cards or filling the air with salty sea-chatter. All of them, whatever they were doing, were studiously ignoring the billowing awning and the muffled noises from within. All, that is, apart from Kev and Bess, who greeted each fresh squeak, sigh or gasp with a knowing smile. Jim, face knotted in confusion, threw down the length of wood he was whittling and took a step toward the awning, whirling as musket fire erupted from the trees.

'What the...'

Barry led the rescue party out of the trees, sword in hand. Most of the pirates had been shocked into instant flight by the sudden volley, though some remained to fight and Barry crossed swords with Jim. 'Where is he?'

'In the tent! In the tent! But...'

'Ollie! Go get him!' Barry drove Jim back with a series of savage blows. 'Die!'

Jim fell to the ground as Barry's blade rapped his thigh and sawed up across his belly. Ollie raced through the chaos to rip aside the flap of the awning. A familiar figure scrambled out, fleeing in a swirl of skirts, but Barry was forced to defend himself from two attackers and by the time he'd dispatched them, she had gone and Ollie was helping a hobbling Danny out from the awning, the boy holding up his unfastened britches.

'My God! What have they done?'

'They –' Ollie paused for dramatic effect '– they took his shoes off!'

'The fiends! Right, we're off! Ray! Terry! Covering fire!'

Ray and Terry disengaged from the melee, loading as they ran back to the trees. The rest of the redcoats fell back – all except Ken who was racing around the camp in a whirlwind of steel, dispatching multiple opponents like a latter-day Errol Flynn.

'Desert boots? Desert boots? Take that! Hah! And that's for your black shirt! Are they gardening gloves? They are! They are! And those trousers are late 19th century!'

'Kenneth!' hollered Barry. 'We are leaving!'

'Not yet! Not yet!'

Barry took a hold of Ken's shoulder and hauled him away as if he was a kid being dragged from the park. Reaching the trees as Ray and Terry's covering shots snapped over him, he released Ken and set off down the path after the others. Great bloody laugh! 'Looks like we got you just in the nick of time, Danny!'

Danny, fumbling to fasten his trousers as he ran, sounded less than appreciative. 'Yeah, thanks. Thanks a lot. Really. Thanks.'

'Don't sound too grateful, will you?' said Ollie.

'No, I mean it, really. Thank you. Thank you very much.'

Tabitha rubbed at Danny's face. 'Is that lipstick?'

A sudden burst of triumphant yelling drowned out Danny's stammering explanation – and prevented Barry from having to confront the unwelcome suspicion that was trying to burrow out of his brain. He pulled up at the edge of the woods, raising his hand. 'Halt!'

'What is it?' asked Ken.

A knot of struggling figures swarmed around the HQ awning. Sneaky bastards! 'They've circled around us – the camp is under attack!'

Horribly outnumbered, the scant forces of law and order were nevertheless putting up one hell of a fight. Swords in hand, Keith, Julian and Steve held the mob at bay, supported by the sailors' boarding pikes. Numbers would soon sway the issue though, an idea that had apparently already occurred to Jane.

'Bugger this! Hold up, shipmates! I'm changing sides!'

To a cheer from the pirates, she turned and thrust her pike at Keith's crotch. *Whoa!* His blade rapped the wooden shaft in a frantic parry that only just saved him. 'Sink me! You traitorous baggage!'

'Me?' Jane thrust again. Again, Keith swept the pike aside with his rapier. '"Coinage in the cleavage"?'

'Just getting into character, dear!'

'Yes? Well, so am I! Take that!'

This time her thrust hit home, a glancing blow that set his testicles swinging like a Newton's Cradle - on karmic reflection he probably deserved it, but that did little to lessen the nauseous billow. 'Oh Jesus!' A ball of flaming ice expanded from his groin to lodge in his guts, though the bark of muskets from the trees stopped him from sinking to the ground to curl into the ball he craved. 'Now you're for it, jezebel! I'll have you taken and stripped!'

Jane blew him a kiss as she fled. 'Promises, promises!'

The balance tipped by the timely arrival of Barry's party, the sea-dogs fled back to the woods in ones and twos until only Kev was left, pinned between Mike and Nick. Sheathing his sword, Keith curled his lip with haughty contempt and craned forward to inspect the grovelling prisoner, stomach still rolling. 'Lud, what a frightful creature!'

'Pirate, sir!' Mike knuckled his brow.

'Then he must be tried!' Julian's voice was colder than a winter graveyard.

Court was in session and their lordships - suitably shaded beneath the awning and with glasses of restorative port at their elbows - were in the chair. Redcoats moved through the watching crowd, selecting for trial those who had caught their lordships' eye. Several had received summary justice already - generally a thinly veiled innuendo coupled with the vague promise of eye-watering punishment - and Keith stifled a yawn. Time to end it before the public got as bored as he was. The next victim was coaxed forward - a redhead in hotpants and crop-top. Maybe they could fit another couple in - it was all to entertain the punters, after all. Thank God Jane was off skulking with the pirates - his jewels had taken enough punishment for one day.

'Gad, woman! I would sue your tailor! Where is the rest of your outfit? Fined for being improperly dressed! A week's hard labour!'

Next up was a woman of, to put it kindly, middling years.

'And what is your crime, crone?' enquired Julian.

'Crone?' She scowled.

'Witchcraft, I'll be bound!' Keith steepled his fingers and touched them to his lips. She'd seen better days, that was for sure, her shrewish features pinched and bitter.

'Is this true, madam?' Julian asked. 'Do you be a witch?'

'Yes, she is!' piped up a brave soul from the crowd.

'Just you wait, Tom!' snarled old Mother Shipton.

'You, sir!' Keith pointed at the offending wit - from the brow-beaten, eroded features, it had to be her husband. 'Silence in court! Fined for having an offensive wife! Now, begone, madam. I tire of you.' He waved the "crone" away. 'Next!' *Oh shit.* Terry had Chase and Jade lined up. Far too dangerous. His faked yawn developed into the genuine article. 'I grow weary! Only one more case will we hear today. Bring forward the pirate!'

Nick and Mike dragged Kev forward and threw him to the floor. Julian peered at him as if he'd just been scraped from the sole of his boot.

'Anything to say?'

Kev wrung his hands. 'Well, your honour, I...'

'Good, excellent.' Keith clapped his hands together like a gunshot. 'No defence offered.'

'But I...'

'Farage!' hollered Julian.

Steve scuttled forward with a pair of black flannels - bought not half an hour before from a nearby supermarket. With great ceremony, he arranged them on the heads of the two judges. Keith turned a suitably solemn gaze on Kev.

'There is only one penalty for piracy and this court has no hesitation in handing it down. You will be hung by the neck until the body be dead, dead, dead!'

'And may God have mercy on your soul!' intoned Julian.

'No! Mercy! I beg you!'

Keith was deaf to Kev's pleas. 'String the fellow up!'

Mike and Nick hauled Kev out into the main arena, Terry following with a length of rope in his hands. The bare arena brought to the fore a pressing issue which he really should have raised earlier.

'Where are we doing this?'

'Should have thought of that.' Mike pointed to the far corner of the grounds. 'Over there?'

They'd never get away with that! It was appalling. 'We can't!'

'We'll have to!' said Nick. With Mike, he dragged the screaming, struggling Kev over to the children's playground. Terry had little choice but to follow, fashioning a noose as he went.

'Make sure you get the harness connected properly, Tel.' Stood beneath the A-frame of the playground swings, Kev dipped forward so Terry could slip the noose over his head.

'Don't worry, I've got it.' The location still didn't sit well, but he had more important matters to worry about as he snapped the safety wire onto Kev's hidden harness. 'There you go. Ready?'

Kev bounced on his toes like a boxer about to go into the ring. 'Do it!'

'Make the dog dance!' drawled Julian.

Mike and Nick hauled on the rope, yanking Kev into the air with a hempen hiss. A deathly hush fell over the crowd, but Kev played it for all he was worth, choking and writhing as he twisted on the rope. The stunned faces hinted that maybe this was a touch too much, but nothing could deny Kev his moment. Finally, after a full minute of gruesome death throes, he gave a final kick, poked his tongue out, and went limp.

Keith cast a gaze over the awed crowd. 'And that is what happens to pirates around here!'

Mike and Nick tied off the rope before heading back to the camp with their comrades. The crowd dispersed, leaving just a couple of small kids looking up at the gently rotating "corpse". One reached out a tentative hand and gave Kev's legs a shove, the pair of them scurrying off when there was no reaction. After a moment or two, Kev dropped his death face.

'Well done, lads.' He cocked an eye open. 'Lads?'

The light had taken on the melancholic tones of late afternoon. The public had gone home, evening meals were being cooked, the first beers were being opened - and Kev was still hanging.

'This isn't funny anymore!'

While he was all for punishment, he usually preferred it in company - abandonment wasn't one of his things. Still, the view out over the sea was impressive from up here and the swinging motion was gently soothing.

'Magnificent!' The sultry tones drew his gaze down. Bess peered up at him, superb in her pirate outfit. 'Want me to let you down?'

'Yes, please... mistress.'

'One condition, though.' She ran a finger along her full lips.

Anything. Anything for his goddess. 'Mistress?'

'You'll find out when we get back to my hotel room!'

Oh God, could this be real? 'Yes, mistress!'

*

158

A sinuous sea-mist hung like silver lace over the froth of foam on the shoreline. Danny sat throwing pebbles into the ocean as if hurling away his troubles, though the ripples caused by each weighty plop seemed directly tied to the expanding waves of frustration. If the rescue party had only waited another five minutes! It had been unbearable to start with (his wrists still bore the marks of the ropes) but the abandoned decadence of Mandy's teasing had left him both dreading and craving the next touch. There was no future there (there may be someone out there who could tame her, but it was not him, and in the meantime, she'd just ride the rollercoaster and who could blame her?) but wouldn't even a few hours of fleshy indulgence be preferable to the perma-frosted limbo of the pseudo-relationship he shared with Tabitha? He'd managed to convince her earlier that the lipstick smudges had all been part of the humiliation he'd suffered at the hands of the pirates, but that hadn't stopped her heading off to the local chippy with her parents, leaving him to his own devices. Shrieks and laughter ebbed and flowed in the darkness and a fire blazed further along the beach, but he was in no mood to join the party. His fingers closed around another pebble and he hurled it into the sea.

'Hey!' came an indignant - and familiar - voice. 'Watch it!'

'Mandy?' A dark shape bobbed offshore like a buoy. 'Sorry.'

'Is that you, Danny?'

'Yeah. What are you doing?'

'Baking a cake! What do you think I'm doing? Swimming, you idiot! The water's not too bad - coming in?'

'I haven't got anything to wear.'

'Neither have I! Come on!'

The water was like a black mirror, merging seamlessly with the night and stretching away forever. Anything could be lurking out in the depths, but the lure of Mandy more than outweighed the thoughts of teeth and tentacles - or Tabitha. He stripped off, the cool night air whispering with coy slyness against his naked flesh. The sense of liberation as he hopped down to the water - gritting his teeth against the harsh nubs of pebbles probing the soles of his feet - was overwhelming. It was as if he'd cast his quandaries aside with his clothes, stripping himself back down to a level where he was free to think unhindered - at least until he splashed into the sea.

'Jesus!' It was like sticking his feet into a bowl of ice. 'I thought you said it was okay?'

'It is when you get your shoulders under!' Mandy splashed him, the water stinging like hail.

'Oi!' He couldn't stand here shivering - it was either retreat or take the plunge. Steeling himself, he took a deep breath and hurled himself full-length forward, crashing down as if the water were a sheet of frosted glass. 'Bloody Hell!' His breath hung suspended, and he thrashed his numbed limbs to keep himself afloat. Water blurred his eyes and guttered in his nose and throat, tasting of salt, but he threw his arms forward in more confident strokes to pump the blood through his faltering body. He circled Mandy like a clumsy shark and then, racing heart still splintered with shards of ice, rose from the water to stand before her with the water slapping at his buttocks.

She was naked, as promised, and her teeth glittered in the moonlight as she glanced down. 'The cold doesn't seem to be affecting you that much!' He put his hands over his crotch, but Mandy pulled them away, her bare breast pressing against his arm. 'A bit late to be shy! Anyway, we've got some unfinished business from this afternoon.'

Releasing his wrist, she wrapped an arm around him and pulled him into an embrace, her free hand dropping down to caress warmth into his water-numbed genitals. Her damp skin was warm despite the chill, and unable to resist, he locked his mouth on hers and searched for her tongue. After a minute of frenzied tongue-wrestling, she broke the kiss to trail her lips down his shivering body, but a savage sledgehammer of guilt made him pull back.

'Sorry.'

'What's up?' She straightened, still holding his most sensitive region, her fingers moving in feathery little strokes.

'Nothing, I…'

'It's Tab, isn't it?'

He squirmed in her tightening grip, knowing it was true, knowing he was too weak to relinquish the meaningless hold on something he had wasted his whole life pursuing. 'Yeah, I suppose. I mean, I've been chasing her for all these years and now that we've actually got somewhere…'

'Have you?' She gave a sensuous little tug that very nearly deposited a swarm of his own little swimmers into a frantic race across the bay. 'Got anywhere?'

'Well, we're going out now. Oh Jesus!' How much longer could he hold on? 'Sort of.'

'And that's enough, is it? Sort of going out?'

'I don't know,' he moaned, the supple finger-work less of a betrayal than the candid confessions she was drawing from him. 'She's driving me mental! Half the time it's like we're a couple, other times she acts as if I'm not there! When we are together though…'

'Poor you!' With a last regretful squeeze, Mandy released him, the consoling peck on his cheek scant compensation for what had been building. 'You need to do what you think is right for you. You can dangle at her skirts for the rest of your life while she strings you along, if that's what you want, but if that means passing up on a sure thing... I'm here, now, and I need warming up. You know where I am if you change your mind.' Sleek as an otter, she whirled and plunged beneath the water, torpedoing back toward the party.

***

Kev eased the door of the hotel room shut and crept out into the corridor. Last night had fulfilled several long-standing fantasies - and sown the seeds of many more. His mistress was as inventive as she was cruel - and she also needed her sleep, which was why he was creeping from her chamber while the first fat fingers of morning light poked through the curtains. He had to be on site in less than half an hour - they were stringing him up as a grand opening today. Safety harness? Check - all in place, though with a new addition. Running a shaky hand around the leather collar his mistress had fastened around his neck as a sign of his devoted servitude, he set off down the corridor with a sailor's gait that had nothing to do with getting into character, wincing as the rough britches further scourged his tender backside.

The public toilets built into the remains of the fort weren't much, but to a man used to the blue perils of portaloos, they were an oasis - especially to one with such an urgent press in his guts. Nodding to Clogger, who had just exited the one viable cubicle, Keith took his place, wrinkling his nose at the unlovely aroma - cat food seemed to be a staple of Clogger's diet. Still, he wouldn't be here for long. He settled down, hitched up the skirts of his coat, and unleashed the hellish by-product of two days' greasy food. Feeling almost human again, he rolled up his sleeves and took the tail of his coat in his teeth while he wiped. Once he'd buttoned himself back up, he gave the chain its requisite two quick yanks and one slow pull, setting off the now-familiar groaning and clanking from behind the walls. The water swirled with a tremendous gurgling and churning but showed no sign of receding. Instead, it started to rise, a horrific muddy whirlpool that slopped at the rim of the bowl, dragging up sopping toilet paper and distressing brown floaters from the depths of the pipes.

'Jesus! No! Good God almighty!' Fumbling for the lock, Keith managed to escape the cubicle, but the brown torrent chased him across the floor. The stench of it burned like mustard gas, stripping the hairs from his nose and throat. Breathing through his mouth - not all that keen to breathe at all - he reached the sink where a bare-chested Jim was going through his morning ablutions, oblivious to the agricultural reek. Keith grasped the taps, head down. It wasn't his fault, couldn't have been - he was a clean-break man, a two-time wiper. Whatever had risen from the depths had been someone else's foul work.

Jim spat a wad of toothpaste into the sink with a companionable nod. 'Now you see why we call him Clogger.'

Terry prodded Kev with his musket-butt, shepherding him toward a rickety set of gallows that had been erected overnight in the main arena. The crowds were currently sparse, but more people were filtering in by the minute.

'Good night?'

'A gentleman never tells!' smirked Kev.

'And since when have you been a gentleman? How was she?'

'Strict. Very!'

Kev shuffled along as if he had a bad case of piles. No accounting for taste, though that Bess was one hell of a looker. 'Each to his own! Surprised she let you go. Everything sorted? You was a bit rushed when you eventually turned up.'

'Yeah, all in order. Is that safe?'

Terry ran a professional eye over the scaffolding. It looked sturdy enough where it counted. 'Jim reckons so, and he was up half the night making it! Had a few complaints after yesterday! Ready?' Terry looped the rope over Kev's head.

'Let's do it.'

'It's alright for you, hanging about all day while we do all the work!' Terry tightened the rope, ran a hand around Kev's sweaty collar to locate the safety harness, and clipped on the cable that would prevent him from being slowly choked to death.

'I need the rest!'

Terry thought in pictures, which was sometimes advantageous. Not now. Scouring away the unlovely images that stained his imagination, he raised a hand to Julian. 'Ready, sir!'

'Let's have him up!'

The gallows creaked alarmingly as Mike and Nick hauled on the rope, but Kev was yanked up without a hitch. As yesterday, he choked and gasped, though the bulging eyes were a new addition.

'He's really going for it today,' Mike observed.

'Yeah!' Nick cocked a thumb to the spinning figure. 'Go on, son!'

'Must be because of that Bess.'

'Well, I would - wouldn't you?'

'Too right! Good thing she likes her men well-hung!' Above them, Kev's breathing rattled and gurgled.

'He's drawing it out, isn't he?' Julian frowned at the grisly antics.

By now, Kev had turned crimson, his face contorted like a gargoyle. Not all the screams from the crowd were kids. Even before Kev went suddenly limp, Terry knew that something had gone wrong. 'Shit! Get him down! Get him down!'

Bess clambered out of her Porsche, smoothing down her captain's coat and screwing her eyes up against the morning sun. It had been a strenuous night and she'd never met anyone with quite the threshold that Kev possessed. Perhaps he could become a repeat offender - it would be a rewarding challenge to fully explore the boundaries of his endurance once he was secured in her fully equipped chambers. Talking of which, there was the gaunt framework of Jim's new gallows over on the festival grounds. Kev should be strung up by now, but the gallows were empty and the crowd around them was too quiet - and was that a siren in the distance? She was across the tarmac in a matter of seconds, pushing her way through the hushed throng around the scaffold. There he was, stretched out on the ground with his friends around him. His face was grey, and he wasn't moving.

'Is he...'

Terry had tears in his eyes. 'He's going to be okay. The harness was faulty - I should have checked!'

'Don't blame yourself.' The collar that she'd locked around Kev's neck last night lay broken on the ground - Terry must have mistakenly hitched the safety rope to that. Shit. She should have thought of that. They'd got him down in time, though, thank God. He would be okay, of course he would, but why was he so still? And... stiff? 'Goodness!'

Terry stood up, a watery grin on his face. 'Yeah, I can see why they used to find all those dead politicians hanging from their bannisters in stockings and suspenders! Someone cover that up!'

Solemnly, Mike placed his tricorne over Kev's crotch. It slowly rotated, like a compass seeking north.

Kev opened a bloodshot eye. 'How did I look?' he croaked.

'Bloody horrible!' Terry told him.

'Brilliant!'

With pyrotechnics adding to the smoke and noise of the muskets, the government forces were making their last stand against the hordes of pirates swarming over the main arena. Ollie and Terry sniped from behind a barricade of barrels, Ray and Annie playing dead at their feet. Smoke curling from his musket barrel, Ollie reached into his cartridge box.

'How many left?' Terry asked.

In reply, Ollie slung his musket and drew his sword. 'That was the last one.' A gaggle of Bess's pirates let off a ragged splatter of shots from the edge of the arena. 'Well, I know where I'm going - let's hope I get taken alive!'

'You won't last long if you do!' Barry had just fallen back on their position, Ken in tow.

'We'll see!' Vaulting the barrels, Ollie charged across the smoke-strewn field and vanished among the welcoming arms of his captors.

Terry groped for a fresh cartridge. Nope, none left. Twenty odd shots in a frenetic fifteen minutes! No wonder the barrel was singeing his fingers at every touch. 'I'm out, Baz. Good luck, mate.' On the next incoming shot, he clasped his chest and fell across Annie.

Barry's options were limited. Most of the redcoats were down, Mike and Nick had just willingly surrendered to Bess's crew, and their lordships were besieged in their awning.

'Well, it's been fun, I suppose.' Grinning over the barrel of his musket, Ken squeezed off a shot. 'Last one.'

'I'm out, too. There's not many of us left.'

'Shall we surrender?' Ken's expression showed what he thought of such a notion.

'To that rabble? Never!' Barry drew his sword. 'After you.'

Humming to get a note, Ken started to sing in a surprisingly on-key tenor. 'Men of Harlech...'

In the midst of the melee, Danny was trying to fight his way through to the palisade on the far side of the field where Tabitha lay hidden. Slapping the flat of his sword across his opponent's bicep, he caught a flicker of movement in his periphery and whirled to parry a wild blow. Over the clashing blades, he locked eyes with his new adversary. Mandy. He lowered his sword.

'Surrender?' she suggested sweetly.

'After last time?' Tempting, but he couldn't so easily turn his back on Tabitha, not after the years he'd invested in her. 'No way!'

She pouted her disappointment, but as Danny raised his sword again, Clogger came barrelling in like a branch of Greggs and bundled him to the ground.

'Alright, alright.' Squeezing his head from beneath Clogger's armpit, he gagged on the fusty odour of unwashed cloth. 'I'm dead!'

*

Though Danny had been taken down by Clogger, Mandy still stood over him, as if claiming him for her own. Tabitha bit down on her nail - Danny had denied anything had happened during his incarceration in the pirate camp but, while he would never willingly betray her, Mandy was a different matter. It would make matters so much easier if something could be proved, but the damage to her pride could prove irreparable. Sod it. Drawing her sword, she sprinted out of cover. Mandy turned just in time to parry Tabitha's wild swing, launching a blistering counter-attack when she saw who her opponent was. Tabitha was forced onto the back foot by Mandy's robust blows, but her quicksilver ripostes evened out the contest.

After a minute of frenzied combat, both girls were breathless, though Mandy waved back Clogger who was itching to come to her aid. 'We'll call it a draw, shall we?' she panted.

By now, Tabitha could hardly lift her sword. Mandy's strength would tell pretty soon. 'Okay.'

'Looks like you're my prisoner then!'

'Over my dead body!' Reversing her sword, Tabitha thrust it under her armpit and collapsed across Danny.

Beneath the awning, only Julian, Keith and Steve were left. It looked pretty hopeless and Keith put up his sword. Jim swaggered out from the surrounding mob.

'Your swords.'

Keith handed over his sword. 'You ain't a gentleman - a gentleman would allow us to keep our weapons!'

'No, I ain't a gentleman. None of us are. We're pirates!' There was a ragged cheer. 'And you won't need weapons where you're going - straight to Davy Jones!'

'You can't mean to kill us?' For a brief second, the wisdom of placing his fate in the hands of Jim and his crew seemed questionable. Despite it all being scripted - and for all the gentle contempt he held for the blank-firing pirates and their raggedy ways - they were suddenly as authentic a horde of merciless sea-dogs as a luckless government agent could ever have the misfortune to run into. They did all know it was make-believe, didn't they?

'What else would we do with you?'

Julian, having surrendered his sword, lay a comforting hand on Keith's shoulder. 'Never mind, my dear. Ruffian, we are gentlemen. We have a man to do everything for us! Farage!'

'Yes, my lord.' Steve dropped to his knees, hands behind his head. 'I will be only too happy to die in your place.'

'We don't want your lickspittle! We want you! Get 'em, lads!'

Rough hands seized Keith, stripping off his coat, hat, wig and boots. He helped as much as he could - the rig was too expensive to get torn, and some of the pirates (not the ones he would have preferred) were a little too free with their hands. Down to shirts and britches, he and Julian were herded toward the sea wall through an avenue of jeering public - he needed to get *The Wicker Man* out of his head and searched the seething mob for the reassurance of a recognisable face. Chase and Jade were there, pointing and laughing with the rest - it would have been a kinder fate if he'd accepted their invitation yesterday, though what Jane would have done to him afterwards didn't bear thinking about. Chase's phone flashed, then a clod of dirt struck Keith above the temple, thrown by the grinning lad who had left Julian so mortified yesterday.

'Lip read this, you little sod!' It looked a long way down from the top of the wall, and the water lapped darkly against the crumbling stonework. Jim had assured them there were no rocks.

'Right! Have them in!'

Jane gave Keith a particularly vigorous prod in the backside with her boarding pike, and his hips jerked forward. He fought for balance and Julian took his hand. The hungry sea churned beneath them. At least it was warm. Locking eyes, they each took a final deep breath and stepped off the wall into thin air.

'Oh shiiiiiiiii…'

7 A BLAST FROM THE PAST

The glitzy central plaza of the shopping centre was usually reserved for Christmas grottos, car shows or other spectacular displays. Today, the content was more modest - half a dozen large tables arranged beneath the soaring ceiling, each one a miniature landscape across which earnest-looking men of middle years moved tiny armies. Around the edge of the plaza, stalls were selling everything the discerning wargamer needed, from trees and bushes through to fresh troops and scale-model vehicles and buildings - there was even an impressive foot-long pirate ship on display.

A giant poster of Barry Reynolds - face set and finger pointing in a Kitcheneresque manner - dominated one corner of the plaza. Ranked display boards held photographs of Harding's in action, and flyers were being handed out by the knot of bluecoats around the recruiting stand. Colour in hand, Trevor stood to one side, oblivious to the hordes of shoppers filing past.

'He seemed pretty keen.' The potential recruit who had just taken Ken's flyer was waddling away toward the nearest burger stand, stopping every few feet to put his hands on his knees and clear his lungs with a horribly moist rattle.

'Yes, just what we need - another heart attack on legs.' Barry had had higher hopes for today - they were catnip for the wargaming types, but the demographic did not exactly lend itself to the rigours of battle. 'I suppose he'll add a bit of weight to the pike block - if he survives the march to the battlefield.'

'He was more interested in shot.'

'Typical!' It generally took a couple of seasons to get someone through their musket test. 'Well, that's fine for the future, but it's not going to do us any good for four weeks' time, is it? I want a big block for Felcham! How many names have we got from today so far?'

Ken consulted his notebook. 'Er, five.'

'And how many were interested in pike?'

'Er, none.'

'And how many were under fifty?'

'Er, one.'

'Oh yes. Him.' God, those eyes would give him nightmares for weeks. 'Make sure you lose his number.'

Keith sheathed the sword he'd been showing to a couple of youngsters. 'Let's face it, Barry, it's a dying hobby - like most things that involve a bit of effort and a whiff of fresh air! I mean, what can we offer youngsters to tear them away from their computers and whatnot?'

'Danny joined, didn't he?' There was something wrong with a modern generation who preferred to be cooped up indoors pretending to kill people on a screen rather than out in the open air pretending to kill actual people.

'Yes - after years of badgering, and he only joined because he wanted to get his hands on my daughter!'

'Dad!' wailed Tabitha. Danny turned puce and looked at his feet.

'That's the best we can hope for.' Keith was up on his soapbox now. 'Just dribs and drabs through friends and families, maybe one or two through gigs like this. It'll never be what it was - people don't have time anymore! Well, they say they don't - if they took a step back, turned off their phones and laptops and stopped watching all the dross they pump through the five hundred channels they get on telly these days, then maybe they'd realise just how much time they actually waste!'

'Okay, dear.' Jane patted her husband's hand.

Keith was probably right, though it was a grim truth to confront on a Saturday morning - especially with other issues peering over the parapet. 'And where's Julian? He was meant to be here.'

It was Jane who answered. 'Yes. It's not like him to just not show up. Mind you, he's been a bit off all season.'

'He was fine the other week at the pirate gig,' said Keith. 'Really came out of himself - like the old Julian again.'

Jane slapped him across the shoulders. 'Yes, you both came out of yourselves there - a bit too much! What's up with him? Penny?'

'I think so.' Keith perched on the edge of the table, knocking over Ken's carefully stacked flyers. 'They've not been getting on for a while, and he's been hooning it around with girls young enough to be his daughter!'

Jane scowled. 'Huh. Typical mid-life crisis. I expected better from him.'

'No, I don't think it's that simple. On the surface, yes, but there's more to it, I'm sure. I've tried talking to him, but he's hard to pin down. Why don't you give Penny a ring?'

Jane snorted, as if to say she'd already done all she could and why the hell did her husband expect any different? 'I've tried - she either doesn't pick up or says she's too busy to talk.'

Like city walls bombarded by Cromwell's mighty siege guns, Barry's frayed nerves took another hit. He didn't need this. Not now. Did he have to deal with everything, up to and including his subordinates' personal lives? Thank God his business - a modest commercial plumbing firm - pretty much ran itself. 'Well, someone needs to sort him! I need him firing on all cylinders for Felcham!'

'For God's sake, Barry!' Jane hammered a clenched fist against the table, making Ken jump. 'There are more important things in life than the August Bank Holiday muster!' Blasphemy! Ken goggled at her and the fire dropped from her voice. 'No, I suppose there's not for you two, is there? Okay, I'll try again with Penny.'

'And I'll see what I can do with Julian,' volunteered Keith. 'I don't want to press too hard, though. He's pretty brittle at the moment - we don't want him buggering off altogether, do we?'

Find a new pike commander less than a month before the biggest gig of the year? 'No, we don't.' Right. Back to business. 'Danny! Tabitha! Stop lurking around the table and go out and pull some people in!'

Danny's hob-nailed boots clicked far too loudly on the plaza's stark white tiles - not that he needed anything else to draw attention to himself. In full kit, with pike in hand, he stood out among the Saturday shoppers like a... like a bloke dressed in armour and carrying a pike trying to blend in with a crowd of Saturday shoppers. Where's Wally? There he is, skulking past John Lewis. God, what if one of his mates saw him?

'I feel a right prat!'

'Why?' To be fair, it was Tabitha who garnered the most interest, attracting appreciative glances from male shoppers trailing behind wives and girlfriends. She placed a hand on her hip and gave a dazzling smile as a phone flashed. 'You've done this for nearly a whole season now - you're just about a pro!'

He couldn't deny it - he'd had a hell of a good time through the summer. 'Yeah. I mean, I'm quite enjoying it all if I'm honest - didn't think I would, but it's a laugh. But we stick out a bit here, don't we?'

Photo opportunity done, Tabitha nodded with a surprising amount of empathy. 'I know what you mean.'

'Look at those two melts!' A rowdy mob of teenagers - probably a couple of years younger than Danny - had grown bored of baiting the studious gamers poring over a 28mm version of the Battle of Blenheim who stoically refused to bite. A handful of sweets rattled against Danny's armour. Little shits! Their faces were frighteningly adult, but he couldn't let them get away with that, not in front of Tabitha.

'Oi! Sod off!' His tentative defiance was greeted with a chorus of jeers and whistles.

'Just ignore them, Danny.' From the way Tabitha flushed at some of the more graphic comments directed toward her, she was finding it hard to follow her own advice. Maybe he should have done, though, as the kids looked ready to square off. Only the appearance of a couple of security guards saved him from having to defend Tabitha's honour - or test his breastplate against a knife.

'Just looking out for my girl.' Thank God for that - the kids were sloping off in a belligerent little huddle.

'Ah.' Tabitha's hedging tone sent his heart plummeting to the soles of his boots.

'"Ah", what?' It was obvious what was coming - he'd been expecting it every day since they'd started going out. It wasn't going to make it any easier to accept though.

'Well...'

'You're not dumping me, are you?' Of course she was. 'I thought we were good together?'

She shook her head, though she didn't meet his eye. 'No, no, nothing like that. It's just, well, we're both off to uni in a couple of months. It's not fair on either of us to tie the other down, is it? I mean, we're going to be different people come Christmas, aren't we? I think we should just, I don't know, ease off a little bit.'

So she was dumping him in all but name. For fuck's sake - the time he'd wasted on her! 'If we ease off any more, we might as well not be going out at all!'

'Don't be angry! We'll still see each other, but just go with the flow, no pressure? Okay?'

Mandy wiggled past through the throng of shoppers, a lad on her arm. What could have been. Bollocks. 'Don't have a choice, do I?'

'Here you go, dad.' Mandy handed Barry a newspaper.

'Thanks.' Passing the paper to Ken, Barry gave Mandy's latest beau what he hoped was a stern, paternally protective gaze. 'Are you going to join us for Little Felcham, Adam?'

'Dad, this is Alex, remember?'

'Oh yes, sorry.' There had been an Adam though, hadn't there? 'Anyway, is he coming?'

'Yeah, yeah, I'll give it a go. I'll give anything a go!' Alex squeezed Mandy's waist, prompting a giggle. Barry turned the temperature of his gaze down a notch or two. Still, the lad was tall, well-built, and probably not too bright. Ideal fodder for the pike block - he had to be indulged.

'Right, we're going.' Mandy wriggled free of Alex's clutches. 'More shopping. Come on, Alex.' She hauled him away. '"Ann Summers" is just down here…'

Perhaps some hints about possessing firearms - or sharp implements - needed to be dropped. Okay, she was no longer his little girl, but that didn't mean he had to like it. At least the lad wasn't Parliament.

'Here it is!' Ken had been leafing through the paper. 'Another bloody hatchet job by William Sneath! Why do they indulge him? He was even on telly the other week! He's really pushing that petition of his, and it's gaining momentum.'

'Give it here!' Snatching the paper, Barry scanned through the article. It was the usual caustic stuff, but in a national paper? 'Bastard!'

'Language!' Jane wagged a finger. 'We've got customers!'

A pleasant-faced woman of around fifty parked a wheelchair by the display boards. In her day she would have been a rare beauty, and though age had robbed some of the finer contours from her features, she still had a youthful smile and her face and figure were just plump enough to plaster over the cracks. By contrast, Barry had last seen something as desiccated as the wizened occupant of the wheelchair in the Egyptian section of the British Museum, though the eyes were startlingly bright and alert amidst the seams of the pickled-walnut face.

'Fuck me, it's Davros,' muttered Keith in Barry's ear. 'Another one for the pike block!' Jane elbowed her husband in the ribs.

'Well, I suppose we could start an armoured division,' Barry whispered back.

'What's this? What's this?' The old man's voice crackled like dried leaves.

'Poor old bugger,' said Jane *sotto voce*. 'I'll shoot you when you get like that, Keith.'

'Oh, great. Thanks!'

'What? What?' The clear blue eyes flicked from person to person.

'I don't think they're talking to you, grandfather.' The woman's voice was smooth as butter. She had the same eyes as the old man, and thick dark hair tied back in an unflattering ponytail.

'Good morning.' Ken stepped forward. 'We are Colonel…'

'Harding's Regiment of Foot,' snapped the old man. 'I know, I know! Stand with some backbone, man!'

Ken flinched, like a slave shown the lash, but was saved from the ancient's caustic attention when Trevor jerked into life like a reanimated corpse. 'It can't be!'

The old man peered up at the aged ensign. 'Is that young Trevor?'

'Freddie! Freddie Bishop! It's been what, forty years?'

'And the rest!'

Bloody hell! Frederick Bishop. The legendary first CO of Harding's - long before any of their time. Except Trevor. A war hero. A commando. Captured but kept escaping. Something of a historian as well. No one had heard anything of him for years.

'I thought he was dead!' Ken looked ready to drop to his knees, like a shepherd in a school nativity confronted by the tinsel-haloed Gabriel.

'Well, give him a moment,' murmured Keith.

'I may as well be dead!' wheezed Freddie. 'Not often I get to escape from Colditz these days! Lizzie here's a good girl, she takes me out when she can, but more often than not I'm left to dribble and fart with the rest of the crumblies!'

The woman smiled apologetically. 'It's a lovely little home he's in really.'

'Bah! All piss and peppermints!' The wrinkled face creased further. 'I was better treated in the stalags!'

'Yes, grandfather.' She took Ken's proffered hand. 'Elizabeth Bishop.'

'Kenne... Ken. Ken Howard. 2IC of Harding's Regiment.'

'2IC?' snorted Freddie. 'Bloody hell, is this what we've come to? My 2IC was Nobby Fowler - or what was left of him after the Japs had finished! Hard as nails - used to blast out our latrines with H.E! Those were the days! Shit in a hole in the ground, not some fancy plastic cabin!'

'I've got a copy of your book, sir,' said Ken, dewy-eyed.

'So you're the one! Always meant to write another, all about Harding. I had reams of notes somewhere...'

'Really?' Ken snatched the newspaper from Barry and passed it down to Freddie. 'This might interest you, then.'

Elizabeth peered over her grandfather's shoulder. 'It says...'

'I do have some faculties left, girl! Wipe my arse, mop up my piss and spoon in that crap they try to pass off for food at the stalag - that's all I need help with! And yes, I know it's a home and not a prison camp - I haven't lost my marbles yet!' He scanned down the article, giving a wheeze of outrage. 'Sneath! That odious little c...'

'Grandfather!'

'I know all about Mr William Sneath and his blasphemous theories!' For a second, the layers of the years were peeled away from the age-ravaged face, and Barry was stabbed with a momentary pang of sympathy for any Kraut sentry whose last sight in this life had been Freddie Bishop's Fairbairn-Sykes glinting in the moonlight. 'Man was military as well! Bad sort! Saw no action but thinks he knows it all! If I was twenty - no, ten - years younger, I'd show him some action alright! Bullet, blade or bare hands, I've killed with them all!' From the steely cast to his eyes, it was no idle boast - what a bastard time was, to reduce such a man to the wreck in the wheelchair.

'Time to be going, grandfather.' Taking the paper from the palsied hands, Elizabeth kicked the brake off the wheelchair. 'I thought he'd like this. I heard you were here and it took me back all those years to when he used to take me along. Good times.'

Removing his hat, Ken smoothed his hair. 'You must have been very young!'

'Flatterer!' Her smile erased more of the fine lines. 'Well, it was a long time ago, it's all a bit hazy.'

'I remember you!' Trevor sparked into life again. 'Pretty little Lizzie bouncing on her grandfather's knee!'

'That's a turn up,' whispered Barry to Keith. 'He can't usually remember what he's had for breakfast!'

'What?' Freddie's gimlet eyes caused a flicker of absurd panic.

'Allow me to introduce our CO,' said Ken. 'Barry Reynolds.'

'A pleasure - and an honour - to meet you, sir!' Barry removed his hat and touched his fingers to his forehead.

'Ever served? For real?' The ice-drop eyes narrowed, judging, appraising.

'Ah, no, no I haven't.'

'And pray you never do! Pray there's never need for it.' The old head shook. 'How's the regiment doing?'

'Blossoming, sir. We've got a muster in four weeks at Little Felcham itself!'

A wistful look crossed the ancient face. 'Not been to one for years - shut away and forgotten.' Freddie looked straight at Danny, who had just arrived back with Tabitha. 'Don't get old, son, don't ever get old.' He frowned, seeing that Danny was holding Tabitha's hand. 'Are you queer, boy?'

'What? Oh, no, no. She's a girl!'

Freddie leaned forward. 'So she is - and a damn pretty one at that! You're a lucky young scamp!' Tabitha dipped her eyes and coloured prettily. Danny just coloured.

'I'd love to bring him to one of your musters,' Elizabeth said to Barry. 'I'm sure he'd enjoy it. Give him a chance to reminisce.'

That would set the cat among the pigeons as far as Sneath was concerned. One in the eye for Mac. 'Four weeks' time - come along as my guests. It would be a privilege!'

'That would be wonderful! Did you hear that, grandfather?'

'Yes! I'm not deaf!'

Ken cleared his throat. 'Mr Bishop... Freddie? I'd be really interested in taking a look at your notes someday.'

'Buggered if I know where they are!'

'I've got an attic full of his old things,' Elizabeth said coyly, brushing a stray wisp of raven hair back from her forehead. 'You'd be more than welcome to pop round one day and take a look.'

'Really?' Ken scribbled on the back of a flyer. 'My number. Please do give me a call - we can arrange your visit to Little Felcham as well.'

'Yes, I will. Thank you. It's been lovely meeting you, K... you all. You've made grandfather's day. I'll ring you in the week, Ken.' She folded the flyer away into her handbag.

'Looking forward to it. Goodbye.'

'Bye bye.' With a last look at Ken - the faintest blush of colour touching her alabaster skin - Elizabeth wheeled Freddie away.

'Goodbye.' Barry sketched a final salute at the old man, admiring the stately roll of Elizabeth's hips. Not large, not really, just... comfortable. Ken was watching as well, a dreamy look on his face, and cogs began to whir. Surely not? From the looks on the faces of the others, similar gears were grinding there, and Ken turned back to find all eyes on him.

'What?'

Belly stuffed with burger and chips, welcome fresh breeze riffling his tee-shirt, Danny strolled past the huge glass blocks of the shopping centre. It was a pity he had to be back in kit in the next half hour or so - being out of the heavy wool uniform and away from Tabitha (who was lunching with her parents) gave him the space to think. The relationship, so long in the making, was a disappointment. If he was honest, it had never seemed right, almost as if they were just going through the motions. A sham relationship was proving to be more frustrating than no relationship at all. Maybe she was right. Maybe it would fizzle out anyway when they went to uni - Business and Management at Warwick for him, Drama at Exeter for Tabitha. The prospect of leaving home crowded his mind with shadows that the sun sparking off the huge silvered windows did little to dispel and, eyes on the ground, he almost collided with a girl coming the other way.

'Oh, sorry.' He sidestepped just in time, barely avoiding the woman at her side.

'Hi, Danny.'

The soft, barely there Scottish burr was familiar, but though the girl's full lips were parted in a smile of recognition, he could place neither the cheerfully pretty features nor the loose blonde curls.

'Hi.' Floundering, his eyes crawled over the snug denim shorts and black tights that showed off the generous curve of her hips and a pair of handsome rounded thighs. The West Highland terrier at her heels met his gaze and, with a whimper, ducked behind the older woman - so alike in looks apart from the greying hair and a few lines on her open face that it had to be the girl's mother.

'What's up, boy?' She had a thicker Scot's accent, but it still possessed the same melodic lilt as her daughter's.

A second glance at the dog (growling from behind the safety of the woman's sturdy calves) was enough for realisation to batter Danny over the head like a sand-filled sock. Jesus! It couldn't be her, could it? She looked so different! 'Hi,' he said again. 'I hardly recognised you! First time I've seen you in normal clothes - in daylight, at least!'

Without the distorting windows of her glasses, Sophie's blue eyes sparkled. 'I know - must be a bit of a shock!' She gave a little hiss of laughter, setting a delicate pink tongue to her teeth.

'No, not at all.' It was the same girl, it had to be, but what a transformation! Admittedly, two or three days of roughing it in a field would be more than enough to rob the vitality from the golden curls, and the round glasses she usually wore did her few favours, but even so... If he was being hypercritical, he would say that the face was a little too round, there was a little too much flesh blurring the line of her jaw into the angle of her neck, but a natural warmth shone through to illuminate her pale skin and highlight her cheeks with endearing pink patches. He'd flattered himself by dismissing her as some needy geek mooning around after him - she could have her pick of guys, though surely there was no way she was single. 'You're... I mean, you look...'

'It's alright, I'm not fishing for compliments!' He could tell she was pleased with the effect she'd had on him, though. 'I recognised you straight away - you can't mistake those schoolboy good looks! This is Danny, mum. He's in Harding's, but apart from that he's okay! Danny, this is my mum.'

The obvious pleasure with which she introduced him further blackened the way he'd treated her last time they'd met. 'Pleased to meet you, Mrs Macintyre.'

'Likewise, Danny. Well, I need to be getting along. Fairfax seems a bit flighty - can't think what's got into him. Sophie, are you...'

'I'll catch up with you and dad later.'

'Of course.' Mrs Macintyre's warm smile raised the intriguing - if moot - notion that Sophie was single. 'Nice to have met you, Danny. See you again, I hope.'

'Yeah, hope so. Bye.'

'I think she likes you,' said Sophie as her mother was virtually dragged away by Fairfax.

'At least one of your parents does.' Although Macintyre had never spoken to him directly, he still got the impression that the Scotsman actively despised him - for being a Harding if nothing else. 'I've not seen her at any of the, what do you call them, musters?'

'No, she's never really been into it.' She curled a lock of golden hair around her finger. 'Just me and my dad - and Andrew when he's around.'

'Andrew?'

'My brother - he's away quite a bit.'

'Oh, right.' He shuffled his feet, knowing what he had to do. 'Well...'

'I…' Sophie began at the same time. 'Sorry.'

'No, go on.'

'No, you go.'

'Okay. Look - last time we spoke, I was a bit of a shit, wasn't I?'

Her ambrosial features darkened. 'No, you were a hell of a shit!' For a moment, it seemed the mask would drop and she'd lay into him with the venom he deserved, then an impudent smile lit her face. 'Luckily, I'm not one to hold a grudge - not for long, anyway! We all have to lash out sometimes, don't we?'

'Cheers.' The ease of her forgiveness was unsatisfactory and the weight of guilt - shame, almost - needed further purging. 'Look, I'm sorry. Really. I've been a dick, haven't I?' He had as well. She'd offered nothing more than friendship, a friendship that his own arrogance had endangered. 'You've looked out for me since that first muster-thing, haven't you? And that's how I pay you back! Look, how about I get you a coffee to make up for it?' He dismissed the frosty vision of Tabitha. 'I'm not due back for another half an hour.'

'Back? Back where?'

'Back to the recruiting stand. We've got one at some wargames exhibition in there.'

Sophie gave an angry little toss of her head, her nostrils flaring. 'I should have known!'

'Known what?' Had he annoyed her? If so, how?

'My dad - he said he'd come here for the wargames show. I bet he's come to have a sniff around your stand as well. He's getting worse!'

Nothing he'd done then. Good. 'You're local then?'

'Not quite.' She pulled a face. 'Corby. You?'

'Aylesbury.'

'Oh, of course. Near Tabitha. How's that all going anyway?'

'Up and down.' She gave him a look of such sweet sympathy that he was compelled to continue. 'Tell you the truth, it's doing my head in! We're on, we're off, we're taking it easy. Why can't I go for a nice, uncomplicated girl?'

'Like Mandy?'

'I think I've probably burned my bridges there - besides, she scares the life out of me!' There was no embarrassment at discussing such intimate topics with her. 'Bit too much to handle.'

Sophie put her head to one side. 'So, you're looking for a nice, uncomplicated girl who isn't too forward and doesn't scare you? How about a nun?'

'A nun? Nah, that would be a bad habit to get into!'

'God, that's awful!' Nevertheless, she tittered into her hand, head down and eyes twinkling through the haze of blonde hair. 'Come on, get me that coffee.'

As he worked his way around the stalls on the periphery of the wargames show - saving the best until last - Richard Macintyre's eye was caught by some 28mm Scottish Covenanters. Just what he needed. The figures rattled in their box as he picked them up. 'How much?'

'Twelve quid, mate.' The stallholder's belly hung out of a faded Motorhead tee-shirt that was several sizes too small. He sounded as though every breath could be his last.

'Twelve! Weesht! Still, I need to finish up my Covenanters. How much for two?'

'Twenty-four quid!'

He could get them online cheaper. 'Come on, man! Some sort of discount for two, surely?'

The stallholder considered this, breath bubbling thoughtfully. 'Do four boxes and I can knock a bit off - forty-five quid?'

Macintyre put the box down. 'I dinnae need four boxes of Covenanters! I'll have to shop around - ye'll be reducing the prices near the end of the day?'

The man shook his head, all four chins wobbling. 'Wouldn't have thought so.'

Macintyre gave up - it was time to pay Harding's a visit.

Barry had seen Macintyre circling like a particularly stout shark - the only surprise was that it had taken him so long to strike. 'Oh blimey, here he comes. Brave-fart!' He said it loud enough for Macintyre to hear.

Macintyre gave a vulpine smile. 'Well, well, well. Look what we have here! Recruiting, is it? I'm sure you've got yourself some prime specimens!'

'Looking for some more toy soldiers to fill out your ranks, Mac? These ones should fit in well with your mob - most of 'em come unassembled.'

'Och, very good, very good.' The smile didn't falter. 'We'll see who's unassembled after Felcham, shall we?'

'Oh, we will, we will.' Smug git.

'I won't spoil the surprises, but I've got plenty in store for you! And I'm meeting up with William Sneath in the week - he's got the ear of the local councillors now. I'd take a few good photos of your monument over the bank holiday because it won't be there next year!'

Ken came in like a pitbull. 'Don't go counting on it - maybe we've got one or two things in store as well!'

Macintyre raised an eyebrow. 'Really? Well, I look forward to it. Good day, gentlemen. Hope the recruiting goes well.'

Barry let him saunter away, visualising the red dot of a laser sight on the broad back. 'Cocky bastard!'

'Don't worry,' Ken assured him. 'I'm going to take Sneath down - and Mac will go with him!'

***

The attic was thick with dust, a choking seasoning sprinkled across the mysterious sheet-covered humps that filled every corner like the wrapped corpses of a defeated army. Cobwebs festooned the rafters and a water tank burped and gurgled like an aged drunk. In the dim light of the single naked bulb, Ken dug mole-like through mound after mound of forgotten junk. Brushing dust and a large spider from his hair, he tugged a sword from a half-buried umbrella stand with a triumphant flourish.

'Bet that could tell some stories if it could speak!'

'I bet it could!' The sword had rounded edges - a re-enactment blade - and was brown with rust. Like everything Ken had pulled out of the jumble, it struck Elizabeth with a painful nostalgia, harkening back to golden summers long since consigned to history. 'I've never really had a decent look through all his stuff.'

'Well, you've got a small fortune up here in militaria, if I'm any judge. His re-enacting gear is probably beyond hope -' Ken shook the sword and flakes of rust showered the floorboards '- but there looks to be a lot of stuff from his army days. Hey, look at this!' He pulled out a large scrapbook, flopping it open to a random page. 'Bloody hell! That's Trevor!'

The black and white photos of Harding's regiment prompted another squeeze of nostalgia, though the tears were surely due to the attic's cloying atmosphere. 'That's grandfather next to him. Look! That's me in the next one! I can only have been five or six!'

Ken was virtually salivating. 'That's John Phillips - he finished a couple of years after I started. I'm pretty sure that's Ginny Williams next to him.'

'You can take it, if you want it.' It would mean more to him these days than to her - and it would re-inter the bitter memories that came welling up.

'Oh yes. Yes, please! I can get some of these scanned in and up onto our website.'

'You can take anything you want - anything for your regiment, anyway.'

'Really? Thank you!' He held up a yellow dress, a child's 17th century gown. 'Yours?'

'Yes! Oh, I haven't seen that for years! I thought it had been thrown away.' Had this been a good idea? The memories that she had thought gone forever were resurfacing with poignant frequency from a sea of bitter-sweet waters, though the delighted look on Ken's guileless face every time he unearthed something was a joy to behold. The first man she'd had in the house - excluding workmen - for years. He was pleasant, undemanding company, so unsure of himself - though she could detect a gentle strength behind the doleful eyes. Nothing was allowed to pass his lips without first undergoing solemn verification, and there was a single-mindedness of purpose that said he would never fail you, never let you down, never drift away.

'And look at this! Beautiful.' It was another 17th century dress, full-size, the colour a rich red, the lace trim faded. 'Yours as well?'

'No. No, that would have been my mother's. I doubt she would have worn it more than once.' Her mother - eaten away by bitterness and wrapped in a premature shroud of her own making.

He folded the dress carefully away. 'I'm sure some of the girls in the regiment would love it, but I won't take it - maybe you could wear it when you come to see us?'

Absurdly, her cheeks flared. 'Maybe - I doubt if I could do it justice though.'

'Oh, I'm sure you could!' It was no false flattery, but an honest, calculated opinion, given with no little thought despite the casual delivery. It was not to charm her, though it did, but just a statement of fact. 'Look, everything's in here. Corset, shoes, the lot. How come your mother wouldn't have worn it? It's quite a piece!'

There was a can of worms for a Saturday afternoon. 'She was never really into it - not like my father.'

'That would be Freddie's boy? Or…'

She sighed, unwilling to rake over old ashes. She owed it to him, though - some of it, at least. 'Yes, he's my paternal grandfather. Mother and father split when I was very young and that was it - I never went to another muster again. Father died soon after - car accident - and mother never really liked grandfather. By the time I was old enough to make up my own mind, he'd given up his re-enacting, so I never got into it. Pity.'

'Yes, a great pity,' Ken said absently, picking out a notebook from a mildewed shoebox. He turned a couple of yellowed pages and his breathing hitched, a modern-day Howard Carter in a dusty Valley of the Kings. 'I think this is it! His notes!'

A methodical scrawl filled the pages, a precise margin bookending the packed paragraphs. 'That's definitely his handwriting.'

Ken was almost bouncing with excitement. 'Yes! Yes! This is it - look! "Colonel Harding took a bullet under the ribs at the storming of Leicester and this would trouble him until his death on the fields at Little Felcham some months later". What's that? Looks like a reference to a chapter in a book. What book, though? Hmmm.' He settled himself down cross-legged on the floor.

'Tea?' Elizabeth asked.

'Mm-mm.'

'Biscuits?'

'Mm-mm.'

She'd lost him for the next hour or so, she could see that. 'I can serve it naked if you like?'

He didn't even look up. 'Mm-mm. Whatever you think, yes. Fascinating stuff!'

Leaving him poring over his discoveries like a little boy on Christmas morning, she climbed down the attic ladder.

There was an air of something very much like triumph in the Macintyre living room, an odious air made all the worse by the cloying waft of William Sneath's aftershave. Sophie kept her attention firmly on her book - an intriguing history of Australian penal stations in the 19th century. Grim stuff, but compelling.

'So the monument is coming down?' Her father swirled the whisky in his glass, though the flush of pleasure on his face was due more to the prospect of defeating Harding's. Why did he have to be like this? It wasn't him.

Sneath smoothed his moustache. 'Well, I've got a good portion of the local council onside - bad PR for them, being associated with the celebration of a murderous scallywag like Harding. The Battlefield Trust and the local history bores are trying to stick their noses in, but the weight of evidence I've got stacked up is overwhelming. I'm meeting with Simon Chatsworth again soon. That should seal the deal.'

'Deal?'

'Figure of speech. It should put the final nail into Harding's coffin.'

'Good stuff - that should wipe the smirk off Reynolds' face! You're empty - another drink?'

Sneath checked his watch. 'Why not? This is cause to celebrate!' His eyes flickered to Sophie.

Her father frowned as he opened the drink's cabinet. 'Och, I'm out. Tell you what, though - I've a bottle stashed away. Something really special - if I left it in here the wife would be giving it away like lemonade! I'll go and get it.'

He bustled from the room. Sneath drummed his fingers on the table and then, leaving his seat, crossed the room to drop down on the settee next to Sophie. She shuffled as far as she could into the corner.

'What's that you're reading? Not mine, I hope?' He gave a laugh of modest self-deprecation that didn't fool her for a minute.

'No, this is by a proper historian!' She showed him the cover.

He snorted. 'Well if you like your history sanitized and fed to you in a bottle, he's the chap for you. You're off to university soon, aren't you? Whereabouts?'

'Birmingham.' The air in the lounge had suddenly gone very still and there was a new heat to it that stirred her stomach, as if she was due on. She wasn't, though, not for a week yet.

'History?'

'Yes.' How long would her dad be?

'Excellent! I've got some contacts up there in Brum, in the history department. Could make things easy for yourself, if you know what I mean?' His hand crept out to rest on her denim-clad thigh, squeezing with a slick warmth. No way! Stuff like this didn't really happen! She'd always known he was a sleazeball, but this? The feel of his clammy, trembling flesh when she tried to remove his hand made her queasier still.

'Yes, I get exactly what you mean. No thanks.' It was an effort to keep her voice steady, but she managed it. Just.

'I thought you were an intelligent gel!' The wiry hairs of his moustache tickled her earlobe, the thick stench of expensive aftershave not masking the livered odour of his skin or the reek of Scotch. 'I could ensure you glide through your course - or I could make life very difficult for you, had I a mind.'

His hot breath slobbered across her neck. Despite her efforts, his hand slid even higher, quivering fingers brushing just beneath the crease of her crotch. The arm of the settee dug into the base of her spine and he leaned closer, grey eyes cold and intractable, though salacious fires danced behind the steel barriers. She drew in a breath to call for help but the cry died on her lips. If she called out now, he'd let her go, and while his touch made her flesh crawl, her dad would catch him if she could bear it a little while longer. All this nonsense about Harding's would be dead and buried then - as would William Sneath.

'Even if I believed you - which I don't - I still wouldn't be interested. What do you think I am? I know what you are and you make me sick! You might have dazzled my dad, but you don't impress me.'

He pouted, a grotesque expression of feigned hurt that didn't mask the predatory lust. 'Just trying to be friendly. Sure you don't want to be friendly back? I could open doors for you!'

'Yes - and slam them behind me!' Her eyes flicked to the door - were they footsteps in the hall?

He saw her gaze, understood, and his hand slithered from her leg. 'Oh, clever girl. Too clever for your own good. Keep him talking, eh?' His eyes hardened. 'Go ahead, tell your father - he won't believe you.' His laughter pierced like needles. 'He'd probably offer you to me himself if I asked! It's so very pleasant to be idolised!'

Free from the probing fingers, she scrambled to her feet. 'Idolised?

You've written a book, that's all. I've seen it - looks like it was written by a sixth-former with a grudge. And not a very bright sixth-former!'

He scowled, his hands clenching into fists. 'You ought to be careful, young lady. You really don't want me as an enemy!'

Seated beneath her on the settee, he was no longer the monster he had been a few seconds before. 'Well, I definitely don't want you as a friend!'

'Maybe not yet, but I'm not going anywhere,' he hissed. 'One way or another, I'll have...'

'Here it is!' Her father bustled through the door, a bottle of Scotch in his hands. 'Hid it so well even I couldn't find it! Having a chat, the pair of you? Good stuff. She's doing history at Birmingham - starts in September.'

'Yes, so she said.' Sneath beamed like a proud uncle and Sophie barely resisted the urge to slam her foot into his crotch. 'A very sharp young gel you've got there, Richard.'

'Aye, you listen to Mr Sneath, Sophie. You could learn a lot from him!'

'Oh, I already have.' She smiled, though she was dead inside. Sneath was right - her father would never believe her. 'More than enough.'

The tears flowed as soon as she made it to her bedroom. Her skin still crawled, and she could still see the pitiless reptilian gaze whenever she closed her eyes. She wanted a shower, needed to wash away the taint of the malodorous presence, but she could not remove her clothes while that slug was still in the house. Hurling herself onto her bed, she tugged her phone from her pocket. She had to talk to someone - not her mother and definitely not her father - and she scrolled through her contacts until she came to the number she wanted. Would he mind? They'd talked for what seemed like hours the other day in the coffee shop, laughing and joking as if they'd known each other for years. That's what she needed now. She hit the screen before she could change her mind, and he answered almost immediately.

'Hi.' She cuffed the tears away from her eyes and then slid her hand across the taut denim of her jeans as if she could brush away Sneath's lingering residue. 'Danny?'

The restaurant was at the high end of high class. The portions were tiny - in inverse proportion to their cost - and marinated in the sweat and tears of the chefs who knew the slightest hint of over or under seasoning, the merest imbalance in the delicately refined flavours, would see the dishes returned and their name blackened for all time.

'So it's on?' Sneath took a sip of the excellent red wine. They were on their second bottle already.

'If you can remove the last obstacle.' Simon Chatsworth pulled his briefcase from under his chair, opened it, and lay a sheaf of documents on the heavy tablecloth. 'The land is ours - or will be. I had to lean quite heavily on some of the more stubborn bumpkins, but they saw sense in the end.'

'Must be costing you a fortune?'

'Good God, no! I'm probably paying half what it's worth. In fact, I'm not paying at all. I've redirected some council funds. Once the idiots sign, the land goes over to the developers.'

'Your brother-in-law's firm?'

Chatsworth chuckled. 'Got to keep it in the family! Then once the bypass is in place, there's the housing and all the associated infrastructure.'

'Sounds like your brother-in-law is going to be a wealthy man!'

'We all are - just so long as that monument goes. Some of the carrot-crunchers aren't fully convinced yet and the heritage mob are still whinging.'

It was Sneath's turn to chuckle. 'Don't worry about that. The petition has more than enough signatures, that Scottish ape Macintyre is fighting my corner, and I've got a few more TV appearances coming up.' How had a cretin like that produced such a pleasingly plump - if frigid - daughter? The moist pink flesh of the butterflied lamb opened like a flower beneath his knife. She'd come around, if she knew what was good for her. If not? Well, he had numbers. He needed something soon - something young, warm and, if not willing, at least artful enough to give the impression that she was. 'People don't want to remember butchers - what better way to cover up a shameful past than to tarmac over the top of it?'

He and Chatsworth clinked glasses.

Sitting on Elizabeth's settee, Ken was more at peace, more at home, than he had been for years. There was a calming aura about the place, with only the regular thud of the clock breaking the silence - maybe it was the sense of ages that suffused the house, hints of Freddie Bishop and his long and illustrious career. He flipped over the page of the notebook - Freddie's notebook - and scribbled in his own. There was so much stuff here - and so much missing! The notes were littered with tantalising references to a manuscript, a contemporary document from the mid-1640s, but there was no hint as to where it could be found. That was the key, the superweapon to blow Sneath and his shady research clean out of the water.

Elizabeth dropped into the seat beside him. 'You'll be setting up home here soon! Not that I'm complaining - it's so nice to have company!'

'Mm-mm. There's nothing else we missed up there, is there? In the attic?'

'No, no I don't think so. Why?'

Again, the knife-twist of frustration. 'He keeps referring to a manuscript. That's the key - if I could just find that then Sneath would be sunk without a trace!'

'No, we cleared out everything. You've got all his papers - all the ones that he gave to me, anyway.'

So close, yet so far. Ken tapped his pen against his teeth. 'He wouldn't have anything else squirrelled away elsewhere?'

'No, no, sorry. He gave me pretty much everything when he went into the home.'

'Colditz?'

She answered his smile with one of her own - shy but warm. 'That's what he calls it. It's quite nice, really. Well, as nice as one of those places can be. Look, why not give it a rest for tonight? I've a bottle of wine in the fridge.'

'I'm driving.' He daren't risk it - what if he was pulled over? Or had an accident?

'I can make up the spare bed for you? Or...'

'Hold on a sec.' She had destroyed his train of thought, but that was probably no bad thing. He'd written enough for one night and he scribbled the last few words to close a paragraph. 'There! That should be enough to put a few shots across Sneath's bow! There's stuff in here that he hasn't even considered. Now, what were you saying?'

'Nothing.'

'Oh, right.' Time to go then. Back to his bare and lonely house. 'Well...'

The phone rang, shrill and intrusive. Elizabeth snatched it up. 'Hello? Yes, yes this is Elizabeth Bishop.' Her face clouded. 'Oh no, really? How is he?' Head cocked to one side, her teeth worked at her lower lip. 'Yes, I see. Yes, yes. I'll get there as soon as I can. Thank you. Bye bye.' She hung up.

Ken was filled with a dreadful foreboding, as if a situation with which he was ill-equipped to deal was bearing down on him like some grim runaway train. 'Something wrong?'

'It's grandfather - they've just taken him into hospital. I have to go and see him.'

It wasn't his business. He had to go home, otherwise he'd be late to bed and where would that leave him in the morning? Her face was paler than ever, though, and Freddie Bishop was currently the most important figure in the world. He had to know how the old man was. 'Come on - I'll drive you.'

The leaden skies were an appropriate framing for the scene below, where sombre yew trees dripped rain onto the little huddle of mourners. The officers of Harding's regiment - Barry, Ken, Keith and Julian - were all there (Ken with a supportive arm around Elizabeth) as was Trevor, his colour furled. Arrayed behind the frail vicar on the far side of the grave, Terry, Ray and Tabitha stood in full uniform with muskets at the rest. The coffin being lowered into the grave by the undertaker's assistants had a battered sword and a green beret on its lid.

'Present!' Keith blinked water from his eyes. The pallbearers stepped back smartly from the grave and the musketeers angled their weapons skyward. 'Fire!'

Despite the drizzle, the three matchlocks fired first time, a crisp, efficient volley to mark the passing of Major Frederick Bishop, DSO and bar, founding CO of Harding's Regiment of Foot. Disturbed by the noise, crows dragged themselves from the trees with guttural croaks while the smoke drifted away across the ranked graves until it twisted away into nothing.

'Thank you for arranging that.' Elizabeth dabbed her eyes with a handkerchief, though most of her tears had been shed long ago. Freddie had lived a life longer and fuller than many, though it was still a wrench - and a relief - to accept that she would never see him again. 'He would have appreciated that.'

The musketeers filed away while the undertaker's assistants discreetly folded up the fake grass that had hidden the bare earth around the grave.

'My pleasure,' said Ken. The few mourners were filtering away, shaking hands with the vicar and making their way back along the rain-soaked paths. 'Shall we go, or...'

'Can we stay a while longer?' It was strangely peaceful here, with just Ken's gentle presence next to her.

'Yes, yes, of course. Do you want to be alone or should I...?'

'I want you to stay.' She'd been alone for long enough. 'Please.'

'Of course.'

Keith slowed his pace, letting Jane and Barry outwalk him until he was alone with Julian.

'Thanks for coming, old boy. It means a lot to Elizabeth - there's no family left, just her.'

'Sad, isn't it?' Even the sombre black cloth and rain-dripping umbrella couldn't spoil Julian's poised elegance - enhanced it, if anything. 'Still, she's got Ken now, hasn't she?'

'So it appears.' For all his faults, as frustrating as he could be, and despite the way they all mocked him behind his back, Ken was a good man.

He and Elizabeth would be good for each other. 'Wonder if he realises it yet?'

'Probably not.' Looking out over the graves, Julian grimaced. 'God, I hate these places. Puts everything into perspective. Makes you think, doesn't it? Playing at war, dressing up as soldiers - are we just glorifying it? Do we ever think about the reality? The death? The misery?'

This was something that had plagued Keith from time to time, though he was easy with it in his own mind now. 'Well, you must do, surely? I do - most of the others too, I think. Yes, it's fun and games, big boys with big toys, but if I ever forgot what lay behind it, then it would be time to give up. It really would be nothing but a game then.'

'I suppose so.'

Julian sounded uncharacteristically gloomy, even given the surroundings. In fact, Julian had been uncharacteristic for most of the summer. Well, now was the chance Keith had been waiting for. 'You alright, old chap?'

'No, not really.'

'What's up?' Don't press too far too fast. 'This place?'

'That's part of it, but no, there's more.'

'Is it Penny?'

Julian gave a heavy sigh. 'Sort of. We've split up, but there's more to it.'

That was little surprise, but what lay behind it? 'Go on.'

'I don't think I can!' The look on Julian's face was one of genuine terror.

Oh God. Keith's stomach dropped. *He's ill or something. Dying. Poor bastard.* 'Come on, old chap. How long have we been friends? You can tell me anything, you know that.'

Julian slowed to a halt, grinding the toe of his shoe into the cinder path. Keith had to lean forward to hear him. 'Well, I need to tell someone. It's all up for me anyway, once it's out, but it's been eating me up. That weekend at Little Felcham - you remember it?'

'I can hardly forget it - there and back in Kev's van! Some things stick with you.' His fears that his levity might be misplaced were proved unfounded when the faintest smile twitched the corners of Julian's mouth. Not dying, then. Thank God.

'Well, you remember I had a B & B a few miles down the road? I had a double room - and it wasn't wasted.'

So that was it! Was that outrage or jealousy burning in his chest? Bit of both, if he was honest. 'Not that young reporter lass, Mel? She was pretty keen on you as I recall.' And quite a piece, to boot.

'No, not her. I managed to stop myself.' Moist, anguished eyes locked onto Keith's. 'I didn't with Suzanne, though.'

'Suzanne?' Poor bastard, he'd thought a minute ago. Now it was lucky bastard! 'The Amazon that came over with the Black Hawk? Good grief! I mean, I can see why, obviously…'

'I don't think you can…'

As a man, Keith wanted nothing more than to high-five Julian. As his friend, he wanted to find out more. As Penny's friend, he wanted to slap Julian across the face. 'But you're old enough to be her father! And Penny? There's a tiny piece of my that's jealous, but really, what were you thinking of?'

'Teresa May. It helped me last longer.'

Julian's calm, almost cynical, flippancy spat in Keith's face. 'Well, I'm glad you can find something to laugh about in all this. I'm sure Penny can as well. Didn't she even cross your mind as you were…'

'Of course she did! Of course she bloody did!' Julian's face twisted with the pain of confession, though there was some small measure of relief flickering behind the clear blue eyes. 'I was doing it for Penny!'

'Really, old chap?' It was shabby excuse for adultery. 'Not sure I understand how that works out. So, the B & B. It can't have been Suzanne, so how many are there? I suppose it shows some sort of conscience that you passed over on Mel to stay faithful to your current squeeze for all of an afternoon, but…'

'Don't you judge me! Don't you bloody well dare!'

'What else am I supposed to do? We've been friends a long time, but it's like I don't even know you. Who was it? You owe me that, surely? Not someone from the regiment? You wouldn't sink that low?'

'No.' Voice bitter with disgust, Julian returned his gaze to the floor. 'What do you take me for?'

'Honestly?' This wasn't a Julian he knew. 'I don't know anymore. Her name?'

'I can't!'

'Well then, I think we're done.' At least the tooth had been drawn, so to speak, but it still left a hell of a lot of poison to mop up, and if Julian was determined to continue with his obstinate stance, there wasn't much more to be done. 'I want to understand, to help, but you seem determined to self-destruct, so…'

'Carl!' Julian looked up, face riven with despair and damnation. 'Okay? His name was Carl!'

'Ah.' *Well, fuck me! Or not, thanks.* Julian? A left-footer? 'I see.' Each to his own and nothing against them, but Julian? Army, police and a string of admiring young girls under his spell. The old school urbane charm. 'Well, that explains a lot! A lot, but not all. Those girls? Well, Suzanne, anyway.'

The confession torn from him, Julian's fire had died. 'I thought Penny would find it easier to handle being replaced by another woman rather than a man. I was trying to kid myself - trying to kid myself that it was just her I didn't find attractive any more. She didn't deserve it - any of it. None of them did, but by the time it got to Suzanne I couldn't stop myself. That's why I went home - I couldn't face her, or any of you. I couldn't even face myself. I hated myself - I wanted to rip out that little black piece of my soul, but I couldn't, because it's part of me. It is me. It's who I am. And I'm ashamed.'

'No need to be, old chap.' It was hardly a big issue, not in this day and age, but Julian?

'Yes, there is!'

'You're gay - so what?'

'Not that! For everything else! For all the people I've hurt trying to prove myself wrong!' Tears were flowing now.

'You could have talked to me - to anyone. You should have talked to someone. Penny, at least. I'm here for you, Julian. We'll all be here for you.' It must have been hell, keeping all that bottled up.

'I suppose I'll have to resign my commission.'

'Don't be an arse! Whatever for? This thing is a part of you as much as the regiment is! It doesn't change you, it doesn't change anything! And if someone so much as raises an eyebrow, they'll have me to deal with! Now come on. Let's get out of here - it's bloody depressing!'

They started to walk. The rain had stopped now, although the thick clouds above promised more to come. Keith gathered his thoughts - would it change anything? Should it? No. Oh, there would be recriminations from Penny and that would most likely be a friendship ended, but for all the way he'd gone about it, Julian had tried his best to do the right as he saw it. This uncomfortable silence wouldn't do, though - it had to be punctured, although at a risk.

'Julian?'

'Yes, Keith?'

'You never fancied me, did you?'

'Fuck off!'

Laughter rolled over the gravestones.

Ken held the cemetery gate open for Elizabeth, almost letting it slam back into her when he saw who was waiting on the other side in a black overcoat of military cut.

'Elizabeth,' said Sneath.

'William.' Elizabeth's lip curled, as if she'd caught a whiff of something unpleasant. *William?* Ken's stomach rolled over.

'Just thought I'd come and pay my respects - didn't think I'd be welcome with the rest of you, though.' The rain stopping, Sneath shook water from his umbrella and furled it away.

'You wouldn't have been.' Elizabeth squeezed through the half-open gate. 'Why are you here? He detested you when he was alive - I doubt if he thinks any different now!'

'Don't be like that, Lizzie. I must say, though, I'm disappointed in your choice of company. The man's unhinged! He assaulted me a few weeks back - did he tell you that?'

'No, but he's gone even further up in my estimation!'

'Oh, come on!' The fact that Sneath didn't even deign to look at Ken only highlighted his contempt. 'The man's a social cripple! And worse besides, I'd bet. He's a lunatic - a dangerous obsessive!'

'He's kind, he's thoughtful, and he's gentle! Three things that you never were - that you could never be!'

'I don't remember you complaining at the time!' sneered Sneath.

Sneath? Elizabeth? Complaining about what? When? Despite Elizabeth's valiant defence, Ken could feel his grip slipping, the slick nausea of betrayal urging him to run and lock himself away. Yet he stayed, a helpless, impotent observer.

'I was young, vulnerable.' There was colour in Elizabeth's cheeks now, cheeks which had been pale since Freddie had died. 'Confused. I had my head turned - it should have been my stomach!'

'We were good together!'

'We were not!' Elizabeth gripped the railings. 'It's taken me all this time to put it behind me and now you pop up again like a turd that won't flush! What do you want?'

'To pay my respects - I told you that!'

'And I don't believe you!' She was shouting now. 'You've never done anything without it serving your own purpose!'

Sneath looked aggrieved. 'That's unfair. I loved the old c... boy in my own way. Admired him.'

Elizabeth dropped her voice to a hiss. 'Well, his opinion of you was somewhat lower. He warned me about you - I wish I'd listened! I don't want you near his grave - you're not fit!'

'You can't stop me!'

'No, but I can!' Maybe it was the spirit of Freddie Bishop, maybe it was the defiant dignity with which Elizabeth held herself, but whatever it was seized hold of Ken with a raging fire that made him step between the pair of them.

'Really?' Sneath raised an incredulous eyebrow. 'I'm not sitting down this time! It would be a pleasure to put you in your place. I spent fifteen years in the forces. You? Thirty years stuck behind a desk still tied to mummy's apron strings - and daddy's purse strings! I'm not wrong, am I? I've got you nailed down pat! What on earth does she see in you? It's sympathy, isn't it, Elizabeth? It has to be! Or are you so used to wiping arses and spoon-feeding broth into dribbling mouths that you just had to find yourself another incompetent after you lost old Freddie?'

'Bastard!' shrieked Elizabeth.

'Just go!' Ken was reeling from the broadside. Sneath mustn't see it had struck home, but his voice sounded feeble in the face of the historian's belligerence.

'Or what?' The glee on Sneath's face was too much to bear - a man who held all the cards and would take a perverse pleasure in laying them down to beggar his opponents. 'Lay a hand on me and I won't deal with you myself - as much pleasure as it would give me! I'll have the police on you.'

Ken didn't lay a hand on him. Elizabeth did. The sound of the slap rang through the empty street.

'Then you can have them onto me as well!

Sneath fingered the red mark on his cheek. 'Looks like my little mouse has grown some claws! You never dared strike me back before.'

'That's been building up for the best part of thirty years! Now go, because if I start, I won't stop, and all your army training won't save you! Nor will the police!'

'Very well, Elizabeth. You've made your feelings clear. I had hoped to spare your grandfather any embarrassment in what is to follow - it pains me to speak ill of the dead - but if you're not going to co-operate...'

'What do you mean?' Elizabeth cut across him, though her resolve appeared to falter.

Sneath's regretful tone didn't fool Ken for a second. 'My dismantling of the Harding legend - the Harding lie. Old Freddie was a vociferous advocate, wasn't he? When the truth is finally realised, your grandfather's works will be exposed for what they are - his memory will be sullied.'

Ken could stand no more. 'That's where you're wrong! It's you who is going to be exposed as a fraud and a charlatan!'

'Charlatan? Much as you may wish it, this isn't the 17th century! You can't call me out and demand satisfaction! These days the pen is very much mightier than the sword!'

'As you're going to find out!'

'What do you mean?'

'I've got old Freddie's notes! Stuff he never got around to writing up - there's more than enough to put a sizeable hole in your questionable theories!'

Was that a flicker of alarm in the florid face? 'Is this true? Elizabeth? Is it true?'

'Yes! Yes, it is.' Elizabeth looked at Ken with such warm admiration that he felt suddenly like a knight errant going into battle with his lady's favour around his arm. Better still was the uncertainty creeping over Sneath's expression. 'Ken has been writing up all his notes - notes with proper references, notes with proper sources!'

Sneath paled, but his voice was firm. 'You're too late - my book has sold enough copies to make it established fact! Anything you come up with will look like nothing more than sour grapes!'

'We'll see.' Ken had lured the enemy forward, exposed them, and now it was time to unleash the cavalry to destroy them. 'There's a Holy Grail in amongst his notes. A manuscript, written at the time. You think that will look like sour grapes?

'You're bluffing.'

'What's up, William?' cooed Elizabeth. 'You don't look so sure of yourself anymore. What will happen when your research is proved to be threadbare and one-sided? Your reputation will be in tatters, your career ruined!'

'I'll buy it.' Sneath thrust his hand inside his jacket and Ken soared with the triumph of seeing the enemy scatter before a well-worked manoeuvre. 'This manuscript. How much?'

'It's not for sale,' Elizabeth told him. 'Goodbye, William. I would like to say it's been lovely to see you again but, unlike you, I've never been a good liar!'

Sneath bristled, glaring at them both, and then strode away, umbrella tucked under one arm, the other swinging with military exactitude.

'You, ah, you knew him before, then?' Ken said after a moment, the raw, open wound liable to fester if left untreated.

'Oh yes, Ken, I knew him.' She spoke with heavy passion but there were no tears in her eyes. Not now. They remained as chill as the skies above, searching some bleak inner place. 'A long time ago. It's a part of my life I'd rather forget. I was at a low point and he gave me a shoulder to cry on. We were together for a while - marriage was on the horizon at one point - and then I realised he wasn't interested in me. Not really. I was just a, I don't know, a concubine I suppose. Someone to keep his bed warm while he tried to further his career. He was interested in grandfather, though. He wanted his patronage for his early books, but grandfather saw through him, saw him for what he really was.'

'And what was that?' He was going to be sick - the thought of them together, Sneath pawing at Elizabeth's warm, unthreatening curves, painted loathsome pictures on his all-too receptive inner canvas.

'A liar, a braggart and a bully.'

'He bullied you?' Had he no other reasons for hating Sneath, here was one now.

'Not physically - not much, anyway. It was all psychological - he enjoyed keeping me in my place, meek and subdued, the dutiful little woman.' Her voice was bitter. 'I wasn't unattractive back then - I was his trophy.'

'You're not unattractive now!' How dare he? How dare Sneath denigrate a great man and treat his granddaughter, this wonderful, handsome, proud woman, like dirt?'

'Thank you.' She gave a great sigh and then the mask of mourning settled back onto her features. 'Look, we need to get on before people start wondering where we are. You'll come back to mine later, though?'

'Of course!' With this business out of the way, he could crack on with the work that had all but consumed him these past couple of weeks. 'There are still a few notes I need to copy up, and I still need to try and find the whereabouts of the elusive manuscript before Sneath realises I was bluffing!'

'That's it?' The hurt on her face had to be a delayed reaction to Sneath. 'No other reason?'

'Can't think of one. Am I missing something?'

'Who knows?'

Still upset from the funeral, bless her - and Sneath popping up can't have helped. She was already moving, heels clipping harshly in the empty street, and he jogged after her. 'Elizabeth? Elizabeth? Wait up!'

Though sparse, Chatsworth's office nevertheless had hints of opulence. Here, it said, is the office of a hard-working man. Would you begrudge him showing off the few modest fruits of success that his tastes dictated? The understated watercolour on the wall was an original and the price tag had necessitated the diversion of several council budgets and some highly creative accounting; the carpet was lush and thick and the rug genuine antique Axminster.

'You're taking this idiot seriously, Sneath?' Chatsworth leaned back in his chair, steepling his fingers.

Too right he was taking it seriously. With a fortune on offer, nothing could be left to chance. 'The man's unhinged - but he's an obsessive.'

'So what? So what if he publishes this Freddie Bishop's notes?'

'Freddie Bishop was a hero - and not just to those idiots who play soldiers. He was a bona fide war hero and a historian of some repute.'

Chatsworth peered over his fingers. 'As are you - or so you assured me.'

Was the councillor's faith in him slipping? 'His word carries weight in certain quarters. If they get enough ammunition, they could make things awkward for us. It will invigorate the heritage and preservation argument if they can do anything to counter the picture of Harding I've built up.'

'But this idiot isn't Freddie Bishop, is he?'

'No, but he's in cahoots with his drudge of a granddaughter and he's got access to all his notes!' It had kept him awake all last night, alternating waves of euphoria and despair spinning his mind into the small hours.

'Ah, yes, your ex. I do hope you've not allowed personal grudges to derail our plan?' Chatsworth's frown suggested that such petty matters were beneath him. 'I would be very disappointed. Very disappointed.'

'Not at all.' Sneath allowed himself a moment of reverie, remembering the days when a young - and subservient - Elizabeth Bishop had warmed his bed. Seeing her the other day had brought it all flooding back - she was way beyond her best now, of course, but still worth a ride or two.

'Perhaps I should send some boys round to see this granddaughter and the anorak she's taken up with? Convince them to see the error of their ways?'

'You could do that?'

'There's lots I could do,' Chatsworth purred, 'and not a lot I wouldn't.'

The councillor's face was implacable - he was not a man to cross. 'Tempting, but I think you could beat the man to a pulp and he'd still refuse to co-operate. You know what they're like, these aspergics. Very single-minded.'

'A beating?' Chatsworth's smile would have chilled a Spanish Inquisitor. 'Oh, I think we could progress far beyond that.'

'Is that not a little extreme?' A warm pulse ran through Sneath as he pictured Elizabeth bound and pleading while the idiot gently roasted before her eyes. A pretty picture, but one that carried the threat of fearsome penalties.

'I didn't have you down as squeamish, Sneath.'

'I'm not, but for the sake of a few words in a book? The risks...'

'Maybe you're right. So, let us weigh up the issues. I - forgive me, we - stand to make a deal of money when the land is sold for development. The landowners - under no small amount of coercion, I might add - are willing to sell, so long as the land loses its monument and status as a site of historical importance. Your diligent work has all but ensured that - will this crackpot really make any difference? If we cannot stop him, we can at least discredit him. Now, this event they're holding - if there was some mishap, this would turn the opinion of the public perhaps?'

'Possibly. The village is all up for it - put it on the map.'

'And any publicity is good publicity? Not in my experience. So, if there was some sort of accident, laid at the feet of the modern-day Harding's...'

Excellent! 'Then everyone would see them for the crackpots they are and no one would give two figs if the stone was torn down!'

'Exactly.' If Chatsworth had a moustache, he would have twirled it. 'There will be explosives at this event?'

'Of course - just black powder.'

Chatsworth eased back in his seat. 'Then I'll have a word with my brother-in-law. See if we can augment it with something that will make things go with a bang!'

*

Ken shuffled from foot to foot on Elizabeth's front step. He'd left a respectable amount of time after the funeral, but he could wait no longer - his notes were in there and the need to finish them gnawed at him day and night. After an age, the door opened.

'Hello,' he said.

'Hello.' Elizabeth's eyes were guarded. 'I thought you'd forgotten about me?'

'No, no, no. I just thought you'd need a bit of space after the funeral. A bit of time to yourself.'

She gave him a weak smile. 'I think I've had enough of that over the past few years. Still, I can see where you're coming from, I think. Come in.' She ushered him into the living room. 'Tea?'

'Oh, yes. Yes, please.' The books and documents were piled on the coffee table where he'd left them, though he couldn't see his notebook.

'So, what have you been up to?' Elizabeth's voice floated from the kitchen over the hiss and gurgle of the kettle.

'Oh, not much. Just work. And sorting out stuff for the Felcham muster.' Portaloos, traders, waterpoints, fencing, beer tent - the list was endless.

'Exciting stuff!'

'Not really - and I've had no time to write up my notes! Just as well. I think I left it here.'

'Left what here?'

'My notebook.' The steady thud of the clock had taken on an insistent clack that fractured the still, timeless atmosphere. 'Good job I've been so busy, otherwise I'd have been fretting over it non-stop!' His fingers raked across the polished surface of the coffee table. 'I can't find it anywhere. Have you seen it?'

'This, you mean?' Elizabeth stepped back in from the kitchen. She had his notepad in her hand.

'That's it.' He reached for his pad and she jerked it away. 'May I have my notepad please?'

'Is that all you came around for?'

It was, but some errant flare of neurons told him that would be the wrong answer. 'I... I... no, but I do need it. Sneath has really ramped up his campaign. Unless we can stop him, it looks like...'

'So you didn't come around to see me?' She spoke in a sing-song voice, as if to a child.

'Of course I did, but I do need the notepad.' He enjoyed her company, of course, but this was far more important. Wasn't it? Surely she could see that? 'So, could I have it please?'

'How much does it mean to you?' She dangled the notebook just out of reach as if he were a dog to be teased, though there was little teasing in either her expression or her voice.

'What do you mean?' Why couldn't she just give it to him? They could have tea and he could write up his notes while she sat with him, like always.

'How important is it to you?'

'It's not me! It's the regiment. It's Harding and his men. If it was just me…'

'You'd what? Throw it away? Forget it?' She ripped a tiny corner off the notepad. He flinched, as if someone had dragged a razor across his skin.

'What are you doing?'

'Destroying the past!' She ripped another corner. 'There's nothing there but misery!'

'Not for me there isn't! Elizabeth, please, the notepad.'

'Look at you! Like a child begging for his favourite toy back! Pathetic! Grown men acting like children - the lot of you!'

'I don't understand…'

'No. No, you probably don't. He was right, that snake. You're obsessed.' She tore the front cover from the notepad.

'Elizabeth!' Hours of work! Hours! She couldn't!

Tears rolled down her cheeks. 'Just when I thought I'd found someone different! You're all the bloody same! Why can't someone notice me as a woman for a change?'

What did she mean? 'You are a woman. Of course you are, but what that has to do with…'

'You really have no idea, do you?' She ripped a page from the notebook. She may as well have ripped out his heart.

'I don't understand what you're… please!' The mocking tock of the clock hammered at his skull. 'Don't rip any more pages. I need it! If we're to sink Sneath, I…'

'Sneath! Bloody Sneath!' She kicked a wastepaper bin across the floor. 'I've had enough of that man!'

'But he's going to blacken your grandfather's name - among other things.' She wouldn't - she couldn't - destroy his work. It was their only hope.

'That's his issue, not mine. If people are willing to believe him, let them! I know the truth!'

'But…'

'For God's sake, Ken! I'm bored of it!' She stood there like a fairy-story witch, a temptress, her thick black hair loose around a face twisted with contempt. 'Grandfather's dead - writing a book isn't going to bring him back!'

'You're emotional!' It had all been too much for her. She'd calm down in a minute, give him the notebook back before she did any more damage.

'Emotional? Emotional? Too bloody right I'm emotional! And not before time! I've got a lifetime of emotions waiting to come out! My whole life I've lived in the shadows of others, quiet, meek, submissive! My mother, then Sneath, then I spent so long looking after grandfather that I was an old maid before I realised it! Well, not anymore!' With savage jerks, she shredded the notebook and showered the torn paper over Ken like confetti.

He batted away the fluttering paper, blinking back the tears that pricked at his eyes. 'No! No! No! What have you done? Why? Why?'

'Work it out!'

Dropping to his knees, he scrabbled to gather in the scraps of paper. Maybe some sticky tape... 'Ruined! It's ruined! No, no.' He could start again. It would be hard work, but what else did he have to do? 'There are still your grandfather's notes - I can go back through them and...'

'These, you mean?' She snatched the papers from the coffee table and hurled them into the empty fireplace. Before he could move, she produced a box of matches, struck one and threw it into the hearth. The paper caught in an instant.

'No! No! No! What are you doing?' Even as the paper curled and blackened, he thrust his hand into the flames, but they bit at his flesh and he snatched his fingers back.

'You can't let it go, can you?' She stared at him with such contemptuous pity that he was a teenager again, being scolded for sitting amongst his sopping bedsheets. 'Go on, get out! Go!'

What had he done to her? Why was she being like this? Sucking his burned fingers, the pain of the scorched flesh nothing compared to the void inside him, he lurched to the front door, pursued by crashes and bangs from the living room. By the time he shut the door behind him, all he could hear were sobs.

'So, while these sorts of re-enactments are good fun and do give a somewhat diluted insight into the times, it is never right to celebrate villains,' boomed William Sneath from the television set in the corner of Barry's living room.

'But the established history...' began the interviewer.

'Is poppycock! As my own book shows. Everyone likes a bit of heroism and romance, but I'm afraid real history isn't like that. So, when these harmless eccentrics have had their fun and games, the stone that falsely celebrates Colonel Harding as a hero will be torn down and that will be an end to this sort of thing in Little Felcham.'

Barry turned the television off with a savage stab of his finger. 'Bastard!'

Ken was huddled like a broken doll on the settee between Keith and Julian. 'If only I had my notes! There's enough there to sink his arguments! There's still hope. If I could just find that manuscript...'

'Ken! Let it go.' Pipe dreams couldn't save them now. 'You've done enough damage - to yourself.'

'What do you mean?'

'Surely you could see... oh, never mind.' This really wasn't his territory.

Keith had a stab. 'She was quite sweet on you, old chap. Surely you could see that?'

Ken frowned. 'I... I thought we were friends.'

'You were!' Julian put an arm round Ken's shoulder. 'But you must have seen she wanted more than that?'

Understanding was dawning on Ken's face. 'You mean...'

'Yes!' said Keith.

'I didn't know!' Ken ran both hands through his thinning hair, his face like cheese. 'I've ruined it! I've ruined everything! Sneath's going to sink us!'

'Maybe.' There was little they could do to stop that now. 'All we can do is make sure that this muster is the biggest and best ever. That will give us a foothold, if nothing else. Agreed?'

'Agreed, Barry,' said Keith with a nod.

'Agreed.' Julian's face was set.

Barry looked to the one man still to answer, his trusted second-in-command. His friend. 'Ken? You with us still?'

Ken rubbed his hands over his face, emerging like a stricken rabbit. 'Yes. Yes, of course. I mean, what else have I got?'

8 THE BATTLE OF LITTLE FELCHAM

It was a typical late summer's afternoon, golden and melancholic with a slight edge to the gentle breeze that hinted of autumn. The lazy pastures echoed to the lowing of cows and the distant burr of a tractor. Birds trilled in the woodlands, leaving their perches to swoop low across the fields that riffled like a great emerald ocean. The perfection was only marred by the frequent bursts of hammering and drilling from the once-empty field where a village had appeared, a modest huddle of plaster and timber cottages.

Up close, the cottages were not so convincing, mere facades that wobbled when the wind blew. Terry said they'd be fine from a distance - and he was waiting on the delivery of some more scaffolding to make them more stable.

'Tea's up, boys.' Working her way through the interconnecting struts that held the fake village together, Annie placed three mugs of tea on a convenient plank.

'Thanks, Annie.' Danny wrapped his fingers around his mug, stretching his back. It had been an enjoyable couple of days helping Terry and Annie (who had all but adopted him) rig up the fake Little Felcham. Being away from Tabitha and all her intrigues was a welcome relief - and a good test for when they were separated by uni - though when he was wrapped in his sleeping bag after a few beers around the campfire, it was Sophie who crept into his thoughts. She was witty, warm, engaging, gorgeous - just bloody lovely, really. Pity he'd only worked it out too late.

Terry finished hammering in a batten and picked up his tea. 'Cheers, love.'

'Your turn next, Tel.' Gulping down half her tea, Annie grabbed a screwdriver and set to tightening the screws in the cottage Terry had just got up.

'Come on! You've tasted my tea!'

'Actually, I don't think I ever have.'

'Then you're not missing out on anything, are you?'

'Looking good, Terry.' Rommel stuck an inquisitive nose into the village, followed by Barry. 'Reckon you'll be done in time?'

'We'll be done in a day - Friday at the latest. The only thing is that standpipe out in the field. I was going to rig up a well or something to hide it - would have looked good for watering - but I won't get chance now.'

Barry shrugged. 'Just wrap some hessian around it.'

Danny had learned over the summer that, as lead was to Superman, so hessian was to re-enactors. It masked a multitude of anachronistic sins and, so the reasoning went, if they couldn't see through it, neither could the public.

'Fair do's,' said Terry.

'You're sure you'll get done by Friday?' Barry still looked unconvinced.

'No problem.' Terry nodded at Danny. 'This young shaver's been a great help.'

Annie looked up. 'What about...'

'And you, love, of course. But it is school holidays, isn't it, so you're at a loose end!'

'So's Danny!' Annie - a primary school teacher - pointed out.

Barry tested the strength of the support he was leaning on. 'Combat, sabotage and now engineering - someone's putting himself forward for the Rex Holmes Sword!'

'What's that?' Danny asked.

'The regimental award for the "Member of the Season",' Terry told him. 'That'll look good on the wall of your university digs!'

Barry frowned, troubled no doubt at the prospect of losing so willing - and young - a recruit. 'You'll still be back next year though, won't you?'

'Yeah, yeah - when I can manage it.' It still seemed unreal that, in a matter of weeks, he'd be leaving home. It was easier not to think about it, but Barry seemed intent on probing.

'Where are you off to?'

'Warwick.'

'Bit of a trek, isn't it? For you and Tabitha? Or is that...'

'Don't!' Terry jumped in. 'Don't set him off again! I've had to put up with his moping for the past couple of days!'

'All over, is it?'

'Buggered if I know - it is, it isn't, I've heard it all!'

Annie put a solicitous arm around Danny's shoulders. 'Leave him alone, poor love!'

Danny was aware of a creeping heat across his face. Perhaps he'd unburdened himself a little too freely during the evenings around the campfire. 'It's complicated - we're on a sort of extended cool-off, before uni.'

'Ah, oh dear.' Barry rearranged his face into sympathetic lines. 'Oh well, maybe for the best. Plenty more fish in the sea, as they say, and I'm sure you'll have your pick up at Warwick! You've made a bit of a splash here - the girls aren't used to having single young men join up. Saying that, Mandy's new boyfriend - Adam? Alex? - is giving it a crack this weekend.'

'I bet he is,' said Terry under his breath.

'What was that, Terry?'

'Nothing, Barry. How's everything else panning out? This stuff with Sneath?'

Thunder clouds gathered over Barry's brows. 'Oh, that? Ken seemed to think he could put a hole in Sneath's theories. Got himself a bit worked up over it and managed to scupper the chances of breaking his duck in the process.'

'Poor old Ken.' Terry's drill whirred into life. 'So, this Sneath thing - the monument and...'

'Let's get this weekend out the way first.'

'Sneath is going to be here, though?'

'Yes, yes he is.' Barry examined the blade of a screwdriver. 'Well, we can't stop him.'

'He's an arsehole,' was Annie's considered opinion.

'An arsehole with influence, unfortunately. Oh well, we'll see what happens. If he tries to get the monument taken down, he'll have a fight on his hands.' Barry flung the screwdriver like an assassin's blade and it embedded itself in the ground. 'Oh, while we're on the subject of arses and holes - Julian. He...'

'I know, I know.' Terry grinned. 'Can't say I'm surprised - I knew he was always trying to catch a glimpse of my arse!'

'Don't flatter yourself!' Annie belted her husband across the shoulders.

'None of that, Tel! We have to be sensitive to his...'

'Sensitive?' Terry snorted. 'Us lot? No hope.'

'Look, we can't...'

'It's Julian! The same Julian I've known for fifteen years! I'm not going to start pussyfooting around him! He'll feel more uncomfortable if we're treading on eggshells, won't he?'

Barry considered this while Rommel nibbled at the toe of his trainer. 'Maybe - just don't push it too far!'

'Only as far as he'll let me!' said Terry with a pout. 'Oooh! Saucy!'

'That's enough! Come on, Rommel, let's leave these chaps to get on with it.'

As always, Friday was a low-key night in the beer tent, though it still seemed full of accusing eyes as Julian walked in with Keith and Tabitha.

'I shouldn't have come! I shouldn't have come!' He dug his heels in, but Keith propelled him toward the corner where Harding's were drinking.

'It will be fine. They're okay with it, really.'

'You told them?' Keith knowing was one thing, but the others? God knew what they would make of it.

'Not really. They guessed. They're not stupid. Well, not really.'

'I can't go through with this!' He'd faced a few situations during his army service, had confronted hardened villains and rioters during his time in the Met, but he'd rather be under fire than go through this.

Tabitha rubbed his arm. 'Julian, no one's going to care. Really.'

'I think I'm going to be sick.'

'Don't be silly. It's no big deal.'

'It is to me!'

'I'll get you a drink,' Keith said. 'Pint? Or Babycham?'

'Dad!'

Julian appreciated the intentions behind the banter but feared he'd lose the contents of his stomach if he risked a smile. 'Rum and coke. Double.' It would settle his nerves, if not his guts.

'Right you are.' Fishing out his wallet, Keith left Tabitha to shepherd Julian over to the clump of Harding's.

'Boys!' she called. 'Oh boys! I've brought someone to see you.'

The chatter of conversation died but no one moved, the broad backs forming an impenetrable barrier. Only Tabitha's hand stopped Julian from bolting for the door. Then, as if choreographed, his judges spun as one. Mike, Nick, Steve, Ollie - and was that Danny? It was hard to recognise the faces beneath the caked make-up and glitter, especially with the apparitions winking and pouting like pantomime dames.

'For God's sake!' Tabitha was furious. 'You immature bunch of morons!'

'Oooh, get her!' shrieked Steve. 'Come on, girls!'

He and his fellow artistes launched into a grandiose, off-key version of "I Am What I Am!", posturing and wiggling for all they were worth - Nick even managed to pull off a surprisingly creditable slut-drop. As the sparkling choir stuttered to a falsetto crescendo, Julian was unable to keep the grin from his lips.

'You bastards!'

Julian was dragged into the circle amid a deal of squealing and good-natured - if crude - banter. Danny took his chance to slope away with Tabitha.

'You've had a busy week, then?' She scrubbed at his make-up.

'Yeah, me and Terry put up the village. Have you seen it yet?'

If she had, it wasn't her main concern. 'How long were you planning that little stunt for?'

'That was Steve's idea!' When Steve had turned up with a bag of make-up and glitter, the rest of them had initially been wary of offending Julian's sensibilities, but Steve had persuaded them otherwise.

'I suppose you think it was funny?'

And Steve had been right. 'Yes, I did. More importantly, so did Julian. Lighten up!'

'So that's why you all did it then? For Julian?'

'Yeah. Like Steve says, we'll take the piss out of him being gay, but we won't take the piss out of him *because* he's gay.'

Her lip curled. 'What's that? Lad philosophy?'

Jesus, she could be up herself sometimes! 'Yeah, if you like,' he said with a little more venom than he'd intended.

'Alright! What's up with you tonight?'

'What do you mean?'

'You seemed fine pratting around with your mates, but you're biting my head off!'

And whose fault was that? 'Dunno. Just been thinking, I suppose.'

'First time for everything,' She gave him a nervous smile. 'Thinking about what'

He hadn't wanted to do this, not yet, but she was forcing his hand. Oh well, sod it. He'd had a decent week and now she was here like a wet blanket to ruin it. 'Me. You. Us.'

'What about us?'

'Like is there?'

'Is there what?'

'An us!'

'Not this again!' Folding her arms, she threw back her head. 'We've been through this how many times? You know the score.'

'Yeah? Well, maybe it's not enough anymore.' He'd thought on this long and hard. It was a wrench, but it would be for the best in the long run. He'd wasted too much time with her, scared to give her up because of all the years he'd lusted after her. Even when he'd found that the reality fell far short of the expectation, he'd carried on like a junkie unable to drop the habit.

'You're splitting us up?'

He took a perverse satisfaction from the hurt on her face, though he knew he was as much to blame for scampering along at her heels like a puppy. Well, time for the puppy to bite back. 'Oh, come on! It's not like we were ever anything much is it? Maybe I've just had enough of being treated like a... a...'

'Like a what?' Her eyes shone with tears, though her face was set like stone.

'I don't know. Oh, sod it. Look, it's our last big weekend before uni. I'm going to enjoy it.' There was still, maybe, the chance to salvage something. 'You know where I am if you want me!'

Tabitha dug her nails into her palm as Danny headed back toward the laughter. How dare he? All the years he'd spent chasing her, and now, when she had finally buckled, he was throwing it all in! Maybe it was for the best - she'd said as much herself a few weeks back - but it hurt when it was coming from him. She cuffed tears from her eyes as Mandy came over to join her, the lad in tow looking like a failed male model.

'Hi, Tab! This is Alex. Alex, Tabitha.'

'Hi, Alex.'

'Hi.'

'Alex is going pike for the weekend,' Mandy explained. 'Where's Danny?'

'Over there.' Tabitha gestured to the mob around Julian.

'Oh no.' Mandy read the situation in an instant. 'You two haven't fallen out again, have you?'

'I think so.' She wouldn't cry!

'What are you two like? I thought that's what you wanted?'

'It is, I think.' Wasn't this the way out she'd been looking for? Why, then, was she so empty inside? 'Or was. Not like this though. I thought…'

'What?'

'I don't know. I just didn't think he'd do that - walk away from me.'

'You mean you don't like the fact that he's finally grown a pair and you can't pick him up and put him down whenever you feel like it anymore?' Mandy's smile robbed the sting from her words. Just.

'It's not like that… is it?' It was. It was exactly like that.

'You tell me - or him! Once you've sorted out what you want.'

The rum had done its job and a rosy glow absorbed the good-natured jibes that flew Julian's way, though when his sleeve was tugged he was ready to defend himself. He needn't have worried. It was Mel, shiny-faced with excitement.

'Hello again.'

'Mel! Hi! Great to see you again! What are you doing here?'

'I'm in for the weekend. Covering the whole lot for the rag.'

'Good stuff. Well, there's not much on tomorrow, just a few displays and cameos about town. Battles are Sunday and Monday.'

'Perhaps we could spend some time together?' She bumped shoulders with him.

'I'd like that.' He rolled his glass between his hands, the ice rattling against the plastic. 'Look, about last time...'

'It's fine, really. I understand. You could have told me, though.'

Keith or someone had been busy on his behalf, sweeping up the mess he'd left behind. 'How could I when I couldn't even tell myself?'

'I think I might try this gay thing, Mike.' Being on his fifth pint, Ollie's whisper could be heard by most of the beer tent. 'He's fighting them off with a shitty stick!'

'I think it's just called being a gentleman,' said Mel, hand on hip.

'In that case - can I get you a drink?' Ollie smoothed back his hair.

Mel looked him up and down, a smile flickering on her lips. 'Go on then. Gin and tonic.'

'What about you, ducky?' Ollie asked Julian.

Best lay off the shorts now they'd done their job. 'Lager, thanks. And don't even think about offering me a Babycham - it's been done!'

'The thought never crossed my mind! So, that's a G & T and a ginger beer!'

Elsewhere in the beer tent, things were not quite as gay - or, to save the sniggers of the pike block, jovial. Kenneth was well and truly in his cups and everyone had abandoned him. Except Barry.

'What's the point?' slurred Ken. 'I mean, what is the point?'

'Of what, Ken?' Barry looked around for support, but no one would meet his gaze.

'Anything! Everything! All this!'

'Entertainment and education, Ken. You know that!'

'Yes, but is it though?' Ken hammered the table with each syllable. 'Is it really?' He slipped from his chair like a discarded blanket.

'Take it easy, Ken.'

'You work at it, put your soul into it, and does anyone appreciate it? No, no they don't - they're not entertained, they're not educated! It's all bollocks! Then someone like Sneath comes along and tramples over everything!' On the fourth attempt, Ken gave up trying to regain his chair and remained on the ground.

'Not this again!' Sneath and Elizabeth, Elizabeth and Sneath. That had been it for the past week - on the phone, via email, in person - though the alcohol Ken had consumed added a new dimension.

'I could have destroyed him! But no, she had to go and ruin it, didn't she? It's over! Everything's over! What's the point?'

'You're repeating now, Kenneth.'

'What's the point in me! I mean, what am I? I can't even see when a woman is interested in me! What's wrong with me? Eh? I've lost her! Never knew I had her and now I've lost her! Bloody notebook - don't care about that anymore! What am I going to do?'

'Chin up, Kenneth. It's always darkest before the dawn! Oh.'

Like a hedgehog, Ken had curled into a ball and was snoring gently.

'Your daughter not around, Mac? Charming girl - intelligent too.' The expression on Sneath's face hinted that the environs of the beer tent were not quite to his taste.

'She'll be out and about with her mates somewhere. She'll be in later.' Honoured as he was by Sneath's kind words about Sophie, Macintyre was more intrigued by the historian's flashy-suited companion, introduced to him as Councillor Chatsworth. If possible, he looked even more uncomfortable than Sneath with the surroundings.

'I'll be back to my hotel by then,' said Sneath. 'Pity.'

'You're not camping?' Surely a couple of nights under canvas would be nothing to an ex-military man? He'd banked on having Sneath on tap all weekend.

Sneath grimaced, sipping whisky from his plastic cup. 'God, no! I need a proper bed beneath me - and something to fill it, what?'

'You've got that number I gave you, William?' asked Chatsworth.

'Yes. Oh yes. Thank you very much. Looks delightful.'

Restaurant number or something, no doubt - a man like Sneath wouldn't care for the delights of "Frying Tonight". 'So, you'll be coming to the battles, Mr Chatsworth?'

'Shouldn't think so! There should be a mob there from the council, but I've managed to wangle my way out of it! Not my sort of thing.'

'Oh.' Macintyre swirled his beer. 'What brings you here this evening, then?'

'Councillor Chatsworth has been very helpful in my drive to get Harding's Stone removed,' explained Sneath.

'Oh yes.' Chatsworth nodded in agreement. 'So you're as keen to see this stone gone as William here, Mr Macintyre?'

He was - or at least he had been. The enthusiastic involvement of the supercilious Chatsworth, without any apparent reverence for history, right or wrong, sat badly with him - and Sneath seemed somewhat distant tonight. It was almost as though, so close to the fruition of their plans, he had served his purpose and could be sent on his way with a pat on the head. 'Well, we need to keep our history alive, but we can't bow down to romance. We can't commemorate butchers. Whatever the truth, men fought and died here and, even when the stone is gone, the battlefield will still be here as a memorial to all those who died, whatever their cause.'

'Oh, indeed,' murmured Chatsworth, flashing a glance at Sneath that suggested Macintyre may as well be standing there in comedy kilt, red wig, and over-sized tam-o-shanter.

Although there had been ominous - if sketchy - forecasts of rain, Saturday morning was bright and sticky. Barry was hurrying past Peter's caravan when the Lord General popped his head out of the door.

'Ah, glad I caught you, Barry.'

'Problem, Peter?'

'No, no, no. No problem.'

Fuck off and leave me alone then! He had problems to spare. The battlefield still needed roping off, the village and defences needed checking, and there were minibuses to be sorted to get armed and armoured soldiers into town. 'Well, I am rather busy this morning - got to get down to the battlefield for the final once over and then we're off to town for...'

'Yes, yes, yes, of course.' Peter cleared his throat. 'Right then. Trevor - when are you replacing him?'

Not this again! Why now? 'Replacing?'

'Well, he can't go on much longer, can he? Needs to be put out to grass, clear the way for a younger model, what?'

Look who's talking. 'Yes, well, I...'

'You've been talking about it all season - for the past four or five, if memory serves me? Is that right, Frankie?'

Francesca had magically appeared at the door, looking very fetching in crisp white blouse and jodhpurs. 'That's right, yes.'

Peter beamed, shark-like, at Barry. 'So we can look forward to a new appointment imminently? Start next season with some new blood?'

'Yeeeesss. Yes, of course.' Okay, he'd been a leading proponent of getting rid of Trevor, but when all the bluster was put aside, it was easier said than done. Must be getting soft.

'Come on, man - it's what you want, isn't it? Man's a doddering old fool. An embarrassment. You needn't be too harsh, but just make sure you're clear. There are other roles he can fill if he wants to stay involved.'

'Yeah,' muttered Barry. 'Lord General.'

'What was that?'

'Nothing, Peter.'

'Good. Excellent. Right.' Peter slapped Francesca on her appealing rider's rump. 'Come on then, m'dear - let's finish up!'

The pair of them vanished back inside the caravan, the door slamming behind them. Barry hurried on. Francesca in the throes of passion was not an unappealing picture - add in Peter, though, and the canvas was soon sullied. Talking of sullied, a thick brewery stench suddenly poked an uncouth finger up his nostril. Ken - looking rather green - had fallen into step with him.

'Morning, Kenneth. How's the head?'

'Better than my heart,' said Ken woefully, then gave an alarmingly solid belch. 'Oh God.'

'You're developing a romantic streak, Kenneth!' Had the frantic phone calls earlier in the week been the right course of action? Soon find out. 'You'll get over it.'

'I'm not sure I want to.'

'Of course you do! Weakens the resolve of the warrior spirit! Anyway, I've got more problems on my mind today than your fledgling love life, thanks to our illustrious leader.'

'Peter? What now?'

'Trevor. He wants rid.'

'When?'

'Yesterday.' Barry stepped over a guy rope. 'Or, failing that, the day before.'

'Well, we have spoken about it.'

'I know, I know. He needs to go, but we can't just out him without a replacement - and I don't want to lose any of the sergeants.' Much as he hated to admit it, no one really wanted to go ensign. He remembered his own tenure, standing around with the colour while everyone else got to give orders or throw themselves into battle. Dull. 'Least of all as we've got no one to replace them!'

'Ollie's next in line for musket sergeant.'

'He doesn't want it - he's already said. It will give him less opportunity to do his Errol Flynn stuff.' He was too young, anyway.

'Ray? Terry?'

'Ray? No, no, he won't do. Terry's a good shout and then that just leaves Neil to convince to step up to ensign. We…'

A baleful roar shattered the morning peace. A battered Land Rover rocketed toward them as if Ben-Hur was at the wheel. The caravan it towed slewed dangerously and Barry dragged Ken to one side as it thundered past.

'Hey, watch it, idiot!'

'Bloody fools!' Ken yelped. 'Who's that?'

10 miles an hour speed limit on camp. As CO of the host regiment, it was his to enforce. 'I don't know - but I'm going to find out. Come on.' He set off at a run after the careering caravan.

'But I feel sick!'

'Come on!'

With a reluctant Ken at his heels, Barry plunged doggedly on through the camp. The flags that fluttered above the various little enclaves, declaring which particular regiment was camped beneath, turned from Royalist to

Parliament. They were in enemy territory now and the standard by which the Land Rover had just pulled up was all too familiar.

'Northern! I might have known!'

'Known... oh no.' Ken doubled over and blurted vomit with a violent heave.

'Come on!'

Without waiting for Ken, Barry strode toward the caravan as it settled with a deal of hissing and creaking. The Land Rover's engine died, and he slowed as the passengers clambered out, the vehicle rising appreciatively on its suspension. There were five of them, all huge and gnarled like some forgotten tribe of sub-humans, beetle-browed, broad-shouldered, slab-muscled and long-armed.

'Oh my God! No way!' He'd been shot on the field many years ago, a burning piece of wadding spat from a musket smacking into his cheek like a miniature meteorite. In terms of sheer shock, this came a close second.

'The Newtons!' burbled Ken.

As one, the five Newtons turned to look at Barry and Ken like Neanderthals catching their first glimpse of Homo Sapiens and wondering whether to eat, fight or fuck him. Five savage pairs of eyes narrowed.

'Mick!' Macintyre appeared, arms open to greet the newcomers. 'Mary! Jez! Darren! Daisy! Excellent! Welcome back!'

'You've done it this time, Mac!' Barry kept half an eye on the Newtons as if they were untrustworthy and savage dogs. Mick Newton, the head Morlock, gave a gap-toothed grin, though even he was over-endowed in the dental department compared to his slab-sided wife, Mary. What she lacked in teeth she more than made up for in tattoos. 'What are they doing here? They're banned!'

Macintyre was bubbling with glee. 'They were banned, correct. That ban has now expired! Oh dear - what's happened to Kenneth? Is he crapping his pants already?'

Barry withered beneath the brutal eyes of the Newton boys, Jez and Darren. Heavily muscled from farm work, fixing (or scrapping) cars, and whatever other dubious enterprises the clan were involved in, they looked like they could take on Harding's pike block alone. Add in the two trolls who had propagated them and... 'Two seasons! A two season ban! That was last season and this season!'

'Ah, no.' Macintyre's grin was threatening to meet at the nape of his neck. 'Well, you see, the ban commenced as of their minor misdemeanour, and...'

'Minor!'

'So the first event of their ban was August Bank Holiday two years ago. They've missed two seasons worth of August Bank Holidays - the ban is over.'

'But that's…'

'Entirely legal and above board.' Macintyre put an arm around auburn-haired Daisy, the youngest of the offspring. Despite being of a size with the rest of the tribe, she wasn't an unattractive girl - in a robust, farmer's daughter kind of way. She was a hellion in the pike block, too. Well, none of them would get the chance to show their prowess this weekend. Whole thing was outrageous!

'I'm going to see Peter!'

'Feel free.' Macintyre waved him away. 'He knows the score.'

What? Peter knew? And had said nothing? Cowardly old scrote! 'He… he… he knew?'

'Aye. Now run along - you're making my campsite look untidy.'

Barry didn't catch what Mick Newton said, but it obviously tickled Macintyre and the rest of the brood as they all fell about laughing like mating seals. Stopping only to collect Ken, Barry beat a retreat back to civilization.

A wan Ken loyally at his side, Barry stormed up to Peter's rocking caravan, gritting his teeth against the slap of flesh against flesh and the frequent giggles that drowned out the creaking suspension. It took several angry knocks before the heaving subsided and the door flew open to reveal a hostile-looking Peter in smoking jacket and cap. A red-faced Francesca squeezed past, buttoning up her blouse as she trotted away.

'Well?' Peter's moustache twitched with indignation.

Barry waded straight in. 'The Newtons! I've just seen the Newtons!'

'No need to sound so excited, man! It's not like you've discovered the missing link, is it? Well, now, come to think of it…' Peter chuckled at his own joke. 'Anyway, problem?'

Barry was fighting a lost cause, that was obvious, but he plunged on in. 'Damn right there's a problem! Those animals were banned! Banned for two seasons! Now here they are, turning up like the Beverley Hillbillies as if nothing has happened, large as life, twice as ugly and same as they ever were - except for old Ma Newton losing a few more teeth and Cleitus and Hank getting a few more scrapes on their knuckles!'

'They've served their ban, Barry.' Peter pulled out a pocket watch.

'Don't try it on with the same loophole that Mac's waving around!'

'Rules are rules, Barry. Two seasons, as of the date of their crime.'

'That's rubbish and you know it! They're animals, the lot of them! It should have been a life ban!' He enjoyed a competitive scrap as much as the next man, but at the end of the day it was a hobby - no one wanted to go home in a wheelchair.

'First offence.' Peter frowned, eyes searching the avenue of tents.

'First one that anyone had the cojones to report! They're dangerous!'

'Well, if they step out of line again they'll be dealt with harshly. Until such time, my hands are tied I'm afraid.'

'I'll remind you of that when they stretcher off the first of my lads.'

'Oh, don't be so dramatic, man.' Peter brightened. 'Ah, Wendy, m'dear! Do come in!'

Letting Wendy in, Peter shot a last meaningful glance at Barry and Ken and closed the door.

'Philandering old fruit.' Barry banged on the side of the caravan. 'Hope it rots off!'

The door swung open and Peter's head popped out like a baleful walrus through an ice-hole. 'Pardon?'

'Nothing, nothing.'

'Good.' Peter peered back into the caravan, licking his lips. 'View hallooooo!' The door slammed shut.

'Bollocks, bollocks, bollocks!'

'We'll be alright.' Despite his assurances, Ken looked far from convinced - or well. 'We've got a big enough block.'

'But it's the Newtons! The Newtons! You know what they're like - they'll eat our lot for breakfast!'

'No, they won't, not if we're switched on - plus it will be like a red rag to a bull for Nick. No one can stop him when he's on a roll. We'll be fine.'

'Maybe - but if they harm one hair of one head of our lot, that's it! Oh Jesus.'

Ken had just been sick down the side of Peter's caravan.

Though the day's cameos and demonstrations around Little Felcham had gone well, Barry was still less than pleased to find most of his regiment carousing in the blare of the beer tent, the pike block downing beers at an alarming rate up at the bar.

'Take it easy, you lot. Big day tomorrow.'

'We're on holiday, Baz!' Mike bellowed. 'You want us to take it easy?'

'It'll be hard work tomorrow.' Okay, they had to lose, but he wanted everyone on their feet and fighting for the last stand. 'You've heard who's back?'

'The Newtons!' There was a feral gleam in Nick's piggy eyes. 'Let's have it!'

'Who?' asked Danny.

'The Mutons.' Steve dropped to a stoop, his knuckles trailing on the ground. 'Bunch of slack-jaws in Northern's pike block.'

Mike traced a curvy - a very curvy - figure in the air. 'Daisy's okay - if you like 'em big! Wouldn't want to get on the wrong side of her though!'

'You wouldn't want to get on the wrong side of any of them!' said Steve. 'They're mental - just come back from a two season ban.'

'Ban?' Danny folded the rim of his plastic cup. 'Ban for what?'

'Don't ask!' Mike told him. 'We'll be fine, don't sweat it - we just need to stick tight and dig in.'

'Just make sure you do!' The amount of crumpled plastic littering the bar did not bode well for the morrow. 'We don't want to get dismantled at our own gig. I've told Peter it's not on, but he's not having it. He's as scared of the inter-bred, knuckle-dragging, sheep-bothering, shit-eating bunch of...' As the mouths of his troops dropped open one by one, Barry didn't need telling who was behind him. He turned - never show a wild animal your back.

'Barry,' said Mick Newton with a nod. His family was ranged behind him, straight from the Misty Mountains.

'Oh, hello, Mick.' Barry's neck crackled as he angled his head to address Newton senior. 'How's it going?'

Mick seized Barry's hand and squeezed like a steel vice. 'Going well. Good to be back.'

The shake was held slightly longer than was necessary, Barry's hand crimping like papier-mache before it was finally released. 'And Mary. Good to see you again.'

Giving him the full benefit of her gap-toothed smile, Mary grabbed his hand. He bit back a whimper, the grinding of bones like footsteps on frost. For an awful moment it looked as though she was coming in for a kiss, her bristled lips puckering, and he managed to extricate his sweat-slicked hand before it popped. It hung limp and boneless and Jez and Darren were advancing, paws extended. Sod that. 'Well, we'll have to catch up soon - things to sort out.' Clapping Jez and Darren on the shoulder - and giving Daisy a wide berth - he hurried away to find a corner to scream in.

'Tosser.' Jez - the bigger and slightly more intelligent-looking brother - gave his opinion of Barry.

'Yeah. Tosser.' Darren nodded, his head barely able to move due to a deficit in the neck department.

Daisy squeezed between her brothers and gave a companionable wave to the Harding's pike block. 'Hello, boys.'

'Daisy,' chorused Mike and Steve.

Her apple-cheeks bunched in a smile as she turned her gaze on Danny, filling his head with images of gingham dresses and romps in the hay. 'Fresh meat! Couldn't you find anyone bigger? You watch that pretty face of yours - don't want that getting smashed, do we?' With a pout on her robust features, she tweaked Danny's cheek, engulfing his face in flames.

'Hands off!' Steve cautioned. 'He's spoken for!'

'Yeah?' Mary Newton looked at Steve and then at Mike. 'Which one? Or is it you, Nick? Nick? Ignoring me, are you? I'm talking to you!'

Nick didn't even deign to turn around. 'I'll do my talking tomorrow. On the field.'

'Not when we've trampled all over you, you won't!' crowed Jez.

'Yeah,' said Darren.

'No way!' Nick crumpled his plastic glass and threw it over his shoulder.

'I hear old Julian's gone a bit light on his feet?' rumbled Mick Newton. 'That right? You hear that, boys? They've got a poof running their block!'

'Poof. Yeah.'

'Each to his own, Darren, each to his own. Bet he likes you, doesn't he, young shaver?' Mick patted Danny on the head with a heavy, hoary hand. 'You his bitch?'

'Bitch. Yeah.'

'Hell of an echo in here,' quipped Mike.

Jez lumbered toward him. 'What's that? Trying to be funny?'

'Funny.'

'No, no, no.' Mike snatched up his pint. 'Well, this has been great, catching up. We'll see you tomorrow. Come on, guys, don't want to leave it too late tonight.' He hustled Steve and Danny away, but the Newtons crowded round to block Nick's escape. For the briefest second, Danny considered staying at Nick's side, but Daisy's flirtatious little wink swept away the misplaced heroism. Like some Rubenesque mantis, she'd kill him once she got bored of playing - if he even survived that long.

'Where you going, Nicholas?' demanded Mick. 'Never had you down for a lightweight!'

'I ain't!'

'Prove it!' giggled Daisy.

'Yeah, come on,' urged Jez. 'Drinking contest! Or is all your regiment poofs?'

'Poofs.'

'Down in one! Come on!' Mick passed Nick a pint. 'Beat our best and you can go - unless you're chicken?'

The jibe had riled Nick. 'Give it here!' Taking the pint, Nick opened his mouth and downed it in about three swallows.

'Not bad.' Mick Newton nodded his approval.

'Your turn,' said Nick, wiping his mouth.

'Me? Not me. Mary!'

Mary took the proffered pint, mouth opening like a boa constrictor. She didn't even swallow - the beer vanished in one smooth pull and she finished by belching in Nick's face.

'Jesus!' Nick's honest farmer's brow furrowed.

Mary slapped him across the cheek with enough force to turn his head. 'Don't take the Lord's name in vain!'

'Never mind, son.' Mick passed over another pint. 'Here, have another go!'

'You sure you want to come on the field tomorrow?' Ollie forced a path to the bar, Mel at his shoulder.

'Yes, definitely! I always wanted to be a war correspondent!' It had been a fun day around the town and Ollie had been very attentive.

'Really?'

'No, not really - but it should make a hell of an article if I can get onto the front line!'

'You remember everything I showed you?'

'Most of it - maybe we can go over a few points later?'

He grinned like a schoolboy. 'Of course we can.'

Mood little lightened by the day's activities, Ken slumped at the bar, alone as was his current preference. He'd always been a little bit different - unkind people would have said "special" - but it had never really mattered so long as he had the hobby to cling to. Now he knew it all to be a sham, knew he had shut out the outside world in the pretence that he didn't need it, where in truth he was just terrified by it. And nothing had exposed that more starkly than the past few weeks. He liked Elizabeth, liked her a lot. She was just the sort of woman he could see himself spending his future with - a future that seemed increasingly barren. She was kind, sympathetic, engaging, understanding - but never in a million years would he have guessed that his feelings could in anyway be reciprocated. And now it was too late.

'Kenneth?' It was Barry. Ken swept away the stack of empty plastic glasses.

'I'll be fine for tomorrow - this is only my second. Or third.'

'Never mind that. I've got someone to see you.'

'Who?' Keith and Jane were ranked behind Barry, even Alice was there, the bitter lines for once eradicated from her features. Grinning like monkeys, they stepped aside to reveal a vision in lace and scarlet.

Elizabeth's hair was caught up in complex disarray, pearls circling her throat and dripping from her ears. The dress - the one from her attic - could have been made for her, the enhancements of the bodice providing a discreetly immodest display of bare flesh that did not distract from her almost regal bearing, though the way she chewed on her lower lip gave her an appealing air of vulnerability.

'Say something then!' said Jane.

'What are you doing here?' She could have stepped straight out of a portrait, could have walked unashamed on the arm of Prince Rupert himself, the king even.

'Smooth, Ken. Very smooth.' Keith shook his head.

'You invited me, remember?' Elizabeth gave him a tentative smile.

'I did? Of course! But I thought after…'

'Barry rung me.'

'Oh, right, good, yes. Well… I…'

'For goodness sake, Ken!' Jane snapped. 'Tell the girl how gorgeous she looks and get her a drink!'

'Oh yes, yes, of course!' The lace around her plummeting neckline was perfect in every detail. 'You look very… authentic.'

'Oh, really!' Jane threw her arms up.

'Do you think so?' Elizabeth twisted this way and that, showing off her generous curves and the exquisite lines of the dress. 'I had to do a little work on it and I'm not sure if the lace is…'

'No, it's perfect.' Ken cleared his throat, rushing the next words out before they had a chance to turn tail and flee. 'And so are you.'

'Bravo!' Jane clapped her hands. 'At last.'

'Can I get you a drink?' That came next, didn't it? What then, though?

'G & T please.' The sweet lavender of her perfume drove away the lingering residues of stale beer, swamping his senses in a purple haze. Her escorts slipped away. 'Look, about the notebook, I…'

'It doesn't matter, really.' What had she said? The past is dead? Maybe that was too harsh for him, but for tonight only the present mattered.

'But I've…'

He placed his hands over hers - she was trembling almost as much as he was and that drove away the fears that circled like vultures, firing him with the courage to plunge into the unknown. 'It's done, gone. History. What's important now is the present - and the future. Wouldn't you agree?'

'Yes, but I really have to…'

With an almost physical effort, he threw aside the thousand and one calculations and permutations sequencing through his head and, for once, took a roll of the dice. He darted in and pressed his lips to hers. The soft red cushions were warm and moist, but he had made a terrible error of judgement, because she stiffened. He repulsed her, of course he did, but before he could pull away and retreat back into his misery, her gentle arms slid around him and the passion of her response awoke regions of his body that had lain dormant for far too long.

'Well, they seem to be getting on just fine,' said Jane. 'Did you really

214

organise getting her here just for Ken?'

Barry looked at his shoes. 'Well, no, I thought that, you know, she...'

'Yes, he did,' Keith told her. He couldn't quite believe it himself.

'You old romantic, you!'

'That's probably the sweetest thing you've ever done!' Beneath the lights of the beer tent, Alice's cut-glass features were mellow, almost like the girl she had once been before bitterness and affectation had carved their harsh lines into her face. Throwing her arms around Barry's neck like an eager teenager, she nuzzled into his ear. 'Don't be too late coming back to the caravan. I might still be up.'

'Big day tomorrow, dear.' Barry's voice was a little unsteady. 'The battle.'

'Then better make the most of it - could be your last chance!' Releasing him, she slunk away with a smouldering glance over her shoulder and a deliberate roll of her hips.

Barry took a sip of his drink before looking at his watch with a casual yawn. 'Right. Well, I think I might call it a night. Lots to do tomorrow. Don't you two leave it too late, either.'

'No, Barry,' said Keith.

'Right. Well. Goodnight then, mate. Jane.'

'Goodnight.'

Barry strolled nonchalantly away before breaking into a jog. By the time he left the beer tent, he was all but sprinting.

Keith still couldn't quite take in all that he had witnessed over the past few minutes. 'Just goes to show you that anyone can surprise you - even the most insensitive pillocks!'

'He's not that bad - at least he isn't when he takes his officer's hat off.'

Looked like tonight was the night for love. Keith slid an arm around Jane's waist, kneading the warm, soft flesh of her delectable contours. He was a lucky bastard. 'So, you, er, fancy an early night as well?'

'Suppose so.' She looked up at him, flushed features framed by her tousled hair.

'Excellent!'

'But only because I've got a teenage girl to console.'

Cold water was dashed on his ardour. 'Oh God, what now? Danny?' Thinking back, Tab had been a bit withdrawn throughout the day, though he'd been too busy to pay it much heed.

'What else? Really, I could knock their heads together! It's not his fault though, poor love.'

'What's he done?'

'Nothing except get fed-up! She knows how he feels about her and she's played on that all summer, dropping him and picking him back up as it suits her. He finally had enough and told her where to go - and not before time!'

'Do I need to have a word with him?' It was a wrench to admit that Jane was right, as it was a wrench to confront the truth; he'd foregone all his reservations for the security of Tabitha's non-relationship with Danny - it had seemed preferable to her knocking about with some knuckle-dragger.

'Oh no, nothing like that, it was just another teenage row. Don't give me that look! I know she's daddy's girl, but you know as well as I do what she can be like! She's taken it badly though - what with the state she's in about going to uni. Pretty fragile at the moment. She'll get over it - and realise it was all her own doing.'

'Not that she'll admit it.'

'No, of course not!'

With hopes of a fleshy encounter all but gone, the arrival of Julian was no intrusion, though the look on his face hinted at something more troublesome than conjugal denial. 'Julian! What's up?'

'That is!' Julian pointed to the bar, where Nick and Mary Newton were downing pints at an alarming rate. The floor around them was strewn with plastic cups and, while Mary was still going strong, Nick swayed gently.

'He'll be fine.' Nick's prowess was legendary. So, to be fair, was Mary Newton's.

'He doesn't look it! The woman's not natural! She'll keep going all night. I've seen it before.'

'Go in and get him then!' said Jane.

'Tried that. Got short shrift from the lot of them.'

'Nothing too near the knuckle, I hope?' Keith knew what the Newtons were like and he also knew how Nick could be after a few drinks.

Julian looked away. 'Well, they are drunk, and...'

'I'm not having that!' Bollocks, he knew something like this would happen.

'Just leave it. Please.'

'Well, if you're sure.' Thank God - he hadn't really fancied tackling the Newtons. At least he wouldn't be facing them on the field - their unopposable thumbs couldn't cope with the intricacies of a musket. No, they'd be Julian's problem, unless Barry had done the sensible thing and edited the script to ensure Northern were nowhere near Harding's.

'Yes, I'm sure. Nick's off his face and the others are animals. It doesn't matter. I can handle it.'

Mary Newton threw back her pint and tossed the glass to the floor. 'This is getting boring! Ready to up the stakes?'

'Wassat?' Nick wasn't feeling all that. His head was whirling and everything was slipping in and out of focus - not that you could really tell the difference with the Newtons.

Mick Newton pulled out a small green bottle. He handed it to his wife who took a long pull before passing it to Nick.

'Finish it!' ordered Jez.

'Finish!'

Bastards weren't going to beat him. No way. Nick raised the bottle to his lips and tipped it up. He had to wait for what seemed like an age as the sticky contents crawled along the neck, but once the first drop touched his lips, it really started to flow. Hints of honeysuckle, aniseed and napalm. Bollocks to them. He gulped down mouthful after fiery mouthful, straining the last drop out before handing the bottle back to Mick. Jesus, he needed to piss! But where was the kharsi? He screwed his face up in an effort to still the indistinct shapes floating around him.

'What's up, my lovely?' crooned Mary.

'Bog. Need the bog.' And soon. Very soon. He set off through the crowd like an icebreaker, barging people out of the way and heading for the exit which he could only identify by the fresh breeze on his face. Outside, he spun in erratic circles until a blue-green blur resolved itself into a rank of portaloos. Thank God - the liquid weight was threatening to brim over and he had to clench. Lumbering over to the nearest cabin, he jerked open the door, threw out the elderly musketeer who was just buttoning up, and stumbled in. The door swung shut behind him, the latch clicking down as he was plunged into darkness. He fumbled for his flies, ripping them open just as his cup spilled over. The explosive stream of urine hammered at the plastic bowl like monsoon rains, leaving a blissful void in its wake. He leaned his head against the wall, legs folding to slide him down into a heap on the puddled floor. By then, he was well beyond caring.

***

Again, the gloomy prophecies of rain had been proved false and Sunday morning was just as dry and bright as Saturday. The battlefield lay serenely in the early sun, though within the fake village, Terry and Ray were hard at work rigging the pyrotechnics for the battle's spectacular finale.

'Must make you a bit sick,' said Ray. 'Knocking all this stuff up just so I can blow it down!'

Terry twisted two lengths of exposed wire together with a grunt. 'With your track record, I reckon it's pretty safe! Nah, it's what it's for, isn't it? Anyway, it's not the whole lot, is it? We need it for tomorrow, don't forget!'

'True.' Head full of smoke and flames, Ray tightened a terminal on his control box. 'Some of it might get a bit singed but there will be more smoke than anything else - after a nice big bang! Got your electric screwdriver?'

'Somewhere.' Terry looked around, patting down the capacious pockets of his cargo shorts. 'No. Bugger. Must be back at the van. Hold up, I'll go and get it.'

Julian peered into the village as Terry hurried past him. 'Ray - you've not seen Nick, have you?'

He really had more important things than errant pikemen to worry about. 'Have you tried "Frying Tonight"?' The burger van did a pretty impressive full English.

'Yes, twice. Not there - and he hasn't cadged breakfast off anyone else.'

'Sleeping?'

'He's not in his tent.'

'Maybe he got lucky?'

'You mean someone got unlucky!' Julian grimaced. 'I'm sure he'll show up - still four hours until form-up.'

Julian jogged off to continue his hunt for the lost pikeman. Left in peace, Ray turned back to his work, only to find a stranger examining the fuses and wires.

'Sorry, mate, this is a restricted area. Explosives.'

'So I see. This is pretty impressive work - you know your stuff.'

'I like to think so. You know a bit about pyros?'

'You could say that,' said the stranger with a smile.

'Really?' Ray's stomach dropped quicker than Richard Cromwell's approval ratings. The bloke wasn't one of the Fireworker General's mob as far as he knew. 'You're not from the inspectorate, are you?'

'No, no. Just taking an interest, that's all, in a professional capacity, you might say. Going to be pretty impressive by the looks of it.'

'Hope so. Biggest I've done yet.'

'Looking forward to seeing it. Well, good to chat, I need to get going. Catch you later!'

Pleasant chap. 'Yeah, cheers.' Picking up his pliers, Ray began stripping the plastic from a length of wiring.

There was still a while to go before the battle, but people were already getting into kit to avoid a manic rush five minutes before form-up. Gathered beneath the telescopic flagpole flying their colour, the Harding's high command were going over the finer details of the script, though Julian's mind was elsewhere.

'You found him yet, Julian?' Ray called as he and Terry made their way back up from the battlefield.

'No, not yet.'

'Found who?' Barry looked up from his clipboard.

'Nick. He's gone AWOL.'

'Well, find him!' Barry's pen bent against the board, splitting to spatter flecks of red ink over his notes. 'You're going to need him today against Northern now the Mutons are back. When did you last see him, Julian?'

'Last night - drinking with the Newtons.'

'Perhaps they took him back to their cave?' Keith said with a smile.

'Don't joke about it!' Barry was not amused. 'What sort of state was he in?'

'Drunk!' said Julian.

Barry rolled his eyes. 'Of course he was - this is Nick! How drunk?'

'Well, he called me a mincing faggot, spat on the floor, fell against the bar and then pinched Daisy Newton on the backside while staring down her top.'

'About average then,' said Keith. 'I'll have a word with...'

'I said last night that I can handle it, Keith. I'm not completely helpless!' The tip-toeing and over-played political correctness were harder to deal with than the insults. He didn't need baby-sitting, for Christ's sake! 'If playground abuse from a drunken pikeman is the worst I get, then I think I can live with it.'

'Why did you leave him there?' demanded Barry. 'Why didn't you get him out?'

'How?'

'Fair point. Well, I... oh my God.' Barry's jaw fell open.

'Jesus!' Keith's eyes widened, as if some unspeakable horror was bearing down on him.

'What?' Intrigued by what could have spooked them, Julian followed their gaze. *What the hell?*

The funereal procession, led by Jane, was made up of nine or ten Harding's pikemen, struggling along with a length of orange mesh fencing slung between them. Whatever lay in the makeshift litter made an inelegant lump, almost dragging on the ground despite the straining efforts of the pallbearers. As the solemn party grew nearer, it became apparent that the lump sprawled in the folds of the fencing was Nick, dead to the world.

'Is he dead?' asked Barry.

'Not quite,' replied Mike.

Julian knelt by the inert figure, careful to breathe through his mouth. 'Where was he?' Nick's damp snores rumbled like a faulty generator.

It was Steve who replied. 'Crashed out in a portaloo - they had to cut him out. He was wedged solid!'

'The Mutons!' Barry gritted his teeth. 'They did this! Sabotage! He's been knobbled!'

Mike smirked. 'I don't think so, Barry - he's still got his trousers on!'

'Not funny! Not funny! Wake him up! Sober him up! Get him some food! We need him!'

Jane shook her head. 'Not today.'

Barry looked close to tears. 'But...'

'He's not going on the field in that state!' Jane stood over the stricken giant as if daring Barry to come and claim him. 'God knows what he's been drinking - raw sewage from the smell! He's out of action for today - if not the whole weekend.'

'Oh God!' howled Barry. 'Oh God! Oh God! Oh God!'

On the battlefield, two furtive figures dressed as 17th century peasants scurried over to the village, lugging a large box between them. They vanished into the cottages, emerging a couple of minutes later. From their steps, the box was considerably lighter.

The Parliament campsite seethed like an ants' nest, a veritable hive of activity. As such, Macintyre had a thousand and one things to consider - what he didn't need was a stroppy teenager.

'Go on, dad,' beseeched Sophie. 'Please!'

'No!' Other girls went in the pike block, but not Sophie. Not his little girl. She'd carry his standard, as always. 'You're not going pike!'

'Go on!' She'd already cadged a helmet from somewhere. 'I'll be fine, honest! Come on - it'll be my last chance to blow off some steam before uni! Please?'

He didn't have time for this! She'd be fine, wouldn't she? The Newtons were back. 'Oh, okay, go on then! But don't tell your mother! And don't go on the front rank! Mick!'

'What?'

'Sophie's coming in pike today - look after her.'

'Right you are.'

'Thanks, dad.'

Led by Peter and his mounted bodyguard, the Royalist army made a fine sight as it marched off to the battlefield, colours streaming and drums hammering. The mood among Harding's - who were to follow on later - was less ebullient. Mutiny was in the air.

'Come on, guys,' Julian implored the pike block, 'I know we're missing Nick, but he's only one man.'

'Yeah, but he's worth ten!' said Mike. 'We don't stand a chance without him - not against the Mutons!'

'We might not even be up against Northern.'

'Julian, we're always up against Northern!' Even the normally reliable Steve was looking shaky. 'They're Macintyre's pets! And you think they're not going to be out for revenge after all the hammerings we've given them this season?'

'So you think we should not come out to play because we're scared of the big, nasty men?'

'You're one to talk about coming out!' A titter ran through the pensive ranks and Mike grinned. 'Besides, I'm more scared of the big, nasty women!'

'You're all for big, nasty men, though, aren't you, Julian?' shouted Steve.

'Big? Yes? Nasty? Not really! And their dress-sense is appalling!' If this was the price for getting his boys and girls on the field, it was a small enough one to pay.

'You could always give them a makeover!' called Danny.

'I doubt it - you can't polish a turd!' Julian teed Mike up and was not disappointed.

'Bet you've nudged a few in your time, though!'

Steve winced. 'That's a bit near the knuckle, mate.'

'As my boyfriend said last night!' To some, the crude banter would have been grounds for complaint, but to Julian it was acceptance and he gave back as good as he got. 'Come on! I thought I was the fairy? Man up! Are we doing this or not?'

'Of course we bloody are!' roared Mike.

'Good boys!'

'And girls!' Jane strode up, unfamiliar in a helmet and with a pike in her hands. 'I thought you could do with the extra weight.'

'Keith?' The more the merrier - he'd have taken any willing body right now, but it was best to check.

'It's nothing to do with him!' Jane looked ready to take on the whole of Northern single-handed. 'I didn't expect any sort of chauvinistic nonsense from you! I'm in!'

Keith shrugged, the knots in his brow testament to the ferocity of the argument that must have raged. 'I tried to talk her out of it, but…'

'Okay, Jane - fill in the back rank there, next to Alex. Who's going to water, though?'

'Elizabeth is.'

Dressed in borrowed men's kit and burdened down with water bottles, Elizabeth coloured beautifully when the pike block greeted her with a rousing cheer. Blowing her a kiss, Ken joined a particularly vinegary-looking Barry.

'About time! Well, let's go and get our arses handed to us!'

'Relax!' said Ken, a beatific smile on his face. 'It'll be fine. I mean, it's a beautiful day, the sun's out, the…'

'Ken?'

'Yes, Barry?'

'Shut the hell up, will you? Move us off.'

'Yes, Barry. Sorry, Barry.' Ken filled his lungs. 'Have a care!' There was a touch of swagger to his commands. 'Harding's Regiment of Foot will march by division to the right! Prepare to march! March!'

The crowd - much larger than expected for the first day of a Bank Holiday muster - was being treated to a rousing skirmish in the middle of the battlefield. Units emerged from a network of copses and ditches, throwing themselves into the fray as cannons roared and muskets crackled. Amongst the skeins of smoke, the Ironsides were locked in a wheeling melee with their Royalist counterparts. Barry, waiting in reserve with Harding's, rubbed his hands, a smug glow warming his belly. It looked brilliant and everyone was on script, giving the impression of men hastily roused from their bivouacs and thrown into battle.

'Okay, Ken, we hit their right flank, have a brief tussle and then we...'

'Fall back into the village, I know, I know. Then hold out there until the pyros go off and march back out for our glorious deaths! It will go like clockwork!'

There was only one cloud darkening Barry's horizon. 'Where are Northern?'

Ken squinted through the smoke. 'Way over there! We won't come up against them.'

The borrowed kit was less than fragrant, hanging off her like a mildewed tent, and the Montero kept slipping over her eyes, but Mel couldn't keep her restless legs still. The battle was as terrifying - the explosions, the guns, made it all seem so real - as it was exhilarating.

'You okay, Mel?' Ollie leaned in slightly closer than was necessary.

'Yes, fine. This is great!' Her ears bulged as a cannon went off, the percussion pounding her guts.

'When the cannon's go off, open your mouth.'

'Why?'

'It's better than covering your ears. Something to do with air pressure.'

Terry, in the rank behind, thrust his head between theirs. 'Plus you'll look like a right idiot! We'll need some dramatic deaths from you, Mel - you're a non-firer, so makes sense to use you as a casualty! You okay with that?'

'Yes, sure.' She was sure she could conjure up some pretty dramatic death poses.

'Good girl - we won't leave you lying around too long. We'll pull you back in so you can die again!'

*

Alex's face was suffused with the same mix of fear, embarrassment and bewilderment that Danny recognised from his first muster. So long ago now, it seemed. A whole summer.

'You alright, Alex?'

'Mm-mm.'

'Just stick close, follow everyone else, and listen out to the orders! You'll get shouted at a lot, but that's only to make sure you don't get hurt - walk under a horse or in front of a loaded musket block or something! I'm sure Mandy wants you back in one piece!' It felt good to play the veteran.

'Advance your pikes!' bellowed Julian. 'Prepare to march! March on!'

'Here we go!' Danny pounded a fist against Alex's back-plate.

'This is it!' whooped Mike. 'Let's get it on!'

'Well up for this!' Steve headbutted the shaft of his pike. 'They're going to get it! Let's do the bastards! Hey, Julian! Do you reckon you could kill a man?'

'Eventually, love.'

After half an hour of glorious mayhem, Harding's had fallen back into the village. Pacing behind the makeshift barricades, Barry watched the battle rage on out on the field.

'Time, Kenneth?'

'Quarter to four, Barry. Here comes Mac now!'

The guns fell silent as Macintyre, accompanied by a drummer, advanced toward the village to parley.

'Right, come on, Mandy!'

The village didn't look half bad, to be fair. A hell of a lot of work must have gone into it, though it grated to give Harding's any credit. An eerie hush fell over the battlefield when Barry emerged from between the cottages, Mandy at his side. A pasty-faced Kev - it looked as though he had not seen the sun in a fair while - hurried over with microphone in hand and set himself between the two protagonists.

'Good day, sir!' Barry's amplified voice echoed around the field with a screech of feedback.

'Good day indeed!' replied Macintyre. 'I'll no beat about the bush, Colonel Harding! The rest of your army is broken. You have done all that honour demands! You may walk out with your arms and colours if you surrender now!'

'And if we do not, sir?' Barry's voice was rich with the contempt reserved for anyone foolish enough to think that Harding's would capitulate so readily.

'Then there will be no quarter, sir.' There was a script, penned by Barry, but there was no way he was going to follow that and give credit to the Harding fallacy.

'What's that?' Barry seized hold of Kev's arm, locking the microphone in place before his mouth. 'You'll burn the village down around us and slaughter any who seek to shelter us?'

'That's no what I...'

'A fig for your quarter, sir, and damnation on those who would terrorize women and children! This is what your Parliament would give us? Then die and be damned, coward and traitor!'

With a shallow bow, Barry turned on his heel and stalked back to the village with Mandy.

'A fairly stiff answer, sir! What will you do now?' Kev thrust the microphone under Macintyre's nose.

'He has condemned his men with his own stubbornness - they will die!' And then some.

'And what of the villagers?'

'I have no quarrel with any man who does not seek to hinder me! However, I think that Colonel Harding is not so welcome as...' Hang on! What was up with the P.A? Why was his voice no longer resonating around the field?

'Bloody mic!' said Kev apologetically. 'Sorry, Richie.'

It was, at best, a Pyrrhic victory for Harding's but it still rankled. 'Aye, I'll bet!'

'Right, people, this is it!' Barry ran his eyes along the assembled ranks of Harding's. Great bloody bunch - this was going to go down as one of the all-time great musters. Even Mac's predictable attempt to change the script had been thwarted. 'We march out, join up with the remnants of the army, and have fifteen minutes of fun before we breathe our last! Okay, Ken, take them out! Watch your ears, guys. Ray? Over to you!'

Ken led the regiment out onto the field. Donning goggles and ear protectors, Ray picked up a control box and tucked himself into a protective cubbyhole. Once everyone was clear, Barry left him to it and headed out to death and glory.

On the field, Harding's were forming ready for battle. Barry jogged over to Ken, tucking his head into his shoulders in anticipation. One big bang and then all hell would be let loose! Or not. When, after a minute, the expected explosion had not ripped through the village, he unfurled his shoulders, exchanged a glance with Ken, and with the expectant hush of the crowd loud in his ears, trotted back to the cottages. It wasn't the most sensible thing in the world - entering what was effectively a giant bomb primed to go off - but if it hadn't gone up now, chances were it never would. Ray was almost in tears, flicking impotent switches on his control box.

'What's happening?'

'Nothing!'

'Why not?'

'I don't know! I checked everything this morning!'

'Bugger!' That was the big finish gone. 'Oh well, make it safe and then come and join us.'

'No, I'll sort it!' Ray pounded the control box. 'It'll go off, don't worry!'

'Okay, but be careful! Ten minutes and then give it up, okay?'

'Okay, Barry.' Ray pulled out a handful of wires, twisting the exposed copper, and Barry scuttled back to the field before he found the right one.

What the fuck? Why couldn't he move? He was trapped, arms pinned to his side. The nightmare was true - some giant spider had him wrapped up, ready to feed! Sod it - the way he was feeling, let the bastard have him. What the hell had happened last night? His head was pounding - he was rarely sober long enough to enjoy a hangover - and his guts rumbled foully. No. What he took to be his innards trying to rearrange themselves was actually distant gunfire. Fuck! The battle! Nick's eyes snapped open. Light filtered through the walls of his tent - it was not the web-shrouded, bone-strewn cave of his nightmare - and he thrashed his way clear of the netting which cocooned him. Burrowing through his heaped clothes, he managed to locate his uniform and rolled from his tent. Screams and shrieks sheared through his throbbing head as, with some difficulty, he hauled the damp wool over his sweating limbs. The eyelets and buttons defied his fingers, so he left them. There was no point in even attempting to buckle on his armour, so he just snatched up his helmet and set off toward the sound of the guns. Picking up a pike from behind Julian's car, he stood for a second, sweat pouring down his face. Smoke rose from beyond the trees to his left. That's where the battle was - and the Mutons! He hadn't imagined them last night - they'd got him into this state. Bastards! He set off again, snagging guy ropes and ploughing through tents. Bollocks to it, he had to get there before it was too late! They needed him! Stumbling against a caravan, something wrapped itself snake-like around his legs, and a buzz-saw scream drowned out the fusillade of yaps that harried him. *Get off!* Jerking himself free, he rumbled on, Rommel at his heels trailing a broken lead.

The remnants of the Royalist army had joined Harding's to face Parliament's final onslaught. Fresh from arranging the rag-tag muskets into a coherent division, Barry turned to Ken. 'Who have we got?'

'Guess!'

'Northern?' The script said not, but he knew Mac too well.

'Who else?'

The Parliament pike blocks pressed forward, driven on by a frenzy of drums. The Newton trolls loomed large in the Northern ranks. Fucking animals. Didn't matter. This was Harding's day - they were invincible! 'Julian? Northern! Take 'em in!'

The usual excitement built as Julian led Harding's pike forward. Danny had grown to love the physical side of his new hobby over the summer, loved the suffocating heat as two blocks ground together, flesh squeezing and bones crackling, loved the relief when the blocks parted and he could breathe once more. He was in the centre of the front rank, flanked by Mike and Steve, his pike held vertically to protect his face.

'Closest order!' roared Julian.

Danny dropped lower, absorbing the pressure building from behind as Mike and Steve squeezed in. Northern. They had Northern. Many of the faces in the opposition ranks were familiar, guys he had fought against all through the summer. The Newtons were there too, huge lynchpins in the block. Daisy was directly opposite him, winking and blowing him a kiss, then Northern surged forward as if their turbo had kicked in. They never came on this fast! Or this hard! The force as the blocks clashed in a shock of armour and flesh was like nothing he'd ever felt before, like being hit by a hydraulic ram. His head jerked like a crash test dummy, a rivet popped on his armour, and his helmet jammed itself down over his nose to limit his vision to a letterbox while exerting a vertebrae-crackling pressure on his neck. Feet lifting from the ground, he tried to free his trapped helmet-rim before his neck or his nose snapped. A shudder ran through the block and then his feet were on the ground, his helmet was free, and all was sweat and heaving.

'Hold them!' Julian's voice was clear above the melee. 'Hold them! Good lads!'

They were holding firm. Danny dropped a little lower, trying to make headway against Daisy, but it was like pushing against a heifer.

'Alright, my lover?' Dropping a hand from her pike, she thrust her fingers deep into his crotch, circling his bollocks and squeezing a nauseous wave through his abdomen.

'Oooh, Jesus! You bitch!'

She smiled sweetly, squeezing harder. He bore it as long as he could, gritting his teeth against the waves of pain rippling around the chilled lead weight in his guts, but when she twisted and yanked he was sure she had pulled them off. There was no escape. He had to call it.

'Man down! Man down!'

The pressure behind him eased but Northern either didn't hear the call or ignored it. They carried on driving and, with no support from behind, Harding's front rank crumpled. A great dark mass filled Danny's vision like a tsunami, and then he was on the floor amidst the pounding hooves of a stampede.

'Have it!' roared Mick Newton.

All was rumbling darkness, his armour ringing beneath the trampling feet. It would clear though, and he held himself still, breathing shallowly, unable to curl himself into the ball that would alleviate the sickening pressure in his abdomen. Finally, he was spat out the back of the block and he picked himself up, although he wanted nothing more than to stay down, curl up, and cry.

'Oi, Derek!' Helping Jane back to her feet, Julian called over to Northern's pike officer. 'Man down - your guys carried on pushing!'

'Didn't hear!'

'Yeah, right!'

Mick Newton shouldered his way past. 'Out the way, Sparkles!'

'You better keep a lead on those Neanderthals,' Julian warned Derek. 'It's your neck if they get out of hand!'

'Just go and reform - unless you've had enough?'

Making the reform point, Danny dropped to his knees and thrust his fists into his crotch. It seemed to ease the pain a little. He accepted a drink of water from Elizabeth, letting her trickle the liquid into his mouth while he massaged his abdomen.

'You alright, Danny?' Julian asked.

'The old Daisy death-grip, Julian,' said Mike with a part-grin, part-grimace. 'Want to rub them better for him?'

Julian hauled Danny to his feet. 'On your feet, Dan! Come on! At the back. The rest of you - watch yourselves in the front rank.'

'It's alright, I came prepared!' Steve rapped his crotch with a flat crack of plastic.

'Alex?' Julian checked on his newest recruit. 'All good?'

Alex was red-faced and panting. 'I think so - this is bloody stupid!'

'Alright to go again?'

'Of course he is!' The awful gripping pain was mercifully subsiding, and Danny shoved Alex into line. 'Come on!'

'Shit!' shouted Mike. 'Here they come!'

'We're not formed!' Julian stepped out in front of the block, hand raised. Northern - with the three Newton males a bulwark in the front rank - bore down on him like a grotesque armoured centipede.

'They're not stopping!' yelled Steve. 'Closest order! Quick!'

It was too late. With a dull clang, Julian was shunted back and driven into his own pike block which shattered as Northern ploughed on. Danny dug his feet in, dipping his hips, but was unable to stop the block being propelled backwards.

'Give fire!' Keith's shout was followed by a volley that sounded horribly close. A second later, Danny and the rest of the pike block were in amongst the smoking muskets, entangled with enraged and panicking musketeers.

'Bloody hell!' roared Keith. 'You idiots!'

'Now kill the buggers!' bellowed Mick Newton.

Northern dropped their pikes and hurled themselves into the mingled block of shot and pike, caring nothing for smoking matches, misfired muskets or the abundance of black powder. Trevor backed away from the chaos but the Ironsides came thundering through the carnage and Sean grabbed hold of the colour.

'Give it here!'

'No!' Trevor snatched the colour away.

'You silly old sod! It's in the script!'

'I'm not falling for that again!' He wasn't senile, not yet.

'It arranged!' whined Sean. 'Harding's last stand and all that! Give it up!'

Never again! 'They didn't surrender their colour - they destroyed it!'

'Give!'

'No!' His time may be short - he couldn't go on forever - but he'd never let down the regiment again. 'My life is my own, but the standard is my regiment's! Pry it from my cold dead hand! Ha!' Drawing his sword in a shower of rust, he unleashed a wild blow at Sean's arm.

'Watch the horse! Watch the horse! Right!' Sean released the colour and slashed back with his own blade. With a flourish, the years falling away, Trevor blocked and let fly with a riposte that Sean only just parried.

It was all over for Harding's, and there weren't many survivors. Ollie was sprawled protectively over Mel while Mandy, her drum smashed, was cradling Alex's head in her lap and mopping blood from his nose. Jane was helping Julian to hobble over to the medic's tent, passing Ken who was defending Elizabeth from the circling Ironsides with his polearm. Hands clasped behind his back, a simmering Barry surveyed the ruin. There were still several scuffles going on - Keith was trying to stop Terry throttling one of Northern's sergeants - and a scream of outrage pulled Danny's attention to where a Parliament pikeman had Tabitha pinned to the ground, slapping her time and again across the face. She may not have been his girlfriend any longer, but she was a Harding. He launched himself at the pikeman, bundling him off Tabitha.

'Ooh! Someone wants to play!' Tabitha's tormentor rose to her feet. Daisy.

'Oh shit!' Danny's hands dropped to his crotch, but before she could lay a hand on him, he was dashed to the floor by what felt like a wrecking ball.

'What you doing with our sister?'

'Sister!'

The boot that slammed into Danny's balls made him yearn for the gentle caress of Daisy's earlier ministrations. A world of pain erupted in his lower regions, unimaginable, impossible pain, and he doubled up while fists and boots smashed into both his armoured and unarmoured areas. His breastplate saved him from a stomach-pounding, but the brutal impacts on unprotected arms and legs bludgeoned them to an aching heaviness and his abdomen burned like ice from the repeated blows to his groin. He needed to be sick, but an iron bar seemed to be clamped across his chest, half-choking him. A boot slammed into his cheek like a sledgehammer, rippling lights across his greying vision. His helmet rang like a bell and he had to snatch his senses to stop them floating away.

'Get off him, you idiots!' The accent was so thick that, for a second, it seemed Macintyre himself had come to his rescue. The avenging angel smacked Jez across the shoulders with a pike before breaking it over Darren's head, but it was only when she hurled herself onto Danny that he realised it was Sophie. Enveloped in a comforting fug, coarse wool fibres tickling his nose, he nestled down into soft, sweet darkness.

Barry could have wept. The scene of devastation was like day one of the Somme. Ruined! They'd ruined it! It was small consolation to know that the Newtons would be banned for life this time. They'd have to be.

'Surrender!' Swords drawn, a knot of Northern's musketeers surrounded him.

'Fuck off!' He ignored the blades, more concerned by the commotion along the crowd line as Nick burst onto the field like a runaway train, a familiar little figure at his heels. Rommel! What the hell? Seeing his master under attack, Rommel gave a piercing yap and hurtled to the rescue, teeth bared.

The world flashed white, the ground rumbling as if a fleet of juggernauts had taken a wrong turn and ploughed through the ersatz village. Barry's last fuzzy thought was that either Ray had really excelled himself or World War 3 had broken out. Then self-preservation kicked in and he threw himself to the ground, battered by the shower of wood and plasterboard.

When he picked himself up, an insistent whine piercing his hearing, the clearing smoke revealed the shattered ruin of Terry's handiwork, hungry flames licking at the charred remnants. Ray! Had Ray still been in there? And what about... 'Rommel? Rommel? Rommel!'

The walking wounded made their way slowly back to camp, a pall of smoke rising behind them. Blue lights flashed on the battlefield - police, ambulance, fire brigade, they were all there. There were even rumours that the bomb squad were on their way.

Danny trailed his pike, his body a seething mass of bumps and bruises - there was nothing that didn't hurt, and it was an effort to turn his neck when Tabitha caught him up.

'Danny! Thanks for that back there.'

'No problem.'

She pulled off her hat and shook her hair free from the loose plait. Chewing a fingernail, she fixed her crystal eyes on his. 'Look, I was thinking. Us. You and me. Maybe we could...'

No way. Not now. He'd made up his mind and he was sticking to it. 'No, I think you were right. It would never survive uni - us, I mean. It was never going to work really, was it? We've known each other too long.'

'Oh, right, yeah, I suppose.' She blinked, hurt. For a second, it looked as though she would say something else, her lips trembling, then she spun around and stumbled away.

He should go after her, but he really didn't have the energy. Throwing down his pike, he slumped onto a fallen tree trunk, unbuckling his helmet and dropping it to the floor. Mike and Steve clapped him on the shoulder as they hobbled past. Mandy, helping Alex along, gave him a weary smile.

'How did she take it?' Sophie lowered herself down next to him, resting her head against his shoulder.

'No too bad, considering.' She looked quite fetching in her armour, hair unravelling from its loose bun and a smudge of dirt across one cheek. 'Probably not the best time, really.'

'No, that was a bit of a mess back there. You okay?'

'I'll live - don't think I'll ever have kids though!'

'They're mad, the Newtons! Animals! That's the end of them - I'll make sure my dad knows everything. At least they left your face in one piece!'

'That's not much consolation.' He rolled his neck and, as she slipped an arm around him, the contrast between the loose warmth of her embrace and the chill cuddles he'd endured with Tabitha forced out a snort of laughter that bulged his aching sides.

'What are you laughing at?'

'Just thinking what an idiot I've been, that's all!'

She squeezed his shoulder. 'You're not the first to have been clobbered by the Newtons - I think you'll be the last though!'

'No, not that.'

'What then?' She lowered her face, but it seemed she was smiling. Putting his arm around her, he kissed the top of her head, the blonde hair matted with sweat and flecked with rust from her helmet. He placed a finger gently beneath her chin and, tilting her face up to his, went to kiss her on the lips.

She pulled away. Shit. He'd been wrong. She wasn't smiling. 'What do you think you're doing?'

He knew then that he'd gambled everything and lost it all. But that afternoon in the coffee shop? The phone calls? 'I thought...'

'Oh, no. Sorry.' She shook her head, the blonde hair falling around those adorably plump cheeks. 'Besides - I'm a lesbian.'

'You what?' It was as if Daisy had grabbed him once more. 'No way!'

She burst out laughing. 'No, of course not, you prat! It's taken you long enough! Come here!' With Harding's hooting and jeering in the background, she hooked her arm around his neck and pulled him down, the press of her lips sweet, warm and eager.

The long-promised rain had finally arrived, drumming a maddening tattoo on the roof of Barry's caravan. Heart as bleak as the weather, he made his way along the portraits hanging on the wall, brushing the dust from them. General Wolfe was there, as were Napoleon, Prince Rupert and Gordon of Khartoum. Beneath each great general was the photograph of a dog - the one beneath Wolfe a particularly savage-looking German Shepherd - and Barry allowed his thoughts to linger on each of the long-gone pets before moving to the last portrait, a black and white photograph of Erwin Rommel. A knock at the door jerked him from his reverie.

'It's open.'

Ken popped his head in, dripping rainwater onto the carpet. 'Ready?'

'I suppose so. Let's get this over with.' Barry thrust his arms into a waterproof, taking a last look at Erwin Rommel - and the bare wall beneath the picture. 'And you're staying here!'

Laying on a cushion, paws and ears bandaged, Rommel thumped his tail against the floor.

The earth was already churned to mud, the rain a downpour of apocalyptic proportions that hid the campsite behind a silvered veil. As Barry and Ken hurried along, a Land Rover came roaring through the grey curtains, a caravan bouncing behind it, and they were forced to duck against the spray of muddy water.

'Good bloody riddance!' Ken had to shout over the hiss of the rain.

Thunder rumbled in the distance. 'We won't be seeing them again! Banned for life.'

Barry had other concerns. He stamped his foot against the earth with a squelch, water pooling in the imprint of his boot. 'We'll be lucky to get off if this rain carries on.'

Trevor was already waiting outside Peter's caravan, standing beneath an umbrella with the rain misting his glasses. Wendy popped her head out of the door. 'In you come, you two. You'll have to wait, Trevor.'

Needing no further invitation to get out of the rain, Barry clattered up the steps, Ken behind him. It was fuzzily warm inside, with a faint, comforting smell of gas. Peter sat at the table, slurping tea from an enormous mug emblazoned with the legend "I'm The Boss" in electric blue letters. 'Ah, Barry. How's the dog, um, er, Ronald?'

'Rommel, Peter.' Little Felcham had an excellent vet's practice, thank God. 'Yes, patched up and on the mend.'

'Good stuff!' Peter brushed droplets of tea from his moustache. 'Well, no point in beating around the bush. Yesterday. Bad show all round! Not your fault, but the inspectorate are all over us and we're expecting a visit from the health and safety people - police as well, probably.'

Barry had spent much of the previous evening flitting between the vet and the local hospital, some eight miles away. 'Well, I'm sure Ray will answer their questions as best he can - once he's out of hospital! I spoke to him last night - he reckons the charges were tampered with! The bloody stuff left a crater!'

'Hmmm. Well, that's out of our hands for now. Not so the other business. The Newton tribe have had lifetime bans slapped on them, as you know. Now, Trevor...'

After everything, Peter was going to focus on that? 'Did nothing wrong!'

'On the contrary, he attacked a rider! You know the rules - stand still and let the cavalry do the work, don't ever strike at them in case you hit the horse. Which he did. Several times. And Sean - I've seen the bruises!'

'So they've slapped a ban on him as well?' How could the board equate Trevor's actions with those of the Newtons?

'Only a field ban. Until he retakes his sword test.'

A stroke of genius on someone's part. He had to admire it. 'They won't pass him again! Not at his age!'

'No. No, they won't.' Peter clapped his hands. 'Right, there you have it! Off you trot, then! There's talk they may cancel today if this rain doesn't let up. Bad form, eh?'

Wendy showed Barry and Ken out. Trevor looked up from beneath his umbrella as the door shut behind them. 'Well?'

Typical of Peter to leave others to do the dirty work. Still, as CO, it was Barry's duty. He cleared his throat. 'Field ban, Trevor.'

'A ban?'

'I'm afraid so, Trevor.'

'So I can't carry the colour anymore?'

A ridiculous tear mingled with the rainwater on Barry's face. 'Not until you've retaken your sword test.'

'But it's a ban? Definitely a ban? I'm not being retired?'

'That's right, Trevor. Disciplinary measures.'

'Disciplinary measures?' Trevor's eyes sparkled behind the rain-flecked lenses and he punched the air with a bony fist. 'Yes!'

Barry's smile died on his lips at the guttural growl of an engine, and he turned to face the Land Rover that bumped toward him. Was this the Newtons, come back to finish him off? No, thank God - for all the mud splashes, the metallic green vehicle was in far better condition than the Newtons' hulk. It rolled to a halt and two men - one wearing a hi-vis vest, the other in a sombre blue overcoat - clambered out and stepped gingerly through the mud that slopped over their shoes. Elizabeth - more sensibly attired in yellow waterproofs - jumped out after them.

'Elizabeth?' Ken frowned like child who, having just found his sweets, had had them snatched away for being bad for him.

'This is Mr Slater from the British Library.' She was fighting to keep the smile from her face as the man in the overcoat produced a transparent plastic folder. The document inside was brown with age, scrawled with ornate script.

Ken's jaw dropped open. 'Is that...'

Elizabeth nodded. 'It is.'

'Why didn't you tell me?'

'I tried to - you wouldn't listen!'

Before Ken could grasp the manuscript, Danny came running up, hand in hand with Macintyre's girl. 'Barry! Ken!'

'What is it?' Barry wasn't sure if he approved of his troops fraternising with the enemy to such an extent, but it would be one in the eye for Mac.

'It's Sneath!' said Sophie. 'He's off up to Harding's monument! With a pickaxe!'

From all Barry had heard, the fate of the monument was signed and sealed - what did it matter how it was delivered? Even the document, the improbable *deus ex machina,* couldn't prevent that now, could it? Gears that took such effort to get moving would not be halted by the petty bureaucrats who delighted in the devilry of paperwork, and after yesterday Barry didn't have the strength or the will to fight them anymore. Stone monuments could always be replaced.

'He must have heard about Chatsworth!' It was the man in hi-vis who spoke. 'Come on!' He and Slater jumped back into their vehicle, the gunning engine rekindling the smouldering embers in Barry's heart. What was he thinking of, surrendering to that git? Maybe it could be stopped, but the Land Rover would have to take the long route round to the stone, and if Sneath had a start…

'Bastard! Danny, round up who you can and meet us there! Ken? Come on!'

Barry and Ken reached the monument at a run. It was a sombre scene, the granite marker nestled in its arboreal sepulchre beneath leaden skies, though the usual tranquillity was absent due to the pounding rain and the baleful figure of William Sneath, pickaxe raised.

'Stop!' bellowed Ken.

'Too late! I've got permission!'

'Not like this!' Barry pulled Ken back before he could hurl himself beneath the pickaxe. 'You can't!'

A breathless gaggle of Harding's arrived, followed by Sophie - and her father.

'Let him do it, man!'

'No! No way, Mac!' The spectre of Harding hung over Barry - to think he'd almost accepted Sneath's victory! 'You've done enough damage this weekend!'

'But he's got permission from the council! One way or another, it's going to go.'

The green four-by-four blasted over the churned fields and slewed to a halt by the stone. 'What's this?' Slater jumped out, sinking up to his ankles in the mud. 'What are you doing?'

'Council business,' sneered Sneath.

'I don't think so!' said Slater's companion.

'Councillor Chatsworth…'

'Oh, have you seen him? There are a few people very keen to talk to him. Us at the council for starters - and the police.'

It was sweet music to Barry's ears. 'What's he done?' He had Slater's companion placed now, one of the council bods he'd been introduced to yesterday.

'Misappropriation of funds - amongst other things. I should think he's halfway to the nearest airport by now.'

'So?' The news didn't seem to surprise Sneath. 'It doesn't change a thing!'

'Actually it does.' Slater again produced his plastic folder. 'This was the property of Miss Bishop's grandfather. It only came to light after his will was read. A contemporary account of Harding's regiment, including their actions at Little Felcham - sheds a fair bit of doubt on your research, I'm afraid. As such - and with the shady actions of Mr Chatsworth - the monument stays.'

'This manuscript - it's genuine?' Macintyre looked like a kid who'd just been told that Father Christmas didn't exist.

'It is,' said Slater. 'Miss Bishop had it verified by the British Library, whose humble servant I am.'

'It's all rubbish, Macintyre!' blustered Sneath. 'My book is…'

'A pile of revisionist crap, it would appear.' Macintyre's expression was unreadable, though Barry took little pleasure from the resignation in his voice.

Sneath turned crimson. 'You Scottish ape! Philistines, all of you!'

Macintyre's shoulders were rounded with defeat, sinking lower when he noticed that Danny was holding hands with Sophie. 'Oh no, that caps the lot! He's a Harding, Sophie!'

'You'd rather have me with someone like your friend, Sneath? He seemed to think he was in with a chance when he put his hand on my leg!'

'What?' It was Macintyre's turn to redden.

'Still up to your old tricks, William?' said Elizabeth. 'The things I could tell you about him!'

'He tried it on with me as well!' Mel had come along with Ollie. 'Like a bloody octopus!'

Sneath rounded on them, baring his teeth like a cornered rat. 'Bugger you all! Retards, old maids, petty tyrants and little sluts!' Throwing down the pickaxe, he pushed his way through the little crowd.

'Sneath?' Macintyre strode after him and, as the historian turned, thundered a punch to his jaw that deposited him into a large puddle with a satisfying splash of brown water.

Sneath shook his head, glasses askew. 'That's assault!' he whined. 'I've got witnesses! You all saw that!'

'I didn't see a thing,' said Barry, envying Macintyre the feel of the arrogant face beneath his fist. 'Ken?'

'I saw Mr Sneath slip in the mud.'

'Anyone see an assault?' Barry asked. Everyone shook their heads. Scrambling to his feet, thick mud smeared down the backside of his fine grey suit, Sneath was swallowed by the rain.

'Looks like it might ease.' Macintyre looked up at the sky. 'We might have our battle after all.'

Macintyre had addressed Barry like a fellow human being and it would be churlish of him not to reply in kind. 'The village is ruined, ah, Richard.' He couldn't bring himself to look his erstwhile foe in the face.

'We'll do without then.' Macintyre was talking to a point a degree or so to the left of Barry's ear. 'We can't cancel. Have a word with Peter. My boys will be on the field at 3 o'clock.'

*

It was still pouring with rain at 3 o'clock, but the armies were drawn up, facing each other across the damp field, the blackened remains of the village between them. It seemed as though the whole of Little Felcham had come to watch, huddled beneath umbrellas but cheering for all they worth. A cannon fired to open the battle and, as the smoke swirled away, the rain magically stopped and a shaft of sunlight slanted down through the clouds to bathe the battlefield of Little Felcham in warm summer light.